W9-CBW-310

Praise for

DAWN'S AWAKENING

"Leigh consistently does an excellent job building characters and weaving intricate plot threads through her stories. Her latest offering in the Breeds series is no exception."
—*Romantic Times* (Top Pick, 4½ stars)

"*Dawn's Awakening* held me captivated and continues to do so a month after having read it." —*Romance Junkies*

"One of the most heart-wrenching of the Breeds series to date." —*Fallen Angel Reviews*

"Erotic, fast-paced, funny and hard-hitting, this series delivers maximum entertainment to the reader." —*Fresh Fiction*

"One of the best Breeds books I've ever read."
—*The Good, the Bad and the Unread*

TANNER'S SCHEME

"The incredible Leigh pushes the traditional envelope with her scorching sex scenes by including voyeurism. Intrigue and passion ignite! . . . Scorcher!"
—*Romantic Times* (4½ stars)

"Sinfully sensual . . . [This series] is well-worth checking out." —*Fresh Fiction*

continued . . .

Harmony's Way

"Leigh's engrossing alternate reality combines spicy sensuality, romantic passion and deadly danger. Hot stuff indeed."
—*Romantic Times*

"I stand in awe of Ms. Leigh's ability to bring to life these wonderful characters as they slowly weave their way into my mind and heart. When it comes to this genre, Lora Leigh is the queen."
—*Romance Junkies*

Megan's Mark

"A riveting tale full of love, intrigue and every woman's fantasy, *Megan's Mark* is a wonderful contribution to Lora Leigh's Breeds series . . . As always, Lora Leigh delivers on all counts; *Megan's Mark* will certainly not disappoint her many fans!"
—*Romance Reviews Today*

"Hot, hot, hot—the sex and the setting . . . You can practically see the steam rising off the pages."
—*Fresh Fiction*

"This entertaining romantic science fiction suspense will remind the audience of *Kitty and the Midnight Hour* by Carrie Vaughn and MaryJanice Davidson's *Derik's Bane* as this futuristic world filled with 'Breeds' seems 'normal' . . . [A] delightful thriller."
—*The Best Reviews*

"The dialogue is quick, the action is fast and the sex is oh, so hot . . . Don't miss out on this one."
—*A Romance Review*

"Leigh's action-packed Breeds series makes a refreshing change . . . Rapid-fire plot development and sex steamy enough to peel wallpaper."
—*Monsters and Critics*

"An exceedingly sexy and sizzling new series to enjoy. Hot sex, snappy dialogue and kick-butt action add up to outstanding entertainment."
—*Romantic Times*

COYOTE'S MATE

LORA LEIGH

BERKLEY SENSATION, NEW YORK

THE BERKLEY PUBLISHING GROUP
Published by the Penguin Group
Penguin Group (USA) Inc.
375 Hudson Street, New York, New York 10014, USA
Penguin Group (Canada), 90 Eglinton Avenue East, Suite 700, Toronto, Ontario M4P 2Y3, Canada
(a division of Pearson Penguin Canada Inc.)
Penguin Books Ltd., 80 Strand, London WC2R 0RL, England
Penguin Group Ireland, 25 St. Stephen's Green, Dublin 2, Ireland (a division of Penguin Books Ltd.)
Penguin Group (Australia), 250 Camberwell Road, Camberwell, Victoria 3124, Australia
(a division of Pearson Australia Group Pty. Ltd.)
Penguin Books India Pvt. Ltd., 11 Community Centre, Panchsheel Park, New Delhi—110 017, India
Penguin Group (NZ), 67 Apollo Drive, Rosedale, North Shore 0632, New Zealand
(a division of Pearson New Zealand Ltd.)
Penguin Books (South Africa) (Pty.) Ltd., 24 Sturdee Avenue, Rosebank, Johannesburg 2196,
South Africa

Penguin Books Ltd., Registered Offices: 80 Strand, London WC2R 0RL, England

This is a work of fiction. Names, characters, places, and incidents either are the product of the author's imagination or are used fictitiously, and any resemblance to actual persons, living or dead, business establishments, events, or locales is entirely coincidental. The publisher does not have any control over and does not assume any responsibility for author or third-party websites or their content.

COYOTE'S MATE

A Berkley Sensation Book / published by arrangement with the author

PRINTING HISTORY
Berkley Sensation mass-market edition / February 2009

Copyright © 2009 by Christina Simmons.
Excerpt from *Bengal's Heart* copyright © 2009 by Christina Simmons.
Cover photos: "Woman bending back wearing panties & bra" copyright © Ben Welsh/zefa/corbis;
"Coyote Snarling" copyright © Randy Wells/corbis.
Cover design by Rita Frangie.
Interior text design by Stacy Irwin.

All rights reserved.
No part of this book may be reproduced, scanned, or distributed in any printed or electronic form without permission. Please do not participate in or encourage piracy of copyrighted materials in violation of the author's rights. Purchase only authorized editions.
For information, address: The Berkley Publishing Group,
a division of Penguin Group (USA) Inc.,
375 Hudson Street, New York, New York 10014.

ISBN: 978-0-425-22633-9

BERKLEY® SENSATION
Berkley Sensation Books are published by The Berkley Publishing Group,
a division of Penguin Group (USA) Inc.,
375 Husdon Street, New York, New York 10014.
BERKLEY® SENSATION and the "B" design are trademarks of Penguin Group (USA) Inc.

PRINTED IN THE UNITED STATES OF AMERICA

10 9 8 7 6 5 4 3 2 1

If you purchased this book without a cover, you should be aware that this book is stolen property. It was reported as "unsold and destroyed" to the publisher, and neither the author nor the publisher has received any payment for this "stripped book."

COYOTE'S
MATE

Del-Rey Delgado, the Coyote Ghost, was alpha leader of the team of twenty-eight mercenary soldiers he had gathered around him from various parts of the Council's ranks. Coyote Breeds that he had rescued, men he had trained himself—hardened, cold-eyed soldiers that the underground world knew only as Team Zero, the mercenary force willing to take on the most suicidal of missions.

They had rescued heiresses, assassinated despots and posed as security for some of the greatest leaders in the world. Men who never knew they were dealing with a shadowy force that had been created rather than born.

There had even been a few times that they had protected Council members themselves. For a while. Long enough to get the information they needed and still keep their reputations intact. Those leaders had always died once payment was collected.

As Del-Rey had told his men, vengeance came after the bills, and supporting the plans they had took an excessive amount of money.

Plans such as rescuing other Coyotes who managed to find a way to contact Del-Rey's shadowy force. This day, he stared into winsome blue eyes and wondered if perhaps the Genetics

Council hadn't truly created a creature without a soul when they created him. Because as he stared into the young woman-child's eyes, he knew he would end up betraying her.

Sixteen and as beautiful as a sunrise. Long red gold hair flowed over her shoulder in a silken braid as she stepped into one of the dirtiest, meanest, jacked-up bars in Russia. Damn, it took courage for her to actually come here.

A breath of fresh air, a single fragile flame of innocence among the most corrupt of men. He tapped his fingernails against the bar in a signal to his second-in-command, Brimstone, and looked to the door as the entire room went quiet.

Even a five-year-old would have enough instincts to run in this situation. But this girl didn't run. Her chin lifted as she stepped into the establishment and moved through the room.

She was a gang rape waiting to happen here. Son of a bitch.

He nodded to his men and watched as they moved from tables, from the corners of the shadowed room, and converged on her, surrounding her as Del-Rey and Brim moved from the bar to the back room that he had selected for this first meeting.

He was waiting when she was pushed through the door, sitting on the corner of the small table, one leg braced on the floor, the other swinging lazily as he watched her. Rounded eyes, parted pink lips, her breathing harsh. And a hint of fear in those eyes.

She should have known fear well before she made it here.

Using his foot, he pushed the single chair toward her.

"Sit," he growled, deliberately letting the animal he was rumble in his voice.

But did she run? She didn't run. She moved slowly to the chair, sat down and gave him a fragile smile. "Del-Rey," she whispered. "It's Spanish, you know, for 'of the king.'"

His brows arched. He was of a king all right, one long betrayed and dead. He didn't mean to follow in that genetic ancestor's footsteps.

He leaned forward, braced his elbow on his knee and let his gaze run over her slowly. Very slowly. Touching on fragile, youthful and yet womanly features. A fucking child. Hell, that Siberian lab had been truly desperate, or depraved, to have sent a child to him.

"I'm going to kill you before I leave here," he sighed, watching her smile falter.

"Kill me?" She licked her lips nervously and stared back at him with a hint of wariness. "You promised I'd be safe."

"And you believed me?" A ghost of a smile played at his lips. "How foolish of you."

"But, you never break your promises." She blinked back at him with such innocence he nearly laughed.

He merely arched his brow instead, a warning that perhaps her information hadn't been entirely accurate.

She looked down at her hands, linked her fingers together then lifted her gaze once again. "There are five females at the lab where my father is security officer." She bit her lip worriedly before continuing. "They said they sent you a message, and you swore that you wouldn't harm the contact sent to you."

His head tilted as his eyes narrowed. "There are no female Coyotes."

"There are five," she told him. "Sharone, she contacted you. It was she that you spoke with in the secured emails. There are four others. Twins, Emma and Ashley. Two younger, Marcy and Chanda. They're the babies of the group."

He stared back at her curiously now. "Where are the males of their group? Coyotes don't let females speak for them, little girl."

She swallowed tightly. "The males are more heavily guarded. The scientists, they like me rather well. I'm one of the few women at the labs. I've been raised with them."

How interesting. She had to be lying; there was no other option. Hell, killing children was one of the few sins he hadn't committed in his life, but this child knew his face. He couldn't risk being identified.

"Sharone said you would save them." She stared back at him, her blue eyes darkening with more than worry now; there might even be a hint of anger in those pretty depths. "Do you know the risks we've taken to contact you? To come to this meeting?"

Yes, that was definitely anger. He stared back at her, frankly amazed. Even his men hesitated to speak to him in such a way. Surely no one else had dared since he had reached maturity. Perhaps even before.

"You risked much," he agreed. "But I warned you in the email I would kill anyone attempting to trick me. Whoever set you on this plot, child, has ended your life for you."

Did she show fear? No. Instead, slowly, she parted her jacket and from inside withdrew several photos. Her hands were shaking as she handed them to him.

Her face was pale, but her eyes were still filled with anger. He glanced at the pictures, brows lifting at the sight of the five young women. Definitely Coyote females if their forced smiles, which revealed their curved canines, were any indication.

"They could be faked." He threw them to the table.

She inhaled roughly. "If I don't return, a message will be sent to the Feline Breed compound Sanctuary that the Coyote Ghost has murdered me. I came to you under the auspices of the newly formed ideals of Breed Law, which you claimed in your email to adhere to. That message will state my name, my age, the labs I am from and a message: 'Breed Law doesn't always survive. Masters control the puppets, and the puppets whisper the wages of death.'"

Shocking. Del-Rey stared back at her as she whispered the code and information that he knew would set every living free Feline Breed on his ass. Perhaps this wasn't a trick after all.

He could smell no deceit. But his senses could be tricked—Coyotes knew well how to trick human and Breed senses alike. A human could be taught, if the human were smart enough.

Anya Kobrin was smart enough. Sixteen years old and already working security and administration with the Siberian Chernov laboratories. He knew the location, knew by now many of the personnel, but rescuing the Breeds there would be much harder.

"These things don't happen overnight." He dropped any thought of killing her. "It could take years. I don't go in blind and I don't risk children. And I sure as hell don't trust big blue eyes and a sincere face. Go home. I'll contact you when I've decided."

She looked at him in alarm. "This can't wait that long. There are over fifty Coyote Breeds here. They die daily." Distress filled her face. "You can't just let them die."

"And I know Coyotes, little girl," he growled back at her. "I know their deceit and I know how easily they can trick pretty little girls. We wait, we watch. I'll contact you. Until then your priority is maintaining the safety of those young women." He pointed to the pictures. "You have no other job, is that clear? The males will know the score. Do they know you're here as well?"

She shook her head quickly. "Only Sharone knows. We haven't told the others."

"Keep it that way," he ordered her, leaning closer, staring into her wide blue eyes, giving her a look that most men saw only seconds before they died. "Betray me, Anya Kobrin, and you die. You die, your father dies, and any friends or family that I ferret out as yours will die as well. Do you believe me?"

She licked her lips and nodded. "I would expect it. But I won't betray you."

He nodded abruptly. "My men will escort you out of the city. Return to your home and await contact."

"Soon?" she asked as she rose slowly from her chair. "Please, soon. So far, the girls aren't mistreated, mostly because my father ensures it. But, they're getting older," she whispered. "The three oldest are already over eighteen. He won't be able to protect them for much longer."

"Then you better be persuasive with your father and your friends," he growled. "Because I don't jump through rings and risk myself and my men as easily as you seem to think I should. Female Coyotes are worth some risk. The men there willing to do what they must for freedom are worth the risk. But never doubt you have spies there, and I'll know who they are before I come in. And I'll know, lovely Anya, if you are friend or foe. Make sure you stay on the friend side of the equation. I don't care about killing a female if she betrays me."

She stared back at him, then her chin lifted in determination and feminine arrogance. Hell, this one should have been a Breed herself. She was that daring. That courageous.

"If one of those girls dies before you make your decision," she whispered, voice trembling, "then you are the one that better be careful, Del-Rey whoever the hell you are. I might be a child in your eyes, but I'd make a very bad enemy."

She was threatening him? He wanted to laugh in surprise at her sheer daring. Instead, he merely chuckled, rapped the wall and waited for Brim to step inside.

"Get her out of here quickly and quietly," he ordered the

other man. "Return her to the train station. She's going back to her nice, safe little home."

Brim gave the girl a hard look before nodding and standing back to allow her to leave the room. She moved past him, then turned and stared back at Del-Rey.

"You should smile," she told him softly, surprising him yet again. "I bet you're really cute when you smile."

He held the smile back until she left, then shook his head as a grin shaped his lips. The little imp. He was going to have a bit of trouble on his hands with this one, he could see. And a bit of a challenge.

TWO YEARS LATER

"This is insanity." Anya jumped from the chair in the back of yet another dirty room and faced the man that entered the room. "You have to move faster than this."

Del-Rey. Dark blond hair grew to his shoulders, black eyes so deep that at times they reflected the faintest hint of blue.

A darker blond brow arched at her outburst as he watched her coolly. He watched her the same as he had two years before, when she'd met him the first time. The half dozen times she'd seen him since had changed nothing in how he treated her.

But something in her had changed. She dreamed of him too often. Thought of him too often.

"I told you this doesn't happen quickly," he warned her. "Those labs are not exactly easily accessible, darlin'. We're doing our best. And if your Coyote friend is as smart as I suspect she is, then she knew the wait would be a long one."

"Breeds are being rescued all over the world," she argued fiercely. "Labs just as secure have been penetrated."

"And many, many lives have been lost," he warned her. "For the moment, your labs are safe from the killings that are everyday business with the other Breeds. They don't kill Coyotes unless they begin to show mercy. So far, those in your group are too young to be in much danger."

"They are already starting to transfer the older ones." Her fists clenched at her side at the memory of the group that had gone out over a month ago. "We can't continue to wait like this."

"Six were transferred, and once they cleared Russian borders, they were extracted. Three died for warning their guards that they were being rescued as we made the attempt." He lifted the camcorder from the desk and switched it on before setting it in front of her. "I believe you knew them."

Shock, betrayal. Anya's eyes widened as she stared at the recording. Three of the Coyotes that she and Sharone had protected countless times had betrayed the others as the rescue group moved in. They had turned weapons on their fellow Breeds. Their eyes hard, they spouted Council bullshit in cold voices.

"The other three are alive and safe at the moment," he promised her when the video finished.

"Get the girls out like that." She jerked her gaze back to his in desperation. "I can arrange their transfers."

He shook his head. "Aren't you leaving something out, little Anya?"

He surprised her with the question.

"What do you mean?"

"Your father had those girls assigned to you as protective detail. I believe you've received an offer from the Genetics Council itself to head an office that would coordinate the admistrative and security duties involved in keeping their organization more secretive."

She frowned. She had received such an offer, but how had he known?

"Doctors Chernov and Sobolova have requested that I stay assigned to the current lab until I'm twenty-two." She let a smile tug at her lips. "They offered proof to the GC that I'm not nearly as proficient in the new programs as they had hoped I would be."

It was deliberate, of course. Her father had warned her such an offer might arrive, and Anya had made certain she began to appear to be lagging in certain areas.

"Indeed," he drawled. She suspected there was a wealth of mockery in that single word. But this man was often mocking, and always hard. But, sometimes, she saw amusement, perhaps a hint of softening.

"Indeed." She rolled her eyes. "Which is totally beside the point, I could arrange for the girls be transferred. It would be simple enough."

"No." His voice was hard. Firm. "Here are three pictures. Do you know these men?"

She frowned down at the photos and pointed to one. "This is Aleski Dornovo, he's a Breed trainer, ex–Russian Elite hit squad. He was sort of black ops for many years." She tapped the next one. "Graco, he's one of the older Breeds at the lab. Very quiet. Colder than the others. This is Cavalier. He's dead on the inside," she said sadly. "He came from another lab just ahead of the rescues. I heard it was a brutal lab to be in."

"And yours isn't?" he asked her.

She shook her head slowly and lifted her eyes to him, feeling the pain that filled her at the thought of what the Breeds suffered. "No. Doctors Chernov and Sobolova believe that loyalty begins with loyalty. They begin training with rewards for proper behavior. They refuse to conduct experiments on the Breeds they created, citing that it would begin a breakdown in that loyalty. They're very high ranking within their fields. The Council rarely refuses them whatever they ask. They kill as example only." She felt the tears that edged at her eyes. "But still, they kill."

"You're too softhearted," he scoffed. "Death happens every day. "This man," he tapped Cavalier's picture, "watch him closely."

"Is he an enemy?" She stared up at him, feeling her heart clench. She liked Cavalier. She never talked to him, she wasn't allowed around the male Coyotes, but there was something haunted and sad in his eyes.

"Enemy or friend, I haven't decided yet. Have Sharone watch him closely. She interacts with the male Breeds more than you're allowed. Correct?"

"Correct," she said heavily. "You're not coming for them yet, are you?"

"Not yet," he told her. "We're going to weed out the chaff before we come in for the harvest. There's no other way to do this, Anya. Not and maintain your safety as well as the female Breeds you're trying so hard to protect."

Sharone had warned her that to do this right, it would take him years. She hadn't believed it. She did now.

"Graco is certainly a spy," he warned her then. "We have proof of it. Have him transferred if you can do so without suspicion."

She nodded. "Father and the scientists make that decision. They normally follow Father's recommendations though."

Her father was head of security and training, and he listened to her opinion, he valued it. The fact that she was betraying him haunted her often. The fear that he could pay with his life for her actions was a constant.

"You won't kill my father?" she asked him again. She asked him each time they met, to be certain. "You won't hurt him?"

"Your father won't die," he promised her. "I promised you I wouldn't harm your family, Anya."

She inhaled heavily. "I'll make certain Graco is transferred. I'll get word to you when it's arranged."

"Be brave, Anya." He surprised her with the words, with the deepening of his voice. "Nothing worth having comes quickly."

She nodded bleakly. "Freedom is worth fighting for," she whispered. "It's worth dying for."

Her friends weren't animals. The Coyotes created in the labs she worked and lived within were created to follow orders, to be cold, to be hard, but Anya had seen so much more in them over the years. She prayed she would soon see them free.

Four Years Later

Del-Rey stared at the young woman standing on the other side of the table as he and his lieutenants studied the diagrams she had brought with her. Electrical lines, water pipes, tunnel access beneath the labs, security weaknesses—she had brought everything they would need. But one crucial key was missing, and he dared not tell her that.

An ace.

Every great mission needed an ace. That one card that he knew would trump all opposition—that trump was Anya herself. Her father was head of security and training. Two cousins were team leaders in security. Various relatives worked within the labs. She was the baby of the family, cherished by father and cousins, and by the Coyotes that remained in the labs, she was seen as their greatest treasure.

They would die for her, die with her or die trying to save her. It wouldn't matter to them. If she said, *Walk through hell for me*, then those men and five women within that damned lab would head to the bowels of the earth with a smile.

There were twenty left. When they came out, they would join the forty men he had already amassed over the years. All Coyote males, hardened and cold as death. They had only their honor, which they had been taught had been bred out of them, and the principles that brought them together.

His men outnumbered those inside, but he was betting when he took the ace, the Breeds in those labs would cheer. There wasn't a one that was comfortable with leaving her behind.

But he knew the cost to the young woman that had become an integral part of his life over the past six years. She had weeded out the chaff, made certain nothing but loyal Breeds remained. She had done her part. He had agreed to her terms, and he was going to break the deal before it even began and she wouldn't even know it before it was too late.

"Father and my cousins Ivan and Donan will have their teams here." She pointed out the general areas that the security teams believed were weak. "They aren't aware of the tunnels that lead from the labs to this cave." She pointed out the cave. "I asked Father if the scientists didn't have secure access underground and he said no. There is no other access. But I found the tunnel myself and followed it."

And she was damned proud of herself. Hell, he was proud of her, even though his guts cramped at the thought of what could have happened if she had been caught.

"We have to do this soon," she told him. "Enough of your excuses, we have only months and the Council will be moving me to St. Petersburg for admin training there in the offices of the Federation Secret Forces. If that happens, then all these years have been wasted."

"And when it happens, what then?" he asked her. "What happens to the humans who worked within your labs?"

"Father will take care of me," she told him confidently. "He's already attempting to have the decision reversed, along with the scientists there. If the Breeds there escape, then the security forces will be reassigned. They will find the fault that will be programmed into their new security system and believe that my trainer overlooked my obvious incompetence to make himself appear brighter for having a protégée. I've seen what they do when this happens. They drop both trainer and protégée, who are then lucky to work in the factories."

"A factory suits you then?" he asked her curiously.

Her smile, impish and teasing, curled at her lips. "I will talk Father into going to America then. It's much warmer than Siberia."

This was true enough, and she would indeed be taken to America. Though her father would not be traveling along with her. Del-Rey would be though. He had plans. Plans he had already set into motion, and Anya figured into many of them. Once this rescue was carried off, they would go to Colorado, petition the Wolf Breeds for an alliance and join the Breed society.

It wouldn't be easy to convince the Wolves to allow an alliance, but he had proof of their work over the past years. Ten years living in the shadows, being no more than ghosts, free yet chained by the bonds of being forced to hide who and what they were from everyone.

"I'll contact you soon," he said.

He was lying to her, and not for the first time. For six long years, he had lied to this beautiful woman-child. He had watched her grow from a gangly teenager filled with fire and a thirst for her friends' freedom. He had watched her plot, plan and implement his orders from a distance.

She was a fucking genius in administration and personnel. Intuitive, she could take a look at a group and damned near size them up instantly. She'd already done it with his men, and he had to grit his teeth when she informed him several of his men were too damned lazy. Hell, they were Coyotes, they needed a few faults or they'd be fucking Wolves.

There was something about her though, something he could never put his finger on, that drew him. Even when she was too young to be amused by or drawn to him, still, she had drawn him.

"I don't want to be contacted soon, Del-Rey," she informed him fiercely. "I'm only months from my birthday. This can't be put off any longer."

"I will contact you before you're transferred," he told her firmly. "The rescue will take place before then, I promise you this. It's time for you to trust me, Anya."

She glared back at him in confusion. "But I do trust you. I've always trusted you and you've always dragged your heels. I'm starting to worry now."

"No worrying, little one." He reached out before he could stop himself and touched her cheek with the tips of his fingers.

It flared then. That connection, that something he had felt growing over the years. And she felt it as well. He watched her lashes lower, watched her lips become fuller, more sensual. A flush filled her cheeks, and the arousal that filled her young body each time they met flared to full, heated life.

He was a Breed. He could smell her dampness, the rush of her sweet juices filling her pussy, her body preparing for him.

She wasn't a child any longer. She was twenty-two years old, old enough. Mature enough, he prayed, because he was still a Breed and still a hard man. It was a bad combination when lust was eating at his insides.

When she tugged her teeth over her lower lip, his teeth ached to nip it. When her tongue dampened it, he nearly groaned at the erection that filled his jeans.

"Tell your people to be waiting," he warned her. "I'll contact you and we'll arrange the date and time. Agreed?"

She nodded slowly. "And you'll not harm my family?" she asked him again. "They don't believe in what is going on here, Del-Rey. This is their job. They're military. They are following their orders, just as your men do. Promise me, you won't harm them."

"I've sworn this, Anya." He let the backs of his fingers smooth over her silken cheek. "My men know which of the forces are your family. We will know where they will be at the time of the attack. It's going to be fine. I promise you."

And he was lying to her. Her father and cousins were soldiers, but they could have taken the responsibility that Anya had taken on her own young shoulders. They could have aided the Breeds a thousand times over, but they hadn't. They had followed orders.

All attempts would be made not to kill them, but they would suffer for allowing this young woman to take the risks she had taken to do the job she was doing.

"Trust me," he whispered again.

The scent of her arousal intensified at the soft croon of his voice. The need that filled her eyes made him ache in regret.

"I trust you." A smile trembled at her lips. "I'll always trust you, Del-Rey."

Sadly, he knew that statement would soon be retracted. Anya knew fierce loyalty, but she also knew how to hate. She was a woman whose passions would always run deep, no matter which way they ran. And before much longer, she would know only hatred for the man she stared at with such longing now.

Regret. It seared inside him. An emotion he had never felt in his life, and it wasn't one he liked feeling.

CHAPTER I

Anya was where she was supposed to be, but things weren't going as they had been planned. Nothing had gone as planned. When she returned to the labs that evening, within hours the attack came.

There was no warning. There was no call. Security alarms were blaring, cell doors were opening, as safeguards were overrode and locks on the weapons rooms deactivated.

She pushed the scientists behind a secure, hidden wall she had found the month before. They hadn't been here long enough evidently to know all the secrets of the labs. Dr. Chernov had replaced the aging scientists ten years before and brought his protégée, Sobolova, a much younger female scientist, along with him.

"Don't leave. Don't move," she ordered them. "Stay here until you hear only silence."

Pale, shaking in shock, the two scientists did as they were told, huddling in the little room as Anya slid the secured door closed and rushed to the exits that led to the cold, desolate land aboveground.

"Anya, get out of here." Sofia Ivanova, one of the administrative assistants, gripped her arm and dragged her down another hall. "Go that way." She pointed to the stairs. "They're free. I'll cover you."

Cover her? Anya stared behind her as doctors raced from labs with weapons drawn. They were firing on personnel? Shock rushed through her, tore through her mind. She knew those men and women. Knew them well. And they were firing on the personnel attempting to escape?

"Run, damn you!" Sofia pushed her to the exit. "Get out of here before I have to shoot you."

Anya ran. As she ran, fury fed the fear and the shock coursing through her adrenaline-laced mind. This was the exact plan she had given Del-Rey for the rescue. Had he not trusted her? He had attacked only hours after her return, giving her no time to ensure her father and cousins weren't here.

No, it had to be something else, she decided in desperation as she raced up the stairs. She gripped an older woman's arm, one of the secretaries, and pushed her ahead of her.

"Hurry, Marie," Anya urged the other woman as she sobbed and nearly fell. "We must hurry."

Other personnel were racing past them as Anya grabbed Marie's arm and all but dragged her up the steps. Marie had children, grandchildren. A husband that was ill. She was needed. And besides, she always brought the Breeds cookies. She was kind and gentle.

The door was broken from its hinges above, lying on its side as security forces were waving personnel through, urging them to hurry, to rush. Masks covered the guards' faces to protect them from the cold. It was bitterly cold outside, and Marie had no jacket, no coat to wear.

"Run for the barracks," she told the other woman. "It will be warm there and safer. We'll hide there."

She ran into the cold, aware of the gunfire, the yelling voices, the clash of forces. Then she was only aware of the hard arm that wrapped around her waist, jerked her against a broad chest, and the knife that lay at her throat.

She could feel the cold blade pressing into her throat, pinching the flesh, within a breath of actually cutting her skin.

"Kobrin, I have your daughter."

Loud, echoing through the valley, she knew that voice, knew

the growl that sounded in it and felt the sob that tore from her throat.

Betrayal. He had betrayed her.

Agony tore through her with such pain she could only gasp at the reality of it.

The sound of gunfire faded away. Personnel were no longer rushing through the doors. She could hear them at the entrance though, feel the tension that thickened the air.

Del-Rey. She felt the first tear fall. Oh God, she had trusted him. She had trusted him so much.

"We're lowering our weapons," her father called out. "Take the Breeds. Go. We'll not stand in your way, but let Anya go."

She stared back at her father's pale face, her cousins moving with him. All three of her cousins were on duty tonight. Her friends were here, those who would have helped her had she asked, but she hadn't.

A shot fired out and her first cousin fell, gripping his leg and screaming out in pain. Two more shots in rapid succession and the other two were left writhing on the ground.

"Stop it!" she screamed, her hands clawing at the arm wrapped around her waist. "No. No. Don't do this."

Fury and pain gripped her. She stared back at her father miserably, sobbing with the shame of what she had done.

"Transport's landing in sixty seconds, Boss." That was the one Del-Rey called Brim. Sometimes he had called him Brimstone.

They had all betrayed her. The small team of men she had become friends with, that she had trusted, that she had trusted her father and her cousins' lives to.

"How can you do this?" she sobbed. "Damn you, how can you do this?"

"Anya, be still, child," her father cried out. "Remember your control, daughter. Your cousins live."

"For now," Del-Rey called back in a lazy drawl. "Tell me, Kobrin, you've been here since the first Breed was created, did you ever think to aid them?"

"They live," her father called back. "I have killed none. This was not a slaughterhouse."

Del-Rey chuckled behind her. "I think I will take your

daughter with me, Kobrin. Insurance, I believe. You will not notify your Russian air force, you will notify no one of what has happened here for six hours. Or she will die. Are we understood?"

"Leave her here," her father called out desperately. "I swear to you no one will follow you."

Del-Rey laughed. "No, they won't follow me. I have the prize of the Genetics Council's young protégées. Your daughter, Kobrin. Don't make me kill her."

Another shot fired and her father stumbled, falling as Anya screamed out for him. Her hands reached out, her fingers curling as she was lifted off her feet, and the sound of a heli-jet arriving could be heard.

She screamed out for her father, clawed and slapped at the arm securing her. She kicked, she cursed, and she sobbed.

Rage ate inside her as the betrayal that filled her burned into her mind. He had lied. From the first moment he had lied, and she would never forgive him.

"Move out!" Del-Rey ordered as he raced into the back of the transport behind the other men that converged on the huge black craft. "Cavalier, get this bastard off the ground."

Cavalier. She had arranged his transport the year before. How many others were here? How many of those she had trusted had betrayed her?

"Stop fighting me, Anya." Del-Rey held her in place as he settled onto the metal bench, holding her secure, and the transport lifted off.

She couldn't see outside it. She had lost sight of her father. Lost sight of her family.

"You bastard!" she screamed, struggling harder as her fists struck back at his face. "You son of a bitch. You fucking bastard. How could you? How could you?"

"How could they?" he snarled, jerking her around to face him, his black eyes blazing in fury as his lips drew back from his lethal canines. "How dare they leave a child to arrange this? How dare they endanger you as they have? They have a bullet in their legs rather than their heads. They should be fucking thankful."

She slapped his face. Her hand slammed into his cheek with

enough force to burn her palm before she slapped him again. Furious, enraged screams were strangled in her throat as he jerked her arms to her side, holding her in place as a growl tore from his throat.

Then his lips pressed into hers. She tried to scream again, but he stole the opportunity to push his tongue past her lips. Spice filled her mouth. She swallowed and sobbed into the kiss, because it was good. Because his lips stroked over hers as she had always imagined they would. Because he tasted like warmth and passion, and because he had lied to her. He had betrayed her. And now he was stealing her mind.

She was still sobbing as his head lifted and his arms locked her to his chest. His hand covered her head, holding her against him as her fists clenched and beat at his shoulders.

She hated him. She hated him. Oh God, she hated him. And she loved him. And she felt as though her soul had been shredded. Her Coyote warrior had betrayed her. He had lied, over and over again, betrayed every vow he had made to her. He had stolen her innocence before he ever kissed her, and she wondered if she could ever forgive him for that.

Del-Rey stared over her head at the Coyotes that now joined him. Breeds, their gazes flat and hard as they watched him. They were a threat—he could smell it in the air; his men could feel it as they surrounded him.

"Mine," he told them all, his voice cold, commanding. "This woman is mine."

The five female Coyotes stared back at him. They were the most dangerous, he thought, especially the oldest, Sharone.

Her gaze flicked to Anya's sobbing form.

"You were wrong," she told him flatly. "You should have left her family alone."

"They put her in danger. They are lucky they live."

"No, my friend." She shook her head. "You will be lucky if you live. You betrayed her, and she won't forget it. She won't forgive it. We see the wisdom of what you did. The retribution we all felt was needed. But we stayed our hand, because she's ours as well." She indicated the Breeds that had come out of the underground facilities. "And what you have done this night, she will make certain you pay for."

Tender Anya? She would rage, she might hate for a while, but he had left her family alive. He would make her understand.

"Stay out of my way," he told her, and he meant all of them. "You swore loyalty to me and to my packs. Not to this girl. Where she's concerned, you will not interfere."

"Then you will ensure she is not harmed, in any way," Sharone told him fiercely. "We follow you, Alpha, but that one"—she nodded to Anya—"that one is one of us. Mistreat her, and you mistreat us all. Remember that."

Mistreat her? He had no intentions of mistreating her. Loving her perhaps. Easing her from her anger, definitely. Fucking her until they were both screaming with the pleasure, that was a given. She would forgive him. He would ensure it. After all, he hadn't killed her father or her cousins. They lived. They would merely hurt. A lot. And it was pain they deserved. Much more than they had received.

He smoothed his hand over Anya's loose hair. Without the braid, it hung well past her shoulders. He cupped the back of her head to him and leaned his own against the wall of the transport.

He was aware of his own men watching him, questioning his decision. They had questioned the wisdom of it when he first told them what he planned. He sent half his men six months ago to Colorado to secretly secure the caverns that overlooked Haven, the Wolf Breed compound. They were preparing things there for his arrival. Arriving in secrecy was paramount though. That meant ditching the transport and going in in small groups. That was easily handled.

Anya might not be as easily controlled, just as he was finding his own response to her was by far less easy to handle than he had imagined.

His head lowered again, his lips touching hers. His tongue was burning for the taste of her. Desperate for another of those hot, passionate kisses, the feel of her mouth sucking at him, drawing the tightness from his tongue.

He was aware of the eyes that watched, yet he couldn't draw back.

"They should have protected you better, little one," he whispered against her lush lips. "They well deserved my vengeance."

Her lashes lifted. Her eyes were dark with misery, with pain as an exhausted sob tore from her throat.

"You betrayed me. You lied to me," she cried. "I'll never trust you again, Del-Rey. I can never trust you."

He stole the words. He couldn't bear to hear them, couldn't bear the pain or the anger in her eyes or her voice. He took her kiss. Her lips parted for him helplessly. He could feel her fighting the need, felt her giving into it even as she cried out in surrender. And even as he kissed her, he realized there was something not quite as it had once been within him. A hunger, a need, a driving inferno of lust building inside him that made no sense, that defied description.

He needed this woman to survive it though. And Del-Rey always ensured he had what he needed to survive. He blamed it on the Coyote side of his genetics. Blood will tell and so, evidently, will DNA. At least in some part. Maybe he should blame it on the human side, he thought wearily. Anya might have accepted that easier.

THREE DAYS LATER

Three days. She burned. Flames licked over her flesh. Fury, confusion, betrayal and pain ate at her mind while the most horrible arousal she could have ever imagined ate at her body.

It had to be the taste of his kiss, she thought. She was craving it. It was killing her, the need for that kiss. And he kept forcing it on her, as though she actually wanted his kiss now.

She paced the bedroom of the cabin she was locked in, dressed in the soft cotton pants and T-shirt Sharone had brought her earlier.

She had begged Sharone to help her escape. She had it all worked out. All she had to do was get to a town and contact the embassy; they would take care of everything. They would contact her father, and she could go home. She could forget Del-Rey Delgado ever existed.

And Sharone had been going for it. Anya had seen it in her eyes until Del-Rey had stepped into the room, furious, and pulled Sharone from it.

Now she was alone. Alone to think, to worry. God, her father was lying in the snow bleeding, her cousins with him. Her

cousins had family, children—who would support them now?
Times weren't good in Russia right now; the economy was
weak all over. They would lose their homes. They would be in
the cold. Her father.

She sniffed. Who would bring him his vodka when he was
tired and worn from trying to manipulate the Council scientists
and members? Who would bandage his leg?

The tears were flowing from her eyes again. She should have
more control than this. Her father had berated her for her loss
of control. But that was something he did. She had red hair, he
told her often, like her mother. And her mother had learned that
holding her temper always helped herself and others more than
losing it did.

She couldn't control her emotions now. She hadn't been able
to since those shots had been fired. Since Del-Rey had kissed
her. Since her world had exploded around her. Since something
had exploded within her.

She pressed her hands into her stomach. Her abdomen rippled and she could feel the pulse of dampness between her
thighs. Her nipples were so sensitive the rasp of the T-shirt was
torture. Her clitoris was engorged and aching. Even when she
had touched herself, she had never been this aroused.

What had he done to her? He had to have done something to
her. There was no other explanation.

She paced the room, she cursed. She would rage and then
she would cry. She reviled Del-Rey Delgado. "Of the king" her
ass. There was nothing kingly about that bastard.

"What did you do to me?" she screamed, picking up one of
the few objects still in the bedroom, a wooden bowl, and throwing it at the door.

It didn't shatter. It hit the door with a resounding bang and
then fell to the carpet as she collapsed on the end of the bed,
curling into herself, moaning at the need rippling through her.

Her eyes closed, and she swore she tasted his kiss, felt his
hands on her flesh. One touch, she told herself. She could allow
one touch, just to still the demand raging through her body.
Maybe one more kiss.

"No!" she gritted out between her teeth. Not even one touch.
One touch would lead to another and she would be begging.
God help her if he ever kissed her. She wouldn't survive it.

And she didn't want that liar's kisses. Lies. Six years of lies. Promises he had broken one right after the other. She would be warned before the rescue. She would have time to make certain her father and cousins were safe. She would have time to ensure that personnel were able to get out safely rather than being murdered in the stampede to escape.

She had seen those doctors wielding automatic rifles and turning them on the innocent administration personnel and lab techs trying to escape.

She hoped the doctors were dead. She hoped they were roasting in hell. Unlike Del-Rey. Oh, she didn't want him dead. She wanted him alive. Alive and well so she could kill him herself.

She whimpered as another punch of sensation slammed into her stomach, her vagina, her clitoris. It was like a racking blow of electricity being shoved inside her. It sizzled and burned and left her gasping in need as the bedroom door opened.

She rolled to her feet, stumbling, staring at the man watching her with those devil's black eyes.

"What did you do to me?" Her fists clenched at her side.

"I don't know." He shook his head wearily. "Whatever it is, I did it to myself as well."

"You bastard!" There was nothing left to throw at him. She had thrown everything she could find over the past three days and the final object, that damned bowl, now lay at his feet. "You're lying. Just like you lied to me all these years, you're lying to me now."

"No, Anya."

The sound of her name on his lips was too much. She snarled, her fingers clawed as she jumped for him. She was going to claw his lying eyes out of his face. She was going to make him hurt the same as he was making her hurt.

He caught her hands an inch from his face.

"Stop this, Anya, it isn't helping."

"Do you think I don't know that?" she cried out, struggling against him, mind and body torn apart by conflicting emotions and needs. "You betrayed me, Del-Rey. You lied."

"I know, baby." He held her hands with one of his, the other touching her cheek, his thumb moving over her lips. "We'll deal with that, I promise. But I need your kiss. Now."

"No," she moaned, a long, drawn-out sob of need and despair as she pressed her cheek into his palm, bit his thumb.

Oh God, he tasted good. So good. Her tongue licked over the pad and her lashes fluttered.

"One more kiss," he growled. "Then we'll figure this out. I promise."

"One more kiss," she gasped. "One more."

She was reaching for him, needing him. Her lips opened beneath his, accepting his tongue and that taste she craved so desperately. She sucked it into her mouth and heard his groan of pleasure. She arched into his arms and begged silently for more.

One more kiss wasn't enough. She needed him to touch her. So bad. So bad that she gripped his hand and shoved it under her shirt. Then her hands were burrowing beneath his shirt, touching hot, hard flesh as she felt his hand cup the swollen mound of her breast.

Oh that was good. His thumb raked over her nipple and it was even better. He lifted her into his arms, and a second later she was stretching back on the bed as he whipped the shirt over her head.

Her hands buried in his hair as his lips covered her nipple. She tore at his shirt until he lifted his head, ripped it off and moved to her other nipple.

His skin covered hard, corded muscle. It flexed beneath her palms, her nails, as she felt his hands pushing at the cotton pants she wore.

It was desperate. She could feel the enraged lust traveling between them, as though electricity connected them, one feeding from the other until she was burning inside and she knew she wasn't going to get enough of him. She needed more of him.

A second later she found herself flipped to her stomach. Her fingers curled into the blankets as she opened her eyes and stared in dazed confusion at the bed. Her hips were jerked up. Calloused fingers ran through the sensitive folds between her thighs, and she was wet. So slick and wet and hot. And it felt so delicious she stretched into the caress.

"Tell me you want me," he growled behind her.

"I want you." She sobbed the answer into the bed, tears falling from her eyes again as she felt him behind her. "I want you."

Broad, hot, the crest of his cock tucked between the wet folds.

Not like this. She pressed her head into the bed. Not like this, where she couldn't hold on to him, where she couldn't find a sense of control or focus.

Why like this?

He pressed inside and she went crazy from the pleasure. Her back arched at the stretching heat, a cry falling from her lips, part protest, part hunger.

She felt a pulse of heated fluid filling her, burning her further. She felt her sex flex and ripple and draw him in. With each heated spurt she became more sensitive, hungrier, needier.

She should tell him she was a virgin. She should tell him she hadn't done this before.

A scream ripped from her throat as he tunneled inside in three hard strokes. Every inch. And he was so thick, invading her, stretching her, tearing through her virginity without the pain she had expected, but with more impact than she could have imagined.

Her thighs parted more, her hips tilted back farther and he was rising over her, his powerful arms braced beside her head as he began thrusting into her. His lips were at her shoulder. Sharp little kisses, heated and fierce just below her neck.

She was filled with him. She could feel every heavy vein in his cock, every pulse of blood through it, and it was killing her. She needed more, wanted more.

And he was giving her more. Surging inside her as she felt her body tighten. The muscles wrapped around his erection tightened, her clit throbbed, pulsed, and then everything inside her exploded in a cataclysm of light and color that had her screaming his name.

She shuddered through her orgasm, jerking beneath him as he continued to thrust hard and fast, gaining speed, pushing into her as she felt more of those pulses of heated fluid.

A second later, she heard him snarl, and felt something shocking. Something she knew couldn't be natural. This couldn't be real. His cock was swelling in one place. Getting larger, separating her farther as she felt his semen began to spurt inside her.

Animal genetics, she thought distantly. He was locking inside her. Held tight and sure inside the heavy muscles of her vagina, he suddenly snarled with animalistic fervor and she felt his teeth pierce her upper shoulder.

She should be screaming in pain. She was screaming in pleasure. Another, harder orgasm ripped through her, shook her, wrenched her senses from her and left her lost. She was so lost, with nothing, no one to hold on to. Thrown into a pleasure so violent, so brutal, she wondered if she could survive it.

Behind her, Del-Rey was growling. His teeth still gripped her flesh, his cock still locked inside her. She sobbed out his name. She wanted to beg him to hold her, but the last shreds of her pride held her back.

He had taken her like this, impersonally, and he had to have done it for a reason. She didn't matter. The same reason he had shot her family, the same reason he had lied to her for so many years. Because Anya Kobrin, and the fragile love that had been building inside her for him, didn't matter.

Which left her alone, at the mercy of a man that she now knew had no mercy.

◆   ◆   ◆

He had made a grave tactical error and Del-Rey knew it. The anger that had festered inside him over the years had overlooked the intense, all-abiding loyalty Anya felt for her family and friends. Del-Rey was a man who believed in retribution. He had been such a man all his life, until he sat here now, staring into the darkness of his own soul, and realized he had wounded a treasure he hadn't known he'd held.

He had known from the moment he met her that he was going to betray her. It was the way of the world. He couldn't fully trust. He never gave complete control or complete trust to another person, outside of Brim. Just as he had known that retribution would be dealt to the guards' leaders, as he had always dealt it. He had always killed before. He'd pulled his punches because of Anya. He hadn't killed, he had only wounded. Her father and her cousins would know they had been dealt with fairly. They were men of war. War had different rules than the fairy tales young women such as Anya lived within.

She was sleeping. Finally. Del-Rey sat in the chair beside her bed, dressed, his head in his hands as his elbows rested on his knees. He had sat down there the minute he could withdraw from her, as soon as the knot that had been swollen in his cock had receded enough for him to pull away from her. He had jerked his jeans back to his hips and sat. To keep from falling to the floor.

And he had remained there as she silently folded herself onto her side, tugged the blanket over her shoulders and cried silently until she went to sleep.

She hadn't sobbed again. She hadn't cursed him or railed at him. She had retreated into herself, and he had no idea how to pull her back.

He lowered his hands and stared at them. Large hands. The hands of a warrior. A killer. These hands had held her beneath him. His teeth had held her in place. His cock had knotted hard and deep inside her.

He had never done that. In his entire sexual life, he had never done that to a woman. Why this woman?

He rose to his feet and fixed his jeans before jerking his T-shirt on. He could hear Brim, his second-in-command moving up the steps to the second-floor bedroom. Del-Rey opened the door as the other man reached it.

Concerned light blue eyes stared back at him.

"Vehicles are here," Brim reported. "Those women downstairs are pissed off though. Watch your back."

He didn't blame them. Hell, someone should shoot him.

"Have you contacted Haven?"

"Messages have gone out; no answer," Brim reported before inhaling with narrowed eyes. "Something isn't right here, Del-Rey. You took the girl?"

Del-Rey growled. Anya was none of his business.

Brim shook his head. "Her scent has changed, shifted, and yours as well. Something whacked is going on here."

That was the understatement of the century. He looked back at Anya.

"Get ready to move out," he told his second-in-command. "Have them send Haven another message. I need their doctor. Now. This can't happen again, Brim. I don't know what the hell happened in here, but it can't happen again."

He closed the door and moved back to the bed.

"Anya." He whispered her name and she flinched.

Was it so horrendous, his touch? The greatest pleasure he had known in his life, and now she flinched from him.

"Get dressed. The vehicles are here and we're moving out. Now. I don't think you want to risk any attempt I would make to try to dress you myself."

He tried to make her angry. It didn't work. She pushed the blankets from her as though the exhaustion that gripped her was painful. He watched as she found her clothes and went to the bathroom, closing the door behind her.

He didn't hear her sobbing, didn't hear her crying. But he could smell her, and what he scented clawed at his chest. Somehow, he had managed to douse that fiery flame that was so much a part of her. At this moment, his Anya smelled of defeat. And Del-Rey felt it. For the first time in his life, he knew the taste of defeat.

· CHAPTER 2 ·

THREE WEEKS LATER

If there was one thing in Del-Rey's life that he knew with all certainty, it was himself. He was a Coyote Breed, and as he informed the Breed Ruling Cabinet weeks later, he admitted to some of that Breed's worst traits. Calculation, manipulation. The ability to look at a situation and instantly size up the roadblocks and dangers inherent in it and find a way over them. He wasn't a charge-into-the-fray type of guy. He was a slice-their-throat-in-the-dark animal, and he fully admitted to it.

For ten years he had connived to ensure that he and his people were part of the recognized Breed society. He was, after all, a man who liked to be on the winning side. Breed freedom was the winning side. But now, the stakes had been raised. Because of his mate.

Hell, he'd never caught so much as a whiff of information about mating heat between Breeds and their lovers. Who could have imagined that the Breed genetics would turn against them in such a way and would torture their females as it did?

Of course, how else did a Breed have a hope of holding his woman once she learned the animalistic nature that came out with mating heat?

He considered it a trade-off. Rather like the flesh wounds he had ordered for Anya's family in retaliation for the risks she had taken for six years. If he had walked away and left those men unwounded, then the Genetics Council would have had them killed. It was that simple when a man came right down to it. The Coyote Ghost wasn't a man of mercy when it came to the enemy. If the Council had suspected he had shown mercy to anyone except the woman he had kidnapped, then they would have instantly suspected those men of having been involved in the plot to free the Breeds from that facility.

Not that Anya had wanted to hear that explanation. She refused to speak to him. Once the Breed doctor Nikki Armani had taken her from the caves, he'd been denied any private contact with her, at her request.

He better understood now why his fury had risen at the thought of the risks she had taken. Why he had put two men on watch at that facility at all times, ensuring that should the Council send soldiers to collect her, she could be rescued.

He'd been too protective of her, and he had known it. His men had known it. They had tread a fine line around him where that girl was concerned for too many years. And the knowledge of the mating heat explained those impulses that Del-Rey would have never risked at any other time. It also explained his awareness, from the first time he had seen her, that in some way, he would betray her.

Calculation and manipulation, cunning and foresight. Those traits were part of the Breed makeup overall, but Coyotes had them in abundance. As well as a healthy dose of near laziness, but no species could be perfect, he told himself. The laziness didn't extend to the job, just to general life, and he was accepting of that in his men as well as himself. They might slouch on their own time, but they got the job done to his exacting specifications.

Now there was a much more important mission facing him. That of acquiring his mate back from the Breed Ruling Cabinet. Rules needed to be established, he told himself. Anya needed her pound of flesh or he would never have his chance to hold her again.

He understood pride. He didn't understand a woman's emotions, but the female Coyotes he'd rescued had informed him rather quickly that he best be learning those emotions fast. They had sworn loyalty to him and the packs seeking the alliance with the Breed society. That loyalty ran deep. They wouldn't break their word. But if he took her freedom of choice from this point forward, then resentment would brew. Both in the woman as well as in the packs he led.

It bit his pride though. It bit at his anger. For three weeks now he had been separated from his mate, knowing she was in the underground Breed research facilities undergoing tests on the mating heat. Knowing inside him that those tests were hurting her. He could feel it, knew it in a part of his soul he hadn't known existed. And he had been unable to force his way into her.

The five female Coyotes stayed with her. They were his insurance that if she asked for him, he would know. If she wanted free of the tests, then they would come for him. They reported to him daily, and each day he was told she didn't want him there. She didn't want to leave. But he saw in the women's eyes the proof that she suffered. His mate suffered and he was helpless to stop it.

Now he sat in the meeting room that had been set up for a Breed tribunal, something he was told had never been held in the eleven-year history of the Breeds' establishment.

A table of twelve men and women chosen from within all species to hear his mate's petition for separation from him.

He knew how it would end. He knew, and the ache that filled him at the thought was surprising. Accepting the truth and the direction each battle must take had never been a hard matter for him. But this time, seeing the path stretching before him and knowing what must be done, tore at him. It tempted the animal genetics that were never far from the surface, and riled the man with burning fury. The same fury he saw glowing in his mate's beautiful sapphire eyes. He ached and he raged, and he watched his life change before his eyes.

◆　◆　◆

A petition for separation from a mate had never occurred, not once in the eleven years that the Breeds had known of mating heat and suffered through it. Not until Anya Kobrin had submitted to three weeks of tests to complete the research the doctors needed to created a base hormonal therapy that would control the symptoms of the heat.

She had been warned it wasn't a cure, merely an aid. She

had been told she would never be free of the man they called her mate, but she would have the time she needed to figure out what the hell had happened to her life and how it had managed to go to hell so fast.

She stared at the Breed tribunal from the table she sat at in front of them. Nine men and three women drawn from every species of the Breeds. Wolf, Feline, Coyote. Del-Rey and Sharone were there to stand for the Coyotes. Her mate and one of her dearest friends.

Her mate, she wanted to scoff at the title as she glared at him. She was furious. Enraged. Scorned. In three weeks she hadn't forgotten a single complaint she had against him.

Her attention was drawn from the man to the young woman at her side. Cassandra Sinclair, daughter of a tribunal member, Dash Sinclair. At eighteen, Cassandra was slender, with long black hair and light, almost pale blue eyes. She had the genetic perfection of features that all Breeds had, though she was what they called a hybrid, a child born of Breed sperm that had fertilized a human egg that hadn't been changed by the genetics needed to create the Breeds. Her mother had then been artificially inseminated and carried Cassandra to term.

She was still Breed though. There was no mistaking the looks or the longer canines at the side of her mouth.

"Ladies and gentlemen of the tribunal," Cassandra announced. "You have before you a petition of separation between the Breed Del-Rey Delgado and his biological mate, Anya Kobrin. I'm acting on behalf of Miss Kobrin and officially request an order of separation be issued and constraints be placed on the Coyote Breed Alpha Del-Rey Delgado and that she be given sanctuary within Haven as long as Alpha Delgado is in residence at the base the Coyote Breeds have established. We further request that Alpha Delgado be refused his counterorder, in effect his petition to have access to his mate, over her wishes. At this time, Miss Kobrin is willing to take questions from the tribunal and has sworn on the tenets of Breed Law that her answers will be truthful and without prejudice to Alpha Delgado."

There was a shuffling along the table as each member except Del-Rey and Sharone took another look at the papers.

Cassandra resumed her seat, her expression composed as the tribunal stared back at the two of them.

"We have only a few questions, Ms. Kobrin. Merely clarifications to your statement." Jonas Wyatt, the director of the Bureau of Breed Affairs, began the process. Eerie silver eyes stared back at Anya surrounded by lush black lashes. His expression was cool and imposing, and perhaps about his lips there was a faint hint of cruel arrogance.

"To start with, I'd like you to clarify for the tribunal that you did indeed work with a man that you knew first as the Coyote Ghost, and finally by his true identity, Del-Rey, for a period of six years, to weed out the spies within the Coyote pack at the facility where you headed administration and inner facility security affairs."

Anya breathed in slowly. She swore she could smell Del-Rey. A subtle hint of spicy male warmth and sexual intensity. Too bad he hadn't been willing to share any of that warmth with her.

"That's true," she answered.

"Did you research the man you contacted before sending that first message?" Jonas asked her.

"I did." She nodded.

"And were you aware of the Coyote Ghost's habit of killing the head of security forces within the facilities he attacked over the years? Facilities that held Wolf, Feline and Coyote Breeds that he deemed acceptable risks to rescue."

"I was aware of this," she stated.

"And what made you believe no harm would come to your family then?" he questioned her, his voice growing colder. "Your father commanded parameter security and training. He was aware of what the facility was and the international laws against those facilities. What made you believe the Coyote Ghost would not kill your father?"

Because she had believed in his word. She had trusted him. And over the six years they had worked together, she had believed there was more binding them than a job.

"He swore before we met that my family wouldn't suffer," she told him. "He swore for six years as I did what he told me, risking myself and my family if I were caught, that they would not be punished or harmed unless there was no other recourse but to wound them to protect their own. We had an agreement."

"You have the secured emails that have been retrieved, Director Wyatt, that back up Ms. Kobrin's statement," Cassandra interjected.

Jonas looked back at her with faint surprise. "I didn't need proof of her statement, Ms. Sinclair," he told her. "I merely needed to clarify that she was aware of the risks in contacting Alpha Delgado before she did so."

"Ms. Kobrin." Merinus Lyons, wife and mate to Alpha Lyons, the Feline prides' leader, spoke up then. "Do you feel that you were, at any time, raped?"

The question had a deadly tension beginning to fill the air. Anya hadn't expected that question.

"I never stated I was raped," she answered.

"No, you didn't," Merinus agreed. "You have instead petitioned this tribunal for separation from a man that we know for a fact is your biological and, we suspect, your emotional mate. No mate has ever done this, no matter the anger or misunderstandings. As a woman, as part of this tribunal, I'd like to understand why you've taken this stance."

"I wasn't raped." She shook her head. "Not by Del-Rey. I feel raped by the insanity of these laws I'm forced to abide by, and I feel raped by a hormonal phenomenon neither Alpha Delgado nor myself had control over. I had no choice but to accept him as a lover because of the loss of control this biological connection forced. I resent that this tribunal feels that I should subject myself to that feeling whenever Alpha Delgado is present. And I resent that the choice could be taken out of my hands. That, Prima Lyons, is the worst sort of rape."

Merinus stared back at her for long moments before inclining her head in agreement. "Thank you, Ms. Kobrin, for that clarification."

Silence filled the meeting room then, as though the men and women heading the tribunal hadn't expected her answer. And she could feel Del-Rey staring at her; from the corner of her eye she could see the dark, brooding frown on his face.

"Would you say, Ms. Kobrin, that perhaps you and Alpha Delgado have been forced into a position that neither of you wanted?" Alpha Lyons asked then.

"I would say that," she stated.

The pride alpha stared back at her relentlessly. "Yet you've seen Alpha Delgado's statement that his intent all along was to take you out of that facility and claim you as his lover. You were sixteen when he first met you. From that point on, he was aware there was no chance he would leave you there. No chance that he didn't intend to convince you to stay with him."

She glared at Del-Rey then. "Then he should have been careful about the order he gave to have my family wounded," she stated. "Once we arrived here, he should have never refused my request to contact my family."

"Even if that contact threatened your family?" Alpha Lyons asked her then. "Ms. Kobrin, by contacting your family, you put them in the position that the Genetics Council has proof that they can be used against you. Their prime objective at this point is to capture Breed mates. Could your father be used to draw you from Haven? Would you give your life for your family?"

Her lips trembled. She stared at Cassandra. She hadn't considered that. The Council rarely struck out at humans any longer, because the propaganda against them was so strong.

Cassandra stared back at her in sympathy.

"No," she finally whispered. "I didn't know this."

"Yet you were sent Alpha Delgado's statement, explaining his reasons and his actions, which he gave this tribunal," Callan further stated. "Did you read that statement?"

She shook her head. She hadn't read it. She didn't want to read it or hear his reasons why.

"It wouldn't have made a difference," she finally told them clearly. "He lied to me, countless times. He destroyed my trust in him, and he knew for six years that he would do it. I don't trust him, Alpha Lyons. Don't doubt that this petition of separation is sincere. I promise you. It is."

"Ms. Kobrin." Wolfe Gunnar, alpha of the Wolf packs, spoke then. "Are you in love with him?"

She jerked in surprise at the question. "My emotions shouldn't come into this, Alpha Gunnar." Did she love him? Until she ached with it. Was she going to allow him to control her body and her life because of it? Not in this lifetime.

Wolfe stared back at her for long moments before nodding his head slowly. "Perhaps you're right," he finally agreed.

"Perhaps that's a question we should ask Alpha Delgado,"

Cassandra suggested then, turning her head to Del-Rey as Anya held her breath in fear. She knew the answer. "Alpha Delgado, are you in love with Ms. Kobrin?"

Del-Rey stared back at her broodingly. "I can't say I'm in love with her," he finally stated. "I'm a soldier, Ms. Sinclair, not a damned poet. I claimed her. As proven, she's my mate. Nothing else should come into this."

Anya lowered her head and stared at her hands, hope dwindling inside her no more than seconds after it had burned through her soul. If he had said yes, would she have followed through with this petition? She knew she wouldn't have. She couldn't have denied him if he had sworn he loved her, even though she knew his word wasn't worth the signature he had scrawled on his statements.

"I see," Cassandra said heavily, her head lifting to stare back at the women on the tribunal. "And we wonder at such a young woman's need to be separated from the man who only *claims* her," she sighed.

"Ms. Sinclair, may I ask a question?" Del-Rey asked, his voice as lazy as his slouched position in his chair.

"Of course, Alpha Delgado," Cassandra said with a hint of surprise.

"We have several mated males on this tribunal. Alpha Lyons, Alpha Gunnar, Enforcer Jacob Arlington, and Enforcer Aiden Chance. Tell me, gentlemen, were you in love with your mates when the mating heat claimed you?"

Each man grimaced heavily. "Maybe we just weren't aware it was love," Alpha Lyons finally said with some amusement as he glanced at his wife beside him. "But have no doubt, Alpha Delgado, we learned quick enough."

"Who is to say that I couldn't learn as well?" Del-Rey shrugged then. "Being a Coyote doesn't make me stupid, merely less willing to recognize emotion, I believe. By separating herself from me, my mate is stealing that chance from both of us."

"He's very clever with words," Cassandra murmured under her breath.

"He is at that," Anya said sadly. "He's very good at twisting words."

"I also noticed that Ms. Kobrin was decidedly less honest in her answer to that same question," Del-Rey pointed out then.

"Ms. Kobrin has the right to request that her emotions not be questioned," Cassandra argued. "Mating heat and the proven psychological effects are clear bases that she not be questioned regarding emotions that she may not be clear on at this moment."

Del-Rey's lips quirked mockingly, his black eyes gleamed in knowledge as Anya lifted her head and stared back at him.

"If I hadn't wounded her family and made it look like a clear attempt to harm them, then they'd be dead," he stated then. "The Council would have killed them and I knew it. But, I will admit, even without that risk, they would have felt my wrath. They endangered her from childhood to the moment I kidnapped her. Their lack of concern for her well-being would have been punished. That was the decision behind my actions, right or wrong. If I knew then what I know now, would I have done it? I have to say yes," he continued. "I claimed her and I claimed all right to exact vengeance in her name. Her tender emotions and lack of understanding of men of war clearly show that she had no idea how little her welfare was considered by those she loved." With that, he leaned forward. "She wants a petition of separation. Very well. She has it. I'll be damned if I'll take a mate or a woman who claims that the bonds between us are no more than rape." He turned to Jonas at his side. "Director Wyatt, I accept your offer as enforcer with the Bureau on the condition that while I'm risking my ass for her freedom, again, that she be required to stay at Base and oversee the Coyote Breeds that look to her for support. Those men and women we took out of there will need time to acclimate and she's a guiding force they look to."

Jonas's brows arched. "How long do you believe this acclimation is needed?" he asked. "I'm certain Ms. Kobrin would like a set timeline. She seems rather talented in the area of setting boundaries."

"One year," Del-Rey stated. "She'll receive advance notice of my returns to oversee the military and financial concerns of the packs between missions. You stated you needed more men for the swift strikes being made against facilities and enemy groups." He grinned. "Looks like I'm your man."

"Those are dangerous assignments," Jonas growled as Anya stared at him in shock. "Mates don't take those missions."

Del-Rey gave a hard, cold laugh as he rose to his feet. "Looks like I'm no longer a mate, Director Wyatt. I'm just the poor bastard with the hard-on."

With that, he moved from the table, stalking past the table Anya sat at, his imposing features savage, tight with anger, as he stalked to the wide double doors, lifted his hands and slammed through them.

The crash of metal against metal as the doors bounced into the walls had her flinching violently as she stared at his back.

"He's crazy," she whispered.

Cassandra snorted. "Yeah. That's a Coyote for you. We've never accused them of being sane."

"Can he do this?" she asked. "He accepted mate status. This is supposed be against the rules or something, isn't it?"

Cassandra stared back at her archly. "Or something," she sighed. "Oh well, look on the bright side, maybe he won't be back very often."

She grabbed Cassandra's arm, glaring at her furiously. "He could be killed."

"We could all be killed, Anya," Cassandra told her, her voice cool now. "We're Breeds. We weren't meant to be free, remember? We're all at risk. He's just accepting a risk other mated males are forced to relinquish. The order of separation changes those rules. He can do whatever the hell he wants to now."

Even risk his life. Anya turned back and let her gaze find Sharone's. Her friend was torn, she could tell. Torn between pack loyalty and friendship. Then, Sharone's expression cleared and a little smile touched her lips as she stared back at Anya. One of triumph. One Anya understood even less than she understood Del-Rey's decision to leave.

EᴵɢHT MᴏɴTHS LᴀTᴇʀ

Del-Rey stared out at the night as the heli-jet neared Haven. The sky was clear; stars studded the midnight expanse and a full moon shone down on the land with vibrant golden rays.

Forests ringed the nearly two hundred acres of valley that the Wolf Breeds now commanded, a far cry from the less than a dozen acres they had held before. Federal land had been granted to them as yet more government officials within the U.S. had been proven to be part of the Genetics Council's lower ranks. Top secret files obtained from select agencies had shown an influx of money through those channels as well as weapons and military trainers.

Two hundred acres of Uncompahgre National Forest, so far, had been deeded to the Wolf Breeds, with another five hundred acres expected to be ceded to them within the next year.

The valley the Wolf Breeds claimed as home was within full sight of the cliff peak that the Coyote Breeds had invaded a little over eight months before. That single mountain had been given to the Coyotes due to the fact that it represented a threat to the valley below and hadn't been in the original land given to Haven. It was a home Del-Rey was now determined to return to.

He'd just finished an investigation into Engalls Pharmaceuticals and a division of that company, Brandenmore Research. The two companies were working covertly on a drug that would control a Breed's free will. The investigation had taken longer than he had originally believed it would. He hadn't been back to Base in over two months.

He hadn't smelled his mate in two months. He'd had too much time to think and too damned much time to regret. And he was sick of being away from Base, being away from his mate.

"Where do you think we're headed next?" Brim smothered a yawn as the pilot contacted Haven's base and neared their airspace.

"We're not going back out," Del-Rey stated, his gaze still narrowed on the night sky.

Brim's silence lasted a little too long.

"You promised the tribunal a year," Brim reminded him quietly.

"I know what I said," he growled. "We'll go fuck off at the beach for a few weeks here and there. Hell, take the girls to fucking Disneyland or some shit. I've had it, Brim. This is bullshit. My mate runs my fucking base better than I do, and on top of it"—he turned to his second-in-command and bodyguard—"did you read that fucking report Sharone finally got around to sending to us? This is a disaster waiting to happen."

He was going to start sweating again. Hell, when he'd read the original report, he swore his hands had shook. His mate was too damned brave, courageous and daring, and those female bodyguards he had allowed her were just as damned bad.

He ran his hand over his face and shook his head. Eight months. A man could do a lot of thinking, conniving and planning in eight months. When it came right down to it though, he knew when he'd reached his limit. Del-Rey's limit had been reached.

"Should be easy enough to put another team on Engalls and Brandenmore with our information," Brim stated. "All we need is the proof now."

"Proof better come soon," Del-Rey snarled.

Brandenmore and Engalls, CEOs of the two companies they were investigating, had nearly been the cause of several Breeds' deaths as well as a librarian in Virginia who had overhead their

plot. Being forced to release them to gain information had left a
bad taste in Del-Rey's mouth. Information had come in. Information that would save a young woman's life, and enough medical knowledge to prepare a fail-safe in case another Breed was
infected with the drug. But damn if he hadn't wanted to kill the
bastards still walking the streets. Smug, superior, Phillip Brandenmore and Horace Engalls were the worst that humanity
could produce. And they called Breeds animals, he snorted silently.

The black heli-jet came in, full stealth, and settled on the
landing pad above the two-story welcome entrance at the gates
of the Wolf Breed compound, Haven. The doors slid open silently, and figures, tall, dark and silent, stepped from the craft
and moved with lethal precision to the steps that led down to
the side of the building and the entrance door.

Del-Rey and his team didn't make a sound as they entered
the secured building, moved through the security protocols,
then entered the enclosed Wolf Breed compound through a
lower door.

"Alpha Leader Delgado, we have a vehicle awaiting you and
your men." A Wolf Breed escort stepped forward in the low
light that surrounded the outside of the structure. "Alpha Leader
Gunnar and the Wolf Breed Cabinet have assembled as per
your request."

Del-Rey gave a sharp nod. He motioned two of his men with
him, the other two he gave a silent signal to return to their own
base within the cliffs that rose high above the peaceful valley.

With him was Brimstone and another member of his team
who was also part of his security as alpha: Cavalier, the Breed
Anya had helped him to rescue before the main facility rescue.

She had never understood why he took only a few at a time.
It had been imperative to weed out the spies, to show her that
often those she trusted would betray her. And when it came to
his packs, he wanted the assurance of loyalty. Cavalier had information he needed and a view into the facility that even Anya
and Sharone wouldn't have known to make note of.

The drive to the pack headquarters in the center of the compound wasn't a long one. The valley was nearly two hundred
acres of pristine grassland and rising, centuries-old cotton-
woods, pines and oak. They sheltered the cabins and buildings

within, and deep beneath the base of the mountains that rose above them was a command center rivaled only by the Felines or the American government itself.

It took time, though, to clear Security in the main building of the headquarters. An elevator ride took them down to the bowels of the base, and then they had another drive through steel and cement to the once abandoned military base that the Wolf Breeds had been given access to.

Over the past seven years since Haven had been established, the majority of work had gone into this defense and operational base. Above them, the serene valley reflected a love of nature, privacy and established camaraderie, if one overlooked the armed guards hidden in the mountains and the sheltering branches of the trees.

Below was the heart and soul of Haven's security, and it ran like a well-oiled machine.

"The cabinet is waiting in meeting room three on the third level," the Wolf Breed guard said and nodded to them as they entered an elevator. "Dash Sinclair and his family arrived just ahead of you."

Dash Sinclair had risen up the ranks of Breed hierarchy quickly since his revelation of Breed status. A Breed with recessed genetics, he had escaped his labs at ten. He had gone into the American foster care system, been educated and was in the military until a little girl's letter drew him back to America and awoke the animal that had stayed suppressed within him.

His daughter, Cassandra, was still a sore point with Del-Rey, but he knew she had been wounded several months before during an operation that she should have never been in the middle of.

"How is Ms. Sinclair's recovery?" he asked. He hated the woman's logic, her ability to argue for everything he had rejected with every part of his soul, but he had seen the tender, compassionate woman she was in her concerned gaze the day she had argued for his mate's freedom.

"She's doing much better." The guard nodded. "She's here at Haven at present under the care of Dr. Armani. We still haven't learned who broke into her hospital room that night."

Cassandra Sinclair had had a visitor as she lay in a near coma state, surrounded by Wolf and Feline Breed guards. Someone had managed to cut a hole into a window more than twelve stories above the ground, slip into her room and send her into screams of hysteria.

The last Del-Rey had heard, she had no idea who or what had been there with her.

Del-Rey clenched his jaw as the Wolf Breed looked back at him expectantly then. Each time he had arrived at Haven, always secretly, always under the cover of night, the Wolf Breeds watched him with the same expression. As though waiting for him to ask the question he had no intention of asking: How was his mate?

"Here we are." The elevator shuddered to a stop depositing them in another steel-and-cement corridor. Water, electrical and various other pipes ran along the walls. Monitors displayed general orders and Breeds—Wolf, Feline and Coyote—moved with an array of humans that had aligned with them.

Some with clipboards, some chatting with companions—they were all heavily armed and prepared.

Del-Rey, Brimstone and Cavalier followed behind their escort until they came to a door, the same gunmetal gray color as the rest of the operational base.

Stepping inside the entrance alone as it slid open, Del-Rey motioned for the other two to wait for him as he faced the Wolf Breed Cabinet that had come together.

There were six of them. Just as there were six in the Coyote Breed Cabinet, six to the Feline Breed Cabinet. Dash Sinclair; the Wolf Breed Alpha Wolfe Gunnar; Aiden, a class one enforcer; Jacob, Haven's head of security; Faith, Jacob's wife and liaison to the other packs; Hope Gunnar, Wolfe's wife; and the lupina, second-in-command of Haven.

"Del-Rey, welcome back." Wolfe and the others rose from the table, hands extended in greeting.

Once the preliminary meet-and-greet bullshit was over with, Del-Rey took his seat and slapped the file he carried with him in the center of the round table, in front of Wolfe.

The pack leader's expression tensed as he opened it and read the report Del-Rey and his men had put together with the help of the Bureau of Breed Affairs, the Feline Cabinet, and the investigations he and his own men had done into the subject.

The file was passed around the table, each member going over it carefully, their expressions telling the same story. Disbelief and anger.

"Will it ever stop?" Jacob murmured, his low voice harsh as he finished the file while his wife read over his shoulder. He slid it on and waited.

Del-Rey watched as Faith laid her hand on her mate's shoulder, her cheek against the top of his head. The connection, the bonding between them ignited a flare of rage in him that threatened to spark out of control. They were mated. The scent of their bond, their emotions and need for each other was an affront to his senses. An insult to everything that he had been forced to walk away from.

When the last cabinet member, Dash Sinclair, closed the file, Del-Rey felt the tension as it began to ratchet up through the room.

"We'll need to convene the full cabinet together," Wolfe said heavily. "This is a risk to all of us."

The full cabinet was something even Del-Rey had never seen. Each species of Breed had their own cabinet. The twelve-member tribunal he had faced eight months before was a selected mix to deal with smaller issues that concerned the society as a whole. Such as when Anya Kobrin had demanded separation from her mate.

The full cabinet was another story. Six members of each species. The Wolf and Coyote packs as well as the Feline pride. Added to that was the six-member board selected from within the Bureau of Breed Affairs, comprised primarily of humans except for the director of the bureau, Jonas Wyatt.

The full cabinet was twenty-four members in all, and Del-Rey had a feeling its meetings wouldn't be as social and well conducted as the few pack meetings he'd been called to.

The risk in not calling together the full cabinet was growing by the day.

"There's not enough evidence to prosecute the pharmaceutical company or the research and development arm that's conducting the experiments," Del-Rey stated. "No evidence that they've used Breeds in that research, either willingly or involuntarily."

Wolfe ran his hand wearily over his face as he pulled the file back to him and reopened it. Del-Rey knew what he would find there. In the past four weeks the Feline Breed scientist Elyiana Morrey had nearly died from the drugs that had been used to attempt to force her to destroy a Lion Breed known to have an anomaly in his blood suspected to induce a primal strength and rage known as feral fever.

Mercury Warrant had developed feral fever in the labs where he had been created and trained. At the time of his rescue the scientists there had developed a drug therapy which, in essence, controlled him, locked the animalistic power inside him and forced him to obey the commands given to him by his trainers and creators.

A variation of that drug had been used on the scientist. The lack of the feral hormone for the drug to attach to in her blood had created far greater, nearly fatal results. It had almost destroyed her mind. Now there was evidence that Breeds unknown to the Breed community were being captured or somehow convinced to participate in the experiments with this drug.

Three Breeds had been found just within the past week, their brains fragmented by the pressure that had built within them. One had nearly killed a human, and keeping that one covered up hadn't been easy.

"This drug could become our personal nightmare," Del-Rey told them. "It doesn't just have the power to steal our will; it also has the power to make us killers and nothing more. The Bureau is working to get more information but their contact within the companies has disappeared. They suspect that person won't show up alive."

"They've found a way to create the killers they always wanted." Hope's horrified whisper filled the room.

"Not entirely," Del-Rey stated. "There are symptoms when the drugs are being slipped into the victim. Our concern is the rumor that the research company has managed to find volunteers. Breeds who were led to believe that this would recess their Breed genetics." He leaned forward slowly. "The Breed that nearly killed the police officer was younger, unknown and unlisted with the Bureau of Breed Affairs. We know there are still facilities holding many Breeds captive, moving them often. He could be one of those, or a volunteer. Whichever, we have a problem on our hands."

Faith spoke up. "Dr. Morrey was given the drug by Breed assistants in her lab. Breeds that showed no signs of being under the drug themselves. Greed."

"Greed," Del-Rey agreed. "The past eight months that I and my team have been chasing down rumors and leads on this, the company managed to actually get the drug into Sanctuary. We need to stop this now."

"And stopping it would require . . . ?" Wolfe asked.

"One of the teams need to be granted full sanction," Del-Rey stated, staring back at them coolly. "Leashing your enforcers and forcing them to hold back in this investigation won't get the answers you need."

Dash sat back in his chair and regarded him silently.

"Full sanction?" he asked. "Very few of our teams are allowed that status, Pack Leader Delgado, and none are available now."

"Then you better make one available," Del-Rey stated coldly. "Do you think keeping a leash on your enforcers is going to work in this situation?"

"Your team has been investigating this since the first," Wolfe said then. "You should still have time to finish it."

His jaw bunched. "I've brought you enough to put a sanctioned team on it," he told them as he rose from his chair. "Go over the file. I should also point out something you've obviously overlooked."

Wolfe frowned back at him. "And that is?"

"One of the first trials of this drug was on a human in Haven, eight months ago. The drug was slipped into her food and drink during visits to her parents in the neighboring town. It was considered a failure because she didn't follow her final order."

They were all sitting forward now, expressions dark, savage.

"Jessica," Wolfe growled.

The young military communications officer was still in confinement, nearly a year after she had betrayed the pack. She was alive only because the Wolf Breed suspected to be her mate refused to allow her to be turned over to Breed Law.

That left confinement until the full cabinet could make a

decision on whether or not her actions warranted death. The matter hadn't been brought before the cabinet because the Wolf Breed Cabinet had yet to decide if that was the action they would take.

"She was tested for drugs," Faith protested. "None were found."

"The drug has a masking agent." Dash's voice was savage now. "It's not easy to detect."

"I'll be returning to my pack," Del-Rey informed them. "There are issues I need to take care of there. I'll no longer be handling the conclusion of this assignment."

He turned and moved for the door.

"Del-Rey, you promised your mate a year." Faith spoke up then. "Its only been eight months."

He stopped, looked over his shoulder slowly, his eyes narrowed on the woman as his lip curled. "You must have neglected to put that provision in the agreement I signed. There's no time stated there, and I have duties to my packs, just as the rest of you do. You can inform my coya I'm back. I may have neglected to do that as well."

He stepped from the meeting room and nodded to his men before making his way from the secured underground rooms. He kept at bay the hard smile that would have curled his lips.

Over the months, he had taken the time to learn about mating heat. He'd made certain he received all Dr. Armani's reports on his mate and he'd studied them carefully. He hadn't hesitated to ask questions.

Getting reports on Base or personal details from Sharone wasn't hard, simply because she was always eager to talk about her coya. Hell, every damned man and woman on base thought the sun rose and set on their coya's ass.

It was the details he had begun to learn that Sharone was leaving out that made his decision for him. Particularly the month before when Anya, coya of the Coyote packs, had convinced her security detail to take her to a bar, in the small town of Advert, nearly an hour from the Haven base. Once there they had proceded to become involved in a barroom brawl that cost his base nearly a thousand dollars in damages.

A drop in the bucket compared to the price his teams commandeered for their private and government security work, but still, his mate had been there. In a barroom brawl where she had been fighting like a man and taking out her excessive adrenaline surges on the unwary, rather than him.

Damn her. What the hell did she think she was going to get away with next? A lover perhaps? He had nightmares about that one. Full, vivid, blood-splashed nightmares where he ripped off the head of any man that dared to touch her, while she stared on in horror.

It was time to return to his place as alpha. Time to show his wayward little coya her place in his life. And it wasn't merely taking over his base while he was gone, not that she didn't do a damned fine job of keeping things together in his absence. It was a job that would be done more effectively if he was working with her. She couldn't train his soldiers. She couldn't make military decisions, and she couldn't aid his pack leaders in choosing the men to be assigned to the Bureau rotation. Every six months teams of Wolf, Feline and Coyote Breeds shifted and moved among the command bases. At present, he had twelve Felines and twelve Wolves on base. Sanctuary had just as many Coyotes and Wolves, and Haven commandeered the same number of Felines and Coyotes.

Two of those Coyotes assigned to Sanctuary were the two younger twin females that had come out of the compound with Anya. They were teenagers now and needed a firmer hand than Del-Rey was comfortable applying. What the hell did he know about female teenagers?

He knew the reports on the older three, and those made him sweat. The price of their clothing, makeup and shoes alone was enough to make a man flinch. Not that Anya spent nearly as much. No, he had to have his gifts sent to Haven and then forced on her by the lupina there, Hope Gunnar.

Stubborn damned woman. She was making him insane.

"Coya is still on base," Brim reported as they stepped into the all-terrain that would transport them along the steep road that had been curved through the mountain to the base entrance. "Sharone says she requests a few additional days as you didn't inform her of your impending return and she considers that grossly unfair." Brim's lips twitched as he gave Del-Rey the message.

Del-Rey grunted. "Tell her that's too damned bad. I'll be

there within the hour." Then he grinned. "Tell her to please apprise my pack leaders that I'll need them in Command when I arrive."

Brim grinned and relayed the message before disconnecting the link to Base that he now wore at his ear. The cylindrical earpiece extended just past the ear. The built-in receiver and mic made communication between Base and Haven much more effective. Separate channels had been built into the interface, and reception was as clear as the satellite phones they used.

"You could be playing a dangerous game with your coya, Del-Rey," Brim informed him. "If she walks, the people she brought out of Russia may walk with her."

Del-Rey shook his head. "They're Coyotes; they know a winning side when they see it. I'll win, Brim."

"Overconfidence, my friend?" Brim asked him. Only Brim could have gotten away with that question.

"Desperation," Del-Rey growled. "Just wait, Brim. When you've gone nearly a year with a hard-on that threatens your sanity, then you question me about overconfidence."

◆　◆　◆

Anya turned to Sharone, staring at her silently for long moments after her friend and bodyguard relayed Brim's message.

"He asked me to do what?" she finally asked quietly.

"Call together his pack leaders to Command; he'll be meeting with them on his arrival." Sharone cleared her throat. "He refuses to wait the extra time you requested to return to Haven."

Anya crossed her arms over the light gray sweater she wore as she tapped her foot irritably against the stone floor of the community room. Around her, off-duty soldiers slouched and watched the huge television screen mounted on the wall or snacked on whatever they had managed to put together for dinner.

It was going to take her days just to figure out what the hell had happened to the supplies in the kitchen area. Either they were eating more, or someone was saving back supplies again.

She'd had that problem in the first months. The soldiers would slip food from the kitchen—it didn't matter what it was—and hide it, just in case they began running low. She suspected it was the younger Coyotes. Food wasn't exactly plentiful in the facility they had been created and trained within. They couldn't get used to the fact that this was no longer the case.

She breathed out heavily as her bodyguard fought to hide a smirk.

"Let that smile free and I won't fix dessert for a month," Anya warned her.

Several growls turned on Sharone. Male Coyotes who had been shamelessly eavesdropping.

Sharone rolled her eyes. "They're worse than that damned Styx when it comes to their sweets."

"Remember that."

"I don't know." Sharone shrugged. "Rumor from Sanctuary is that Del-Rey has told Jonas to take a flying leap. He's returning to Base for good."

Base. She was tired of hearing it called Base. It wasn't the damned base. It was home. Just as Haven was home to the Wolves and Sanctuary was home to the Felines. Yet Coyotes called home *Base*. Like *soldiers* rather than men.

"He wouldn't dare." Anya tossed Sharone an irritated look before turning and heading to the exit tunnel that led to her quarters. "Contact the team leaders and let them know to be waiting on their alpha in Command. Get Emma and Ashley back here, tell them playtime in town is over. Their alpha has returned."

She didn't question why she was following his orders. She should have contacted him herself and told *him* to take a flying leap. But if she did that, then it would affect the team leaders and the soldiers under them. That was uncalled for. Her personal battle with Del-Rey shouldn't affect the men, and too few women, who worked within the caves and caverns the Coyotes had taken over.

She listened as Sharone relayed her orders. She couldn't leave yet; there was still too much to do and she hadn't been given warning. If she left without preparation, then the place was a mess when she returned, sometimes weeks after Del-Rey arrived.

She ignored the leap of excitement building within her though, the little ember of warmth that burned low in her stomach at the thought of seeing him again. If she didn't ignore it, then she was forced to remember everything that was sure to piss her off. To hurt her.

She hadn't quite gotten over the hurt yet. Her father and cousins had healed without complications. They were back to full strength; the flesh wounds they had received had healed nicely. But Anya's heart hadn't quite healed, and she knew it. She still woke in the middle of the night crying out for him, and she still remembered the feeling of complete isolation as the pleasure of their sexual encounter eased away.

She had been cold. So cold clear to her soul that sometimes she wondered if she would ever be warm again. At the time, she had known she wouldn't. And she would never forget his answer to the Breed tribunal when Cassandra Sinclair had asked him if he loved his mate.

Had he actually suggested he could learn to love her? As if she wanted him to learn anything.

She stomped into her personal quarters, casting a glare at the door that led to Del-Rey's. She had started to move her rooms, until the pack alphas had come to her, refusing to allow it as per Del-Rey's orders.

Everything was Del-Rey's orders. At least everything he could get away with. She still hadn't seen her father, despite his transfer to the United States. He and her cousins and their families now lived in California, having been slipped from Russia by a combined Wolf and Feline Breed mission.

Because she was now Del-Rey's mate, her family represented a threat to her welfare if they remained where the Council could easily reach them.

She was coya of the Coyote packs. Second-in-command when Del-Rey and his lieutenants were off playing heroes. When he was back, she had always been moved to Haven, where she paced and worried and knew all the hard work she had done at the base was being ruined by Del-Rey.

Coyotes had a tendency to be a little deliberately lazy. Not so much on the job. They could be counted on to do their jobs. But keeping the kitchen in order, the community room free of debris and the reports flowing smoothly weren't always as easy to ensure. Because Del-Rey let them slack off.

Sharone piped up. "Maybe we'll have an official ceremony soon. With the alpha back, he could decide it's time to seduce his coya. You know you can't get out of officially accepting your title much longer. Whether you sleep with that bad-assed Coyote or not, that ceremony is serious shit. Even the soldiers that came out of Russia with us are looking forward to it."

The ceremony. That's all she heard about was that damned ceremony. It was a wedding, pure and simple. But for some reason it held much more significance to the Breed community than it did to some humans.

"I'd be satisfied if he'd just learn how to clean the dirty clothes out of his quarters while I'm gone," Anya snorted. "The man excels at deliberate messiness."

"At least he excels," Sharone laughed.

"This isn't going to work," she stated, swinging around to stare back at Sharone as she closed the door behind her. "I haven't managed to straighten out the messes he left me last month when he returned. I can't leave yet."

Sharone's hazel green eyes gleamed with amusement. "You're going to stay while the alpha is in residence? Oh, Coya, very brave," she drawled. "And here you're a day late on hormone therapy injections? Guess you should have gone to see the doc yesterday, huh?"

There was another problem. That Wolf Breed quack was starting to get on her nerves. There was something wrong with her, she didn't care what Dr. Armani said. The dreams were coming back. Bright, sensation-ridden dreams of sex. The kind of sex where Del-Rey wrapped around her, whispered all the lies women liked to hear and left her aching for release. It had to be the mating heat. Armani had to be wrong about her hormone levels, there was no other option.

"Contact Armani and tell her I'll be in first thing in the morning." Anya worried her lower lip as she thought. "Maybe I can convince her to up the dosage a bit with Del-Rey here." She looked at Sharone questioningly. "If that worked, then I wouldn't have to leave every time he got a wild hair up his butt and decided to come back."

"Del-Rey? Get a wild hair up his butt?" Sharone snorted. "No body hair, remember?"

That was Sharone, mocking and sarcastic.

"Don't pick on me, Sharone," she ordered her. "This situation is bad enough with Del-Rey returning as it is."

Her emotions were ready to overload. Excitement. Anticipation. She was tired of hiding from something that wasn't her fault. This mating heat crap was kind of under control. The mating heat hormone levels were steady. She had periods of arousal, but Armani kept arguing they were normal. Baloney. What she was feeling was not normal. It couldn't be. Otherwise, it meant she was actually missing that wisecracking, lying, mangy Coyote and she refused to do that.

"So, should Emma and Ashley get the cabin in Haven prepared?" Sharone asked.

Anya grit her teeth and stared back at the other woman in fierce determination. "I don't think so. Let's see how long he can actually stay with the coya in-house so to speak," she bit out. "A hundred says he's gone in a month."

Sharone laughed. "A hundred says you're knotted again within the week."

They shook on it. Anya had no doubt in her mind who was going to win.

CHAPTER 4

He had changed.

The next afternoon Anya walked into the open community room, a large cavern that housed the recreational area of the base, and stopped.

She stared at the man lounging in a recliner on the far side, his pack alphas similarly relaxed, beers in their hands as they talked.

Del-Rey looked happy. There was a grin playing about his lips, his dark face was creased in amusement, his devil's black eyes filled with mirth as one of the pack alphas talked.

His dark blond hair was shorter. It had once fallen to his shoulders, the long, coarse strands thick and healthy. It was now cut a bit above the shoulder and it was shaggier than it had been before, as though he'd cut it himself.

One jean-clad leg was stretched out, the other bent. His wrist rested on his knee and he held his beer loosely. The shirt he wore buttoned up the front was wrinkled, clean but not exactly neat.

In his opinion though, if it were neat, he would be a Wolf rather than a Coyote. She snorted silently at the thought as she let her gaze caress him again.

He was just as gorgeous as ever. Not pretty-boy gorgeous, but rough and rugged. Strong features defined his face; arched brows, a high forehead. His entire body was a golden bronze, as though perpetually tanned. His lips were sensual, the lower lip just a bit too lush for a woman's peace of mind perhaps. The full curve tempted the imagination, made her remember what his kiss had felt like.

Hot. Destructive. Hungry.

At that moment his head jerked around, his gaze meeting hers. As though he had felt her eyes on him, felt the caress that her hands itched to give in the middle of the night.

She swallowed tightly as he watched her, his hand moving as he brought the bottle of beer to his lips and tilted it back. Her breathing became deeper, harder. Sweet mercy, she was going to break out in a sweat.

"Call that damned quack Armani and tell her to get her crap together," she ordered Sharone.

"Really," Sharone muttered. "Damn, Anya, you're getting hot."

"Shut up." Anya threw her a hard glare before stalking through the community room and heading into the kitchen.

Okay, the alpha leader was in residence, he could damn well approve kitchen help now. She needed a cook, assistants and a cleanup crew. And she didn't want Breeds. Breeds were military trained; it was part of their genetics, part of their training. Breed soldiers did not make good cooks, or neat cooks.

She stepped into the kitchen and automatically started rinsing dishes and loading the dishwasher as Sharone, Emma and Ashley began putting other items away.

"I wasn't created to clean a kitchen," Ashley informed all of them as she flipped her cosmetically enhanced blond hair over her shoulder and looked at her nails. "I'm not washing skillets."

"You get the first stack," Anya informed her. "I'll take the second."

"You're so kidding," Ashley laughed.

Anya turned back to the younger Breed girl. She and Emma might be twins, but they were worlds apart.

"Do I look like I'm kidding?" she asked the other girl coolly.

"You're just doing that because I got my nails done yesterday and you were stuck here." Ashley pouted. "That's so not fair, Coya."

"I'll give you a list of not fair later," Anya told her.

"Oh boy," Ashley hissed. "Alpha coming."

Anya stiffened. She was put out with Dr. Armani, herself and the fact that the first thing she did on seeing him was crave the warmth she knew his body held.

Not just his warmth. His touch. She wanted to be tucked into his arms, and it was the one thing she knew he truly didn't want.

She swore she felt him step into the room. The temperature in the large kitchen area shot up drastically, burrowed beneath her flesh and left her flushed.

"Coming to clean up your mess?" she asked as though she saw him every day rather than just twice in the past eight months.

He paused and looked around the room, his brows drawn into a frown. "I didn't make the mess."

"Neither did I," she informed him sweetly as she shoved a plate into the machine. "Someone did though."

He looked around at Sharone, Ashley and Emma as they made themselves very busy. Too busy actually. They usually balked at kitchen duty.

"How did this happen?" he finally asked her.

Anya straightened slowly and glared at him. "Do you ever read my reports?"

"With diligence and exacting attention," he drawled. "What does this have to do with your reports?"

He leaned against the door frame, watching her curiously as she straightened and fought to control her temper. Damn him, she'd never had a problem controlling her temper before she met him.

"I'll tell you what." She smiled tightly. "Clean up the kitchen, then go read one of my reports with a bit more exacting attention than you read them before and see if you can't figure it out."

With that, she shoved the dishwasher closed and stomped to the opposite entrance, which led to a narrow tunnel running behind the community room.

Her bodyguards were moving quickly behind her, as though

they bothered to follow her every step in Base. She was so safe here it was enough to offend her need for adventure. It did offend that need.

"Wow. You walked out on the alpha," Ashley said and whistled behind her. "No one walks on the alpha, Coya."

Anya rolled her eyes. No one argued with the alpha. No one sassed the alpha. No one disobeyed the alpha's orders. The list was almost never ending and never failed to send Anya's nerves into chaos. She wasn't the alpha's puppet and she wasn't going to pretend to be one.

"Maybe he'll get mad enough to finish loading the dishwasher," she bit out.

Sharone laughed. "Wanna bet?"

"Ten bucks he doesn't," Anya shot back.

"Ten bucks he does and the kitchen sparkles when he's done. Alpha doesn't like messes unless he makes them."

Well hell, she had nothing to worry about then, because she was the biggest mess there.

She wasn't much better by evening. Adrenaline was racing through her system and Dr. Armani wasn't being helpful. Natural arousal her ass. There was nothing natural about her reaction to Del-Rey, and no one was going to convince her otherwise.

She waited until darkness fell to check the kitchen and turn over the ten bucks to Sharone, then she and the three other girls slipped out into the night.

The guards on duty were used to her slipping out; they didn't even blink. As usual, when Del-Rey was on base, there was a strangely relaxed atmosphere. She'd slipped into the base a few times while he was there, when she had forgotten something she needed. She had noticed the difference. There was more of an air of camaraderie, a warmth that was lacking when he was on a mission. It made her feel curiously lonely, and aware that the Coyote home wasn't complete when their alpha was gone. Their coya just wasn't a fitting replacement.

◆   ◆   ◆

Del-Rey stared around the kitchen and at the younger soldiers that had completed cleaning up the mess that had been made.

"How long has your coya had kitchen duty?" he asked one

of them, strangely enough one of the men from his own group, not the group that came from the Russian facility.

The young Breed shrugged, glanced at his feet, then lifted his gaze to Del-Rey. "Whenever you aren't here, Alpha," he finally admitted.

"This is the reason I have the request for kitchen staff, in bold, in my coya's list of requirements?" he asked the Breed.

"It's not just me, Del-Rey," the Coyote Breed breathed out roughly. "Sometimes we just forget to do things. You know how we are. If we were perfect, we'd be Wolves, right?"

His own words thrown back at him. He growled in warning. The Breed cleared his throat and stepped back, but there was a glimmer of amusement in his eyes.

"Make a roster for kitchen duty," he told the other man. "Put the Felines in first."

He almost chuckled at the idea. Damn, he could see those Felines having fits already.

The Coyote Breed whistled soundlessly. "Alpha Lyons will protest."

Del-Rey shrugged. "So, I'll just protest right back the next time he puts our Coyote team on babysitting duty. Last time they were out, they had to make mud pies with the babies."

"Yeah, but we liked that," the soldier laughed. "Man, those Feline kids know how to pitch a mud ball."

"Yeah, but Alpha Lyons protested," Del-Rey reminded him. "So now his Felines can start off kitchen duty."

They both chuckled as Del-Rey made his way from the kitchen and went searching for his coya. He found her scent in Command, in laundry. He found her scent in the new barracks being built within one of the caverns, and he found her scent in her bedroom. It was strongest there. The scent of feminine heat and delicious female.

Damn, why hadn't he taken the time to go down on her when he had her in his bed? To run his tongue between the luscious folds of her pussy and lap at her like candy? He'd kicked himself a dozen times a day for missing out on that.

He found her scent in damned near every area of the base, but he didn't find Anya. Activating the communications link, he clicked into Brim's channel and waited while it beeped.

"I'm in Command, what's up?" Brim answered him.

"Everything okay?"

"We picked up hunters on the eastern side of Base. We have a team heading out to cover them," Brim answered.

"Pull in security monitors; see if you can find Anya."

"Manage to lose her already?" There was a chuckle in Brim's voice.

"Laugh at me later," Del-Rey grunted. "For now, find her before I have to kick your ass."

"I'll let you know when we've cornered your coya, then," Brim promised.

The line disconnected as Del-Rey propped his hands on his hips and frowned at the disappearance. Dammit, one woman shouldn't be so hard to keep up with. There were security monitors through every area of the damned caverns.

He flipped to the general channel. "This is Alpha Delgado, report on coya whereabouts ASAP."

He could just imagine Brim's laughter over that one. Not to mention his coya's irritation if she found out.

He strode from her bedroom and headed back through the tunnels toward the community room as his link beeped.

"Yeah?"

"Del-Rey, it's Thomas, I have entrance duty tonight. Your coya and her three bodyguards exited Base twenty minutes ago on their way to their evening training session."

His teeth clenched. He disconnected as the link from Brim beeped at his ear.

"She left Base twenty minutes ago and headed to the east." Brim's voice wasn't easygoing now. "Those hunters we were tracking disappeared from sight and the team I sent to track them can't be reached. We have a possible penetration into Base territory."

"I want team three at the entrance now," Del-Rey yelled as he began running for the entrance. "Fully armed and in gear. Have someone get my gear as well. Get the heli-jet revved and ready to move, and I want team six moving in as backup. And get on those fucking heat sensors we put out there. I want Anya found and I want her found now!"

He raced through the tunnels as he switched to the general

channel and listened to the reports coming through. The two-man team sent out to track the hunters wasn't answering; that meant they were down. His mate was out there with three body-guards and God only knew what tracking her.

"Teams three and six waiting," Cavalier reported into the communications link as Del-Rey raced through the community room.

The cavern was empty now; all soldiers were moving to assigned duties and preparing to move out.

He rounded the curve to the entrance to the exit tunnel as the twelve men there turned to him expectantly.

"Team three, get your asses out there, I'll catch up ahead of six. Finding your coya is priority. Team six will provide backup and another team is heading out to locate the missing team."

He jerked the mission jacket out of Cavalier's hands and shrugged it on quickly, checking the pockets for extra ammo, knife and backup weapons. As the first team moved out, he was strapping a handgun to his thigh before grabbing the PDW sub-machine gun from Cavalier and clipping it to the jacket. The lightweight personal defense weapon was loaded, safety off and ready to fire.

"Move out," he ordered as he pressed the secured line on the link and waited for Brim to target his identifying signal. A minute beep signaled that Brim had him, and he moved out.

He caught the faint hint of her scent as soon as he moved into the scrub and pine rising around the base entrance. The eastern edge of the mountain cliffs they called home was less steep, covered in pine, oak and a variety of foliage. The western edge overlooking Haven was pretty much sheer cliffs.

He caught up with team three within seconds, motioned them into a new direction and headed east. The same direction where his mate's scent lingered.

It was subtle and light, and would be harder for the others to detect as it blended so well with his own scent. Mating made the female scent harder to track unless she was aroused or ovulating. Her body adapted, her scent changing to match the mating hormones and the male's scent rather than her own.

Camouflage maybe. A natural protection of some sort. Nature was weird as hell where the Breeds were concerned, so who the hell knew. All he knew right now was he was the only person that could track his mate effectively and danger was stalking her.

◆　◆　◆

"We're in trouble," Sharone whispered as they lay flat on the ground, knives gripped in their hands, watching as the five figures moved below them, their voices carrying up to them easily.

"The bitch is here," one of the men hissed. "She goes out damned near every night to this area. We've been tracking her for weeks."

Bitch. Okay, well, there were only four so-called bitches on base, so it had to be one of them. Anya was betting it was her.

"She doesn't have her link enabled," another voice retorted. "I have her channel and the secured line. Nothing's showing on her or her bodyguards."

Okay. That meant her. Well golly gee, didn't she feel so special this week. First her mate returns unannounced and now these yahoos were playing hell with her only downtime.

"We've got to strike before that filthy Coyote Delgado returns," the other voice ordered the others. "Once he's back, security steps up."

And just how did they figure that? No, Del-Rey was just less subtle about security. Over the past months, Anya had been hypertense and looking for a fight. She'd let a few areas appear lax, though she had known they weren't. She'd learned a few lessons from Del-Rey over the years. She tested the strength of Security and Command often. Too bad she wasn't in Command right now tracking these bastards. Instead, she was stuck out here, almost the hunted rather than the hunter she was training to be. And she couldn't risk activating her link or the others' now, not if these men had a way to lock on to their signals.

She stared down at the five men then turned and motioned to Sharone that they needed to back off and get back to Base. At the moment, they were ahead of the men and upwind of any Breed help they might have. Sometimes rogue Coyote Breeds helped the fanatics that still thought they could eradicate the Breeds and steal their freedom.

As long as they stayed upwind and moved quietly, they had a chance. The only weapons they had on them tonight were the knives Sharone and the others used to train Anya. They were sharp, lethal, but they weren't much protection against a gun.

Moving back silently, though not nearly as silently as her bodyguards, she waited until the voices became more distant before giving the order to move out.

Crouched, they moved as quickly as possibly, which was slower than she knew Sharone and the others could have moved, as they started back up the mountain to the faint animal trail they used to access the area. It was still steep here, though not as steep as the western edge of the mountain. But this particular area was close. Part of the way back was particularly steep. They would be at their most vulnerable then.

"Move," she hissed. "We need to make speed, Sharone."

"If they have a rogue Breed with them, then speed is going to get us caught," Sharone retorted. "Because you're not quiet enough."

That was Sharone, blunt and to the point. She didn't cut slack for anyone.

"Did you smell Breed?" Anya asked as they surrounded her, leading her through the underbrush at the quietest possible speed.

"Doesn't mean anything," Emma whispered. "They've learned how to disguise their scent. We were taught that in the labs, remember?"

Oh yeah. She remembered that now. They'd found a way to disguise Coyote Breeds' marker scent. It wasn't easy, and it was irritating to the Breeds' senses, but they could do it.

"We need to contact Del-Rey," Sharone said, voice low. "Ashley, get ahead of us. Run hell for leather and find help. I have a feeling shit's going to get ugly if those bastards catch us on that trail. We'll be sitting targets."

Ashley moved ahead and disappeared. Silently. Damn, Anya wished she could do that. She'd trained for years, even before Del-Rey had kidnapped her, to be quiet like the Coyotes, to race through the night without making a sound, and no matter how hard she tried, she still hadn't achieved it.

At least Ashley was out of danger. She was the most innocent of all of them, Anya sometimes thought. Their girly little Coyote Breed with her fake nails, polish and hair dye. Her makeup, girly clothes and sexy lingerie. She was what they all wished they could be, Anya also sometimes thought.

"This way, Coya." Sharone was leading her through a pine thicket, out of sight and edging closer to the trail. "When we start up, we have to move fast. Emma will go ahead of you, I'll cover the back."

Anya shook her head, fighting back tears. They would give their lives for her, and that wasn't what she wanted. She wanted them safe, and she was realizing that her own incompetence merely made her a danger to them.

They had reached the base of the trail when they heard a shot ring out from behind them. Anya flipped around, staring into the night with wide eyes.

"They didn't see us," Sharone said carefully.

"Ashley," Anya whispered. "Oh God. Oh God, not Ashley."

"Snap out of it, Coya." Sharone's voice was hard, unemotional. A clear indication that she was flat pissed and worried now. "Get moving. The shot was aimed higher up and to our right. The trail is in shadow, and we should be able to reach the top and belly crawl from there into the thicket of juniper growing to the right. Don't worry about quiet going up the trail. We'll have time to get up there before they're in position to take a shot."

They hit the trail and pushed their way up. Anya could feel her chest, tight with tears and rage at the thought of Ashley. God help them if she was hurt, because once Del-Rey caught them, and she knew he would, then she would demand justice herself. Her knife across their throats. She wasn't proficient enough yet that it wouldn't hurt.

◆   ◆   ◆

Del-Rey heard the shot, his head jerking in the direction of the sound. He cut through the mountain echo, pinpointed direction and sent six men toward the shot, and six with him to where it was most likely aimed.

They were racing through the darkness, aware that once the first shot was fired, time was of the essence. One shot. Anya had three Coyote guards with her. There wasn't a chance of getting to her without taking the others out.

He was racing around the top of a particularly steep area of the cliff, using juniper and holly, piñon and pine for cover, when he glimpsed the fallen form.

Fuck. Ashley.

Motioning his men around the perimeter, weapons aimed into the mountain below, he moved for the fallen form. Gripping her shoulder, he pulled her to her back and found her knife nicking his throat as he jerked back.

"Oops. Del." Her smile flashed in the dark. "Hey, find that fucker shooting at me 'kay? Coya's coming up the pass now. And turn off those fucking links, they have our codes."

He flipped off the link and turned to pass the message. How the hell had they gotten the link codes?

"Are you hurt?" He crouched beside her, scanning the darkness, his night vision picking up the movement in the pine below.

"Naw. Broke a nail though," she hissed. "Good thing they guarantee me for forty-eight hours, because this one is going to have to be fixed. I might have even skinned my cuticle."

Fuck. He would have gaped at her if he hadn't scented his coya moving up the trail.

He pushed her to the waiting Breed lying on his belly, and watched as the Breed dragged her into the cover of the boulders to his side.

Lying flat, he motioned the men behind him to do the same as he made his way to the trail. There were areas he could crouch and run, but getting to her was torturous.

◆   ◆   ◆

"I smell alpha ahead," Emma announced as Sharone pushed at Anya's back, forcing her faster up the trail. "He's close."

"Get on your stomachs." Del-Rey's growl sliced through the night, enraged, echoing with fury and sending relief thundering through Anya.

"Belly," Sharone reminded her, pushing her down as they started crawling quickly toward his voice.

"Ashley?" Anya hissed into the night. "Did you find her?"

"I found her." He was suddenly there, gripping her wrists and dragging her over the rise. "Stay down. I'll pull you."

"Ashley?" she whispered again, terrified.

"She broke a fucking nail," he snapped out. "She's fine until I get my hands on her. Now move." He pushed her toward the Breeds, who pulled her around the boulder.

Sharone followed, collapsing against a boulder and breathing out roughly.

"Martin, Jax, Ryan and Cross," Del-Rey snarled. "Get those four back to Base and lockdown until I contact. Apprise Brim we're on comm blackout. Shut down all comm until I arrive."

Nothing was said. Sharone was crouched, pushing Anya ahead of her again as they moved with the four Breeds who surrounded them at Del-Rey's command. All four had been in the Russian facility. They were hard and well trained, and they knew well how to kill and how to protect.

"The moment we get to Base you turn right back around and go back for your alpha," Anya hissed.

"Sorry, Coya," Ryan said miserably. "He didn't say come back; we don't go back. We could mess him up being in the field and him not expecting it."

Anya locked her teeth together as they ran now. Dammit, Ryan was supposed to obey her, not Del-Rey. But it made sense. Okay, that made sense. Del-Rey would know this territory well enough. He had staked it out long before they had arrived here.

She couldn't help but worry. She knew better than to worry; a few trespassing bastards looking for the Coyote coya, their alpha female, didn't have a chance against Del-Rey. She knew that. But something inside her insisted on worrying. Aching. And fearing. Because she had seen his eyes. When he made it back to Base, there was going to be hell to pay.

· CHAPTER 5 ·

Anya paced Command through the night. She ignored Brim's firm suggestions that she should retire to bed, glaring at him each time he suggested it, even though she had sent her body-guards to their rooms hours before.

She chewed at her thumbnail; she growled at the techs when they told her time and again there was no way to pinpoint their alpha's position without comm going back online, and she wasn't willing to risk that either.

She ached from head to toe; exhaustion was a bitch she fought tooth and nail, and she railed at herself for not having the same stamina and endurance the Coyote Breeds had. She was supposed to be their coya, their female alpha, and yet she couldn't manage two days without sleep? They could go for days; she had seen Sharone go for more than a week with barely more than a twenty-minute nap here and there, while Anya had collapsed more than once and slept like the dead.

Daylight was peeking over the mountains as she stood by the silent communications techs and waited. All communications was shut down. Soldiers had been sent to Haven to inform them of status and to secure their own communications. Safeguards would go into effect once Del-Rey and his men returned, but as she had told the communications techs months ago, Del-Rey should have already placed safeguards for just this eventuality.

As they had told her, he was never on base long enough and those safeguards required not just his permission, but also his help.

It hadn't been stated, but she had seen the look in their eyes. It was because of her that he was never there long enough to fulfill his own duties.

So now she was staring at a silent comm board with no way of knowing if the Breeds in the field were alive or dead. No way of knowing if Del-Rey was safe or wounded. She couldn't consider anything else.

The two missing soldiers had been brought in an hour after her return, slightly dazed and bleeding from several wounds. Med tech had been forced to send them to Haven as they didn't have the supplies or the experience to treat them.

They needed their own damned doctors. What if Del-Rey was seriously wounded? Dr. Armani didn't know enough about Coyote genetics to do more than stitch them up. And sometimes, with the Wolf Breeds, severe wounds caused unexplained infections, fevers, almost rabid behaviors in some cases, if the wounds were bad enough.

If that happened to a Coyote Breed, then they could die. Del-Rey could die.

It had been nearly eight hours since she had returned, she estimated; looking at the clock again, perhaps closer to ten. They had left the caverns late to go on the training exercise, later than usual. Otherwise, those hunters would have managed to slip right up on them. They were usually much farther toward the base of the mountain.

Someone had been watching them. They had known about the exercises. Somehow, security had been penetrated enough that the enemy had nearly blindsided them.

"Pacing the floor and glaring at the comm board isn't going to make time pass any faster," Brim told her as he stepped back into the command room carrying coffee. Two cups. God bless his heart. She took one of them.

"That cup was for your communications tech," he pointed out.

"Comm is down; he can go get his own," she muttered as

she sipped at the caffeine-laced brew. It was rare that she could sneak the real thing past her bodyguards. And they always managed to make her spill it or find a way to steal it.

Several times Ashley had found a way to just spit in it before she smiled back at Anya impishly, knowing damned good and well she wouldn't be drinking it then.

She caught the smile the communications tech threw Brim before he pushed back his chair and headed into the lounge.

"You can get hyper as hell for all I care." Brim shrugged. "It's not going to change anything. He's going to come in here tearing ass over this one, and it won't be my ass he's tearing this time."

She narrowed her eyes at him over her coffee cup. His thick black hair was cut short, short enough that sometimes it would spike on his head. Light blue eyes regarded her coolly. He always watched her coolly, ever since the first time she had seen him. Nothing seemed to touch Brim. He never worried, he never got in a hurry, he never got excited. He just wisecracked and glided through life.

"He has no reason to tear anyone's ass here," she finally retorted. "It's not our fault those bastards found a way to access our comm codes."

"You think that's why he's going to be pissed?" He let his lips quirk as though in amusement. None of that amusement showed in his eyes though. "Coya, you were out there with comm links deactivated, and without apprising Command you were outside the caverns. He's going to tear the asses of every soldier that saw you slip out and didn't report it. Then he's going to strip your bodyguards to the bone. Ashley's going to cry those pretty alligator tears for him and probably get off easiest. Emma and Sharone are going to take it like the soldiers they were trained to be, and that's just going to piss him off more because he hates it when they go all stoic soldier on him. Then by the time he works his way to you . . ." Amusement might have touched his eyes at this point. "Well, let's just say, he'll probably have his most fun where you're concerned. He's been rather upset over that separation order, you know. Maybe you should start planning that official acceptance ceremony. You'll need it once the two of you come up for air."

He was laughing at her. As though a wedding ceremony would do anything more than assure the Breeds of all species that Del-Rey had accepted her as his mate and their female alpha. She could refuse him, as Hope had explained, but if he refused her, then she could become fair game when it came to the more savage qualities that were a part of the Breeds' genetics. Respect came in many forms. An alpha leader earned it. A human female could only marry into it in Breed society.

"The poor baby," she expressed mockingly. "Really, Brim, why don't you just go ahead and have a laugh over it? I'm sure we'd all love to join in. Later maybe."

He chuckled then. "Ashley's rubbing off on you. Or are you the one that taught her all that girly crap?"

Her nostrils flared as she turned away from him and sipped at the coffee. Neither Ashley, Sharone nor Emma was here to steal this cup from her; she was going to enjoy it.

Where the hell was Del-Rey anyway?

"Do you think everything's okay?" She turned back to Brim worriedly. "If he was hurt, we would know, wouldn't we?"

He looked at her in surprise. "He's not hurt, Coya."

"How do you know?" She followed him when he turned away from her and picked up the e-pad he'd been filing reports on earlier.

His gaze moved back to her. "If the alpha was hurt, a comm link would have been activated with an emergency distress well away from him. We would have received it, and every soldier on base and in Haven would have streamed over that mountain like killer ants. Satisfied?"

She breathed in roughly and stared up at him in regret. "You don't like me, do you, Brim?"

Surprise flickered in his eyes then.

"Why would you think that? You're my coya, same as Del-Rey is my alpha. It's against the rules to dislike you."

Was there amusement in his eyes? No, she must have been mistaken, but it was obvious he had no intention of playing fair this morning. He and Del-Rey were too much alike for that.

"Thank you," she whispered before turning away and pacing back to the lounge, where she sat down on the long couch that sat inside the glass-enclosed room.

The caverns were inordinately quiet for this time of the morning. The Coyotes seemed to walk on tiptoes through the area as they moved about their duties. Teams hadn't been called out, but that didn't mean teams weren't ready to go. Every soldier on base was armed to the teeth and ready to move if needed. They were dressed in their plain military uniforms, the ones with the Wolf Breed insignia on the shoulder.

They needed their own insignia. It would promote a feeling of pride in their own endeavors. They were too often mistaken for Wolves, and she knew they often remarked on it.

There was a deliberate laziness about the men that had originated with Del-Rey, one that had been picked up by the others. After all, as Del-Rey often stated, if they were perfect, they'd be Wolves.

She finished the coffee slowly as she waited. When the cup was empty, she set it on the table and paced the room, her hands shoved into the pockets of the comfortable cotton pants she'd changed into after showering the night before. A long T-shirt fell to her thighs and her bra was irritating the crap out of her.

She paced the room several times before throwing herself into the corner of the couch and glaring into the command room again.

Brim was sitting in her chair. That was her chair when he and Del-Rey were off base. Unfortunately the order of separation gave him command of that chair while Del-Rey was on base, rather than allowing her to retain it. Brim should have been second-in-command to her with Del-Rey gone. Or out there protecting his alpha's superior, arrogant butt.

She leaned her elbows on her knees before pushing her fingers through her hair in frustration.

Okay, so they weren't going to be able to slip out and play their games anymore. At least, not without backup. She could handle that. She was so used to Base and communications being secured that she had deemed the threat acceptable. She had nearly made a deadly mistake, and that mistake weighed heavily on her shoulders.

Sharone, Emma and Ashley weren't just bodyguards. They were her dearest friends. She had been raised with them; she thought sometimes they were the sisters her parents had never given her.

She rolled her shoulders, which ached from exhaustion, then shivered against the chill filling her. She felt chilled all the time, and she had grown colder still after Del-Rey hadn't returned within an hour of her. How long did it take anyway to catch five bastards looking to kill? One of the Coyote snipers could have taken care of them easily.

Breathing out in irritation, she curled up in the corner of the couch and dragged the little blanket that rested over the back of it over her. She was too cold. And too worried. If he was hurt, it would be her fault. And it wasn't fair, she thought with an edge of self-pity. If anyone got to hurt him, it should be her. Not strangers that didn't know him.

The problem was, she thought, she didn't want to hurt him. She was too worried to consider hurting him. She just wanted him home.

◆　◆　◆

Once again, Del-Rey was forced to follow his mate's scent through the caverns to find her. With comm down, there was no calling Brim to locate his once again missing mate, and that was pissing him off.

He checked her room first, but she wasn't there. She wasn't with her bodyguards and she wasn't in the community or rec rooms. She wasn't in the kitchen, or if she had been there, she was gone now. He thought perhaps he caught the scent of her there.

Finally he stalked into Command and faced Brim.

"Where is she?" he asked the other man as he slouched in the chair that sat at the back and to the side of the room.

Brim glanced up from the reports he was filing on his e-pad, with a quizzical look on his face. "You've lost her again?"

The unemotional expression, the chill in his voice warned Del-Rey that he and his second-in-command just might be coming to yet another disagreement where Del-Rey's mate was concerned.

It was becoming a common, ongoing fight between them.

"Don't fuck with me, Brim," he growled as the other man laid the e-pad to the side of the command chair and stared up at him.

Glaring down at Brim rarely fazed him. There were few things that did. The bastard. Del-Rey often wondered if his friend challenged him for leadership of the packs, which one of them would come out the winner. Or if either of them would. They knew each other too well, faults and all.

"It's a little early to be chewing her ass," Brim finally

answered. "She paced the command room most of the night worrying after your worthless hide. Let her sleep." His response was voiced in a low tone that carried no farther than the two of them, but the deliberate insult had the animal inside Del-Rey rising along with his temper.

"She's not in her rooms sleeping, Lieutenant," Del-Rey told him, his tone warning. "Now, I'll ask you one more time, where is she?"

Anger flashed in Brim's gaze. "She's safe. Let her sleep awhile longer." He had reached his hand out for the e-pad again, when Del-Rey gave a low, savage growl.

Brim's jaw clenched. "She drank coffee not too long ago. You know what that does to her; Sharone has already reported it. A confrontation at this moment isn't what she needs. She needs to sleep."

Del-Rey stared back at him, unblinking.

"You let her drink coffee?" Del-Rey bit out. "Have you lost your fucking mind?"

Brim's jaw clenched as his light blue eyes flashed in anger.

"Well, I wasn't willing to spit in it like Ashley does," he retorted mockingly. "Somehow that just seemed rather rude to me."

As though Brim cared about rude.

"She's not supposed to have coffee," Del-Rey snarled. "She's like the damned Energizer bunny from hell and you know it. She's irritable and confrontational and threatens to kill anyone that gets in her way. Usually me the minute she sees me again."

Mating heat and caffeine did not mix well at all. Unless the male mate in question was into a little BDSM and a whole lot into a defiant, challenging mate.

"She can't eat chocolate, she can't drink coffee, she can't see her family, she can't take a fucking walk at night." Brim moved from his chair and glared back at Del-Rey then, the unemotional facade falling away. "You take everything from a woman that once had freedom and control and expect to play these asinine games with her that you've developed to get her back into your bed and then you wonder why she doesn't inform you of what she's doing whenever she's doing it. Hell, Del-Rey, it's a wonder she hasn't shot you."

"And a wonder you haven't loaned her the gun," Del-Rey

sneered. "I'm getting sick of battling you over her. You're not her brother."

Brim's lips quirked. "I think she rather needs a brother. Perhaps I'll petition the tribunal for adoption. Someone needs to see beyond their own wants where this woman is concerned."

If it wasn't for the fact that Del-Rey was damned certain Brim was seriously brotherly rather than in lust with Anya, then he would have taken him out years ago. They had been fighting over Anya since she first showed up in that damned bar, and the confrontations had only grown more frequent over the past eight months.

"I'm losing patience with this, Brim," he warned him.

"Try being honest with her then." Brim crossed his arms over his chest and glared back at Del-Rey. He was possibly the only man in the world who could get away with it. "You should have been honest with her from the beginning."

"Oh yeah, I should have told a sixteen-year-old virgin I intended to fuck the hell out of her after she grew up, and that I was going to shoot her father and cousins for the hell of it because they allowed her to endanger herself. Now, wouldn't that have just inspired confidence in me? We'd have really managed to get her and those Breeds she protected out of that underground facility, wouldn't we, Brim?"

This argument had played out for nearly seven years now. For some reason Brim had all but adopted Anya since the moment he saw her. There was no lust, there was concern. And Brim rarely concerned himself with others besides Del-Rey. They had been fighting together since they were kids. They had been created in the same labs and plotted to escape them since they first understood they were prisoners and expected to kill.

Five, Del-Rey realized. Brim had been five and Del-Rey had been ten when they first began planning. Brim had been fifteen and he twenty, and both were hardened killers, before they'd managed it. That had been nearly sixteen years ago, and until Anya, Brim had never questioned Del-Rey's plots and schemes.

"You should have warned her before you shot her father about what you had to do." Brim repeated his years-old refrain. "All you had to do was tell her that if you didn't do it, it would endanger their lives. She would have understood that. You didn't have to shell-shock her."

"Well fuck, let's just get our little time machine and go back and fix it," Del-Rey sneered.

Brim grimaced.

"Where the fuck is my mate, Lieutenant?"

Brim sighed. "She's asleep in the lounge. She just went to sleep less than an hour ago, Del-Rey. She's worried herself sick about you while you were out there. She already looks like she hasn't slept in months. Leave her the hell alone for a while."

That was it.

Del-Rey's hand snapped out, wrapped around Brim's throat and applied just enough pressure to assure the other man he was dead serious now.

Brim's gaze flickered.

"We haven't fought since you were fifteen years old and you decided you could take me and the alpha position in my pack. Do you want to try me again?"

Brim stared back at him for long, tense moments before he sighed. "I swore loyalty to you. I won't go back on it."

Del-Rey's gripped slackened. "Don't get between me and Anya, Brim. I swore when we returned I'd deal more fairly with her. Accept that, and let's put this behind us."

"When she accepts it." Brim shrugged. "Until then, you're stuck with my shit."

Del-Rey almost grinned before shaking his head at the mess he had made for himself.

"I'm going to take my coya to her room. You will tell her bodyguards, you will inform every soldier in this base, that any order she gives that would give her access outside this base is to go through me first. Are we understood?"

Brim grimaced. "Wrong move."

"Are we understood?" he repeated.

"Of course, Alpha Delgado," Brim finally replied mockingly. "I understand English very well."

Mocking son of a bitch Coyote, Del-Rey thought fondly.

"We brought back a prisoner," he told Brim then. "He needs transport to Haven. We haven't finished the detainment cells here yet and I don't want to risk him escaping. See if you can find some secure communication with Haven and let them know that we're bringing him in. Tell them I want to be involved in the interrogation."

Brim nodded and turned away to do that as Del-Rey moved toward the lounge. The door was closed; the interior was sound-proofed for meetings when needed, that was the reason he hadn't caught her scent when he stepped into Command.

She was curled into the corner of the couch sleeping. A small blanket was wrapped around her, and she appeared chilled. He wondered if she got as cold as he sometimes did. There were nights the cold went clear to his bones, the need to wrap him-self around her warmth eating at his insides.

It wasn't all sexual. He'd had six years to form the bond he had with this woman, letting it go was impossible.

He should have known when he first realized he was claim-ing her for his own that games wouldn't work with her. She was too damned sharp, and too easily hurt by them. She didn't see the cunning manipulations as he did. She didn't play those games that other women caught on to so easily. She, quite sim-ply, was just Anya. Unlike any other woman, unlike anything he had known in his entire life.

He moved to the couch and hunkered in front of her, staring into her sleeping face. Hell, she looked sixteen rather than twenty-two. Her looks hadn't changed much in the years since he had first met her. She still had that innocent curve to her soft lips, that impish tilt to her red gold brows.

She liked to tease, and she liked to play. Sharone had sent video after video of his mate over the months. Catching her in a snowball fight with Ashley, recordings of the three women sparring in the gym as they trained her to fight. She laughed with them. She used to try to laugh with him.

Hell, Brim should have shot him as soon as he realized what Del-Rey was doing. He'd have deserved it.

Moving carefully, he slid his arms beneath her knees and around her back before lifting her against his chest. She'd had coffee; if she woke up, she was going to go ballistic on him. He hoped she slept for a while longer. A whole lot longer, if he was lucky. But she wasn't sleeping on this couch in the command lounge. She had a bed. Two actually, his and hers. If she needed to sleep, then she could do so in comfort.

As he moved from the lounge, she cuddled closer, her cold little nose burying itself against his neck as a little shiver worked over her.

She was cold. A surge of possessiveness shot through him at the realization. The caverns weren't cold. They were a comfortable seventy-one degrees almost all year long. If by chance any part of them grew chillier, then there were heating units in place to take care of that.

He held her closer as he moved through the stone- and steel-reinforced tunnels to their quarters. Her bed had been turned down for her, he knew, the lights left low, but he was damned if he wanted to put her in her own bed.

He wondered if it were possible that she would sleep through him putting her in his bed. He was more than willing to leave her dressed, though he wasn't as sacrificing where his own clothes were concerned. Tucking her against his naked body would tickle the hell out of him.

It was worth trying. Better to fight it out with her now than to try to seduce her there in a week or so. Maybe he just needed to put his foot down a bit. He'd never done that with her. Never given her boundaries other than that of not allowing her father on Haven or Base without his presence.

She had simply forgone seeing her family rather than do it in front of him.

He frowned darkly as he entered his own room.

Or had she forgone seeing them?

He glanced down at her. Dammit, he had stated she couldn't see them at Haven or on Base without his presence. He was betting money she had seen them somewhere else. Why the hell hadn't he considered that loophole? Anya would not have gone this long without seeing her family, even if it meant dealing with him.

Cunning, conniving little imp. How had he been so wrong about her? And he knew clearly that he obviously was. Anya was stubborn as hell, but she loved her family with a devotion he was frankly jealous of.

He knew clear to the bottom of his gut that she had met them somewhere else. No doubt with her bodyguards' full endorsement. He was going to have to do something about the damned women running roughshod over him on his own base. His coya. That flighty little genius Ashley that so loved playing the dumb blonde. The too quirky Sharone and the quiet, manipulating little Emma. Hell, he hoped the Felines managed to temper some of that shit in the younger twins they were fostering.

Shaking his head, he settled his mate carefully on his own turned-down bed and eased the little blanket she had tried to use for warmth away from her as he lifted the sheet and comforter over her. He didn't bother with the lights. He stripped to his skin, slid in beside her and eased her into his arms.

He almost groaned at the warmth of her body against his own chilled flesh. The way she settled in against him, mumbling, grumbling a bit with charming feminine irritation until she was as close to him as she could get, her nose buried against his shoulder, her rounded body tucked into his until he could feel her warmth seeping into him.

His eyes closed as emotion threatened to swamp him. Fuck, he didn't deal with emotion. It wasn't his damned strong suit. In the labs he'd been created and trained within, he'd learned to let no one but Brim know his weaknesses. To let nothing touch himself. To never feel regret. To never know possessiveness. They were lessons that had been taught to him in the most exacting of ways. Lessons he had adapted to, too easily at too young an age, supposedly due to his Coyote genetics.

They had rushed in on him the first time he had seen this fragile young woman though. Gently rounded, she wasn't exactly slender. She was a nice handful for a man. Some might have accused her of being a little heavy. But she was perfect for him. With her rounded little rear, her plump breasts and silky thighs. He could hold on to Anya. She wasn't skin and bones, nor was she muscular and hard. She was just soft. Soft and warm. And she was his.

He let his hand smooth down her hair with the lightest touch as he ignored the heavy, desperate throb of his cock. He had learned how to push that pain back over the months. It wasn't easy, but being able to hold her, being able to warm the ice that often tormented his insides, was worth it.

For the first time in over eight months, Del-Rey felt warm. He wasn't willing to give that up. Yes, he was going to have to put his foot down. She would sleep here, or he would sleep in her bed. Sleep. Hold her. He couldn't demand anything more. He wouldn't demand more. But by God, this he was determined to demand.

CHAPTER 6

She was warm. So warm she felt toasty and relaxed all over. Well, almost relaxed all over. There was that pesky arousal she couldn't seem to get rid of in the past months. The dampness between her thighs, the ache in her clit, hard nipples.

And she had worn her bra to bed for some damned reason. She hated wearing a bra to bed. She would wake up enough to take it off, but that would mean pulling out of the pocket of warmth she had managed to find, and she wasn't willing to do that.

She shifted closer, and realized she had to be dreaming again. Because it wasn't a furnace she was hugging, it was a hard, clearly aroused male body.

Her lips tilted at the corners. She must be surely desperate to be dreaming this well. She hadn't dreamed like this in, well, days maybe. But she had never been warm in those dreams. She had been cold and frightened, confused and begging him to help her. To warm her, while he stared at her in confusion.

Del-Rey.

She still had moments when she was amazed that such an incredible creation had ever touched plain, plump little Anya Kobrin. Her father had always told her she was mother material, and that one day she would find a good man that would appreciate that in her. The men she knew went for the tall, slender, beautiful women. Not the short, plump ones like her.

But from the moment she had first met Del-Rey, when she was around him, she didn't feel plump or plain. She had felt excited and warm, tingling all over. At sixteen she had had her first seriously sexual dream, and they hadn't stopped.

So yes, this was definitely a seriously whacked dream, because Del-Rey wouldn't be holding her. He hadn't held her after he'd had sex with her that first and only time, and he wouldn't be merely holding her now to keep her warm. Not with that erection she could feel pressing between her clenched thighs.

He was just as large as she remembered, she thought with sleepy wonder. So thick and heavy. She'd felt every rasp of every bulging vein in that wide shaft as it pushed inside her that night. The pleasure/pain of it had been nearly more than she could stand. The shocking events that came later, though, had nearly thrown her into a catatonic shock.

He had been large already, but as he'd begun releasing inside her, another secondary swelling had grown in the middle of that hot, hard cock. He had knotted her. Animal genetics had kicked in like a bitch—that's how Dr. Armani had explained it.

It was part of the mating heat. Part of the changes that occurred in both male and female once mating occurred. It was something the world wasn't aware of, and something Anya knew wouldn't help the Breeds if it were known.

She let herself touch him. She was asleep, and this was her dream. She liked this dream better than most too, because she could feel the warmth of his body. She could pet him as she wanted to.

Wouldn't the big, tough Coyote Breed alpha be shocked to know that she longed to pet him? Even when she had hated him the most, she had been on the verge of begging him to just let her touch him, let her share the warmth of his body.

Her hand smoothed over his shoulder, his biceps. Timid fingers tested the hard muscles beneath tough flesh. She stroked down his arm as it lay over her hips. She let her nails scrape over his skin, enjoying the ripple of response beneath her touch.

Okay, that was a new sensation in her little dreamscape. She didn't normally feel that.

Beneath her lips, more warmth beckoned. The taste of salty male flesh met her tongue as she licked over a hard pectoral muscle. A response rippled there as well, tightened beneath her tongue. She liked that. This dream was incredibly more satisfying than any other.

She thought perhaps she heard a groan or a growl, and filed it away to think about later. Would he growl when she touched him? She doubted it. He hadn't wanted her touch before, just her kiss. He hadn't wanted foreplay or warmth, just the main event.

She pouted at the thought, and for damages ensued over the months, she nipped at his flesh, just to be contrary. Her dream lover would love that little nip.

And he did. He definitely growled. A sound of rough pleasure as his arms tightened around her and his cock twitched between her thighs.

That hard flesh was pressed against her sex, heating it as his hips moved, pressing it deeper between the notch of her thighs. He hadn't bothered with just pressing against her belly. Nope, the dream Del-Rey was just as arrogant as the one she knew when she was awake. He had just gone ahead and pushed between her legs as though it were his right.

Arrogant Coyote.

Sometimes, she liked that arrogance a little too much. She didn't like admitting it. She intended to take that secret to the grave with her, because she didn't care what her father said to excuse Del-Rey's actions, she wasn't willing to excuse his lack of trust in her.

She had trusted him. He should have trusted her.

And he should have cuddled her after fucking her, it was just that simple, rather than mounting her like he'd bought her off the streets and couldn't bear looking her in the face.

She nipped at him again for being so damned inconsiderate. Her dream. Nips allowed.

But then she licked over the little bite and moaned at the taste of him. God she loved his taste. She wanted to taste all of him, from his lips to his thighs and all parts in between.

She wanted to feel the heavy heat of his erection between her lips, she wanted to lick the broad head, wanted to taste the hot essence of the man. She wanted him until she was burning for it.

A distant corner of her mind was warning her to beware, that this dream was too intense, too rich with sensation. But she didn't want to wake up yet.

Her hands petted his arm, then traveled to his hard waist and hips. He was just so damned hard all over, and so warm.

She let her thighs clamp on the erection between them, creating a friction and pressure against her clit as she heard a muttered curse above her. She smiled at the sound. His voice was very husky, very rumbling and primal. She liked it. She wanted to hear more of it.

Later.

First, she wanted her kiss. She had longed for his kiss for so many months. Sometimes she swore she could almost taste the spicy hot wickedness of it in her mouth. Sometimes she swore she was still in heat, though Dr. Armani assured her that her hormone issues were stable.

"Kiss me," she ordered him. It was an order, a command. She wanted to be kissed and she wanted it now. And he'd better comply. Her dream. Her kiss. It was time the coya got her due.

Del-Rey knew he was going to die. He was going to go up in flames right there in that damned bed and go to hell for every sin he'd ever committed. And kissing her would send him there.

He arched his neck back from her inquisitive little lips. No kisses. But damned that order to give it to her had sent a punch of lust slamming into his gut. She'd sounded commanding, hot. Fuck, he was so perverted. He could see his wild little coya straddling him, on her knees, demanding his cock. Instead of *Kiss me*, she'd order *Fuck me*.

He was so close to panting it was fucking pathetic.

He let one hand tangle in the red gold curls of her hair as he held her in place. No damned way he was pushing her away from him, but if he kissed her now, he was likely to find himself in front of the Breed tribunal again.

No kisses, Dr. Armani had warned him months ago. Not without Anya's permission. And he was sure the good doctor didn't mean her sleeping approval. The hormonal aphrodisiac in the glands of his tongue was like a damned erotic TNT. He knew. Been there, kissed her and burned in the flames.

Kissing her was only going to make it worse.

But God help him, he ached to kiss her. To sink his swollen

tongue into the hot depths of her mouth and feel her sucking that hormone into herself. Then, he wanted her lips lower. Sucking his dick with the same hunger she was reaching for his kiss with now.

He sure as hell wasn't cold now though. He was burning from the inside out, so fucking desperate for the taste of her that he wondered if he could actually hold out.

"Kiss me." Her voice deepened, sexy and rough, that hint of command causing his hips to jerk against her, burying his cock deeper between her thighs.

"Anya." His hand tightened in her hair. "No kisses."

Cunning, manipulation, calculation. He was a Coyote, that was what he was good at.

He pulled her head back, staring into the dazed features of her face, the drowsy sensuality. She moaned, a lost little sound that tore into his soul.

"One kiss," she whispered.

"Anya. Wake up." His voice was such a hard growl it surprised him. "I won't go before another tribunal for tricking you."

Her lashes fluttered open; her blue eyes were darker, sexier. She looked tousled and ready to be fucked. He was sure as hell ready to fuck her.

"Wake up, Anya." He glared down at her. "The next time I kiss you, it will only be because you know what's coming. I will not stand before another tribunal and be flayed for taking what's mine."

Awareness shifted into her eyes. Heat rushed into her cheeks, staining them a perfect pretty pink as he watched realization transform her features.

"Oh my God. It's not another dream." She stiffened, her fingers curled against his shoulders, and Del-Rey knew what was coming.

Anya was out of the bed as quickly as she could untangle her legs from his and tear herself out of his grip. She stumbled at the side of the bed, fighting to get her weak legs beneath her as she stared back at Del-Rey in horror.

She was in his bedroom. In his bed.

"How did I get here?" She heard the squeak in her voice as he shifted lazily and lifted himself on an elbow.

"Your pussy is so wet those thin little pants are damp," he growled. "Fuck, Anya. I can see it."

Outraged horror exploded inside her as she looked down, seeing the faintest of dark prints against the light gray material where his cock had rubbed her pants against her sex. She hadn't worn panties. Why hadn't she worn panties again? Oh yeah, they had rasped her engorged clit and irritated her.

"Why am I in your bedroom rather than my own?" she snapped back at him.

He grinned slowly. "Sleepwalking? My, my, Anya, trying to accost me in my sleep? Should I protest this myself in front of the tribunal?"

She started to shake. She had actually done that a time or two. Gone to sleep in her bed and awoken in Del-Rey's. Just a few times though. And never had he been in it.

She shook her head, feeling herself pale. "I did this?" she whispered, shuddering at the knowledge that she could have set herself up like this.

His brows lifted as he grinned again. "Actually, I carried you here from the lounge and tucked you in myself. You sleep deep, baby. I could have had you fucked and knotted before you knew what happened to you."

Oh shit.

Anya swallowed tightly. He had carried her from the lounge and put her in his bed. And this was what had happened the first chance she'd had to forget what a lying snake he was.

"You bastard!"

"Yeah? So?" He smirked. "We've established this already, haven't we? Are you going to start throwing things now?"

He was laughing at her. Daring to laugh at her because he had done this to her. This, made her sleep with him. But she remembered the dream clearly. She knew who had started touching first and who had been demanding. It hadn't been him. It had been her crawling all over him like a bitch in heat.

Heat. The mating heat. She threw him a contemptuous stare before rushing across the room and throwing open the door to her own bedroom.

Was comm still down?

She picked up the secured landline at the side of her bed and stabbed her finger into the button to connect to Command.

"Yes, Coya?" Brim was still there.

"Is comm up?" She was breathing hard, heavy. She felt on the verge of panic. On the verge of rushing back to him and demanding he give her that damned kiss.

"Not yet. We're still awaiting Del-Rey and Jonas Wyatt from the Bureau of Breed Affairs to go over the diagnostics on the electronics that were found with the hunters. Is anything wrong?"

"I need to see Armani," she bit out. "Now."

Silence filled the line for long moments.

"Are you unwell?" His voice was calm, cool. Typical Brim.

"I . . . I'm having an odd reaction to the hormonal therapy." She swallowed tightly. "Is there any way to contact her?"

He was silent again. Longer this time.

"I can have a team waiting to take you to Haven as soon as I talk to Del-Rey and receive verification to do so. Would you like me to contact him?"

Contact Del-Rey? Her eyes swung to her still-closed door as she swallowed tightly. "No. No." She shook her head; she was losing her mind. "Forget it."

She disconnected the line before punching in Sharone's number.

"Yes, Coya?" Sharone answered warily.

"Get one of the soldiers," she ordered her. "I need a message out to Armani that I need to see her. Quickly."

"I can't," Sharone answered her regretfully. "Brim contacted me earlier. I can't take any orders from you that involve anything outside Base, without going through the alpha first."

Anya turned slowly as the door opened and Del-Rey stood naked, aroused, in the doorway.

"Need to see Armani?" He lifted a brow in amusement. "Let me know when you're ready, I'll take you there myself. I'd like to discuss a few issues concerning your mating heat with her."

Anya hung up the phone and gaped at him.

Oh Lord. His erection was huge, heavily veined, the crown flared and damp, and the sight of it had her entire body weakening for precious seconds. She had to force strength into her legs. Had to force herself to straighten and jerk her gaze from his cock to his face. And the bastard was smirking.

Standing there, all hard and bronzed flesh, a cock that made her mouth water, and those sexy lips tilted into a half smile. She felt her sex grow more heated, her juices gathering between her thighs.

"It's none of your business," she informed him through gritted teeth. "And you do not need to talk to Armani about my body."

"Of course I do," he told her, his tone mildly curious. "It's obvious you need further hormonal treatments to control the mating heat. You were flowing over me like honey on a comb, Anya. I have a few things I have to do first, but I'll be ready in three hours. Meet me in the community room."

He stepped back and slammed the door closed as she picked up the wood paperweight on her desk and hurled it at his head.

It bounced off the door, and she knew, *knew*, she heard his laughter echoing from the other room.

Be ready her ass. She wasn't going anywhere with that snide, smirking, too damned sexy for her own good Coyote.

Damn him. Let him go by himself.

She pushed her hands into her hair with a snarl of outrage before dragging them through the strands. And it felt too much like that damned dream that wasn't a dream. Del-Rey's fingers in her hair, tugging at it, sending sharp, burning little sensations of pleasure racing through her.

She shivered at the remembrance. Oh man, she was in so much trouble here. He was right, she needed to see Armani, because the heat was building again and she had a feeling she couldn't control it this time.

It had changed. It was insidious, growing by small measures, burning inside her when she least expected it and leaving her aching for his touch, even though she knew the culmination of that touch was cold, lonely emptiness.

She sat down on her bed and breathed out with a small, strangled groan. She so didn't need this right now. Of all things she didn't need, it was the mating heat returning.

◆   ◆   ◆

An hour after Del-Rey had heard the paperweight strike his mate's door, he was sitting in his office beside Command and staring across his desk at the three Coyote females his packs had adopted.

He'd darkened the windows as they stepped inside, ensuring that his little mate couldn't wander into Command and see him talking to her bodyguards.

Sharone Bryce stood tallest, military straight as she stared at the wall above his head, her expression composed. She hadn't even shifted during the minutes she had stood there. Her dark brunette hair was pulled back into a fussy little braid that worked its way down her head. French braid, he thought he'd heard it called. Her hazel green eyes were cool, but he could detect the flicker of wariness in them.

Emma Truing was standing similarly. Still and straight, her lighter brown hair cut short and framing her pretty face. There was the slightest crook to her nose where it had been broken in her teens. Her lips were firm, her gray eyes steady.

Ashley Truing was a whole other ball game. Del-Rey liked to tease her that she was a true Coyote: lazy, shiftless, too charming for her own damned good, cunning as hell and filled with fun.

She was a genius. A stone-cold killer standing before him with lightened hair, nearly blond, her gray eyes twinkling back at him, though he knew they could fill with crocodile tears at any moment. And she wasn't even trying to hide the fact that she was chewing gum between those perfect teeth of hers. She wasn't standing straight; one hip was cocked and she was on the edge of looking bored.

"Okay already, chew my ass out. I told you I have to get my nails fixed today. And there's this shoe party that Young Leaders of America or some bullshit is throwing. I'm gonna be late, Alpha." She pouted back at him. "Come on, we weren't totally bad. Right? We got her to you."

He'd known Ashley would break first. Emma winced. Sharone closed her eyes for a brief, irritated second. He would have chuckled if the lives of his mate and these three women weren't so important to him.

"And if you hadn't gotten her to me, Ashley?" he asked, a warning growl in his throat. "If the four of you had died on that mountain, what then?"

Her eyes widened. "They didn't have a prayer," she scoffed.

"Come on, Alpha, I knew you'd be looking for her the minute we left on 'no comm.' I figured you'd catch up with us sooner than you did. I mean, come on, you're totally hot for her. She's not going to be out of your sight that long when you don't know precisely where she is."

Cunning, manipulative, charming and too intuitive—because she was fucking right.

"That's not the point." He leaned forward in his chair. "What would have happened if that bullet had struck you at the top of that trail and left you dead?"

She stared back at him blankly. "Umm. The coya would cry. I'd be dead. And if that had happened, I would hope you would dress me really fine and give me one of those cool funerals, you know? Like real people have. And roses."

She was utterly serious. *Like real people.* His chest clenched at the words, as though in her soul she believed she wasn't 'real people'.

"Coyotes would have gone to war," he stated clearly, powerfully. "None of those hunters would have escaped. I let them go, all but one last night, Ashley, to track where they went. Had you, your sister or Sharone died on that mountain, nearly a hundred Coyote soldiers would have broken Breed Law and descended on Advert with the full fury of killing rage."

She blinked back at him. "Why?" She looked to Emma and Sharone's surprised faces. "We're just Coyotes, Alpha. We were born to die." She flashed him that fucking fearless smile that tied his guts into knots.

"Your allowance has been pulled for the next four weeks." He rose from his chair, his hands braced on the desk as he glared at her, fury beating at his temple. "In four weeks you will come to me and tell me why, Ashley, that Coyotes would have shed blood in that amount for your life."

True distress filled her eyes. He suspected true tears.

"My allowance?" she whispered fearfully. "Oh please, Del-Rey, just like, knock it down. Don't take my allowance." She spread her fingers out. "Look at my damned nails. I need my allowance."

"If a single Breed—Coyote, Feline or Wolf—pays for those fucking nails," he stabbed his finger at her hands, "then I'll make damned certain he pays for it in ways he doesn't even want to imagine. Are we clear?"

The tears cleared; the lips trembled; her gaze shuttered.

"I don't know what your deal is." Her voice was perfectly composed. "If the coya were hurt or killed, you'd take out my throat. Fine. I'd expect it. She's my damned coya too, so you really don't have to play up any loyalty here. And fuck the nails, I don't need your allowance."

He growled, a low, lethal sound that had her flinching.

"Four weeks," he told her. "One more smart-assed remark and we'll go for six. Would you like to chance that?"

She crossed her arms over her breasts, hip cocked, and glared back at him.

He turned to Emma. "Why would I have gone to war over your death, Emma?"

She cleared her throat. "We're pack?" she suggested.

He glared back at her. "I hope you enjoy kitchen duty for the next two weeks."

She gasped.

"Two weeks?" Ashley bit out defiantly. "You're punishing me for four."

"Six!" he snarled back at her as she jerked back and stared at him, horrified.

"Sharone?" He was all but yelling. He was fucking pissed off, and realizing that only made him madder. "If you died? Why the fucking hell do you think I'd go to war?"

She blinked quickly. "Because . . ." She swallowed. "Do you love us, Alpha?"

He sat down in his chair and breathed out roughly as he stared at the three women. "The three of you, Marcy and Chanda, who are presently charming the hell out of the Felines, are the females of our packs and are the same as sisters to me. You are more to me than any man in this base." He could feel the anger churning in him. "Because I love you, I would have gone to war." He turned to Sharone. "What would I have done if my coya had been captured or killed? My mate, Sharone. The other half of everything I am. What would I have done?"

Her eyes were wide as she shook her head slowly. "I can't imagine anything worse, Alpha, than going to war."

"Worse is having my soul ripped from my body," he told

her. "We, who are told we have no soul. I found mine nearly seven years ago when a kid walked into the roughest, dirtiest, meanest bar I know of, to save her friends. If I lose her, I lose who and what I am." He rose threateningly again. "And if you tell your coya I said that, then all three of you, no matter which one spills her guts, will be separated from the coya's security detail for six months. Are we clear?"

They nodded slowly, fearfully. They had never been separated from Anya. The four of them were like kids together, learning how to be free, how to play. They were playmates, perhaps even sisters.

"Alpha?" Ashley asked. "May I ask a question?"

"Will it piss me off?" he growled.

"Yes. Probably."

That was his Ashley. She didn't balk. Shaking his head, he sat back down and stared back at her. "What?"

"Why would you love us? You didn't raise us. You've known us only as long as you've known your coya. Why do you care?"

He wiped his hand over his face wearily. "I've known you for nearly seven years, Ash," he sighed. "Your coya talked of little else but five young girls that were her best friends. Her confidantes. Her family. In those years, she made me love you as fiercely perhaps as she does." He shook his head. "You are Coyote Breeds. You are not simply coyotes. You are not unfeeling animals, and you're worth more than a fucking funeral. Are we clear on this?"

She bit her lip. "Can I have my allowance back?"

"No!"

She pouted, but she wasn't hard, she hadn't fallen back on her training to show her displeasure.

"The three of you will ensure, from here on out, that if your coya even thinks of leaving these caverns without me at her side, I'm notified. If she wants to train, I as well as a backup team will oversee it. If she wants to fucking pick flowers, she will have a backup detail and I will oversee it. If she just wants to step outside the fucking door and breathe in the mountain air, what will you do?"

"Notify you, Alpha," they snapped at once.

"Emma, you're on kitchen duty when you're not with your coya outside Base. Ashley, you better hope you've saved back enough to fix those nails. They look like shit. Sharone, you're assigned to Brim for two weeks when you're not needed by your coya. He'll let you know what he needs."

He could have sworn Sharone whimpered. Brim enjoyed the hell out of the girls and loved every chance he had to torment them. It was his hobby, his fun. Like the older brother he had never been.

"Dismissed." He waved to the door, waited until they filed out, and as the door closed behind him, he smiled and shook his head. Damn, if this was any indication of what human men dealt with when it came to daughters, then he was damned glad he was a Coyote.

· C H A P T E R   7 ·

He had her timed perfectly. Ten minutes after the girls left his office, Anya was charging into it. Her blue eyes sparkled with fury, her red gold hair tangled around her face and fell to her shoulders in such charming disarray that he wanted nothing more than to mess it further.

She slammed the door and faced him, arms crossing over the snug, thin white sweater she wore as she glared at him furiously.

"How dare you punish them!" She shoved a finger toward him. "You had no right."

He sat back in his chair and forced control on himself.

"I'm not ready to head to Haven yet. I need about forty minutes at least. Could you wait to start throwing things at me and calling me names until then?"

"Wait?" she snapped in mockery. "Wait for you to do what? Devise more ways to torture my friends? You have no right. Now fix it."

Oh, she was fucking beautiful. He could feel his cock hardening impossibly. He was so damned ready to fuck that smart mouth it was almost impossible not to jump from the desk and take what he wanted.

"What did you think would happen, Anya?" he asked her carefully instead. "I could have been much harder on them. I could have had them sent to Haven and celled for endangering their coya's life. Instead, I did what I felt would teach them quickly not to fuck with your life or theirs."

"And you think we didn't learn our lessons last night?" she yelled. "Trust me, Del-Rey, we did. You didn't have to punish them this severely. Now damn you, fix it."

"I don't think so." He straightened and braced his arms on the desk to look at the files on the e-pad lying before him.

Not that he read a damned word that was on there. It was the impression that counted.

"You can't do this," she argued.

"I'm alpha." He shrugged. "I can and will do this." He lifted his head. "By the way, since I can't punish you in the same manner, would you like to know what I've come up with?"

Her eyes widened. "You do not punish me, you slack-brained, dim-witted mongrel. I'll shoot your ass with your own gun."

God bless her. He was going to fuck her until she was begging for mercy. Right there on his desk if she wasn't damned careful.

"Your punishment is a week in my bed, every night, eight hours, while I'm sleeping. Beginning tonight."

"I'm returning to Haven, along with my security force." Her voice was strangled. "You can't order me anywhere."

"Check our separation agreement," he suggested casually as he scrawled his signature on the document and sent it to Brim. "While I'm here you're only allowed off this base if your safety and security isn't endangered. I've deemed both in jeopardy. My report was filed no more than an hour ago with the members of the tribunal and has been returned with their agreements." He lifted his head. "As for sleeping in my bed, yes, Mate, I can order that as well under the same conditions. I'm certain you'll consider that your punishment, rather than your reward for actually managing to stay alive."

He pushed the e-pad to the side and watched as her breasts heaved, her nipples spiked. Caffeine and anger. They were a destructive combination with the mating heat and he knew it. Keep her pissed off enough, he might get a chance at that kiss that he was dying for.

"You're not serious!" she exclaimed. Her blue eyes were shocked. Her face was flushed.

Oh, he was serious. As serious as the hard dick in his pants.

"Give me forty minutes, cupcake." He smiled back at her. "And I'll let you go bitch about it to the lupina while Dr. Armani is upping your hormones. I can smell your arousal. I like it."

Her fingers curled at her sides. "You've lost your mind."

"Nope, not this week," he laughed back at her. "I'm really pretty sane for me right now. Ask Brim, he can tell you, sometimes I'm actually trying to have fun."

Anya stared back at him in outraged amazement. The man took idiocy to a new level. He was sitting there grinning at her as though he were actually having fun. Calling her "cupcake." She was going to poison his cupcake if he didn't find a measure of intelligence in that thick skull of his.

"Look." She tried for calm. "You can't take Ashley's allowance. Getting her nails fixed, buying her shoes and girly stuff keeps her grounded. Emma will break everything in the kitchen if you put her in there. And Sharone will end up shooting Brim. Not that he won't deserve it. But I'd prefer she not have to deal with the guilt later."

He relaxed farther back in his chair, lifted those long, powerful legs and propped them on the corner of his desk as he stared back at her, his lashes lowered over his eyes.

"If Sharone shoots him, then he'll have deserved it." He shrugged. "As for Emma, inform her if she breaks anything I'll add a week. And Ashley will survive without her nail treatments for a while. It will remind all of them who the alpha is around here."

His smile was all teeth as he crossed his arms over his chest and let his gaze drift down her body. And she felt it, almost as though it were a phantom touching her.

"I will not sleep with you either," she bit out. "Get it out of your mind."

"Fine. I'll sleep in your bed with you." He shrugged. "Either way, you're gonna be my cuddle bunny for a week. It gets damned cold at night for some reason, Coya. You can keep me warm."

His what? His cuddle bunny?

"Oh, you are so reaching," she said scathingly. "Warm your ass on a brick, because it's not getting in my bed."

"It's not my ass that gets cold," he laughed. "Come on now, my little coya. What's wrong, afraid you'll have another of those hot little dreams and let me actually get a taste of that wet little pussy?" His gaze dropped to her thighs. "I'll make sure you're awake for it. I'm a gentleman like that."

"You're a sorry excuse for a Breed and an even sorrier excuse for a mate," she snarled. "How dare you order me to sleep with you. You didn't buy me off the street, you crackpot."

His brows lifted. "I'm going to wash your mouth out with soap. Be civil or we'll try for two weeks."

"You bastard!"

"Three?"

She was shaking. Anya couldn't remember a time in her life when she had been more furious. It swept over her like a tidal wave, slammed inside her and sent heat searing her insides for vital seconds.

She stumbled against the onslaught, almost gasping as it peaked in her clit and sent a shot of pain racing through her system.

"Anya!"

Del-Rey's chair slammed into the wall as he tore from his seat and raced to her, catching her before she hit the floor. Her face was suddenly pale, sweat gleaming on her forehead as her blue eyes stared back at him in stark pain.

"Brim!" He tore the door open as he held her to him, then picked her up in his arms.

Brim and Sharone raced from Command as Emma and Ashley moved from the lounge, fear flashing across the girls' faces.

"I need transport," he called out. "Contact Armani and tell her to be waiting at the door."

Anya moaned, a low, pain-filled sound as she tried to curl against him. Sweet God in heaven. What the hell was wrong? He ran for the base exit as Brim shouted out orders for his personal security detail to be waiting. Behind him, Anya's friends followed, weapons being strapped on as they ran, concern filling the air with a dark, fear-tainted scent.

What the hell had happened? One minute she was sniping at

him and the next she was nearly passing out from pain? This wasn't mating heat. Mating heat didn't do this. He'd researched that fucking curse and it simply didn't do this.

"Del-Rey." Her voice was weak as he stepped through the doors swinging open into the late evening air. "What's wrong with me?"

Fear filled her voice as her body tensed. Del-Rey swore he felt the pain that tore through her slight body. She moaned, her forehead pressing into his shoulder as a Coyote threw open the passenger door to the all-terrain/all-duty vehicle they used on the rough passes they called roads.

Sharone, Emma and Ashley jumped in through the back access door and braced themselves as the soldier moved quickly behind the wheel and set the vehicle into motion.

"Hurry, Martin," he ordered the Breed furiously as Anya moaned again. "Get us to Haven as fast you can get through those fucking passes."

He held her tighter, wishing he could take the pain, hating the cold sweat that gleamed on her pale face as he braced her against his broader body for the rough ride into the valley.

Each time she flinched, gripped her stomach and cried out from the pain, he swore he lost a part of his control. He was enraged, fury roaring through his veins and, yes, fear tearing through his mind. Nothing could happen to her. God, nothing could happen to her, because Del-Rey knew, if anything did, he would lose himself.

◆　　◆　　◆

Anya had never felt anything like the agony undulating in her lower stomach. She swore it felt as though something were being ripped out of her body in pulsing waves. Ice lashed at her, then heat. She was sweating and she was freezing everywhere except where Del-Rey was touching her.

What the hell had happened? She remembered the anger coursing through her, tasting it in her mouth, wanting to claw his eyes out. Then she remembered the wave of heat that swamped her an instant before the pain began clawing through her system, and the ride down the mountain at breakneck speed before Del-Rey rushed her into Armani's examining room.

She was breathing through another wave of pain when the

doctor's gloved hands touched her arm. Excruciating, unbeliev-
able pain ripped through her, causing her to cry out as she
fought to get away.

She heard a snarl filled with fury. That was Ashley. She
opened her eyes to see the three women in front of the bed,
bodies braced as the sound echoed around her of a door crashing in on the room.

Del-Rey had seen it through the window on the other side of
the exam room as Wolfe and Jonas waited with him. Anything
that happened to one mate where the mating heat was concerned had the potential to affect the other.

He watched Dr. Armani steady Anya's arm, a syringe poised
to draw blood, when Anya cried out and jerked away. Instantly,
three enraged female Coyotes were blocking her, throwing the
doctor back, death echoing in their feral growls as Del-Rey
crashed into the exam room.

Anya was curled into herself, crying again, her neck arched
and thrown back as she gripped her stomach through spasms of
pain.

"I need blood, Del-Rey." Armani was frantic, her dark gaze
filled with worry as she faced off with the three women poised
to protect their coya. "Get those feral little monsters out of my
exam room!" she ordered.

Ashley turned on him. "I won't leave her. Take my allowance
for life. You let that bitch hurt her again and I'll rip her apart."

Sharone was growling; Emma had drawn a blade and
watched the doctor silently. She was the most dangerous at the
moment.

"Emma, sheathe that blade," he snapped.

"I regret, Alpha, that I must deny your request." Her voice
was barely human. "She won't hurt Anya like this again." She
turned enraged eyes on him. "You let them do this to her the
first time. I swore then it wouldn't happen again."

Del-Rey moved to the bed, his hand brushing against Anya's
flesh as she suddenly turned to him, shaking, shivering as
though freezing.

He eased onto the mattress, letting her crawl into him, easing her into his arms as she panted for air.

"What's she talking about?" He looked from the doctor to
the bodyguards standing so fiercely over her.

"She ordered us to stand down the first time they had her screaming in agony. Those three weeks they tested her to create that fucking drug they pump into her every week. They won't hurt her again."

Del-Rey looked down at Anya before lifting his head and staring back at Armani where she now stood at the foot of the bed with Wolfe and Jonas. "What are they talking about?"

"No." Anya gripped his shirt, her voice laden with pain. "I ordered them not to tell you. It was my fault," she sobbed. "Don't punish them. It was my fault."

Wolfe's gray gaze was dark with regret; Jonas's was as cool as ever.

"The three weeks she submitted, to testing," Jonas told him. "It's extremely painful. Though I don't remember it being as painful as this for her. The scent of her agony is thicker now."

Del-Rey stared at Wolfe coldly. "You allowed them to harm my mate?" he asked carefully.

Wolfe sighed heavily. "We monitored every second of it, Del-Rey. Hope, Faith and her bodyguards begged her not to complete it when it was at its worst. She refused."

She had hurt like this? In this agony and they hadn't told him?

"Sharone?" She was Anya's lead bodyguard; the others followed her, no matter what.

Sharone glared back at him. "I didn't know you. You had hurt her. The hurt you dealt her went so deep I would have sliced you alive before letting you near her then. I followed my coya's orders until I gave you my loyalty. I still follow my coya against anyone who would dare hurt her again." There was a warning in her voice.

These three women weren't the ones that had faced him earlier. Submitting to his position of leadership, accepting his terms of punishment. They would fight even him to protect her.

"No one's hurting her again," he promised quietly, maintaining his control, realizing how close the girls were to losing their own at the sound of Anya's strangled screams. "Emma, do you trust me to protect your coya?"

She stared back at him furiously. "You didn't before."

"Did I know?" he asked her softly.

Her shoulders relaxed only marginally.

"Put away the blade, Emma," he told her gently. "Sharone, pull your team back. We're going to fix this in a way that isn't going to hurt your coya. I swear it."

"Del-Rey, she has to be examined," Dr. Armani said urgently. "Do you think it was easy for the others? That they didn't suffer? I need that blood to see why the hell she's in pain. Her hormonal levels have stayed normal. She shouldn't be doing this."

He held out his hand. "I'll get the blood. I'll do what must be done, Doctor. I'd suggest, for all our safety, that we do it this way."

Wolfe and Jonas stepped back as Armani glanced at the women guarding Anya, then back to Del-Rey.

"I know how to do it," he promised her. "Give me the syringe."

She handed him the laser syringe with its vial capped to it.

"Anya." He brushed her hair back from her face. "I need some blood. Can you let me do this?"

She was shivering in his arms but managed to nod slowly.

"Good girl." He kissed her forehead, stretched her arm out and extracted the first vial of blood and then the second.

"We need vaginal samples as well as oral." Armani was moving quickly for the supplies as Del-Rey eased from the bed.

He hated hearing Anya cry. She was sobbing, both in pain and in embarrassment as he was forced to take the vagina samples. The oral was easier. He petted her as he took the samples, ran his hands along her sweating flesh, then laid his palm against her trembling stomach.

She gasped. Shuddering just for a second before he felt the tightness in her muscles ease. The scent of her pain, the hole shredding through his soul, eased just enough that he wasn't ready to tear the walls down in his rage.

"I want my clothes on," she whispered roughly, another tear easing from her eyes. "I don't like being naked here."

She wasn't naked. She had her bra and sweater on, but he knew what she meant.

He eased her panties on, a bit of silk that covered very little. He helped her with her jeans, drawing them over her hips as she hiccupped and tensed again.

His palm pressed into her stomach, massaging the spasming

muscles as she turned her head away from him and shuddered again.

"Has this happened before?" He turned to Sharone.

Sharone shook her head. "I haven't seen her like this since the first tests. And Dr. Armani's correct. It was never this bad. Extremely uncomfortable, but it wasn't agonizing. Not like this. I would have told you, Alpha. I wouldn't have let her suffer like this." She nodded to Anya's shaking body.

"Stop," Anya groaned. "Just stop."

He gave the girls a warning look, stroking Anya's stomach slowly, easily, almost shaking himself with the fear that the agonizing contractions would return.

◆   ◆   ◆

"Shit! Dammit! Fuck! Breeds are going to drive me into an early grave." Armani slammed back into the examination room from her lab a half hour later, her dark face creased into a scowl, a million tightly woven braids bouncing with her movements.

Del-Rey's head lifted.

"Hormone levels are normal." She stopped, stared at Anya as Del-Rey felt fear crawl through his belly. "They're normal, Del-Rey. This isn't mating heat."

"Then what is it?" he asked dangerously.

"I don't know." She looked on the verge of tears. "I ran every test. Everything. I have the best fucking analysis system that can be bought, begged or stolen. I rival the U.S. fucking government. And everything is showing normal."

"Not possible," he snarled, flashing his canines in warning. "Rerun your tests. She's in pain, Armani. Do something. Give her something."

"Like what?" she demanded. "Damm it, Del-Rey, Coyote physiology is just different enough to make me crazy. Your DNA has affected her; that means she's just different enough to make it dangerous. Tell me what to do and I'll do it."

"She was angry," he muttered out roughly. "I slept with her this morning, all morning. Then I punished her bodyguards because she was out last night and in danger." He fought frantically to try to figure out what to do. "I touch her and it eases," he snarled, showing Armani how his hand lay on her stomach.

"I was pissing her off. I wanted her angry with me. She was furious, ready to throw something at me. For a second I could smell her arousal." He shook his head. "It was hot and bright, and then this." He turned back to Anya's damp face. "This. What happened?"

Dr. Armani's expression grew thoughtful.

"She had coffee last night." He was desperate for answers. "God damn you, do something."

She narrowed her eyes on Anya before moving closer to the bed, ignoring the bodyguards' growls.

"Coffee is a no-no, Anya," she said gently.

"She was aroused when she awoke this morning."

Anya groaned in embarrassment. "Dammit, Del-Rey."

"She was dreaming. She wanted my kiss." He was close to losing his mind.

"Anya?" Dr. Armani moved closer. "Have you hurt like this before?"

"Duh," she managed weakly. "I would have been here."

"Smart ass." The doctor smiled fondly. "I want you to let Del-Rey take another sample of blood for me. I may have an idea."

She moved, collected the syringe and pushed another vial onto it before handing it to Del-Rey. Swiftly Del-Rey drew the blood, tensing as he felt the pain in her rising from the loss of the pressure of his hand.

Armani moved quickly back to her lab as Del-Rey returned his hand to her stomach.

"Mate, you're going to give me a stroke," he sighed as he moved closer to her and brushed damp hair back from her cheek.

A weak smile crossed her pale lips. "I should get a treat for being a good girl while you took the blood."

"Anything," he whispered, knowing what she would ask. That she would ask to be relieved from his bed, out of his arms.

She sighed. "Get Ashley's damned nails fixed. Her whining will drive me insane."

"Whenever she needs it." He caressed her hair and laid his lips at her temple. "Nails are no longer included in punishments."

She sighed, slowly relaxing. The tension eased, bit by bit,

until her muscles relaxed beneath his palm. The heat of his hand and her flesh melded them together. He swore he sweat buckets while he caressed her rounded tummy.

Finally, she breathed out in exhaustion and turned her head to Emma. "Em. I need some water."

"Yes, Anya." Emma rushed to the outer room as Ashley and Sharone stood by her side.

"Anya." Del-Rey eased up.

She shook her head. She was still pale, but she wasn't sweating and normal color was returning to her cheeks.

"Pain in the ass, Coyote," she snorted, but there was a smile in her weak voice. "I scared you, huh?"

"Terrified the hell out of me, Coya," he admitted.

He wasn't supposed to kiss her. He was to keep the hormone in those glands to himself, but he wanted to kiss her. Until hell wouldn't have it.

"Hey, Breed." Armani's determined voice had him lifting his head. "Open." She shoved a swab at his mouth.

"What?" Del-Rey jerked back.

"Oral swab. Now." She shoved the damned thing in his mouth, swiping it over his swollen glands before turning and rushing back to her lab.

"Coya, your water." Emma moved back to the bed as Del-Rey helped her sit up and sip at the water.

"I want out of here," Anya muttered after Del-Rey handed the cup back to Emma. "Now."

"Not yet." There wasn't a chance in hell. "Stay still a while longer, Anya. You're going no place until we figure this out."

"I'll live here then," she retorted. "I want my own doctors. We need Coyote Breed specialists."

He snorted at that. "I killed them all. Remember?"

Her expression became mutinous.

"I trust Dr. Armani. She'll figure it out."

"Not without a Coyote Breed specialist she won't figure crap out," she groaned. "What if this happens to Ashley, Del-Rey, or one of the younger twins? Sharone or Emma? How will we help them?"

"Anya, there are no Coyote specialists left. Those that were left that the Council didn't kill, I took care of. They're murdering bastards with a god complex. Armani will fix that."

She eased up on the bed and glared at him. "I want our own doctor."

"Find me one then." He threw his hands up in defeat. "If you can find one you trust your friends with, then go for it. Have at it. But they're all dead. Six feet under and can't help us."

She wasn't going to find one. When the Russian facility was breached, the doctors that returned to the Council had disappeared, their bodies turning up one by one over the months. The Council had suspected one of them of conspiring with the rescuers, so they had killed them all.

Over the years, Del-Rey and his men had taken care of the others. If the bastards weren't alive, then they couldn't create more. The process wasn't easy. Coyote Breeds were the most difficult to create and to keep alive until age five. It seemed their mates were going to be difficult in other areas as well.

"Coyote Breed mates are just different." Armani reentered the examination room. "Amanda Bear, Kiowa Bear's mate and wife, is the only Coyote Breed we've been able to test. The Felines took care of that unfortunately," she sighed. "But they did share the results of the tests with me. Kiowa is more or less a hybrid, conceived naturally, so his genetics are slightly different, but we might have something here."

"Meaning?"

"A hormone that only shows up when semen has been spilled inside the womb. There's a hormone caused by the one in your tongue that acts as a blocker to prevent conception. It quite literally forms a barrier against viable sperm. Now she has that hormone in her system because you've kissed, you've had intercourse."

Of a sort, Anya thought sarcastically as she watched the doctor.

"It's been eight months," Anya pointed out. "I've never hurt like this before, Dr. Armani."

"Because you've not been in contact with him," she stated. "Your hormonal levels are showing steady. But I wasn't looking for that additional hormone, as you weren't having sex. Were you?"

"No," Del-Rey growled.

Anya gave him a hooded look. Maybe if she bought him an instruction book. Surely he could learn more than doggie style if he saw the pictures? Of course, knowing male Breed training as she did, he probably knew all the moves. He just hadn't practiced them on her.

"Okay, so, this hormone just dropped off the radar, but it wasn't gone."

"Meaning?"

Armani sighed as though they were dim-witted children. "So there was no addition to your hormonal therapy for it. You're ovulating, and that hormone is building."

"So?" Anya asked again. "How many months have you tracked ovulation with me, Dr. Armani? I've never hurt like this."

"And your mate was never around to tempt you or to arouse you. I keep trying to beat it into you guys. Mating is not all about the physical. Emotions cause hormones and chemical reactions as well. Love, hate, anger, irritation, satisfaction—they all trigger separate chemicals within the body."

"So I was angry." Anya nodded.

"Pissed off, horny, ovulating and perhaps, Anya, you don't hate your mate near as much as you once convinced yourself you did. Bam. That hormonal blocker is in place. But added to it is another hormone that also releases with it. One that tries to force the female to have intercourse, to get more seed, to break through that barrier. The Wolf Breed mates share that chemical barrier with the Coyote Breed mates. I hadn't adjusted the hormone to allow for any change. Your hormonal levels were showing normal, because it takes more than a vaginal swab or blood to detect it. The test is much more in-depth and painful for the female; it requires actually penetrating the womb itself. That's how it was found the first time. Dr. Serena Grace, she was there before Ely Morrey, found the differing chemicals and hormones and figured out how to adapt the hormonal treatments to that. But we weren't able to get enough of that hormone until you submitted to those tests after you came here."

"I didn't hurt like this then," Anya stated. "You're not making sense."

"Emotions are the difference, Anya," she said, her voice

gentle. "It's not your hormones that are changing; it's the chemicals released due to your emotions at any given time. I've adjusted your hormonal therapy for that additional chemical and hormone. This should prevent that pain from returning." She handed the pressure syringe to Del-Rey. "Upper right arm, Del-Rey."

He pushed the loose sleeve of her sweater back, his fingers going over the slight blemish on her skin where the syringe was used regularly.

"Next month, during ovulation, we'll be on guard for this. Until then, we'll need to step up the hormonal injections. Perhaps every few days." Armani sighed deeply. "But damn, don't scare me like that again."

"Get a Coyote specialist," Anya told her fiercely. "They might have answers you don't."

Dr. Armani shook her head. "I've looked, Anya. There are only a few that haven't turned up dead, but they're missing. Likely dead as well. I'm doing my best." She shrugged heavily.

Anya thinned her lips. No, they weren't all dead, but that didn't mean she trusted Del-Rey to contact them. She would have to do this one herself. Because that pain was scary. And even scarier was Dr. Armani's supposition that it was emotional changes causing it. Because Anya knew she only wished she could hate him.

CHAPTER 8

"My nails look so pretty." Ashley sighed as she threw herself beside Anya on the couch in the community room and lifted her hands up for inspection three days later.

French-tipped, a brilliant stripe running diagonally across each of them through a rich, lustrous vermillion. They were pretty nice.

"Cute," Anya stated as she flipped a page in the magazine she was pretending to read.

Ashley curled her legs under her and stared back at Anya.

"Get a haircut?" Anya asked her.

"Oh yeah." Ashley flipped the shorter back and sides. "Alpha sprang for it. But I'm still six weeks without new shoes, video games or splurge money for the mall. That sucks. He's being mean about cutting weeks off too. Remember, though, you can't have that ceremony until after my punishment. I want to look really pretty for it."

Anya had thought about that ceremony, though Del-Rey hadn't mentioned it. Hell, she had even looked at dresses herself, as though it meant something to her.

"Hmm," Anya muttered as she flipped another page.

"You're horny," Ashley whispered. "Alpha make you sleep with him last night?"

Anya glared at her. "I had to have been out of my mind when I bargained for your nails rather than my bed."

Ashley grinned impishly. "It's because you love me best. I've been rubbing it in too. Sharone and Emma are so put out with me."

"Emma doesn't have kitchen duty," Anya informed her. "Del-Rey put her in the office instead."

"Only because she put that knife of hers under a Feline Breed's throat when he wanted a sandwich," Ashley laughed.

Anya closed her eyes and laid her head back on the couch. "I want kitchen staff, Ashley. A cook, someone that can bake."

"Ohh, chocolate. Yummy," Ashley sighed. "I had chocolate cheesecake and coffee in town."

"I hate you," Anya muttered, uncurling from her seat and moving away. "Get away from me, chocolate breath, before I kill you."

No caffeine, no chocolate. No masturbating. No nothing for the bad little Coyote mate that didn't want to fuck. She snorted at the thought of it.

"Hey, let the alpha give you a little somethin'-somethin', and you can do coffee and chocolate." Ashley caught up with her easily.

Anya harrumphed at the thought. "I'm not that desperate yet." She was dying for him. So aroused she was liquid heat, and Dr. Armani was scratching her head over it. All hormone levels were fine and dandy. Just great. Emotional response, Dr. Armani had said and smirked.

Emotional her ass.

"Come on, Anya, you know you want him." Ashley skipped beside her, her pouting lips spreading into a smile. "You could just eat him all up like he's chocolate himself, couldn't you?"

"I'm going to shoot you," Anya mumbled as she headed for her room.

"Where are you going? Don't you have coya stuff to do?" Ashley asked her. "I heard Brim bitching at Sharone over your reports."

"Did them," Anya stated. They hadn't taken long.

She was dying for Del-Rey's kiss. It was eating her alive.

She wanted to bite that lower lip and then lick it all better. Then she wanted to get serious about it and lick him all over.

"Don't you have a party tonight?" Anya asked. "I already bought my dress. Thank God I didn't wait till the last minute on that one."

"Yes, something. City council shindig. Their yearly schmooze fest from what I understand."

"Yeah, Del-Rey has a team out now going into place in case of snipers. He says his neck is itching." Ashley reached back and scratched at her own neck. "So is mine. Do you think he's messing with my mind?"

Anya had to laugh. "Did they dye your hair again, Ash? Sweetie, that stuff is rotting your brain."

Ashley pouted. "And here I thought you loved me."

Anya shook her head as she opened the door into her bedroom and came to a complete, hard stop. In a flash, Ashley was in front of her.

"Oh boy," Ashley squeaked as the woman pushed away from Del-Rey's arms. "Oh hell. Oh shit. Alpha, you fucking suck."

◆   ◆   ◆

Del-Rey watched as Anya stepped slowly into the room. He watched her carefully as Sofia Ivanova moved slowly away from him.

Hell, he was up shit creek now and it damned sure wasn't what it looked like.

"Anya, you know this isn't the way it seems," he told her.

"Why is this woman here?" Anya was glaring at Sofia, her sapphire eyes glowing between lowered lashes. "This is my bedroom."

"I'm sorry, Anya, this is my fault." Sofia's smile was nothing if not confident. "I came to see Del-Rey. We argued and I meant to leave the room. I was upset and used the wrong door."

"Don't insult me by lying." She turned to Del-Rey, her nostrils flaring as she fought to control her breathing.

A perfect cloud of beautiful blond hair framed the other woman's aristocratic features. She was slender, tall, willowy, and Anya had never liked her.

"Why is she here?"

He pushed his fingers through his hair with a grimace.

"She's one of our plants within the Council. She always has been. She came with information and I didn't want her seen so I had her slipped in."

"To my room?" Anya drawled. "Did you think my body-guards wouldn't know another woman had been in my room?"

"She's going to be difficult about this, isn't she?" Sofia whispered loudly. "She always was such a temperamental little thing."

"She assumed the room was my office. I didn't have time to inform her otherwise."

He didn't look the least uncomfortable. He was still dressed, his wrinkled white shirt hanging over his well-worn jeans. Boots were on his feet. Sofia was still dressed.

"I expect a little trust here, Coya," he said darkly.

Anya snorted at that. "Get her out of my bedroom."

Her fists were clenched, her teeth ground together.

"The next time you need to meet with someone, find a room other than my bedroom if you don't mind."

"Jealous?" Sofia gave a soft, tinkling little laugh. "Really, Del-Rey, don't tell me you're still sleeping with her?"

"Enough," Del-Rey snapped, his expression growing forbidding. "I apologize for this, Anya."

"Get out!" She jerked her door open and glared at Sofia. "Now!"

"Oh dear." Sofia blinked back at her as Ashley growled behind her. "Del-Rey, perhaps I should leave. We can talk later."

"I think I have everything I need," Del-Rey snapped. "Ashley, take Sofia down the east tunnel. She has an escort waiting there. And be nice."

"I'm always nice, Alpha." Ashley's smile was all teeth. "Come along, Ms. Ivanova, I know the way. Boy, whoever did your hair sure messed up. Bad dye job?"

Sofia's lips tightened at Ashley's "dumb blonde" routine. Anya didn't even bother to warn her or Del-Rey that Ashley was going to make sure Sofia suffered before she left the tunnel. Even if it was only with words.

Watching the bodyguard warily, Sofia edged around the room and out the door, leaving Del-Rey and Anya alone.

"Your arms were around her." Anya closed the door. "Doesn't hurt to have another woman touch you, huh?"

"Just like a thousand needles slamming into my flesh," he bit out. "Dammit, Anya, you know I wouldn't touch her willingly."

"What about before?" She stared back at him furiously. "She was an informant within the Council. She was part of your network even before I came to you, wasn't she?"

She watched his jaw bunch. "Yes."

"You already knew about the facility, and you still waited?"

"Sofia wasn't in a position to do anything but get information out to me. We couldn't have breached it without your help."

"Too bad for me." She smiled tightly.

God, that bitch had been right, she was jealous. So jealous it was eating her inside. She wanted to push him into a shower and wash the touch of that woman from his flesh.

"Because you really wouldn't give a damn if I were fucking someone else, would you, Anya?"

"Should I?" she retorted. "Yeah, it was really pleasurable. Mounted, fucked and knotted, then left to figure out what the hell was going on by myself. I'm really anxious to repeat the experience. Can't you tell?"

Del-Rey stilled.

He couldn't believe the words that came from her lips. She had refused to discuss that single night they had been together. She hadn't spoken to him afterward. In the intervening months she'd only spoken when she had no other choice.

He could feel a curl of shame in his gut.

"It's not always like that." He stared at her, feeling the lash to his pride as it seemed to shrivel beneath her withering glare.

It would bounce back easily enough. Del-Rey had immeasurable pride and he knew it. Simply because he knew himself.

"It would never be like that again, Anya." He would damned well make sure of it. "Do you think that was enough for me? That it was anything close to what I needed?"

She smirked. "Well, you were the one that flipped me on my stomach and decided on the position. Have you learned something since then?"

He snarled silently. "Mate, you're pushing my temper."

"Oh come on, Del-Rey." Dampness glittered in her eyes. "Tell me, those years Sofia was helping you, did you ever fuck her?"

He wasn't going to lie to her. He couldn't lie to her, not about this. Something unimportant, something that got him what he knew they both wanted, that was different. Harmless. This wouldn't be harmless.

"Briefly."

Her chin lifted and he could smell the tears that sparkled in her eyes. "Did you spend more than a few thrusts and grunts with her? Or was I just the anomaly?"

"Anya."

"Answer me, Del-Rey." Her voice was calm, though it throbbed with pain. "Come on, Coyote Man. Tell me. Did you spend hours with her or minutes?"

"What I did to you was unconscionable," he stated heavily. "And I regret it, Anya, with every fiber of my being."

"That doesn't answer my question." Her lips trembled before she firmed them quickly. "Hours or minutes, Del-Rey?"

"Hours."

She was breathing roughly. Pain emanated from her with a scent that was mixed with more than just pride.

"Well, can't call you a liar now, can I?"

"Anya." He shook his head. "I would give my life to go back and make that night what it should have been. I lost control, and when it was over, I had no idea how to deal with it, or what I felt coming from you. The mating heat cheated us, together. I tried to explain that to you afterward, after we arrived here. It would never be that way again."

She stared at him accusingly. "I was a virgin."

"I know that, baby." He ached with that knowledge. Ached with a fire and a fury he couldn't quell, hadn't quelled since the moment he realized what he had done.

"Leave me alone."

Anya knew she was going to cry. She had never imagined Del-Rey had slept with a woman she could possibly know, let alone spent hours pleasuring her body. Touching her. Stroking her.

"Anya, we need to talk about this." He pushed his fingers through his mussed hair. "Ignoring it isn't going to work. I won't let you go."

She shuddered at the sound of his voice, part growl, part rasp of anger.

"You should have cared!" she cried. "You should have cared enough to at least hold me when you finished. You left me, Del-Rey. Cold and alone, and suffering that damned heat as though something were inside my body tearing it apart. You couldn't even hold me."

Oh God, don't let her cry. Don't let him see how bad this hurt her.

"You fucking bastard!" Her fists clenched and there was nothing to hit. "You screwed her? The slut of the Chernov facility? You spent hours fucking her? Or just hours giving her pleasure?"

"Enough of this!" He crossed the room, gripped her arms and gave her a firm shake. And she wanted to hate him. She wanted to hate him so bad it ate into her soul like acid, and all she could do was hurt, because one of the few people in this world that she did hate had fucked the man she loved.

"Listen to me, Anya, what happened that night will never, ever happen again. I swear it to you. The next time I touch you it will be in gentleness. Hours, baby." One hand cupped her face as his expression twisted.

Anya couldn't stand it. She didn't want to see gentleness on his face now. She didn't care.

"You break your promises, remember, Del-Rey?" she whispered painfully. "Did you break your promises to Sofia?"

"I made no promises to Sofia," he rumbled. "Stop this."

Her head jerked up as she forced herself to contain the pain rising inside her. It hurt. It hurt to the bottom of her soul to see that woman in his arms, to know he had pleasured her, spent hours doing so, and she hadn't deserved so much as a few moments of foreplay.

"I'll be more than happy to stop it." Her breath hitched with the pain. "As soon as you leave my room. I have a party to get ready for, remember?"

"You do not order me, Mate," he growled. "Don't make the mistake of believing you do."

Anya watched his eyes flash, the black deepening, showing a hint of raven's blue as his expression tightened, his hands flexing on her arms as she felt herself backed into the wall.

"Oh so fierce, Del-Rey," she snapped. "I catch another woman in your arms, a woman you spent *hours* fucking, and I shouldn't feel cheated? Doesn't work that way. You cheated me and you know it and now you expect me to just accept that things will be different? That you can control yourself? Go to hell!"

"Keep running your mouth, Mate, and we'll see how fast that mating heat can jump back into your system. Don't push me like this."

"I dare you!" The words were out of her mouth before she could stop them.

Cassandra had warned her: never dare a Coyote. She'd been pushed past the point of caring. Sofia had had what should have been hers. Hours of pleasure, and she should just calmly accept it?

"What the hell did you say to me?" His voice deepened, roughened.

"You heard me, *Alpha*," she sneered. "I dare you."

It was the wrong thing to say. He'd warned her years ago never to dare him. He took dares and bets seriously. Both challenged that core of animal genetics within him, and in some situations, well, in this situation, he had no intention of pulling back.

He jerked one hand from her arm, speared it into her hair and jerked her head back.

"You little witch," he snarled down at her. "You're not pissed off because of some long-forgotten affair with Sofia. You're pissed because you believe she had something you didn't."

"She had plenty that I didn't," she ground out. "She had a man. What the hell did I have, Del-Rey? Slam, bam, knot you, ma'am? It sucked. And you sucked for daring to allow me to walk into my own bedroom and see that affront to the paltry excuse for sex you gave me."

Enough was enough. He growled low and hard, his lips coming down on hers, his tongue striking sure and deep past the parted curves, as she met his kiss and gave her own.

Her nails bit into his biceps for long, shocked seconds as he felt her lips close over his tongue and her hungry moan filled the room.

There it was. Fuck. Hell. Control. He vowed control. Had sworn for eight months he would love her slow and easy if he ever had the chance again, but all he could do was devour her mouth, her lips.

The glands at the side of his tongue throbbed fierce and hard as he fought to push back the animal rising inside him, striving for satisfaction. Nearly nine months without her. Too many months, too many weeks craving her. He could count the hours if he could clear his head enough.

She drew on his tongue, moaning that soft, feminine little sound of hunger that he remembered only in his dreams.

He pumped his tongue between her lips, fucking her mouth with it as she sucked at it. The mating hormone flowed free now, drawn by the heat of her mouth and the unique taste of her kiss.

He could feel fire gathering at the base of his spine. His balls drew tight and hard beneath his cock, and his muscles locked as he fought for control. Fought to please his fiery little mate.

"Damn you." His lips jerked back, moving over her jaw, nipping roughly as she arched in his arms. "You'll drive me insane."

He jerked at the neckline of her snug sweater, pushed it over her shoulder and attacked with lips and tongue the mark he had left between her shoulder and neck. He stroked it; he sucked at it. He worked his tongue over it and scraped it with his teeth, as his other hand moved from her hair to the hem of her sweater and pushed beneath it roughly.

She was his. His mate. His sweet, tempting little Anya. So soft and defiant. A challenge and a pleasure. She was the perfect mate for him, smart-mouthed little hellion that she was. He loved that about her. She gave him that spark of challenge he needed and kept him on his damn toes.

He intended to keep her on her back.

He picked her off her feet, one arm behind her back, the other at her hips as he laved and caressed the sensitive mating mark.

As he bore her back to the bed, his lips caught hers again. He didn't want to hear objections. If she dared push the word no between her lips, then he might lose any control he had on the fragile leash of his lust.

Her back met the bed as he pushed her legs apart, settling

between them with a groan of triumph. He had her where she belonged. Beneath him, locked in his embrace, his lips moving over hers as he pushed her sweater over her breasts and palmed the lush, full curves.

"Bra off. Off." He tore the fragile lace, but her breasts were released to him, her hard little nipples like ripe berries. A delicate, fragile pink. Hard, stiff.

He growled, a demented animalistic sound, as his lips covered one, his tongue licking and stroking, laying that powerful hormone along the throbbing tips.

Oh, dare him, would she? Push him to show her who her alpha was, would she? She would learn better than that here and now, right here in her own bed where she would never forget his possession of her. Then, he would take her to his bed. If he could still walk.

Her nipples were so damned sweet. She was too sweet. The taste of her fueled the flames burning in his gut as the glands in his tongue became sensitive, swollen again.

He lifted his head from her breast, pulled the sweater from her then stared down at her in amazement. She was perfect for him. Beautiful. So sweetly rounded. Lush breasts, curvy hips, thighs that could hold a man through the night.

He eased his hands down her waist. Slow, he reminded himself. Slow and easy. Love her. Touch her. Feel every inch of her silken flesh.

He pulled the button of her jeans free, watching her face, her eyes. His fingers brought her zipper down.

"Toe off the shoes," he growled.

He expected her to object, to deny him. God help him if she denied him.

She moved, pushed her sneakers from her feet as he pushed his hand beneath the material of her jeans. He was breathing so damned hard it hurt his chest. His fingers slid over her lower stomach, into the band of her silken panties, and he found paradise.

Slick, saturated curls. He loved curls between a woman's thighs. Breeds had no body hair, though over the past months he had developed chest hair, since mating her. But there was none on his genitals. He was fascinated with his mate's fiery curls.

He let his fingers pet the sweet curls, scratch through them, feel her heat and the promise of her passion as her hips arched to his hand.

His tongue was throbbing as he lowered his head, his lips taking hers again, capturing the deep, tongue-thrusting kiss he craved from her.

She sucked his tongue into her mouth, moaned at the taste of him, her arms digging into his hair, clenching in the strands and holding him to her. His fingers slid through the thatch of wet curls again, then delved into the narrow, swollen slit of her pussy.

"Fuck!" He snarled the word against her lips as he found the luscious, juicy flesh beyond, filled with her sweet syrup, the temptation of it filling his senses as she lifted to him again. He was drowning in her, and he wanted nothing more than to sink farther.

Anya's lips parted for air. She couldn't seem to draw enough into her lungs, couldn't seem to drag herself from the heated haze of hunger and need that enfolded her. Her thighs parted farther, allowing his fingers privileges she'd sworn she would never give them. Privileges she ached for now.

"More," she whimpered, desperate for his taste.

It wasn't like the first time. That freezing, burning, clawing agony. This was just hot, desperate pleasure. So much pleasure she pulled at his hair, dragging his lips back to hers, wanting more of his kisses.

The taste of him was addictive; even with the hormonal therapy in her system, his taste was like a drug she couldn't get enough of. Was this normal or mating heat?

It was a stronger need than the one she had known before he had betrayed her. Before he had lied to her. It was that same driving, intense need to explore. But the pleasure. Oh, the pleasure was exquisite.

Hours. He could keep this up for hours?

Could she?

She tossed beneath him, sucking his tongue into her mouth and tasting the spicy heat of the hormone that spilled from it.

She could feel his body tensing, growing steel hard as he held himself above her. Her hands moved from his hair to his shirt. She wanted to unbutton it, but couldn't. Her fingers fumbled; they slipped. She gripped the secured edges, one in each hand and jerked, feeling the buttons pop, tear.

The growl that tore from his throat was primal, feral. It was pure animal hunger and sent racing tingles of electric energy spreading through her body. She could feel them, like little sizzling fingers beneath her flesh as his calloused fingertips rasped around her clit.

"You make me crazy." He tore his lips from hers, his teeth nipping at her jaw, her neck. "I'm going to come in my fucking jeans."

She smoothed the shirt back from his broad chest, relished the warm mat of chest hair beneath her fingertips. That was so sexy. Most Breeds had no body hair, she'd heard.

But Del-Rey had a light mat lying over his chest, arrowing down the center of his body to just below his navel. And it was sexy. And warm. And she wanted her tongue in it. She wanted her lips on it. She wanted to lick his flesh, taste him all over.

Her head lifted, her tongue swiping over a hard, flat male nipple as his lips moved to her shoulder again. He froze.

She let her lips, her tongue, play around the bit of flesh. She tugged it with her teeth and pushed her hands beneath his shirt, flattening them on his back, relishing the heat of him.

He surrounded her now. She liked being surrounded. She liked having him all over her until she was melting beneath him.

"I say we castrate the alph—Oh fuck!" Ashley's shocked voice was a splash of ice water she didn't need.

"Get the fuck out!" Del-Rey's voice was feral. "Damn you, Ashley!"

He was poised above Anya, head turned, snarling. His black eyes gleamed with that hint of blue and his hard expression was savage, hungry.

It took a moment for her to realize exactly what she had done. What she was doing. She was pawing him, so desperate for him she had dared him. The same as begging him.

She pushed against his chest. "Stop!"

His head jerked back to her. "I have my fingers all but up your pussy and you're saying stop?" Incredulity filled his tone. "Have you lost your mind?"

"Have you lost yours?" she cried. "Let me up, Del-Rey. Now."

She had to get her bearings. She had to figure this out. This wasn't heat, but it shouldn't be arousal either. It shouldn't be natural. She had just caught another woman in his arms and she was all but pleading with him to take her. Whining because he hadn't loved her, because he hadn't touched her, pleased her.

"Now!" she cried out again, pushing against his shoulders as his fingers slid slowly from beneath her jeans.

His expression hardened; his eyes were midnight and navy blue fire. Then he lifted his fingers, still glistening from her juices, and curled his lips around them.

"The next time I get my hands in your pants, Mate, you're fucked," he growled. "Be very, very careful the next time you dare me. This one was free."

With that, he jumped back, landing on the balls of his feet as she lay back on the bed, panting, chilled, weak from the sensations still racing through her.

"The next time I catch Sofia in your arms, I'll make you wish you were dead," she shot back, sitting up and jerking her sweater over her head. "You made this situation, now you can live with it."

His smile was slow, dangerous. "Remember that, Coya, the next time I get between your thighs. Because next time I'll show you exactly what you've missed out on."

"What you gave Sofia?" She was shaking again, furious. She saw that scene again—Del-Rey gripping the other woman's arms, her hands on his chest, her head lifted to him as though for a kiss. It made her want to kill.

He shook his head first, then his finger. "Jealous, Coya? She might have had a taste, but I intend to give you the full banquet. A few hours would never be enough." He glanced over her body, a flush mantling his cheekbones. "I think I'll be fucking you all damned night long when I get my cock inside that snug little pussy again. Think about that. Because I will be."

· C H A P T E R   9 ·

Del-Rey stood at the bar and watched his mate. She wasn't wearing the black silk he'd bought her and sent to her the month before, though he'd heard she'd definitely claimed it and thanked the Breed that delivered it nicely.

No, his fiery-haired mate was dressed in sapphire blue silk that made every cell in his body ache to feel her rubbing against him again. The bodice cupped and held her breasts like a lover, hugged her trim waist and hips before flowing around her legs.

There was some kind of burgundy trim at the bodice and the straps that went over her slender shoulders. A burgundy wrap had been given to the doorman earlier along with a tiny matching purse.

His coya was exquisite. She moved like a flame, danced over his lusts like a tempting promise held just out of reach.

He glanced over to Brim, with whom Ashley was flirting outrageously. When had his female Breeds learned how to flirt? He would have shaken his head, but it would have indicated his confusion. Never show weakness, he reminded himself as he collected his whiskey and a glass of wine for his mate.

Striding back to her, he hid his smile. She watched him, no matter where he moved. His mate was jealous. Enraged with it.

It indicated more than a surface lust, and he craved her emotions as much as he craved her body.

"For me?" She reached out and took his whiskey. "Thank you."

He watched, cock throbbing, his senses suddenly heightening further as she sipped the smooth whiskey without a grimace. Hell, he should have known better. She had drunk vodka with the same relish at several of their meetings and laughed at him the first time he'd shown his surprise.

As she sipped, she let her gaze slip along the room. A dance floor was set off to the side, and a band was easing into a slow, seductive tune as waiters worked to clear the tables of dinner dishes.

Del-Rey handed the glass of wine to a nearby waiter and turned back to Anya, his fingers covering hers, surprising her, surprising himself. He pulled the glass she held to his lips, tipped it and finished it for her. His lips covered the spot hers had, and he swore he could taste her on the glass.

The sweet taste of her pussy was still in his senses, tempting his tongue. The need to lay her back and lick her slowly and thoroughly was nearly overwhelming. Anger or not, he'd show her, prove to her the pleasure he could give her. He had but one goal. To wipe the memory of that first time out of her mind and replace it with the ecstasy he knew would grip both of them.

Her brow lifted as he finished her drink; her blue eyes sparkled with the challenge. Then she licked her lower lip slowly. "Very practiced," she murmured. "Who taught you that?"

The clear little jibe pricked, but he shook it off easily enough.

"I had to be taught?" he asked her, moving closer as he took the glass and set it on the table beside her.

"I would imagine," she drawled, "if you've learned moves like that, then someone must have taught them to you."

Damn her. He should have known she'd pick the worst possible place to tempt him.

His jaw clenched at the memory of that afternoon's pleasure, and need burned inside him like wildfire.

"That didn't count," he assured her, lowering his head to her ear, letting his cheek rub against hers. "Just because I lost control then doesn't mean I will now."

"A loss of control?" she murmured. "An interesting excuse."

She shifted, her breasts brushing against the front of his tux as she spoke. "I don't remember any reports of sexual training for the Coyote Breeds. Maybe you really just didn't know any better."

She was deliberately challenging him and he loved it. She wasn't going to ask him for anything. She was pushing him, daring him without saying the words. Pushing to see if he was worthy of her. Damn her, she was invading his soul.

"A man doesn't need training to know how to touch his woman," he finally stated, allowing his hand to rest against her hip, his senses to inhale her scent. "But remember, Mate, I was out of those labs for a hell of a lot of years. Trust me, I know well how to please you."

She stiffened at the reminder. He could feel the fine tension radiating through her.

"Took advantage of it, did you?" she asked. "Perhaps that was where I made my mistake. I didn't take advantage of any chances I may have had. Maybe I should have gained the experience you didn't take the time to show me."

His teeth clenched. He loosened them to nip her ear.

"I would have ripped out the throat of any bastard who touched you."

"Would you?" Her hand settled on his arm as his fingers tightened on her hip. "You wouldn't have known."

"I would have," he whispered against her ear. "I would have known. And I would have killed."

"You're rather handy at the killing part," she snorted, pulling back from him, the deep blue of her eyes peeking up through her lashes. "Tell me, Del-Rey, how many times have you used the freedom of the hormonal therapy to touch another woman?"

"This is the wrong place to push me, Anya," he warned her. "Don't make the mistake of believing a public event would stop me from throwing you over my shoulder and carrying you out of here. I will. And once we're back in that limo, I promise you, you'll learn to not defy me in such a way again."

Her lips twitched. Sweet, pouty lips. They glistened as though a layer of dew had been laid to them. He was so damned hungry for her kiss that the glands beneath his tongue were now twice their size. He wanted nothing more than to pump it between those lush lips again, feel her suckling at it, meeting and stroking it.

"Del-Rey," she murmured, her fingers tightening on his arm. "What do you think you'll gain by wining and dining me at this very social event?" She looked around the room before her gaze returned to his. "Do you think this is going to keep me in your bed?"

He let his lips curl suggestively. "Actually, I was more concerned about keeping the bars safe tonight. I hear the last time you visited one, the accounts in the Coyote coffers dipped drastically to pay for the damages caused."

She blinked back at him, and he had to applaud how well she kept her expression clear and composed.

"A total misunderstanding." She sighed dramatically as she waved her free hand. "I didn't start that fight. I was just there."

He laid his forehead against hers, moving closer. "You broke a whiskey bottle over that cowboy's head. He was in the hospital for several days. I believe Sharone made another sing a high note when she stomped his testicles, and Ashley pulled a swath of hair from another woman's head. Coya, I've been regaled by tales of the exploits the four of you have managed in the past eight months. Just because Sharone didn't report it didn't mean I didn't hear about it. I'm amazed you weren't locked up for your own safety, let alone the safety of the public in general."

She rolled her eyes at him. Eyes that were brilliant, highlighted by cosmetics, tempting and mysterious.

"Everyone survived intact." She shrugged.

"It won't happen again. It goes on my list of rules to be followed," he informed her. "Your safety is not to be risked, in any way."

She frowned, her eyes glittering with irritation now. "Well hell, Del-Rey, why don't you just lock me up in a padded room and hand-feed me?" she snapped. "Get over yourself and get a clue. I don't need your permission any more than you obviously need mine to bring another woman to my bedroom. Consider it a trade-off for all those hours Sofia enjoyed your very manly body."

With that, she jerked away from him, moving smoothly, gracefully, to the small bar that had been set up. Her soldiers followed her, including Ashley, who somehow managed to drop the dumb-blonde act she was giving Brim long enough to realize her coya was no longer with her alpha.

Del-Rey exhaled roughly as his lieutenant moved to him slowly.

"We could make dungeons in the lower caverns," Brim said thoughtfully. "We could lock all four of them up in them."

Del-Rey grunted at the observation. "They'd find a way out."

Anya ordered vodka and sipped at it with an expression of pleasure.

"Have you learned anything during the vastly unentertaining hours that the good city council has spent attempting to show their appreciation of the animals that funded their new school?" Del-Rey asked.

They were there for more than food and drinks. The reports Del-Rey had brought with him linked that Breed drug to Advert and one of the soldiers who had worked at Haven a year ago.

"Not a lot." Brim shook his head. "The others aren't learning much either. Mayor Raines is still grieving for his daughter. It seems there's still no information as to why she disappeared during that attack eight months before."

Jessica Raines hadn't disappeared, except from sight. The secured cells in the mountain that rose above Haven had been her new home since the attack she had participated in.

Del-Rey let his gaze wander around the room again. "We have five pack leaders here. Wolfe Gunnar and his mate. Hawke Sanders. Dash Sinclair, his wife and daughter. Myself and my coya. Jacob and his mate. Only Aiden and his pregnant mate, Charity, aren't in attendance. You have near the full Wolf and Coyote Breed cabinets and their families in attendance and a lot of social pressure to get them here."

The others were aware of that as well. Each Breed in the room was on high alert, prepared for trouble. Del-Rey could almost feel that trouble brewing, like a storm easing in, trying to slip up on them.

"Sentries outside aren't reporting anything suspicious," Brim murmured. "I can feel the tension, Del, but I can't figure out where the hell it's coming from."

"Any further information from Sanctuary on the drug situation?" Del-Rey asked.

Brim shook his head. "Nothing new so far. We know the drugs went out with specific individuals in mind, but no names. Sanctuary has their own men watching the pharmaceutical and research company involved, but they don't have much. Plenty of suspicion, not enough to prosecute."

"Jonas Wyatt is waiting for evidence?" Del-Rey grunted. "That's a new one."

"He has a new secretary," Brim explained. "I think he's afraid to make a trip to that volcano until he's certain she knows how to keep her mouth shut."

In other words, the new secretary Merinus Lyons had hired had the security of knowing Jonas couldn't fire or kill her. Del-Rey was betting Jonas was loving that one. Breed enemies had a habit of disappearing, proof or no proof. And Del-Rey knew there were several particular volcanoes that had been receiving more than their fair share of human sacrifices over the years since Wyatt had achieved directorship of the Bureau of Breed Affairs.

"Jonas, with said secretary in tow, will be arriving at Haven again tomorrow," Del-Rey stated. "She's breeding. You can smell the scent of the child she's carrying. I can't believe Prima Lyons hired a pregnant female to work for Wyatt. It's certain to scar the poor kid before it's even born."

Brim nodded. "Hell, he should send her to Sanctuary. A breeding female has no place around any of us. Even our own females. Our lives are too dangerous."

With that, Brim strolled away, moving about the room once again as Del-Rey checked for the feel of the weapons he carried beneath his tux. The city council had asked that they come unarmed. They had come with their weapons hidden instead. Unarmed was undefended. Del-Rey went nowhere undefended. Especially where his coya was concerned.

Del-Rey caught Sharone's eye, gave her a silent signal to make certain Anya stayed close to the three of them, then moved to where Mayor Timothy Raines was holding court across the ballroom.

Raines wasn't a man that Del-Rey could make himself like. He was deceitful. His blue gray eyes barely hid his maliciousness, but there was no hiding it from Breed senses. Del-Rey could smell it, a subtle acrid stench that sickened him.

"Ah, Pack Leader Delgado." Timothy gave him a twisted little smile as he moved toward the group. "Join us. We were just discussing those nasty tabloid stories that are making the rounds again. Really. You'd think if Breeds were so animalistic, they would have never achieved human status." There was the barest sneer in Timothy's voice.

Del-Rey lifted his brow. "I don't read the tabloids, I'm afraid. What are they saying now? Are we eating our meat raw again? Howling at the moon?"

"Knotting your females," one of the men said and snickered with avid curiosity. "Turning them into nymphomaniacs with some kind of hormonal release from a kiss."

Avid eyes latched onto him as he scratched his cheek, as though in confusion. Breeds didn't deny the mating heat, but they didn't admit to it either.

"They're still harping on that?" He grinned. "From what I understand there were several of our Breed males that volunteered to prove differently. Did that ever happen?"

Del-Rey knew it had. Some of the younger male Breeds had publicly named lovers for several journalists. It had stopped the rumors for a while.

"That doesn't stop the gossip," the gray-haired public works manager chuckled. "Your genetics are still a mystery to too many folks, Delgado. Makes you good gossip fodder."

Del-Rey shrugged. "Whatever works for them. It does keep the women interested in us though. I'm sure quite a few of our males appreciate that."

The men laughed, then looked around as though making certain none of their women were listening. It was amusing at times, and at others offensive. Del-Rey could imagine the furor that would erupt if the world learned the truth. That only with certain women did their animalistic nature show itself, and when it did, for now, there was no permanent escape from it.

Del-Rey caught the mayor's gaze once more.

"Mayor Raines, when you have a chance, I'd like to discuss the request you put into the Coyote Cabinet last month."

Timothy's gaze sharpened, too much, and Del-Rey swore he caught the scent of death on the man. The request was to assign several Coyote males to the local police department and as security guards at city hall.

The little town outside Haven's boundaries wasn't large; it hadn't attained the popularity of Sanctuary's neighboring town, Buffalo Gap. He wanted to know what made Mayor Raines believe they needed the advanced talents of the Coyote Breeds for any security.

Raines's gaze moved around the room before a smile shaped his lips. "I didn't mean to bother you with that decision, Alpha Delgado," he apologized with the utmost insincerity. "I assumed the lower members of the cabinet would take care of that."

"There are no lower members of the Coyote Cabinet," Del-Rey informed him. "I'm but one of six pack leaders, Mayor. Each of us chairs the cabinet."

"Every army has a general, Delgado," Raines laughed. "You head it, correct?"

As he did, by strength and by will. That didn't make any of the others below him, they were his equal, they merely chose to follow him.

"Incorrect, Mayor, but we can discuss that as well when you get a moment. As you're busy tonight, we could meet in the Coyote base sometime this week if you prefer. I'd like to see the proposal you promised the cabinet."

Something flashed in Raines's gaze. Something triumphant, certainly dangerous. "I'll be sure to do that." He nodded. "I'll call soon."

Like hell. Del-Rey made his excuses and moved from the group. He lifted his wrist and spoke into the small mic beneath the cuff of his tuxedo jacket. "We're going to have problems. I suggest an exodus."

"Grounds?" Wolfe murmured into the earpiece Del-Rey wore.

"Instinct, use yours. I'm getting my people out."

He nodded to Brim and headed for the bar, where Sharone and the other females surrounded Anya, their expressions filling with dangerous tension.

Ashley shifted, hiding the fact that she had reached to the holster strapped to the inside of her thigh and the small handgun she carried there. Sharone was blocking any access to the side and Emma was covering her back.

"This one stays."

Del-Rey heard the bartender's voice, dark, ugly with menace through the bodyguards' comm links.

Emma turned to Del-Rey, her expression icy, and mouthed, *Weapon on coya.*

"We have a weapon on my coya," he announced into the mic. "Get your women the fuck out of here."

He moved for the bar, aware of Brim striding quickly toward it and a young Breed, Carlen, moving for the females. The Breed was Wolf. He wasn't Coyote, nor was he one of the Wolves assigned to Anya's small protection detail.

"Jacob, call off your man," Del-Rey ordered as he heard Jacob screaming through the link at Carlen. He moved faster, breaking into a run as he watched the young Breed jerk a weapon from inside his jacket and attempt to push past Sharone to get to Anya.

"She has to die, Sharone," Carlen growled, his gray eyes too dark, too dilated. Fuck, they were going to lose another of their people to that fucking drug. "You know she has to die."

Carlen managed to lift his arm enough to aim.

Del-Rey's mate was going to die before his eyes.

Sharone pushed Carlen back, then threw him several feet across the room when he lifted the weapon and fired at her instead. At the same time, a knife streaked from her hand and buried itself in his chest as he stared down at it in shock.

Emma was on the floor covering Anya even as she struggled; Ashley had jumped the bar and taken out the bartender. She cocked the sawed-off rifle she'd jerked from him and leveled it on the room as she moved from behind the bar.

"Sharone." The Wolf Breed went to his knees as Del-Rey jerked Anya from Emma's hold.

Emma was on her feet, catching a swaying Sharone around her waist as blood seeped from her shoulder. They both stared at the young Breed as he gazed at them in confusion and fear. He didn't even know what he had been about to do. Del-Rey knew the effects of that fucking drug, and this Breed, it appeared, was a victim of it.

"Why did you hurt me?" He sounded like a child.

Del-Rey was aware of the shouts, the orders filling the room. The Wolves had the city council surrounded, but Del-Rey was watching the death of an innocent young man before his eyes.

"What did I do?" Carlen coughed, blood spraying on Sharone's white dress as a whimper left her lips. "What did I do?"

He toppled over, still trying to lift the pistol, still trying to focus on Anya as his eyes glazed with death.

"Get this taken care of," Del-Rey shouted as more of his own men surrounded them. "Grab that Wolf off the floor and get him to the labs at Haven. I want full blood work done. The rest of you surround me until I get my coya to the limo. Emma, Ashley, get Sharone to a transport and get her back to Base. Now."

They were moving quickly through the ballroom, aware of the Wolves moving just as effectively. Breeds were covering the humans, weapons drawn, eyes hard as mates and family were whisked from the room and into the late evening cold.

Secured limos were pulling into the drive, then moving out as quickly as they'd come in, as Breed Enforcers worked to get the pack leaders and families out of danger. Enforcers and soldiers stayed behind, covering them while still others took the rooftops, ensuring that snipers weren't in place.

"I want that bartender in custody," Del-Rey told Brim through the mic as he pushed Anya into the waiting limo. "I want him ready to be fully interrogated the moment we hit Base."

"He's in custody and rolling now," Brim barked back. "Get your ass back to Base. Ivan should be your driver. There's no way he could be compromised by that fucking drug; we just had him tested after our return."

"I have Ivan. I want you at Base ASAP," Del-Rey ordered him. "Don't take chances and don't bother with that fucking city council. I'll take care of them myself."

He slammed the door closed as he slid in, and Ivan sped away from the banquet hall. He could feel the fury filling him now. No other mate had been targeted. Carlen had gone after Anya. The bartender had been prepared to hold her there. Why?

He turned to her, his gaze meeting hers and seeing not one iota of fear.

"They have my purse and my wrap," she stated. "Morons kept my gun and knives. If they had left me alone, Sharone wouldn't have been wounded."

Shock resounded through him. Where was the anger, the terror, the sheer fear she should have been showing? His mate shouldn't be staring at him with furious brilliant blue eyes and a determination that normally only blood could quench. Others' blood.

"Sharone will be fine," he told her. "It was a shoulder wound. The worst it's going to do is piss her off."

"I'm past pissed," she snarled. "You didn't tell me to expect trouble, Del-Rey. That was damned unfair of you."

Unfair of him? As though he had knocked her out of some sport? His mate was becoming more aggressive than he had ever anticipated. The thought of it made him hard.

"If I'd expected trouble, your ass wouldn't have been here."

Before he could stop himself, he was nose to nose with her. "Do you think for a moment I'd take my mate where I expected bloodshed? Expected some crazed fucking bartender and Wolf Breed to take a shot at her?"

He was yelling at her. Anya stared back at him, adrenaline and fury pumping through her. She was shaking with it, desperate with it. She'd fought Emma as the other girl held her down, fought not to protect herself or her soldiers, but to get to Del-Rey.

It had been the only thought in her mind. To get to him, to protect him. As though he needed her protection. As though he really needed anything from her outside of sex. But the knowledge, sudden and swift, had slammed into her. She needed it from him, and right before her eyes, it could have been stolen from her.

"I don't know what you would do," she cried. "My bodyguard is wounded and you could have been killed in front of my eyes, Del-Rey. I'm not a happy little camper right now."

She was terrified for him. She was shaking, desperate; she needed to touch him, just to be certain, as though only touch would assure her that he was actually there with her.

"And you think I am?"

That growl sent a shudder up her spine. It sent sensation crashing through her adrenaline-laced bloodstream, and lust and emotion to sear her mind.

She could have lost him. It could have been him carrying a bullet rather than Sharone. Though he would have probably pretended the damned thing had never hit him, despite any blood he shed.

Man of steel. Unconquered. Undefeated. Oh God, she needed

him. Needed to assure herself he was alive, that he was hers. That nothing could take him away from her.

"I really don't care if you are." She pushed against his shoulders, trying to shove him back, and he wasn't moving. His hands were braced on the seat at her side, his nose nearly touching hers, his black eyes glaring into hers.

"Oh, I know just how much you don't care," he bit out. "To the tune of eight months. Without my mate."

"Oh yeah, I can really see how you suffered." She was shaking with emotion now. So many months of loneliness, fear and even, at times, guilt raging through her. "I saw that when I walked into my bedroom and caught you all but fucking Sofia. Damn you to hell." She shoved harder, and was surprised that he moved back, even more surprised that she followed him.

She was in his face. Nose to nose. "You let that bitch touch you."

"It's not as though you attempt to touch me." He bared his teeth at her. "You ran. Like the child you were, rather than facing what you knew couldn't be changed."

"I changed it. I suffered those damned tests and I got what I needed to make sure you couldn't control me again." She slapped one hand to his chest, then the other. She gripped the lapels and jerked.

Buttons flew as his gaze reflected surprise, then burning lust.

"And I'll change it now if I want to."

Desire and need was like a demon inside her. Not like the mating heat, but like a surge of pure, white-hot lust that didn't need hormonal help. Like it had been earlier. Powerful. Desperate.

It was helpless emotion, caught in a grip of fearing for his safety, terrified, aware that anytime in the past months she could have lost him. A knowledge that she might never have the chance to touch him again.

Nights of tossing and turning. Dreams that didn't stop. An aching hunger she couldn't rid herself of. And fear. In one striking moment she could have lost all those dreams. He could have died in front of her eyes because she wasn't prepared, because she was a liability. She had to be protected for his sake because she was too damned frightened to accept the place he had made for her. As his mate. As his coya.

Well, he had to be protected too. Because he was hers. Mate, lover, man, whatever. She couldn't name the possessiveness that rose inside her, not yet.

Her hands pressed against his chest, feeling his heart racing beneath her palms, the muscles that bunched and rippled at her touch. Her fingers curled, her nails scratched across his flesh, and she reveled in the rumbled growl that left his chest.

"Did you want Sofia after me?" She shocked herself with the question, then with the actions that followed it. She bit his lower lip, and it wasn't a love nip.

"Do you care?" His voice was graveled, so rough it was feral.

Did she care? Oh hell yes, she cared, but she'd be damned if she would give him the satisfaction of hearing it from her lips.

"Do you care if I fuck another?" she asked him. "Maybe I should have found someone else."

She was challenging him and she knew it. Daring the Breed, part man, part animal, to claim what was his. To claim what she didn't know how to give him.

He buried his hand in her hair and jerked her head back as he snarled in her face. "Don't make that mistake."

"Why?" Her nails scratched his hard abs. She felt the flexing power in them, heard the growl of hunger that parted his lips. "Why would you care?"

He didn't answer the question. He bore her back until she was beneath him, stretched along the leather seat, arching against him as his lips covered hers, his tongue driving into her mouth.

Fire and lightning sizzled around her. Hunger and need clashed inside her head. Her arms wrapped around his neck, her fingers speared into his hair as she met the kiss, sucked his tongue into her mouth and gave them both what they needed.

He hadn't fucked Sofia since he had taken Anya. She could feel it. She knew it. Sensed it. The female part of her, the woman who knew when something had touched what belonged to her, assured her of that. And she was going to make damned sure the bitch never touched him again. The man she held in her arms belonged to her. And she was going to claim every inch of him.

Her common sense was screaming, *Mistake*. Her independence was clawing against the need thundering through her system, but something stronger, something more vital had Anya pulling Del-Rey closer, holding on to him tighter, her lips moving beneath his, tempting his kiss deeper, hotter, stronger.

He kissed her as though he were starved for her, just as he had earlier. And she kissed him, *knowing* she was starved for him. Not just for the taste of the mating hormone, but for the man. The man who filled her senses even when he wasn't touching her. The man who could have been lost to her forever.

When had it begun to matter?

It had always mattered.

As she felt the hem of her gown rising above her stockings, Anya admitted that to herself. When she heard his hungry growl, felt his hand on the bare flesh of thigh, she knew it would always matter.

Twisting, arching beneath him, she held on to him, her lips caught by the pleasure of his kiss, by the storm tearing through her.

"Part your legs." His voice was so deep, filled with such

rough hunger, that she whimpered, her lashes lifting to stare into the fierce, black depths of his gaze.

"No woman has mattered to me as you do," he rasped, one hand cupping her cheek, holding her still as his thumb curled under her jaw. "I've taken no woman since I touched you. Desired no woman. I've craved nothing but the taste of you, Anya."

His body lowered, his hips wedged between her thighs as he lifted her leg and laid it along his hip.

"Feel how hard." He nipped her lower lip. A tiny sting against the sensual pleasure raging through her. "Feel how I've needed you, Coya. Your touch and your heat. Only yours."

She licked her lips, staring back at him as she fought to draw enough air into her lungs just to breathe.

"The hormonal therapy." She knew there was a therapy for the males as well. A way to tame the raging need that burned in them, though it was said not to be as torturous for them as it was for the females.

He shook his head. "Do you think I wanted to lose a single moment of knowing something in this world belonged to me?" he asked her, destroying her. "One thing, Anya." His thumb ran over her lips and his hips rolled against the mound of her sex. "In this world, God granted me one thing for the honor I chose rather than the evil I could have followed. He gave to me the woman that I saw as a tender woman-child, and desired above all things. When you were no more than sixteen, tender and so innocent, I claimed you. I don't want to lose a moment of knowing, even if you walk away, that there is proof that I'm worthy of something that isn't marked by blood."

She shuddered, her heart clenching as tears filled her eyes. His gaze was liquid black now, dark, haunted and sinking so deeply inside her that she wondered if she would ever be free.

"You can't base that worthiness on me," she finally whispered, torn, aching for him in ways she couldn't name.

"I base my worthiness all on you, Coya. My Anya."

Before she could protest, his lips settled back on hers, parting them, his tongue licking over hers like a promise. She felt herself gasp, felt the damp heat that spilled between her thighs as his hips rocked against hers, stroked her clit, sent unimaginable sensation tearing through her.

"I want to touch you." She was pushing at the jacket he wore, the edges of his shirt that she had torn.

His flesh was hard and warm beneath her palms.

"Anya." He tensed as she pressed against his shoulders.

"I need to touch you. You took before, Del-Rey. Now let me have what I need. I need this."

She needed her control.

Del-Rey could feel the force of the lust tearing through his balls, his senses. He couldn't let himself lose control again. Not this time. Not this close. She wanted to touch him. She wanted to stroke him.

He eased up, following her direction, his teeth clenching furiously as rumbled growls echoed in his chest.

Oh fuck. Sweet God have mercy.

Her nimble finger faltered only a little, pulled at the button of his pants, then eased the zipper over the raging erection it covered.

Del-Rey could feel a snarl building in his chest as her slender fingers wrapped around the swollen flesh. His erection was thick, the engorged head throbbing, threatening to spill the slick ejection that Wolf and Coyote males produced once mating heat began.

"Ah hell. Anya. Sweet Anya."

Her lips touched the heavy crown, slid over it as her tongue flicked over the tiny slit at the tip. Holding back was killing him. He knew how shocked, how frightened she had been the first time he had taken her. He didn't want that for her now. He wanted her to explore as she needed to. To taste. To touch.

He wrapped his own hand at the base, feeling that sharp bite in his balls that warned him the first sharp ejaculation of pre-cum was building.

He shook his head, feeling the rivulet of sweat that ran down his chest as sharply as he felt her hot little tongue circling the head of his cock.

Looking down, he was torn by the sight of her—her lips glistening, those blue eyes staring up at him—then her lips parted and covered the throbbing head, sinking over it as her tongue flicked over the swollen, sensitive flesh.

When she began suckling, her cheeks hollowing, laying an exquisite pressure along his nerve endings, Del-Rey shook his head. Ah God. He couldn't hold back much longer. He gripped the base of his shaft tighter, but he couldn't hold back the spurt of pre-cum that jerked from his cock.

The silky, slick fluid had its own purpose Dr. Armani had warned him. The hormones contained in it excited the nerve endings in the vagina, even as they relaxed the snug sheath and allowed for the swelling that came when a male Coyote spilled his seed fully.

Anya's eyes widened as a second spurt filled her mouth. Her lashes lowered and a little moan escaped her lips before she was sucking him deeper, more firmly, as though she craved more of the taste that spilled from him.

He couldn't do this. He didn't have the control for this. He wanted inside her. He had to fuck her, fill her, take her. Hold her hips and pound inside her until the ravaging waves of hunger were stilled.

The fingers of one hand held his cock as he reached out with the other to touch her face, his thumb caressing over the side of her lips as she worked her mouth over him.

Need. The need was more animal, the clawing hunger demonic in its intensity. He couldn't wait. He was going to take her here. Now. He had to. If he didn't, he'd lose his mind forever.

"Incoming!" Ivan's voice screamed through the intercom between front and back. A second later an explosion rocked the limo as a mortar struck the road in front of it.

Anya fell back as Del-Rey pushed her from him, zipping his pants and latching them as he hit the switch to lower the window between the passenger's and driver's sides.

Another explosion rocked them as Del-Rey's eyes narrowed on the vehicles ahead of them. Behind him, Anya was scrambling, the brush of her dress assuring him she was now crouched on the floor of the limo.

"It's coming from the mountain," Ivan yelled as another streak of fire filled the night air. "Someone's going to get hit, Del-Rey, we have too many vehicles together."

"Air support?" he clipped out.

"It's coming in. We had a team airlifting from the army base camp in the area, but I've not had radio contact."

The next explosion took out a chunk of road, raining sparks

and fire over the front of the limo as Ivan swerved and kept moving.

"They're going to get lucky," Del-Rey snapped before reaching into the front and jerking the radio from the dash. "Brim, are you there?"

"Dragging in behind the convoy," Brim yelled back. "Mortar fire is coming from the north, at the head of the mountain. Cheap bastards. They should have invested in heat-seeking rockets."

"Don't give them ideas," Del-Rey snarled as he jerked the cuff of his jacket up to reveal the mic at this wrist. As he flipped it on, the receiver at his ear activated. "Wolfe, are you in the lead?"

"We're lead and hell's coming down on us." Wolfe was snarling.

Del-Rey stared ahead. "In two clicks. Sharp right, then left—it's going to bounce like hell. The dry creek bed there runs for three miles and takes us out of the line of sight."

Wolfe repeated the orders to his driver.

"Ivan, get that to the rest of the vehicles," Del-Rey ordered before lifting the radio he could hear Brim screaming into. "Brim, you have weapons?"

"Enough." Brim's response was cold, furious. "They're targeting the vehicles with the bartender and the body of the Wolf Breed, Del-Rey. I have a line on location."

Del-Rey reached forward again, hit the sunroof and tore the jacket and shirt from his shoulders. The hanging material would only get in his way at this point.

"I'm bailing from the limo. Ivan can't slow down for the exit. Watch for the falling body and pick up the pieces."

"Here." A leather jacket was shoved in his face. "It will protect against the fall. Here." A lightweight submachine gun was pushed into his hands as he noticed that the backseat of the limo had been raised.

Another, closer explosion rocked the car, nearly tilting it as Ivan cursed, swung the wheel, then made the turn into the creek bed they would be using for a road.

Del-Rey quickly pulled on the jacket, zipped it, jerked the gun from Anya, then launched himself onto the roof of the car.

As he gripped the edge of the sunroof, his eyes narrowed on the dark landscape passing them. He knew the best place to jump. Grassy, soft earth leveled out in one place. The impact would be lessened, and the chances of being run over by the vehicles speeding through the pass would be nonexistent.

He waited, poised, then lauched himself from the limo, curled and rolled as he hit the ground with enough impact to steal his breath and assure him he'd feel the damned bruises for weeks to come.

The bastards. Del-Rey knew he should have expected the ambush. Hell, the others probably had. The only problem was that there was only one clear road into the town and a lot of mountains rising around them.

Coming to his feet, he gripped the weapon as he ran for the all-terrain Brim had swung to the side of the creek bed. The vehicles were built high, light, and made for mountainous terrain. Heavy shocks supported the dirt-gripping tires and a powerful motor gave the ATV the edge needed to effectively cut through some of the roughest passages.

"Move in on them," Del-Rey yelled as he swung into the passenger seat.

Behind him, two of his men were braced in the attack supports. One carried a handheld missile launcher; the other gripped the mounted machine gun.

"All vehicles are in the pass," Jacob, Haven's head of security, barked into the receiver at Del-Rey's ear. "Good luck, Alpha Delgado."

"Move!" Del-Rey shouted the order to Brim as another explosion sent rock and earth flying into the air.

The all-terrain jerked and sped off at his order, climbing the pass and shooting across the road as another explosion sprayed chunks of earth around the vehicle.

"They'll be waiting in line of sight when they come out of that pass." Brim jerked the wheel and headed up the mountain.

"Give them a new target," Del-Rey ordered harshly. "Let them see us coming. Pull the fire off those limos, Brim. If so much as one of those women is injured, there's going to be war."

The peace between human and Breeds was always tenuous at best. They were aware that it would take only one wrong move to change the balance in peace. The death of a mate, especially an alpha leader's mate, would create chaos.

Breed loyalty to pack was everything. Their women were their future, their survival. The death of even one of them would not be taken lightly, and the Council knew that. They knew the Breeds would descend on the murderers with a fury that the humans of the world only imagined them capable of.

Del-Rey's eyes narrowed along the terrain. His night vision was perfect, drawing from the moonlight above, the shadows around them, each detail highlighted.

"We have incoming," Brim yelled. "Brace. Brace."

Del-Rey clenched his teeth in a grimace of fury as the all-terrain rocked and sped along the mountain. It zigzagged among the trees that crashed down around it as the explosion ripped through the forest.

"When we reach them, stay the hell out of my way," Del-Rey ordered.

"We need to question them," Brim growled in irritation.

Sometimes, Brim was too fucking logical. That was why, Del-Rey decided, Brim wasn't pack leader.

He smiled, hard and cold, as the all-terrain avoided another explosive mortar shell and raced toward the ambushers' location. Within minutes, they'd have them.

Del-Rey turned to Brim and snarled, "Question their fucking ghosts."

A second later, the world exploded in a haze of color and sound as the all-terrain flew into the air.

♦   ♦   ♦

The limo raced up the mountain to the Coyote Breed stronghold as Anya sat silently, staring into the distance at the explosions on the mountain.

She knew a team of Wolf Breed Enforcers had followed Del-Rey and his men up there. A helicopter was now streaking across the sky, as was one of the lethal weapon-equipped stealth heli-jets that the Breeds used.

She'd listened to the reports that echoed through the limo and flinched, barely holding back a cry when she heard that the Coyote vehicle had been struck.

Del-Rey was fine, she assured herself, feeling the tears that marred her cheeks. He had been through worse than this. He would have been prepared. He was fighting even now, his teeth clenched, a killer's smile on his face.

"Coya, we're pulling to the entrance," Ivan told her fiercely. "Soldiers are waiting at the entrance to escort you into the caverns."

"Find your alpha, Ivan, don't worry about me," she ordered him. "Which team are you taking?"

He shook his head. "Your protection—"

"Take team two, they know the mountains around here best. Is our jet still waiting here?"

"We're not armed, Coya," he stated.

"Get that jet ready to roll and get yourself and team two to your alpha," she stated fiercely. "You bring him back here alive, Ivan, or I'm going to skin your hide. Do you understand me?"

"Yes, Coya," he snapped before picking up the radio and ordering team two to detach from her protective detail and replacing them with another team.

Coya was second-in-command now, and their alpha was in danger.

"Doctors are waiting at the entrance for Sharone and she'll be taken straight to Medical. Get ready, Coya, it's going to be a hard stop."

The limo skidded, the back end sliding to the side as he threw it to a stop. The door opened and the soldiers assigned to her were pulling her out.

"You." She was in one of their faces, she had no idea which. "Take me straight to Medical."

"Coya, we need you in secure quarters . . ." the soldier began.

"Do you want to piss me off, soldier?" Anya snapped, aware of the other limo jerking to a stop and the medical personnel racing to Sharone. "I said Medical and I mean now. The only way you're going to get me to my supposed quarters is if you carry me there. What would your alpha think of that one?"

She didn't give him time to respond.

"Samuel, Mordecai," she yelled at two of the Coyote enforcers. "Get your butts in the air with Ivan and team two." They were two of Del-Rey's best men.

They looked to each other, then her.

"Is your alpha here?" she yelled back at them.

"No, Coya." Samuel shook his dark head quickly.

"Then you obey your coya. Now go!" she snarled. "Now!"

They surprised her. They turned and ran, barely catching up with Ivan as he straightened the limo to head to the top of the mountain and the waiting heli-jet.

She could hear the hum in the air and, over it, the explosions across the mountain. Lifting the hem of her gown, she moved into the caverns, following the medical team that was bearing a still-cursing Sharone through the stone hallways to the lower-level medical rooms.

At least one attack had been made on this mountain while Anya had been here. A stealth jet had managed to penetrate the Breeds' air defenses and had slammed "cave busters," mountain-penetrating missiles, into both the Coyote Breed base as well as the mountain that overlooked Haven.

Anya had led then. It had been her first command situation.

There had been damage, but not a single Breed had been scratched. There had been more damage to the Haven buildings and homes, but the rumored base in the mountain that sheltered the valley hadn't been hurt. Twenty-four hours later Del-Rey had returned and taken over.

"Coya, Sharone's threatening to leave Base and head to the mountain." Emma rushed to her side as Ashley flanked her. "She's cussing up a storm, and it was all we could do to keep her in the limo."

"Tell the doctors to shoot her full of a sedative if she can't keep her butt on the gurney and out of trouble," Anya ordered her. "Ashley, get to Command. Have one of the soldiers get me a headset. I want to know everything that's going on as it happens."

Ashley rushed away as one of the male Breeds took her place.

"You!" She pointed to another soldier, watching his eyes widen almost in panic. "Find me some information and find it now. And make damned sure your alpha is still breathing."

The soldier hurried off as Anya entered the medical caverns and stood back, watching as Sharone cussed out the Coyote Breed medical staff.

If she was cussing, she was just pissed. Sharone could get eerily silent if she was really hurt. Almost deadened.

"Emma, get one of our enforcers down to Haven. I want

information on that bartender they brought back and I want to know what he's saying. Get another to Dr. Armani's office and see what's coming out of there, then contact our enforcer in the Wolf Breed security detail and see what he has. I want everything tapped into me, via the link Ashley better have to me within the next second."

"Yes, Coya." Emma stepped to the side as Anya wrapped her arms around herself, slowly rubbing at the chill invading her body.

"Coya, I found a blanket."

A soldier stepped forward, unfolding a thick gray blanket and helping her pull it over her shoulders.

"My wrap and purse are still at the ballroom," she told him. "My knives are in that purse. When it's safer, I want a team flown into town and all our belongings collected. Get a list together. If we don't get everything back, then we're going to break a few rules and start breaking into houses. Whoever was behind this won't be expecting us to come back to collect anything."

The soldier grinned. "I like how you think, Coya. I'll get the information and get everything ready."

"Prepare a plan," she told him. "When your alpha returns, we'll submit your ideas to him in the eventuality that anything is missing. Because I'm betting you, someone is collecting it and splitting the goods now."

The women invited had all left their purses and wraps with the doorman. Some were exquisite creations donated by some of the world's premier clothing makers on the off chance that the Breed females or mates would show off their creations and give them the cachet of knowing their designs were worn by the women chosen by the notorious Breeds.

"Coya, I'm a lower-ranked soldier," he finally said. "I'm not an enforcer. I should take this to an enforcer to prepare."

She turned on the man, her gaze going over him. "Were you considered defective in your lab, soldier?"

"No, Coya." His voice hardened, a deadly growl reflecting in it. "I was considered a class one stealth and exterminating specialist."

"Then here's your chance to earn your bar as an enforcer," she retorted. "You got lucky tonight, soldier."

"Yes, Coya." He straightened. "I'll get that information together now."

"Emma, I don't have my communications set," Anya reminded the other woman as she turned back to the window that looked in on the medical room.

"It's coming, Coya," Emma promised her, then paused. "Our alpha is fine. No matter what."

"Of course he's fine, and he's going to be growling and snarling and tasting blood when he stomps into this mountain. Get on the radio, get me that communications set now. Tell those boys in Communications they better be anticipating every shred of information he's going to need before he gets here. If I hear again that the information needed to defend this mountain isn't available to him the minute he's ready for it, then heads are going to roll."

During the last attack, she knew, Del-Rey had spent hours getting much needed information together because Communications and Security had been so surprised by the attack that they had been scrambling to figure out what was going on.

"I should be in Communications," she decided. "Keep a soldier here. I want reports sent in on that stubborn Breed's status every five minutes. And if she tries to pull her usual get-up-and-fight bullshit, then have her sedated."

She turned and headed along the passageway as the other Breeds watched her assessingly. This was her first time as second-in-command while Del-Rey was considered on base.

Coyote Breeds had a love-hate conflict in regards to their coya sometimes. She didn't reside in their mountain while their alpha was there. They had felt deserted by their leader's other half, and Del-Rey's original team felt as though she had deserted their alpha.

Now Emma almost smiled. She, Sharone and Ashley had done well. Eight months. In only eight months Anya was automatically taking her place as Del-Rey's second-in-command and his mate.

"Call up to Communications and have them ready for her," Emma ordered the soldier. "Make certain she has a cup of coffee or she's going to crash and burn on us the way she's using adrenaline at the moment. I also want the doctor standing by for hormonal injections if needed. That adrenaline crash sometimes retriggers the heat."

And Anya could get pissy if she went into heat without warning. Not to mention the fact that Del-Rey would have all their heads if Anya ended up in pain again.

The soldier nodded and made the calls as they stepped into the elevator and made the descent into the well-protected communications center.

She glanced at Anya. Her coya's shoulders were straight, her head held high, sapphire eyes glittering in her pale face. And for the first time, Emma noticed the little sprinkling of freckles across Anya's nose.

"He's fine," she murmured again.

"Of course he's fine," Anya snapped. "Have Medical be prepared just in case. And tell me again why the hell we don't have our own operating rooms and surgeon in-house." She turned and glared at Emma.

Emma shrugged. She knew the answer; Anya knew the answer. "Dr. Armani . . ." was their designated specialist.

"Is a Wolf Breed specialist," Anya snapped. "I've had enough of this."

"Hard to get a surgeon to perform surgery when he's dead," Emma reminded her.

She remembered. Just as she knew there were at least two Coyote specialists well adept in surgery, Coyote genetics and general Breed medicine that would be well able to treat them.

Anya pulled the blanket tighter around her shoulders and turned to stare at the Breeds watching her curiously.

They were hardened killers. But standing there, they were staring at her as though she represented more than a pretty face or a singular title she had refused to acknowledge outside the most basic of duties.

She let her gaze connect with one of the olive green–garbed soldiers. Her gaze flickered over the plain military uniform he wore. Wolves and Felines both had a uniform for each designation of their forces. Something else Del-Rey hadn't been able to take care of.

"Find me some damned jeans," Anya muttered as the doors opened and they swept into the huge communications network set up underground. "This dress sucks."

If there was a bone or muscle that didn't hurt in his body, then Del-Rey couldn't find it. Brim did a rough stitch on the laceration on his arm after he managed to reset the dislocated shoulder.

Blood fury had raged, though, the second the all-terrain went flying through the air. Jumping from it, they had moved in on the position of the men attempting to ambush the Breed limos.

They'd run like rats, but humans were no match for the Breeds' night senses and tracking abilities. They'd captured five of the bastards; one had died as he fired a bullet that managed to lodge in Del-Rey's other shoulder.

They were still trying to find all the pieces of his throat after Del-Rey had managed to tear it out.

Wolfe, his heads of security, Jacob and Aiden, as well two Wolf Breed and two Coyote teams were present. Del-Rey was still staring at Ivan in disbelief as he was relating how Anya had sent out the second team of Coyote soldiers along with three of his enforcers—Ivan, Samuel and Mordecai—in the heli-jet to make certain they brought back their alpha, breathing.

He wanted to shake his head. That wasn't the Anya he knew,

but as he'd learned in the past week, the Anya he had known had grown in ways he still didn't fully understand.

"She has control of Communications." Brim covered the mic of his communications headset and stared back at Del-Rey in amusement. "She hasn't cussed yet, but she's demanding a report."

"Tell her I'm breathing," he grunted.

"She's ordered a team to Haven," Brim told him then. "And an enforcer to interrogate the bartender we brought back with us. She's been in contact with the lupina, Hope, and they're coordinating—umm—defenses."

Del-Rey winced and looked at Wolfe, who didn't seem in the least concerned.

He finally shrugged. Hell, Hope, Faith and Anya's body-guards had prepared her for this. At this point he had no choice but to trust in her abilities.

"She threw Sofia out of Communications. Did you know she was headed back to Base?" Brim asked. Del-Rey gave him a negative shake of his head. "While her soldiers turned their backs and covered her, she tossed her dress aside and within seconds had on jeans, a T-shirt and sneakers, and she was barking out orders the whole time. Our men are scared, Del."

Del-Rey snorted at the thought of that. His men were scared of nothing, least of all a coya they all but revered.

"Damn, she's running the place like she was born to it." Brim looked worried. "What the hell is she doing learning how to run Command this way?"

Del-Rey lifted his head from where he had glanced at the ground, processing the information Brim was giving him. God, he fucking hurt.

"She's going to make our lives hell and in the end most likely have us thanking God for it," he finally told his enforcer. "Get the heli-jet ready to fly. I need to get to Haven for medical assistance before I return to Base. Our medical techs aren't experienced enough to deal with my wounds."

He might have a cracked rib. He probed at it and winced, hoping it wasn't too severe. He'd had every intention of mating his little mate at the first opportunity. He had a feeling that wasn't happening tonight.

"She's demanding a detailed report," Brim suddenly hissed.

"Down to that last scratch on that mangy Coyote's hide, as she's calling you. Del-Rey, I'm not dealing with her."

"Then deal with her when we get back to Base," Del-Rey sighed. "Is that heli-jet prepped yet?"

"Fuck! She finds out you went to Haven for medical and she's going to be waiting on all of us with a gun."

There was something more serious than his coya's irritation. Del-Rey forced himself not to sway as he felt the blood seeping from his side from the branch that had punctured it earlier.

Blood loss definitely. Possible internal damage. He listed the injuries in his mind, searching for any other problems. Sometimes, Dr. Armani needed help in diagnosing Coyote medical problems.

"Hell!" Brim suddenly caught him, his hand uncovering the mic at his mouth. "Get that heli-jet ready," he yelled out. "We have alpha three in distress. I repeat. Alpha three in distress. Notify Armani we're flying in."

He should have told Brim about the puncture, Del-Rey thought caustically. The leather of the jacket had helped, but that damned wood had been spiked.

He felt the helping hands and pushed them away as he pushed himself to his feet and waved his men to the transport. He could still walk under his own steam. He'd been wounded worse and made it back to pick up plenty of times; he would damned sure make it to Haven now.

◆　◆　◆

Anya froze as she heard the order. "Alpha three in distress. Notify Armani."

She could have sworn she felt the blood leech from her face.

"Well, it seems he managed to get himself hurt," Sofia drawled in amusement from the doorway of Command.

Mocking and filled with cold amusement, the other woman had Anya's fingers curling to keep from trying to tear her eyes out.

"We're going to Haven," she ordered Emma before turning to the lieutenant in charge of command personnel. "You have Command. Keep me updated every thirty."

"Base is under lockdown, Coya." The computer tech stared

up at her in concern. "We can't unlock without the alpha's authority."

"You'll unlock or I promise you, you'll be on perimeter duty, sleeping on the dirt outside, for the next month," Anya snapped. "Get a door open and get me out of here."

"I'm sure he's fine." Sofia was leaning against a wall, inspecting her fingernails. "I saw him take a bullet to the belly four months ago. He was up and moving around hours after they removed it and bitching orders right and left. He's tough."

"Alpha three has lost consciousness." The voice came through the communications speakers.

All the Coyotes in the room raised their heads to the monitor that showed the heli-jet lifting off.

"We have a deep puncture to the left side, possible kidney damage. Bullet, right shoulder. Laceration left biceps, laceration left thigh. Possible cracked rib."

Anya could feel her legs weakening.

"Emma!"

"Exit found," Emma called out. "Team three is waiting, Haven has been notified that you're arriving. Armani is prepping Surgery."

"Move!" Anya turned, pushing at Emma to move faster until they were practically running for the elevator. The Coyote soldiers surrounded her as she, Emma and Ashley stepped into the cubicle.

The ascension was quick, though each second seemed a lifetime to Anya. As the doors slid open, she was moving to the second team, waiting at a narrow access door leading through a narrow stone tunnel.

"All-terrains are waiting outside," one of the soldiers informed her quickly. "You'll be riding with your two personal bodyguards. As well as three soldiers. Two vehicles ahead of you, two behind."

"One ahead of me, three behind," she informed him, flashing him a hard look. "Missiles generally aim for the middle vehicle and you know it."

"An armed ambush would go for the first two vehicles first," he argued. "We don't know what we're dealing with yet."

She turned on him, eyes narrowed, rage shaking through her.

"Delay me a single second longer and I'll have you reported to the Coyote Cabinet for reprimand. Don't assume, soldier, that I'm not well aware of our security and protection protocols, because I am. Now, get your head out of your own egotistical ass and get me to Haven before I have Emma shoot you."

Emma smiled and laid her hand on the butt of the weapon strapped to her side.

"Why can't I shoot him?" Ashley pouted. "Emma gets all the fun."

She ignored them, waving to the team ahead of her to proceed. She wasn't ignorant. She knew how to run Base; she'd studied everything about the Coyote base that she could study and spent hours upon hours working command simulations with the techs in charge of the command center. She'd thrived on the challenge of learning. But now she was terrified she wouldn't get to Del-Rey in time.

Exiting the caverns, she moved quickly to the second all-terrain and jumped into the back, knowing damned good and well no one was going to let her ride up front. Emma and Ashley sat on either side of her as the Coyote soldiers filled the front and back weapon areas.

Within seconds the five vehicles were racing back down the mountain, swinging around the curves and entering the secured pass into Haven.

Minutes later she was jumping to the ground and moving swiftly into the medical bunker, moving through the secured area and down the incline belowground to the surgical and medical areas.

"Brim." She moved quickly to Del-Rey's personal bodyguard and second-in-command. "How is he?"

Brim looked harried.

"You shouldn't be here, Coya," he admonished her. "You're safer at Base."

She was tired of everyone acting as though she didn't belong in the places she wanted to be.

She glared back at him. "I didn't ask for your opinion; I asked for your report."

He gave it, and when he finished, Anya felt her frustration rising. Dr. Armani was fighting against genetics she didn't understand, but Del-Rey had stabilized. The blood kept on hand for just such an occasion had been used to replace what he had lost, but his system was moving sluggishly, accepting the drugs the doctor had created to treat Coyote wounds, but those drugs still weren't as effective as they could be.

Unfortunately, there was very little information on the treatment of Coyote Breeds in the labs. Coyotes were slightly more paranoid than the Wolves and Felines. Talk about the destruction of records. All records. Nothing had been saved, on the off chance that anyone would find a weakness they were unaware of.

This couldn't continue.

"Emma," she murmured as Brim moved away. "I need a contact."

"No. Don't ask me to do that." Emma sighed. "I nearly got caught last time, Anya. I'm telling you, breaking that rule is such a no-no that it could get me killed."

Contacting her father was expressly forbidden unless by phone. Twice Anya had managed to slip out to visit with him on the other side of town.

"He has the information I need," she hissed. "What he doesn't have, he can get. We're going to end up losing men if we don't get a Coyote specialist in here. Now, set it up."

"I hate you, Coya." She grimaced. "Del-Rey will kick my ass personally, then slit my throat."

"Him or me, take your choice." Anya shrugged before turning and pacing to the doors that led to Surgery.

She couldn't see in here, as she could when she'd watched the techs treat Sharone. She was barred from Surgery, barred from seeing him herself.

"Anya?" Hope touched her arm.

Anya swung around to face the slightly Asian, exquisite features of the Wolf Breed lupina, the mate to the alpha leader Wolfe Gunnar. At her side was the Breed pack and pride liaison Faith, a Wolf Breed herself.

"Thanks for coming, Hope." She smiled back at the other woman. "Is Wolfe okay?"

Hope nodded. "A few scratches, nothing more. He's in a meeting room going ballistic with the army again over a gunship that didn't get out in time. Jonas Wyatt is en route along with the pride alpha and his prima, Callan and Merinus Lyons.

They're considering a protest against the army base. They should have been prepared. They were on alert for any trouble tonight, but didn't respond."

"Typical," Anya sighed.

"Wolfe sends his regards and says if you need anything, you've only to let us know."

Anya nodded. "Base is secure and we have information coming in. I'd like a copy of anything you have as well as full sanction for Del-Rey's enforcer, Brim, to interrogate your prisoner as well."

Hope nodded. "I'll contact Wolfe immediately. He mentioned you might want to want to do that but he wasn't certain of your priorities."

What had changed within her? The moment Del-Rey had jumped from that limo, everything she had learned about Base and the pack had kicked in. As though she had been born to stand at Del-Rey's side and do what had to be done when he couldn't.

That was the alpha female's job. Hope had always pulled Anya along with her when Wolfe was required to lead certain missions. The weight of command seemed to sit comfortably on the other woman's shoulders. Anya had noticed that about Merinus Lyons, the alpha pride leader, or prima as they called her. Both women knew how to lead, how to snap from mate to commander in the blink of an eye.

Something Anya had done without thinking as well. As though the entire time she'd been observing Hope, Anya had also absorbed the ability and the knowledge to begin stepping into her role of coya, the alpha female, the other half of the Coyote alpha pack leader.

Anya had always been a quick study. Anything that interested her, that caught her curious mind, was easily learned.

The Council had already chosen her for advanced admistrative and covert intelligence work. She had been scheduled to leave the labs within days before the Breeds' escape.

"Come with me for a few minutes, Anya," Hope encouraged her, leading her from the doors to a small sitting area. "Is everything going well with you and Del-Rey now?"

Anya turned back to her, watching the other woman intently. "We still snap and snarl at each other."

Hope's lips twitched as she smoothed back her shoulder-length straight black hair. "Proceeding as expected then," she stated.

Anya shook her head. "I don't understand him. I want to, but sometimes . . ." She shrugged. "He told me tonight that I'm what makes him worthy." She frowned at the thought. "You can't base your worthiness on someone else, Hope."

Hope's expression eased into a smile. "You're talking about a man that's aware he's not natural," she said softly. "One who was created and trained with the understanding that he wasn't natural. That nature or God, or whoever you attribute the beginning of life to, didn't breathe that life into him. Now, suddenly, nature or that God has given him something that's marked solely as his. His other half. A comfort, a warmth, someone that eases all those lost, lonely dreams he didn't know he had. That's a part of being a Breed male. They base who and what they are on the acceptance they gain from that mate, Anya. You can't change that."

And maybe that was part of what terrified her when it came to Del-Rey. An innate knowledge that she was the woman this man had chosen, among all the women he had been with, those he had known, or could have known. He had chosen her. His body had chosen her. His soul had chosen her.

Which meant she belonged to him and everything he was. Even more, he belonged to her in the same way.

"Jonas showed me your file," Hope admitted then. "Our director of the Bureau of Breed Affairs is amazingly efficient. That file listed your IQ as pretty much off the charts. Notes in the files state that anything you 'want' to learn, you excel at quickly and I've seen that. You've taken your place as the coya of your pack in a matter of months. You knew inside you couldn't escape it, Anya. You didn't want to escape it, or Del-Rey. Did you?"

"At the time, I had to." And she had known that then as she knew it now. "That doesn't mean I know how to be the woman he needs or that old hurts are easily forgotten," she whispered. "Being coya is a far cry from being a Breed's mate, isn't it?"

Hope nodded slowly. "Yes, it is. But being a Breed's mate can quickly become even more important than anything you ever imagined, Anya. His lover. Letting him be the man you love. It's growth. Just as you've grown in the past eight months.

Because you wanted to grow. It was in you to do it, and you did it far quicker than any of us anticipated."

"You were working me." She saw it now. Eight months of being worked, slowly, surely.

"Only in the most loving ways. We're pack, Coya. We stick together and we help our own. It's the only way we'll survive in this crazy world we've been drawn into," Hope said softly before her gaze shifted past Anya.

Anya twisted around, watching as Dr. Armani moved from surgery, her dark face creased in a frown as she pulled the mask from her face and found Anya's gaze.

Anya was on her feet and moving to her, even as Brim stepped between them.

"Status," Brim snapped.

Anya laid her hand on his arm and moved in front of him. She was aware of his irritation, the tension in his body as he stepped aside.

"Coya, I need a Coyote assistant," Armani sighed. "Why did they kill all their scientists? We could have used one."

Because their scientists were mad—not evil, not cruel, but their search for the perfect unfeeling warrior had been relentless. Letting them live hadn't been an option. The two Anya had hidden were the exception.

"Something's wrong?" Anya asked carefully.

"He's already started healing." Dr. Armani grimaced, shaking her head. "The wound was healing around the bullet, which made it harder to extract. He'll be conscious within an hour, I predict, and back on his feet within a few days, but the bruising has gone bone-deep. He's going to be growling for a while."

"He growls anyway," Anya stated. "Can I see him?"

"I need to talk to him first," Brim protested. "He's going to have questions I need to answer. He'll have orders to keep Base moving effectively."

Anya turned back to him slowly. "I'll see him first. Base is covered for the moment with all security protocols enacted until further word from Del-Rey, myself or you. You can allow me five minutes before he turns back into the big, bad Coyote."

"The big, bad Coyote returns the moment he opens his eyes," Armani snorted. "I do want to keep an eye on him. The branch he landed on nearly punctured vital organs. His Coyote genetics still aren't familiar enough to me. White blood counts, hormonal levels, shift in the mating hormones." She shook her head. "Even heart rate and pulse are different from Wolf Breeds. I'm flying in the dark with him."

"He'll heal," Brim challenged her. "He always does."

Anya nodded at the doors. "I want to see him now."

"Anya, I need in there first," Brim countered her again.

"Now, Dr. Armani." Anya ignored him.

"Mates come first, Brim," Armani told him. "Come on, Coya, I'll show you to your mate." She turned back to her, and they pushed through the surgery room doors. "While you're here, its time for your hormonal shot. We need to do that before you go in to him. We don't want to forget it."

Anya paused. She stared at the doctor as she let herself mentally scan her body and its reactions. For eight months a part of her had felt almost dead inside. She attributed that to the hormone, and she realized she didn't want to feel it any longer. She knew what she intended to do; she didn't need the hormone shot any longer. Del-Rey would ensure she didn't hurt, because he would ensure she was taken often.

"No more shots," she said softly as Armani arched her brows.

"You know what will happen," she told her. "It could happen in phases or it could slam into you, catching you unaware. Be certain, Anya."

"I'm certain."

As Anya stepped into the recovery room and stared at Del-Rey stretched out on the white hospital bed, she affirmed that decision. She was ready to take her place, ready to accept what she had once thought she could never accept.

Right now, she had a hard time believing he was hurt in any way.

The sheet covered bandages; the raw scrapes and scratches on his face and upper torso were already healing. Coyotes, her father had once told her, were a sheer work of art. Their genetics were exceptional. They healed faster. They ran faster. They could process information faster and make decisions faster than any other Breed. Then he would shake his head and say, "Too bad they're still just killers. They could have been a benefit to mankind rather than soulless beings created to kill."

The scientists, soldiers and trainers that oversaw Breeds didn't see them as possessing a soul. Not Wolf, Feline nor Coyote. But the Coyotes least of all. For more than a century human scientists had worked to find a way to eradicate what they called the human genetic that promoted a conscience. And they thought they had found that in the Coyotes. The animals were scavengers—primal, brutal. And for a while it seemed as though the Breeds created from them were as well.

She touched Del-Rey's arm, amazed at the heat radiating from it. She lifted her gaze to the doctor. "He's running a fever?"

Dr. Armani shook her head. "Not like you or I would. The heat is part of the healing abilities. I'd be worried if it wasn't there, though it's higher than normal. I suspect it has something to do with the off-the-chart mating hormones racing through his blood."

"Did you give him anything for it?"

"No. He's already made certain his files were notated. At no time is he to be given hormonal treatments himself. He refuses. But, most male Breeds do."

"They'd rather suffer?" She remembered the pain herself, the brutal, soul-suffering pain that stole control from the mind and made her a creature of lust and little more.

"It's different for male Breeds than female mates," Armani told her. "The females suffer the pain, the need for a hormone that isn't natural to their body. Like a withdrawal from a narcotic, only worse. Male Breeds are more aggressive, more territorial. The constant lust isn't as painful, but it has no cycle. Females go into mating heat, then it eases for periods of time, only to return. Rather like ovulation. For the males, that need never goes away. One of the males told me it's like having a dagger continually stabbed into his balls, the need to release is so imperative. Masturbation only makes it worse. The scent or taste of another woman's lust is so distasteful they can't find release there either."

"Another person's touch is excruciating for female mates." Anya remembered that well. "Is it the same for the male mates?"

"Not to the same extent as it is for the females. No Breed male mate that I know of has ever attempted to have sex away from his mate. Some have waited years. In some the mating heat finally eased. It's almost as though each mating is individual, Anya. But the physical reactions in the male Breeds aren't well understood simply because most of them refuse to discuss them or allow tests to control them. The mating heat is their affirmation somehow. A who-and-what-they-are type thing." She shrugged, as though helpless to explain it.

"It gives me a soul." Del-Rey's rough, scratchy voice surprised them both.

Anya looked down at him, realizing she had been stroking his arm.

"You would have to get yourself hurt." She had to force back a wave of emotion that threatened to overwhelm her. "So much for seducing you tonight, huh?"

Surprise was reflected in his eyes. "If I'd known you had that planned, I would have stayed with the limo."

"Liar," she laughed softly.

"Where's Brim?" he asked then. "I need to make sure Base is secured and on lockdown."

"Taken care of."

He exhaled heavily. "I knew I could count on him."

She pressed her lips together and clenched her teeth at the comment.

"Get a transport ready." He turned to Armani then. "I'll be ready to go back to Base in an hour."

"I hate Breeds," Armani muttered. "You need to be under observation. It's the only way I can get any damned information to work on you again later, Del-Rey. You're not helping me here."

"I have a base to run," he told her. "I promise, next wounded soldier, you can have him for a week."

She snorted at that. "Yeah. Those berserkers? No, thank you."

Anya stood silently. She ached to touch him again. To push his hair back from his forehead. To wrap her arms around him or something. She ached to do something.

"I need to see Brim," he told her again. "Could you call him in here?"

Anya swallowed tightly and pushed back the hurt.

The seducer, the man who had kissed her and claimed his

worth was tied to her, didn't need her here. He needed his second-in-command, which is what Anya should have been. She was his coya, automatically second-in-command. Until she had denied the position.

She stepped back slowly. "Sure. I'll get him."

Anger surged inside her. Fear. Hurt. She pushed it back and tamped it down. She fought to keep her expression, her emotions, contained so he wouldn't so much as scent the pain that bloomed inside her.

She had refused the title of coya while he was on base. She had no right, no right to be hurt and angry that he would want to talk to Brim rather than her. He was the alpha leader. There were things he had to do, assurances he needed that Base was operational and secure while he was outside of it and weak. It was those damned animal genetics. That was all it was. Security over emotion. All that good stuff.

She pushed through the doors as Brim straightened from the wall and gave her a piercing look.

"He's waiting on you." Her smile was tight. "I'm returning to Base. Please let me know when you return with him. Emma!" Her voice sharpened as she turned to her bodyguards.

Emma and Ashley both stood watching her strangely.

"I'm heading back to Base."

She headed for the exit, striding quickly through the corridors and up the incline into the entrance area. She kept her head high, her shoulders straight, and she didn't cry. She wanted to. She needed to. But not the first tear fell.

✦ ✦ ✦

Del-Rey stared at the door, a frown on his face at the subtle, barely discernible scent of feminine anger and pain that lingered behind Anya. Now, that didn't make sense.

He turned to Dr. Armani. Her arms were crossed over her chest and she was glaring at him.

"I hate Breed males," she told him, eyes narrowed, feminine outrage filling her gaze.

"What the hell is wrong with every damned woman in the world this month?" he muttered. "What the hell did I do?"

"You didn't do a damned thing," she stated harshly. "Not one damned thing, Alpha Delgado. And that just might be what gets your balls in a wringer and your ass in a sling. And when it happens, I think I want to sell tickets to the event."

With that, she swept out of the room, passing Brim as he entered. The other man stared at Del-Rey, perplexed. "What the fuck?" He questioned the alpha, "Being your charming self?"

To that he could only shake his head. *What the fuck* just about described it.

CHAPTER 12

The first person Anya saw as she entered the main living area of the base was none other than Sofia. Anya made a mental note to decide she herself hated vodka, period. If the other woman enjoyed it with the same relish, then there wasn't a chance in hell Anya was drinking another drop of it.

Slouching seductively on one of the stools that sat at a long teak bar, the Russian was sipping vodka and watching with avid eyes as Anya walked into the community room.

Communications and Security had been notified that the alpha would be returning within the hour; preparations were being made for the twenty-four- to seventy-two-hour length of time it would take for his body to completely heal.

"What are you doing back here, Sofia?" Anya asked as she moved to the bar. "Del-Rey said you were a secret contact. Secret contacts don't show up flashing their pearly whites and interfering on the base."

Sofia smiled with superior amusement. "He didn't tell you my cover has been blown? I'd nearly returned to my apartment before the Breeds assigned to my security detected that assassin waiting on me. I'm now a security risk. I was kindly offered protection here."

No, she hadn't been told.

Anya extracted the cylindrical link from the pocket of her jeans, attached it to her ear and beeped Security.

"Yes, Coya." Command came online immediately.

"Sofia Ivanova is banned from Communications, Security and all areas deemed proprietary until further notice from your alpha. Is this clear?"

"Understood, Coya. Order is being coded in as we speak."

She smiled back at Sofia as the other woman frowned.

"Del-Rey won't thank you." She pursed her lips, perturbed. "He considers my opinion to be valued in all areas."

"Then he will be unconsidering it," Anya promised her.

Sofia shook her head slowly as a light laugh left her lips. "So confident. I was his lover, you know, several years ago of course, but we've remained close."

Several years. Much longer than Anya had suspected.

"Sofia, you're wasting your time here," Anya informed her, determined not to play the shrew.

She was Del-Rey's mate. They might have trust issues. She might want to rap his head against a wall. But he was hers, just as she was finally accepting that she belonged to him.

"I never waste my time, dear." Sofia smiled. "He'll grow tired of your childishness soon." She looked around at Emma and Ashley, who stood prepared, watching her carefully. "I nearly raised the three of you, Anya," she said as she turned back to her. "Trust me, I'm a woman, not a child. Del-Rey understands that."

"Wow, she doesn't know about that whole commitment thing, Coya?" Ashley piped up innocently. "Did you tell her he made you coya of the packs?"

Sofia might have paled. "You little brat." She swung around to Ashley again. "You always were a very practiced liar."

Ashley popped her gum and frowned. "She doesn't know?"

"I didn't tell her," Anya drawled. "It appears you have though."

Anya straightened from the bar as Sofia's face flushed with fury.

"Sorry, Sofia, I am his coya. I am coya of this entire base. What I say goes. And be very careful, because trust me, if I tell

Del-Rey to kick your ass to the curb, the curb is where you'll go."

"He wouldn't dare!" Sofia was shaking now. "He may have made you coya for now, but you won't hold that title for long, you little bitch. Remember, it takes more than wanting it. He has to give it to you. Officially."

Anya smiled slowly. "Sorry, Sofia. I'll hold that title forever. Bet on it. And maybe I'll send you an invitation to that ceremony."

Mating heat didn't go away. It was forever. And as soon as *her* mate was healed, she'd ensure it. Then they'd see about that little ceremony.

✦   ✦   ✦

Del-Rey walked into the narrow access tunnel, paying close attention to the soldiers that stood on alert, their gazes sharp, their hands ready on their weapons as he limped through the passageway. Normally they were lucky if a single guard wasn't dozing. Red alert secured the inner base, the soldiers outside rarely had problems, and if they did there was always advanced warning, so they normally weren't at their sharpest here. Until now.

Passing the access tunnel, he waited as the reinforced doors leading into Base unlocked and slid open. On the other side waited a four-man detail, at the head of which was a younger soldier, Dorian.

"Alpha, med tech is waiting in your quarters. Coya asks that after you've rested you have your enforcer inform her when you're ready to see her. We have communications reports and security details." The electronic pads were pushed into his hands as he glanced at Brim in confusion.

Since when had Brim gotten the additional time needed to kick ass? Base was secure, but general work ethic hadn't been at its best in recent months when he had been here.

"We also have the heli-jet lowering into the bay with diagnostics being prepared. I need your signature on that if you don't mind, so the techs will get cracking. And we have all-terrains being pulled in for repair. Sign there too." The soldier pointed to the X's made on the electronic file.

Del-Rey scrawled his name and continued to limp toward his quarters. His people were moving at a quick pace through the corridors, and the community room was empty. No one at the billiards table or in front of the television screens.

"Meetings with our pack leaders have been scheduled for a time after you've healed. They send their greetings and request that you let them know if they're needed."

Pack leaders, besides Brim, were normally waiting in the corridor for him harping about everything from funds for their teams to the cost of parts for their equipment. Where the hell had the insanity gone? Hell, he'd been dealing with it for over a week now.

"Are you looking for a raise, Brim?" he muttered as they neared his rooms. "How the hell did you manage this?"

"I didn't manage this," Brim grunted. "I don't know what the hell has happened here. Should we have Dr. Armani check them for a virus?"

"Or something," Del-Rey said as he opened the door to his quarters and stepped inside.

Sure enough, medical technicians were waiting for him with all their little vials, scopes and various torture devices. He endured it but paid close attention to the somber expression of the techs who performed the checkup. They were intent, serious, as though their own lives hinged on his health. The best he'd gotten the last time he returned wounded was a perfunctory call to make certain if he felt he needed anything.

"You're healing well. That Wolf doctor doesn't seem to have done you much harm." The tech chuckled as he stored his vials in his little case. "We do need a Coyote specialist though, the coya's right about that. I hope she's willing to consider additional equipment. She wasn't happy when we didn't have the sedatives for Sharone. You know how she cusses and throws things when she's been shot."

Del-Rey lifted his gaze to stare at the tech. "She's been known to do that," he said carefully.

The tech nodded his sandy-colored head. "We ran out of sedatives several weeks ago when team three was flown in with so many injuries. Coya hit the roof then and radioed Haven for extras at the time, but their supply was low as well. I'm waiting on a new batch. We should have the new analysis machines in soon as well."

Del-Rey turned to Brim, giving him a speaking look. The other man gave a quick nod and moved to the adjacent office to begin making calls. Was Anya somehow responsible for all this? In a matter of months had she managed to whip fierce Coyote Breeds into the measure of discipline they had somehow lost since Del-Rey had signed out for mission status rather than overseeing the base and other pack leaders himself? They slacked when he was there because it was something he had a tendency to do himself in order to rest and prepare for the next mission.

"Glad you approve, Harding," Del-Rey finally answered as the tech rose to his feet.

Regan Harding hadn't been trained just for killing and bloodshed. He was a trained Coyote med tech. Not a surgeon or specialist, but as close as Coyotes were going to get to one.

"Good to see you back, Alpha." Harding nodded his shaggy head before collecting his supplies and heading to the door.

Del-Rey moved from the chair to his bed and lay back with a weary groan. Damn. Armani was right, he was bruised clear to the bone and it always took longer for the bruises to heal. As though his body considered them unworthy of the effort of a quick healing.

He was running low on sleep, food and sex. Hell, the sex part he hadn't had in two years until he took Anya eight months ago. He'd have been damned if he was going to fuck a woman with the image of Anya in his head. And since the day she'd turned twenty, that was where she had stayed.

The mating hormone had his tongue swollen despite the kiss he'd shared with Anya earlier that night. His cock wasn't as hard as normal, but he had had significant blood loss, he thought. Give it time; it always managed full mast at little more than the thought of his mate.

Dammit, she was on base because he'd forced her here. No doubt the minute lockdown was reversed she'd run just as fast back to her cabin at Haven now that he was too weak to stop her. Her and those female Coyotes that followed her like faithful little puppies.

So where was she and why wasn't she here waiting for him until then? He closed his eyes tiredly, aching at the loneliness that suddenly wrapped around him.

He remembered the impulse he had nearly given into to steal one last kiss before he jumped from the limo. If he had, he might not have been able to tear himself away.

Touching her was like a drug. Hell, it pumped a drug straight into his system, if one wanted to consider the mating hormone. She kept him hard and ready for her. She stayed in his thoughts, and lingered around him like a dream he couldn't escape. One he didn't want to escape unless he escaped in her arms.

Damn, he should have stolen that last kiss, he thought.

"You're not going to believe this."

His eyes opened as Brim stalked into the room, his expression a mask of disbelief but not of danger.

"Bet me," Del-Rey said and yawned.

Brim moved to the monitor on the wall, picked up the remote and flipped it on.

"Security recordings," he announced. "Watch this."

Del-Rey leveled himself up and watched. And watched. A sense of triumph, of satisfaction, sizzled within him at the knowledge that the coya had taken her place.

From the moment she was rushed into Base, she took over like a little general. He could see her in the circle of Breeds, their backs turned to her as she quickly shed her dress and dressed in jeans.

She handled Communications and Security as though she had been born to it. Which, in essence, perhaps she had been. Her father had been a whiz at the labs. Rumor was, Petrov Kobrin as well as his deceased wife were geniuses in their field. One of the reasons Del-Rey had planned their escape so exactingly. And still he had been surprised that so many of them had escaped. Petrov almost had a sixth sense for escape attempts.

As he watched, he saw echoes of her father, saw the intelligence in her eyes, the composed features and the confidence she had seemed to have lost in the weeks after he kidnapped her.

She wasn't a woman-child any longer. She was a full-grown woman and taking her place. Her voice snapped and Coyote Breeds came to attention. She didn't harass or harangue; rather, her tone was filled with command.

That added to the fact that she was the coya, the alpha in charge when he was away, and she had done what even Brim had been unable to do—instilled a sense of discipline in them while he was away.

She wasn't bitchy, she wasn't confrontational; she was confident, assured. She knew what the hell was needed and she was putting it into effect.

And it made him hard. He was as stiff as a board, and he could feel the fever working inside him, the need that crashed into his system and came close to stealing his breath as he watched her. Those brilliant eyes cool and focused, her expression composed, an aura of command settling on her shoulders as it had in those labs when she ran the administration wing like a young general.

"Son of a bitch," Del-Rey muttered.

"She knows Sofia's here too. She has her barred from Command, Security and proprietary areas."

Del-Rey lifted his head with a sense of foreboding.

"She knows Sofia was given asylum?"

"She knows."

Did she throw her out? Had Emma or Ashley killed Sofia?

Admittedly, the woman he had once considered a friend was becoming an irritant with her determination to get back into his bed.

"Hell." He leaned his head back on the pillows and stared up at the ceiling. "Where is Anya now?"

Hopefully far away from him, because if he saw her, if he smelled her, he was going to fuck her. It was that simple.

"Looks like she's in Communications at the moment." Something in Brim's voice warned him.

Del-Rey lifted his head again.

"She seems to have several of your pack leaders in attendance over that issue we've trying to resolve with team participation." Amusement filled his tone. "Our teams, one and two, are working like the good little puppies they are. The rest, it would appear, are being shifted and sorted as any good little general would shift and sort them. So, you going to go play with her?"

Del-Rey snorted. "I'm going to sleep. Let her play. She's damned good at it while I'm on mission. Maybe I'll get some rest this time."

If she was running Base as he knew she could, then he could tell Jonas to shove mission status, and Del-Rey and Brim could take their place in training the Coyote Breed soldiers more effectively and getting them into enforcer status.

That was a priority he had left the other pack leaders in charge of. Unfortunately, they weren't as well trained themselves as they could have been. They were killers, not investigators or interrogators. Making that switch wasn't as easy as it could have been if Del-Rey and Brim had been on base to train them.

"She has a junior soldier working up a proposal to slip into city hall and collect the purses and articles left there as well as to investigate any items missing and conduct covert searches of leading city council members' homes to detect if they have said missing articles. According to the memo just sent to me, the soldier expects to have a full proposal prepared by tomorrow afternoon."

Del-Rey blinked up at the ceiling.

"Did you consider that angle?" he asked Brim then.

"I'm sure one of us would have soon," Brim answered laconically.

Del-Rey wasn't so certain.

He sighed as weariness pulled at him and his healing body demanded sleep.

"Get everything together. We'll go over what she's done in the past hours and see how it's affecting Base in general. I want a full report from all pack leaders, and I want Sofia's input on that intel that came in last night concerning the drugs we're trying to track. Tell her to be prepared to give her report. Once I'm prepared, then I'll see about facing my mate."

He had no intention of being ill-prepared when they came face-to-face once again. He wanted her in his bed, and he wanted the upper hand with her. That wasn't going to happen if he didn't have his shit together.

If her feelings were hurt, he'd have to fix that.

Added to dealing with a mate he realized he truly didn't know, he was also faced with the fact that, for some reason, she had been targeted at that attack tonight. It hadn't been just any female. Carlen, the Wolf Breed soldier, had gone for Anya, just as the bartender had. The entire event had been a stage for a planned execution. And Del-Rey wanted to know why. Then he wanted to know by whom, because he wanted to know whose throat to rip out.

Haven was attacked often, though this was the first time Breeds had been attacked in the small town that resided outside the lands the government had granted the Wolf Breeds. And with each call sent to the army base outside the pack lands, delays had resulted.

Typical, he thought tiredly. So typical. Prejudice had found a new focus when the Breeds revealed themselves. Humans who had no acceptable scapegoat to hate had found one with the mysterious new beings that had been created without their knowledge. They'd found something to fight against, something else to fear. And Del-Rey often wondered if they wouldn't, in time, find another war to fight in their battle to destroy what they didn't understand.

No divine deity had given the Breeds life; therefore, they could have no soul. That was what the Breeds were taught, and that was how many saw them. Creations shouldn't have rights. They shouldn't have freedom, and there were those that would take every freedom, every right the Breeds had managed to acquire and steal it from under them.

That was the battle they faced, and Del-Rey often wondered if there was a way that the Breeds could ever triumph.

With that thought in his mind, he let sleep take him. The healing process came with its drawbacks. Twenty-four to seventy-two hours of complete weakness and weariness. The need to sleep. That weakness had hampered the Genetics Council several times as they tried to fix what they considered a defect in the Coyote genetics.

Del-Rey had, at times, considered it a blessing. It was the only time he slept deeply, the only time he didn't awaken searching for the warmth and the sweet relief that only his mate could give him.

CHAPTER 13

"We still have four pack leaders working against each other," Anya mused as she went over the notes she had made through the hours Del-Rey slept. "Teams one and two, Del-Rey and Brim's personal teams, are working efficiently, though not at peak, in Security and Communications. We still have a rivalry with teams three and four, though they're working together in those areas. Team five seems to be the most efficient at the moment, medical and joint administrative, with team six working perimeter patrol. Too few of the soldiers have achieved enforcer status though."

There were six pack leaders, a total of only sixty-four Coyotes. There were more coming in, a possible ten to twenty that had managed to escape a facility in the Middle East. The pack leader there had agreed to step down and aid his group in the integration into the packs that were already established here at Base.

Tapping the electronic pen against the side of the e-pad, Anya bit her lip and considered that information. Over the years, she'd dealt with several administrators of various labs and facilities. If she wasn't mistaken, the facilities in the Middle East had been training surgical and scientific personnel from those Breeds that showed a predisposition to medical knowledge, rather than killing them, as many other facilities did. Coyotes were bred to kill, not to save lives, even those of their own kind. A predisposition to such talents, the Council had feared, was also a disposition toward mercy. That wasn't what they wanted or needed in this species.

She made a note to check into that before going to Del-Rey with this information. They could use any medical personnel that could be acquired, or even kidnapped at this point.

"Coya, the pack leaders have all promised a full report on their team areas, duties and complaints within the next seventy-two." Ashley turned to her from where she'd stood, her back turned, talking to the pack leaders via the internal base link. "They're so cute, have I mentioned that?"

"I think you might have." Anya grinned at Emma, who was rolling her eyes.

"Has med tech sent their report on Del-Rey's condition?" She turned to Sharone who was working frantically on her PDA.

"His condition is stable and healing," Sharone told her. "Brim reported he's sleeping like the dead and promises you his team report once he can leave the alpha and resume his regular duties."

Ashley snorted. "She's supposed to be in there watching over him, not covering Base while Brim sits on his tush and does her job. Cute though it may be." She waggled her brows.

"Emma, make a note to watch the dye that goes in Ashley's hair the next time she bleaches it," Anya ordered. "I think it's beginning to hamper cognitive abilities."

Ashley snapped her teeth at Anya playfully before going back to work.

"She's right," Sharone hissed furiously, her voice low. "You're supposed to be gathering reports and watching out for the alpha at this point. This makes us look bad."

Anya clenched her teeth. "I know what I'm supposed to be doing, Sharone," she bit out. "He wanted Brim with him. I'm not going to go beg."

"Who says beg?" Sharone told her. "Go in and be the coya. Damn, have we wasted our time all these months teaching you how to take over?"

Had they? Anya looked up from the e-pad and considered those options. She was aware of the Coyotes in command center sneaking her covert looks. She was well aware that this was Brim's job now that he was on base, not hers. It was a job that needed doing though, and Brim was busy with her duties.

She was also aware of her own bodyguards watching her thoughtfully. They'd had enough belief in her that they had trained her even as she hadn't realized she was being trained.

She tapped the e-pad closed and turned to glance around the command center.

"Let's go!" She turned and moved from the electronic center and began making her way through the tunnels toward Del-Rey's quarters.

She'd been putting this off. She hadn't slept since the night before, and her own temper was fraying. She was out of sorts, frustrated, and there was a slow, simmering burn between her thighs from her inability not to remember exactly what she and Del-Rey had been doing before that ambush.

Her lips wrapped around the head of his cock, tasting the essence of his lust as it spilled between her lips, feeling him, taut and hard, growls rumbling in his throat as the arrogant alpha was replaced by the seducer.

Now, nearly eight hours after his return to Base, weariness was dragging at her and the need to see him was eating her alive. Even if he was just sleeping.

But he hadn't asked for her. He hadn't sent for her.

He was healing, she told herself. The healing process was exhausting for Coyotes, even more so than other Breeds.

As she turned into the alpha's section of the base, she nodded at the security team she'd put in place. They were Del-Rey's pack members and, she knew, more loyal to him alone than the others would be.

"Should we wait outside?" Ashley asked.

"Yes, you should," Anya answered her. "I don't need protection from your alpha." At least, she hoped she wouldn't. "As a matter of fact, the three of you can return to quarters while I'm here. Get some damned sleep or something, Ash. You're getting dark circles."

"Those are fighting words, Coya," she growled, though the playfulness still filled her tone.

"We'll spar later." Anya laid her palm against the palm plate that had been installed, and waited to see if she would be accepted.

She wasn't. She closed her eyes against the pain.

A second later the door opened and Brim stepped back, his gaze remote as she entered the room. She slapped the e-pad into his hand.

She could almost feel his disapproval that she was there; the fact that if he had the authority, he might even order her out.

"You'll find my notes, unencrypted, there," she told him. "You're needed in Command and Security. While you're there, have a talk with your pack leaders about cooperation in areas you share before you need to knock some heads together."

He stared back at her silently.

"The packs have been cooperating fine," he said coolly. "They're working together when they were never meant to do so. I consider that a rather amazing occurrence on a good day."

She stared back at him with the same measured look. "They're not working together well enough then. It's your job to see to this, and you haven't."

"I have been rather busy." The mockery slipped free then. "I'm Del-Rey's bodyguard and part of the team now assigned to the Bureau. It's rather hard to be in two places at once and to see to my duties in Command and Security as well as be bodyguard and general overseer."

"You should have assigned someone in your place," she retorted calmly.

"I did so," he informed her, his voice clipped. "Things have worked well enough."

"Well enough isn't working anymore," she told him. "And you are not needed as general overseer. I think I can handle that well enough."

"Coya, this isn't a place to play games," he said quietly. "You can't walk in and take your place for a few days, then run screaming when things begin to get out of control for you where the heat is concerned. Let this be until Del-Rey awakens and he can decide how we'll handle it."

"My place is here," she gritted out. "Yours is in Command and Security now that you're on base. Are we understood?"

She wasn't going to argue over who belonged where. She

belonged here, and she would be here. Her decision had been made; mating heat or not, as arrogant as all of them could be, it was time to finish this, one way or the other.

"Completely, Coya." He inclined his head slowly, though his expression never changed. "I'll collect my PDA and get to where I belong then."

"Have you slept?" She propped her hands on her waist as he started to turn from her.

"For several hours," he admitted. "There's a sleep chair in the office that I made use of."

He took her e-pad and held it in one hand with his PDA and stared back at her. "When he wakes up after healing, he's a prick. I don't want to hear you crying later if you end up with your feelings hurt or, worse yet, you find yourself back in his bed."

Coyotes didn't beat around the bush, she had to give them credit for that.

"Agreed." She nodded sharply. "I've left notes where I need to be updated if you don't mind. My PDA code is notated in there so you can send it straight to me."

Brim nodded his dark head, his light blue eyes shifting as though amusement threatened to touch his gaze, before he left and closed the door quietly behind him.

Breathing out roughly, Anya stepped fully into the room, then felt, saw, the haze of red fury that began to wash over her. She felt her fingers curl as the need for violence rushed through her system. She wanted to kill. To see blood flow and kick some damned Russian female ass.

Sofia was sitting on the side of his bed staring back at her, a damp cloth in her hand, a bowl of water on the bedstead as Del-Rey lay sleeping, stretched out, all but naked before the other woman's gaze. Her Del-Rey. Naked. Covered by nothing but a sheet, and another woman was touching him? Brim had dared to allow another woman to touch him?

Sofia rose slowly to her feet. "Fever." She cleared her throat, her hazel green gaze flickering for a moment. "I was merely helping Brim."

Merely helping Brim? Brim had called this woman in, allowed her to touch Del-Rey, to care for him as he left Anya in Command and Security?

Anya's head lifted. "He's not going to fuck you, so we both know you don't have a chance of achieving the status of coya in this base, are we agreed?"

Sofia's gaze darkened, almost in amusement, as she licked her lips slowly. "We're agreed, the status of coya will never be mine. But you haven't officially accepted it as of yet either."

"Don't play word games with me, Sofia," she warned her. "I'm not in the mood for them, or for your cattiness. Get the hell out of these quarters and make damned certain you stay out of my sight for a long while. We might both regret it if you don't."

"Possessive, Anya?" she asked. "I've heard you really don't give a damn, and haven't given a damn in over eight months. Why begin now?"

"Playing gossip, Sofia?" she sneered. "You should know better at your age."

Sofia's lips curled into a mocking smile. "Poor guy. He needs a lover that could balance him, that can be just as determined as he is. You ran from him."

"Do you want to die today?" Because Anya was definitely in the mood to shed blood.

"Today is as good as any." Slender shoulders shrugged expressively. "But, I have a feeling it's not going to happen just yet. I'll be on my way, Coya. If you need any help, let me know."

"Oh, I think I can manage all on my own," Anya assured her, her voice calmer than she had expected it to be.

"I'm sure you can." Sofia's low laugh grated on her already stretched nerves.

"Sofia." Anya stopped her as she passed.

"Yes, Coya?" she asked with a mocking smile.

"Let me catch you touching him again while he's unaware, and I'll make certain you never enter this base again."

Better yet, if she didn't manage to get a handle on her rage, she'd make certain no one found the body.

Sofia's brow lifted and amusement sparkled in her eyes. "You don't have that authority, Anya. But I'll play along and promise to be a good little girl while he's sleeping, how's that?"

"I don't need your promises," Anya informed her coldly. "Get out of these rooms, and don't make the mistake of entering them again unless I'm present."

"Once again, no authority." Sofia wagged her finger at her. "Only a full mate can make that demand." She paused and looked at Del-Rey's sleeping form before turning back to Anya. "Separation order. Remember?"

Anya hid her shock, though she knew she should have expected Sofia to know about the mating. She had worked with Del-Rey all these years, been an informant against the Council. She was here at Base; Del-Rey wouldn't have allowed it unless he trusted her to keep her mouth shut.

That didn't mean Anya liked it. It sure as hell didn't mean she liked the other woman.

She strolled past Anya then as she said, "He needs to be bathed with cool water as he sleeps. Mating heat and healing don't work well together when the heat isn't being satisfied. Poor little Coyote. He's suffered."

The door closed softly behind her moments later as Anya fought to still the shudders racing through her body. That woman's hands had been on him. Stroking him.

She stared at Del-Rey, stretched out, only a sheet covering his hips, leaving long, powerful legs bare, giving a full, tempting view of hard abs, a powerful chest. Naked, he was imposing, arousing and aroused. The hard length of his cock pressed clearly against the sheet.

Brim was going to pay for this. It was his job to watch over Del-Rey, to ensure he was protected during the healing phase when he was wounded.

Sofia was sensual, sexual; would she have dared to do more than simply wipe the sweat from his body? A part of Anya was certain the woman was capable of any perversion; another part of her knew better. Conflicting knowledge and emotions were whipping through her, tearing through her mind as she felt herself flushing, felt emotions she'd kept carefully contained rising inside her.

She knew Sofia too well. She had known the other woman all her life, and she knew the games she played. She was as calculating and manipulating as any Coyote Breed. Anya remembered Sofia directing her out of the labs, from the direction she would have gone, into the direction Del-Rey would be.

Yeah, she hated Sofia. She always had. But more because of

the other woman's mocking arrogance and air of superior knowledge than for any other reason.

Del-Rey shifted on the bed. Where he had been comfortable, locked in a haze of dark peace, he suddenly became aware of something more.

First, the heat. It tunneled through his cock as he heard Brim talking. That wasn't normal. The mating heat was always pushed back when healing took over. It was the only time he slept peacefully, the only time he didn't ache like the bastard animal he knew inside that he was.

The mating heat pushed forward, locked inside his mind. He heard Anya, scented her. He swore he could almost feel the warmth of her body against him. He needed it, he admitted to himself. Here in this dark nothingness, he needed her to lie against him, to warm him. God, sometimes the cold went clear to the bone and chilled him until he feared he would never feel warm again.

He shifted on the bed. He knew he should be sleeping deeper, that the near unconscious state the healing put him in should be blocking whatever was rising inside him. Hunger. Need. A craving for Anya he was never long without.

His Anya. Like a flame in winter, soothing the cold and the fears that haunted the man who wasn't fully a man, and tormented the animal that wasn't fully animal. Sometimes the battle between man and beast inside him was so tenacious that he wondered how long he could contain the conflicting urges.

The animal demanded that he take what belonged to him. That he steal her, kidnap her again. He wanted to throw those fucking hormonal treatments to the wind and force her to suffer as he suffered. He was ready to howl with the hunger inside him for the relief he knew they were both desperate for.

The man ached though. The man needed her acceptance. The man needed her touch given voluntarily, without the demand of the mating heat that surged between them. The man, arrogant and filled with his own sense of hunger, craved her acceptance.

"I've missed you."

He heard her voice, like summer rain, washing over his senses as a cooling touch covered his brow. It didn't ease the heat raging through his body, but it was better than nothing. At least in this tortured, demented nightmare, she was speaking to him rather than taunting him, just out of reach, always slipping past his desperate touch.

"Brim's a dead Coyote, Del-Rey. He shouldn't have let her in here. Let her touch you."

She must have meant Sofia. He had warned Brim to never allow Anya to know Sofia had bathed his brow and chest while healing from that gunshot wound months before. Had he told her?

It had hurt Anya. He didn't want her hurt.

"God, just being close to you makes me wet."

Her little sigh had him tensing in need now. She was wet? She wanted? He was hard and willing to give. But he knew better than to open his eyes and reach out for her. When he did, the dream would be gone, as would her touch. And he needed her touch like the land needed the rain. He needed to soak it in, feel it inside him, soothing him, refreshing him.

"I've missed you so much, Del-Rey. Like you were before you kidnapped me. Teasing me. Just your eyes would smile and I wanted to see your lips smile too. I wanted to feel that smile in a kiss and know it was all mine."

He wanted to give her such a kiss. A kiss filled with the promises he wanted to keep, the security he wanted to give her.

There was so little security in a Breed's life. So little they could depend upon. They had nothing to truly believe in except this. This promise that nature gave them with the mating heat. That there was a place for them. That at least in nature, they were accepted.

Del-Rey twisted against the bed, that agony of need raging through him. His hands clenched in the sheets he could feel beneath his body, the bed he'd picked out with Anya in mind. Large so they could roll around on it. Comfortable and warm, and now it felt like a bed of bricks.

His body was on fire for her. Just one more touch. He wanted to feel her hand, not whatever that cool touch was. He wanted her flesh. Flesh to his flesh. But he knew better than to reach for her.

"Anya." He forced the word past his lips. "Warm me."

He could smell her, so warm and sweet. He wanted to wrap

around her, just for a while. He couldn't drag himself far enough from the healing to still the mating heat.

He was lost in this need. The need to just feel her warmth. He had ached for her warmth. It had driven spikes of agony into his soul for months, unceasing, always there, reminding him that what should have been his would never belong to him.

"You're burning with fever." Her hand stroked over his chest and something inside him unknotted. Flesh to flesh. That was how he needed her.

"Warm me, Anya," he sighed, wishing he could touch this dream, feel it, just for a while. "Flesh to flesh."

Then she was gone. He wanted to howl in agony. The sweet gentle touch was gone. The warmth was gone. He could smell her scent, but only barely. Only enough to know she had been there.

Anya stared down at Del-Rey, uncertain why she was toeing off her sneakers, pulling free her T-shirt. Stripping down to flesh.

"Flesh to flesh," he had whispered as his fingers dug into the sheet and the fever raged in his body. He could be cold. Fever made one cold. Chilling clear to the bone. She remembered the one time she had really been sick, just before the Coyotes' rescue. She had ached with the cold as she ran a fever.

She felt her breath catch in her throat as she unlatched her bra and pushed her panties from her hips. He was aroused. He could take her even as he slept and she couldn't blame him if he did. She wouldn't stop him if he did.

The longer she sat beside him the hotter his flesh seemed to get until touching him was almost like touching a flame. And he was shuddering, shivering.

The healing was excruciating by itself, and she knew the mating heat was hell. At least, it had been for her.

"Del-Rey." She whispered his name as she moved onto the bed, felt him stiffen, then growl her name again.

Pulling the sheet over both of them, she settled slowly against his side, trembling with wariness, wishing she knew more about this man that nature had decided belonged to her. And that was her fault. She had forced the separation, he hadn't.

She had no more settled beside him than he moved. Anya

almost whimpered in fear as he flipped her to her side and moved. He shifted, shifted her. Pulled her over him, then under him.

Confused, she followed his mumbled directions, moved here and there until she realized they were in the exact center of the huge bed. Finally he settled, draped over her, her head tucked beneath his chin, his leg thrown over hers, his arms wrapped around her, and then he eased.

She felt it; almost a muscle at a time, she felt him relax until he was limp, curled around her, his breath stirring her hair, the inferno that had fired his body somehow seeming cooler. And if she wasn't mistaken, she might have heard a soft little grumble, almost a snore slip from his chest as his hand curled around her breast and his heavy weight held here beneath him.

She lay there, tense, silent, uncertain what he would do next. When nothing came, when he continued to sleep, she felt her own lashes drifting closed, felt her own weariness dragging her down.

Being a coya was damned hard work, she decided. She would sleep here, just for a little while. And maybe slip away before he awoke and she found herself pinned by a fully aware, fully aroused Coyote Breed in mating heat.

But she couldn't help the smile that edged her lips as her eyes closed. He was like a puppy. Rumbling here and there, twisting and turning and dragging her to suit his comfort until he slept peacefully.

It was kind of cute.

Hell, she had to admit, Del-Rey had a charming side that had mesmerized her before the mating crap managed to scare the hell out of her. Until she had convinced herself he had lied, deliberately, that he had taken his promises and her heart and trampled them.

He had trampled her sense of confidence in herself when her body had gone crazy with the heat. He had taken her, as lost in the pounding lust as she had been. She had convinced herself that he should have had the control to make it easier for her. That he should have taken responsibility for something neither of them had expected. That he should have been the charming, in control, teasing Coyote Breed that had spoiled her with the hint of laughter in his eyes and his promises that he would care for her. Take care of her. That he would make everything work out.

It had worked out. He had protected her. He had made certain she had what she needed even above what he needed. And like a child, she had blamed him for the results.

He was still arrogant. He was definitely too dominant. But she had learned that that was a male Breed. It was a part of them. It was even a part of him that made her crazy to touch him, even when she wanted to hate him.

She hadn't seen a single Breed mating that went easily. They fought, they yelled, they clashed, and they challenged each other. And as Hope had once told her, once it was over, they laughed and they loved and they knew they belonged. No matter what happened in the world around them, they belonged.

Could she be lucky enough to find that with Del-Rey?

She still had issues to resolve with him, Anya knew that. But she also knew that until they clashed, fought and yelled, those issues would never be resolved and they would never have that chance to laugh, to love and to belong.

As she slipped into sleep, she prayed she hadn't waited too long to attempt that resolution.

CHAPTER 14

He was warm. The only time he was ever warm was when Anya had slept in his bed.

He usually awakened from a healing chilled to the bone, damp with his own sweat and feeling like an animal that had lain in a gutter for two days.

He shifted, moved to stretch and realized, in one heart-stopping moment, one instant of cognition, why he was so warm.

His eyes opened and he stared into a sleeping face. Anya's face. Spiked red gold lashes lay against her creamy flesh; her lips were parted as she breathed, her breath whispering over his chest.

Their legs were tangled together, his erection, fierce and engorged to the point of agony, throbbed with brutal insistence where it lay, pressed between her thighs, surrounded by the slick, creamy essence of her arousal.

She was wet, and her wet heat slicked his dick and reminded him of how much hotter it was deep inside her body.

What the hell was she doing here? He was wrapped around her like a vine, holding her to him, tucked against him, and he had managed to sleep through this for how long?

She moved against him then, her hips shifting as she rode the thick length of his cock against her clit.

Damn. Damn.

He felt his hand clench her hip, then relax. Did he want her to stop or to continue? Would she find her pleasure in her sleep as he watched?

His hand smoothed over her hip and down the curve of her ass to her thigh.

"Anya." He swallowed tightly as he felt her move against him again.

He barely remembered awakening several times, moving to the bathroom or forcing himself to eat before collapsing again. He didn't remember her being here at those times. He remembered the chill in his bones and the need for sleep or for water or food. He would have surely known if she had been in his bed.

He glanced at the clock on the wall. Forty-eight hours since he had first returned to Base and collapsed in the bed.

His teeth snapped together as she moved again, spreading her slick, hot cream along the painfully engorged shaft it cuddled. Damn her. Damn the heat. Damn his weakness.

Her thigh lifted along his, the side of her knee rubbing at his hip as she opened herself farther to him and rubbed her swollen, hard-tipped breasts against his chest.

Hell. He was supposed to control his lust in the face of this temptation and the mating heat combined? Was he supposed to be fucking made of steel?

Well, except his cock. It felt hard as steel and as hot as newly formed iron.

"Anya, wake up," he groaned, hearing the growl in his voice.

She rubbed against him again, her hips tilting until the swollen bud of her clit was in direct contact and the fiery heat of it threatened to blister him.

Sweet merciful heaven. He held her hip, but was he smart enough to ease her back? Hell no, he was moving her, encouraging her to ride him, to stroke the brutal length of his dick as she gave herself pleasure.

"Wake up." He lowered his head and nipped at her lip. "Damn you, do you expect me to be strong enough to simply walk away?"

Her tongue peeked out, swiped over the area he had nipped,

as her lashes lifted and sleepy, aroused sapphire gems stared back at him.

"Watch the teeth," she muttered as her lashes lowered and an expression of sublime pleasure filled her face.

Her hips rolled again as a little moan broke past her lips and the silky flesh of that perfect little pussy rode his dick again.

"Anya. Move," he growled.

And oh how she moved. With a slow, wicked roll of her hips that had the head of his cock pushing against her entrance before it slid in her creamy juices and only glanced it.

This was torture. It was agony. No hell he had endured could come close to the hell of being this close and knowing he couldn't take what awaited just within reach.

He was sweating. Del-Rey could feel the sweat building on his flesh, but he was too dick-dumb to pull away from her. If she wanted to ride him to her own release, then slip back into sleep, God knew, he'd try to give it to her. But he knew he didn't have the control to sustain that patience in the face of a hunger that ate into him like acid. It cramped his balls, his abdomen. He swore it was setting fire to his brain as he felt the hormone attributed to mating rushing through his system.

The glands beneath his tongue were torturously swollen; the need to release the hormone into her system was damned near killing him.

"Del-Rey." Her lashes lifted again. Gem-bright, her eyes stared back at him. "If you tease me one more time, I might have to kill you."

"Tease you?" he groaned.

"You've teased me for two days." She shifted again, rode his cock and then paused as she had the engorged head lined up against the entrance to the sweetness beyond.

"How have I teased you?" he muttered.

"Your lips all over me, but never enough. Then you tuck your cock between my legs and just sleep. That's torture, Del-Rey. The worst kind. I bet its punishable or something. Should I take your allowance?"

He'd done this? In his sleep, without taking her?

Del-Rey shook his head.

"Kiss me," she whispered. "I'm late for those damned hormonal therapy shots. It's killing me."

"No." He couldn't do this. "You should have called Armani. She would have come here."

"Lockdown." She stretched against him. "Snipers in the woods and all kinds of stuff."

"You should have told Brim," he snarled. "He would have gotten you there in the heli-jet. Damn you!"

He didn't want to take her like this again. Not in the full fury of mating heat, where the scent of her was like a drug itself, whipping control from his mind.

"Brim offered." She nipped his chin, then licked it as he tried to find sanity. "I want you the way nature meant for you to take me, Del-Rey. This is the way it's supposed to be."

Ah fuck. He was going to die. Her hips moved, the tip of his cock invaded the snug confines of her pussy, and he felt flames shoot up his spine.

Not like this. He wanted to kiss her, taste her. He wanted so much more for her than just the mating.

"Do you know," she whispered roughly, "when you rub against me like that and you fill me with your pre-cum, you make me burn? Even before I felt the mating heat coming back, I felt that. You were tucked against me, and I was so wet, so wicked, I let you do it. And I felt that. And all I wanted was you inside me."

He knew what Wolf and Coyote pre-cum did to their mates. Armani had explained it in humiliating detail. The silky fluid was filled with the hormone that induced heat as well as one that relaxed the tight flesh that would surround his cock. It would raise the female mate's arousal, make her more sensitive, make the pleasure sharper as it prepared her body for his final release and the tight secondary swelling halfway up the shaft as his cum tore from him. It would lock him inside her, make it impossible to pull free as his seed shot into the heated depths of her pussy. And it would hold him there—the last time, he had been locked inside her for over half an hour, feeling her climaxes as though they were his own, as she begged him to make it stop.

That memory gave him the strength. God, he never wanted that shame again. To stare into her tear-drenched eyes as she begged him, pleaded with him to make it stop and he could do nothing to stop it.

"Enough." He jerked back, pushing her away before swinging around and shoving his feet to the floor. "I'll call Armani and tell her."

He froze. A sense of vertigo rushed over him as he felt her at his back, hot nipples stabbing into him as her teeth raked his neck. "Call Armani, and I'll take my injection like a good little coya and return to that dead little world where my dreams torment me, and my emotions overshadow the truth?"

"Honest arousal," he snarled. "Give me that. I'll take it. But not like this, where you have no control over your need."

He couldn't fucking breathe. The scent of her pussy was washing through his senses like a tidal wave, like an eruption of white-hot heat piercing his brain.

"I don't want something else controlling me either," she whispered. "I want all of you, Del-Rey. Don't you want all of me? Mating heat and all?"

"What do you want in your bed then, the animal?" he sneered.

"And the man," she whispered as he glared down at her, holding her down, his hands manacling her wrists to the mattress, his hips pressing against hers. "You're both. I want both."

"So you had to do without the injections to take both?" Self-disgust tore through him.

"Is that what you think, Del-Rey?" She stared back at him, her eyes so brilliant with arousal it hurt to stare into them. "That I have to let myself become drugged by the heat to take you? That isn't why."

"Then why?"

"Because the hormone therapy they were giving me deadens certain nerve endings and makes anger, frustration and fear worse. It was the only way it would work. It blocked the receptors to areas that receive the most arousal, while heightening other emotions. I don't want anything deadened or heightened unnaturally. I want to feel you," she whispered. "All of you. Was that so wrong?"

He shook his head. He was supposed to make sense of this right now? When need was tearing through him with a force he had never known before?

"I want your kiss, and I want to taste it, feel it. I want your touch, and I want to know all the pleasure. I want you inside me, and I want to feel the emotions I felt before. All of them, Del-Rey."

"You're lying," he growled. "I can smell the fear inside you and the lie that falls from your lips." He pressed his forehead against hers, his balls cramping with the need tearing through him. "God, Anya. Why are you doing this to us?"

"I can't be a little bit afraid?" Tears sparkled in her eyes then. "Del-Rey, I don't want the hormone therapy because I don't want to cheat whatever it is that does this to us. If I don't face it now, I'm never going to."

No, it wasn't a lie, it was courage and fear. She was coming to him, all of him, and she was trying.

"And what do I do when I knot you?" he snarled. "When I swell inside you and the fear overwhelms that pleasure? When you beg me to make it stop, Anya? What do I do then? Because there is no stopping it."

"Whatever you need to do, as long as you hold me, Del-Rey. Don't leave me alone. Don't let me get cold," she finally answered. "But if I take another of those injections, then I won't come back here until it wears off again. We'll do this right, and we'll both become accustomed to it, or we'll not do it at all."

Anya could feel the old fears trying to rise inside her, the need versus the unfamiliarity of the Breed body and the mating heat. He made her wild, and control had always been her focus. He made her lose that control. He made her want to lose it, made her want to be wicked, and he had never known that was the most terrifying thing of all.

Now, as she stared into his raven black eyes, she knew the chance she was taking. If she didn't overcome those fears, if she lost herself and the fear returned, it could damage something more between them.

She had never considered how Del-Rey had felt when the mating heat tore through both of them. When she had cried and fought him, feeling him locked inside her, becoming hysterical at the brutal pleasure that tore through her. She had begged, pleaded with him to stop it. And she had cried. Hysterical tears that had dampened her pillow and left her exhausted even as the heat rebuilt.

"We won't resolve this by hiding behind the hormone

treatments." She breathed in raggedly as a wave of furious need swept through her. "This was my decision, Del-Rey. I won't blame you for anything."

"Anya." Agony flickered in his gaze. "Do you know what you're doing to us? To me?"

"I'm not a child," she told him, willing him to believe her. "I'm not the woman you probably expected. I'm your mate, and you can take me as your mate, or I can walk away."

A growl rumbled in his chest. It was sexy; she had always found that sound to be soul-searingly sexy. It sent shivers racing up her spine, and even before the mating it had made her wet.

"Growl at me again," she tempted him. "Kiss me while you growl, Del-Rey. I dare you."

Never dare a Coyote. Ever. It was a law, even the Council knew to never dare them. They always accepted a dare. They always triumphed.

His lips were on hers in an instant, his tongue sinking inside her, and Anya realized what she had been missing for eight long months. Even in the past week his kiss hadn't been just right.

The taste hadn't been just so, because of that damned therapy. This was Del-Rey's kiss. Primitive and primal. The hormone that spilled from his tongue was spicy and addictive. There was nothing sweet about it, nothing gentle, it was hot and sensual, and she stroked her tongue against his, drawing more to her, needing more.

This was the taste, the heat, the hunger. It merged and melded with her own, stoked the fire waiting inside her and sent it blazing. Without the fear.

She strained in his grasp as she heard the growl in his throat that rumbled into their kiss. Strong thighs bracketed hers; the feel of his cock throbbing against her lower stomach had her trying to arch closer. She couldn't touch him as she wanted to, as she needed to.

She tore her lips from his. "Let me touch."

He growled harder, rougher, but didn't release her hands. He stared at her breasts as they rose and fell swiftly, the hard tips of her nipples standing tight and a blushing pink beneath his gaze.

"I kissed you here while I slept?" he asked her, his gaze lifting to hers.

"You only kissed them," she admitted. "I wanted to beg for more."

His expression shifted, turned arrogant and dominant as sexual tension tightened his features. "You wanted more?"

"I ached for more."

His head lowered and she nearly screamed at the sensation. Her nipples had always been incredibly sensitive, until the hormonal treatments. Now that sensitivity had returned tenfold. She swore she was going to orgasm from his mouth sucking her in, drawing on a tight, hard tip and lashing it with his tongue.

The pleasure was exquisite. She arched against him, drowning in it now where it had terrified her before. It raced over her flesh, streaked to her clit and spasmed her womb in one heated second as she gasped his name.

The sight of him suckling at her nipple did things to her that she couldn't describe. The pleasure was incredible, but the visual sensation, his black eyes, heavily lashed, watching her, his lips drawing on her, his dark face ravaged by lust. It was the most incredible sight of her life. It clenched her thighs, had her straining to create friction at her clit as pleasure invaded every cell of her body.

"Don't stop," she moaned as his head lifted.

He moved to her neglected nipple, sucked it into his mouth and with his free hand used his fingers to plump the damp tip he had abandoned.

Shards of sensation were tearing through her now. She wanted him and she wanted him now. Waiting didn't seem to be a viable option. Then his lips lowered. He kissed and nipped his way down her torso, her stomach, as he released her wrists and loosened his thighs about her legs.

"The scent of your arousal makes me hungry." The growl in his voice was deeper, darker. "I wanted to taste you before and didn't get to. I swore, if ever you gave me the chance again, then I was going to lap every drop of cream from your sweet pussy."

Anya lost the ability to breathe for precious seconds. When she finally managed to inhale, he had her legs spread and his lips lowered.

He kissed her first. His lips pursed and he kissed her clit, so gently as he watched her. As she watched him.

A heavy flush mantled his cheekbones now and Anya could feel the same heat flushing her body. She couldn't drag her gaze from the sight of him though, his lips delivering sensual, hot kisses as his hands pushed her thighs farther apart, opening her to his lips and tongue.

"So sweet."

She jerked as his tongue licked through the swollen slit.

"You taste like pure nectar," he whispered, his voice hoarse, low. "Sweet and hot as sunshine itself."

Who knew her Del-Rey could be so damned seductive? She'd known he was, but not to this depth.

"Taste again," she panted. "You might be wrong."

She watched in anticipation as he smiled, flashed those wicked curved canines and licked again.

Her lashes fluttered. She was nearly lost. She was sinking into a whirlwind of sensation and she didn't want to escape.

"Lay back, my coya." He pressed her back until her shoulders were against the mattress once again. "Let me show you how I love your taste. How I love the sweet heat flowing from your body."

Would she survive it? She didn't think she would. The sensations racing through her were unlike even those first destructive times Del-Rey had taken her. This was deeper, hotter, it was filling parts of her that had never been touched before.

His tongue was like rough silk licking from the entrance of her sex to her clit. Stroking and lapping, little growls vibrating against her flesh as she tried to get closer, tried to get more.

She wanted to come. She needed to. It was burning inside her like wildfire searching for escape.

Anya spread her thighs farther, her heels digging into the bed as she arched to him. One hand went to his thick, coarse hair, the other to an aching nipple. Gripping it between her fingers she pinched and rolled the tip, her head thrashing against the sheets as pleasure rolled through her like a cataclysmic wave of heat.

"Fuck, yes," Del-Rey snarled before he was licking her with male greed, his tongue pressing inside the desperate, clenching entrance of her vagina, thrusting into it as she cried out his name and begged for relief.

"Yes, baby," he groaned. "Beg me. Beg me to take you, to touch you."

He licked, stroked, his hands pressed beneath her, cupping her ass and lifting her to his ravenous tongue. She felt it press inside her again, a slow, heated stroke before he licked at the juices easing from her and growled into the caress.

"God, I dreamed of this, prayed for this." He kissed her clit again, flicked his tongue over the violently sensitive bud as Anya plucked at her nipple and tried to force his lips closer.

She was so close to release. Seconds from it if he would just let her have it. She could feel the pressure building inside her, tightening through her. The need licked over her flesh with nearly the same destructive results as his tongue licking through her sex.

"I need," she cried out hoarsely, loosening his hair to bring her fingers to her other nipple, to increase the friction and the torturous sensations. "Del-Rey. I need."

"Anya." He kissed her thigh, ran his tongue over the flesh there before returning to the liquid center of her body. "Sweet and hot. My Anya. My coya."

She arched as his lips covered her clit again, this time with the heated pressure she knew would send her flying into the oblivion she had once fought against. Now she raced toward it.

Increasing the pressure on her nipples, she felt her breath catch as he sucked the bud into his mouth and drew on it seductively, as his tongue flickered over, around, heating it, spilling the mating heat on it, and then sending her screaming into orgasm.

She felt her upper body jerk upright. It wasn't controllable. Her hands flew out, reaching for him, a thin, ragged wail leaving her body as pleasure exploded through her in a rush of sizzling energy.

And he caught her. His hands gripped hers, his gaze caught hers, as his lips held on to her pulsing clit and his tongue wrung every harsh explosion of sensation from her body.

She could hear his growls. She could feel them. She strained into his lips, her head tilting back as the world rushed around her in a dizzying display of color that left her shuddering in the aftermath.

Del-Rey eased her back to the bed, his hands stroking over her waist, her stomach and thighs, easing the violent shudders of her body as he slowly, regretfully released the swollen, throbbing little button of her clit.

He could taste her release on his tongue. Sugar and fire. Earth and air. He licked his lips as he pressed a kiss to her hip, then nipped the sweat-dampened flesh with his teeth.

He couldn't wait. His head was filled with the taste of her, with the scent of her. It called to him, teased him, tempted him.

Moving over her, he gripped the base of his throbbing cock with one hand. He'd spilled the slick pre-cum to the bed as she exploded beneath him. He was amazed he hadn't shot every ounce of cum from his body as she screamed his name.

"I'm burning," she moaned, her head twisting on the sheets as she stared up at him, panting for breath, perspiration dampening her forehead, her hair.

Her eyes were slumberous, brilliant in her flushed face as the mass of red gold curls cascaded around her.

"I'll ease you," he promised.

He would ease them both. The hunger was clawing at him now, brilliant red-hot sparks of need exploding up his spine, traveling to his tortured balls as he pressed her legs farther apart and moved to her.

He prayed for control. His erection was thicker than she would have known with a human lover. Coyote and Wolf males were cursed not just with the knot that would lock them inside their mates, but also with a heavier, thicker shaft. As though they wouldn't frighten their mates enough to begin with.

"Anya. Look at me, baby. Look at me."

Her eyes opened again, brilliant, dark within her heat-flushed face.

"We'll go easy, I swear it," he groaned, allowing the head of his cock to press against the tender opening.

His teeth locked together as the first pulse of heated fluid erupted from the tip. Rich with the mating hormone, it pulsed inside her even as he fought to hold it back.

"Oh God, that feels so good." She arched closer, pressing him deeper. "Like it's burning me, easing me, making me crazy for you." Her gaze sharpened. "I don't like crazy, Del-Rey. I like control. You know I like control."

He did. He knew this.

He cupped her cheek with one hand, feeling his chest clench in agony. "I know, little love. You want control."

There was no control here, for either of them. But he remembered that now. He should have remembered eight months ago. His Anya was always composed. Even with that brilliant red gold hair and the fiery temper that could light her eyes, she had always maintained control. And there was no control amid the mating heat.

Her breath hitched as another pulse of fluid filled her and a sound, nearly a sob, escaped her throat at the feel of it.

She shuddered beneath him as her hands gripped his biceps, her nails digging into his flesh as he eased farther inside her, his teeth gritting at the too tight grip of her silken flesh.

"Oh. Oh, Del-Rey." She lifted to him, her lashes lowering as he pressed deeper and a growl tore from his throat.

He felt every ripple, every convulsive tightening of her pussy around the crown of his cock. It was like sinking into pure ecstasy the pleasure was so violent.

The pulsing pre-cum came faster now; each spurt was another thread broken on the thin expanse of his control. His patience was wearing; the need to drive into her was eroding his every sense.

"Anya." He laid his head against her shoulder, continuing to work himself inside her, his teeth clenching into the sheets rather than her tender shoulder as his instincts demanded.

Slow and easy. He repeated the refrain inside his head. Control. Patience. No taking. He couldn't take this time.

He jerked, his head lifting as a snarl of furious hunger exploded inside him. His hips jerked, driving his cock inside her deeper.

It was rapture. It was incredible. It was pleasure that tortured his dreams and his waking hours with the same driving force. The memory of this. Of Anya, slick and tight, clenched around him like a milking fist.

"Yes. Oh yes." Her hips jerked to him. "More. More now."

His head lifted as he fought to breathe, staring into her enraptured expression as her nails bit into his arms. Her neck arched, her hips rolled beneath him, working him in nearly to the base of his cock.

He couldn't maintain this, he knew he couldn't.

"Look at me, Anya," he snarled. "Open your eyes."

If she didn't open her eyes, he would never hold on to the control he needed. He had to see her. He had to remind himself he was a man, not an animal. He was loving his coya, his other half. His woman.

He had sworn if he ever had the chance to touch her again, he would hold on to his control. He would show her the pleasure, not the fear.

"Look at me, Anya," he growled again. "See me, damn you. Hold on to me, and there will be no fear. I swear. No more fear."

CHAPTER 15

Anya's eyes opened, dazed, almost unseeing as she tried to focus on Del-Rey.

She was lost in the sensations whipping through her now. The feel of him, huge, hard, sinking into her as the heavy pulses of pre-cum continued to spurt inside her.

It would, until he was fully seated, she knew. And then the pleasure would only burn brighter. This was the part that had begun the nightmare the first time. This raging need, the way she clenched around the thick length of his cock, her hips moving frantically, desperate for more.

But this time, he was facing her. When he had taken her before, he had turned her to her stomach and lifted her hips, giving her nothing to hold on to. She'd had no sense of warmth, no sense of the man taking her as she did now.

"Anya." His breathing was ragged, his broad chest moving with rough breaths as sweat eased down the side of his face. "I can't—"

He shook his head, his eyes clenching before they opened once more and focused on hers.

His jaw clenched as his hips jerked, driving that last inch of his heavy erection in to the hilt. Anya felt her breath ease from her body for precious seconds. She was filled, overfilled. She was burning and so desperate for more that she wondered if she would survive it this time.

Swallowing tightly, she fought to stare into his eyes. As black as midnight with the faintest hint of blue. As though the color hid within the darkness, a shadow of light to hold her to him.

"Ah hell." One hand clenched her hip, the over buried in her hair as he braced his elbow at her shoulder. "I can't." He swallowed tightly. "I can't hold back, baby."

"Don't hold back," she panted. "Just hold on to me." Her voice broke. "Hold on to me, Del-Rey. Don't let me get lost."

His eyes seemed to widen then his expression twisted as lust transformed his features and he began to move. Each heavy thrust pierced her deeper than just the clenching depths of her vagina. Sensation tore through her with excruciating pleasure/pain. It stroked along once hidden nerve endings, reached to the depths of her and burned into her soul.

She held on to Del-Rey. She stared up at him, and felt the spinning whirlwind whipping inside her latch onto her. Hunger. An agony of need so deep, so desperate she couldn't fight it any longer. Her hips lifted and her legs wrapped around his hips as she met each thrust, each stroke with a broken cry.

She was filled with midnight colors as she stared into his eyes and held on to him. Thick, dark blond lashes, so thick she would be jealous later. She felt the muscles of his biceps beneath her fingers as she dug into them, clenching at him as he drove into her, his hips thrusting heavily now, harder, faster as she felt the ever narrowing spirals of pleasure whipping through her.

"Yes." His voice was part animal, part man. "Fuck me, Anya. Take me, baby. All of me. Take all of me."

She knew what was coming. She felt her own orgasm building inside her, and she knew what it would do to her, what it would do to him.

In those years that her heart had settled on this Breed, she had never expected this. Scientists and techs used Breeds as sex toys, often having their favorites, calling them their pets, and this had never happened then. There were no animalistic results to those sexual adventures.

But Anya knew there would be now. She knew where the

whirlwind would throw them, and she fought to hold back. Not yet. She didn't want it to happen yet. She didn't want the fear, she didn't want that total loss of self that came with it.

"I have you." His voice brushed over her senses. "Hold on to me, Anya. I have you. Always."

He drove inside her, fast, furious, shafting inside her with a power and a pleasure that took that control, took that last edge of strength and tore it from her grasp.

She heard her own screams of release. Breathless, pleading, an agony of pleasure ripping through her as she felt the first convulsive eruption tear over her senses.

Then, she felt his release. She felt the swelling, the burning stretch of muscle and tissue, the violent throb of heavy veins pounding into nerve endings that screamed from the additional intensity. She heard his shout, then a sound that was part snarl, part howl as his head lowered and his teeth pierced her shoulder.

It wasn't pain. It was too intense to be pleasure.

Anya was locked in a world of sensation so brutal she screamed out his name as she felt the first furious blast of semen erupting into her already too sensitive sex, and the additional width, locking him into the clenching muscles of her pussy, set off a harder, stronger eruption that seemed to center in her womb.

She was coming hard, each detonation jerking her muscles, tightening them until she cried out in fear and in wonder. Because she wasn't lost. She could feel Del-Rey, his growls at her shoulder, his shoulders beneath her clawing nails, his thighs powerful and flexing as her legs wrapped around them.

She wasn't lost without him, she was lost within him, holding tight as flames raged over her, pleasure tore through her, and for the first time in eight months a sense of completion overcame her.

How long it lasted, she didn't know. They shuddered together, jerking and moaning, each pulse of his release triggering another smaller explosion inside her as the mating knot throbbed hard against sensitive nerve endings and sent another current of electrical pleasure sizzling through her.

She was aware of his teeth buried in her flesh, but this time, there was no pain. There was the feel of his tongue touching the wound as he gently extracted the curved canines and licked over the mark with sensual enjoyment. The feel of his hands, one buried in her hair, one holding her hip with what she was certain was bruising force.

Then the knot pulsed again and she shuddered, a weak cry leaving her lips as another detonation of release gripped her, spasmed through her.

It was too much pleasure. Too much sensation. She was crying. She could feel the tears falling from her eyes even as she buried her face in his shoulder and bit him back.

She would be shocked later, she promised herself as she felt her teeth clench the hard muscle of his shoulder. Later, she would debate the wisdom of the action. For now, she heard his shocked exclamation, felt his hips jerk against her, the swelling inside her throb and semen pulse. Anya moaned low and ragged as the taste of male flesh filled her mouth and Del-Rey seemed to fill her very soul.

Nothing should be this good, this torrential, this overwhelming. No pleasure this intense and all-consuming could survive. But if it didn't, then Anya feared that this time, if she lost it, she could not hold on to her own sanity.

✦ ✦ ✦

Del-Rey held on to her. It was all she had asked of him. To hold on to her, not to let her go. He held her against his chest until the swelling eased and he was able to withdraw from her. A grimace of surging pleasure twisted his expression at the feel of her still-snug grip against the overly sensitive flesh of his cock. Another small ripple of sensation fluttered through her muscles before she relaxed against him again, curling against his chest as he collapsed beside her and wrapped his arms around her.

This was what he had craved all those months ago.

"Are you okay?" He tried to keep his voice low, keep the growl out of it. There was no way to hold back the satisfaction that filled him though.

For the first time in eight months he wasn't tortured with the need. He was semi-aroused, but that desperate throb of agony was no longer present.

"Hmm," she mumbled against his chest.

He almost grinned at the grumpy, slumberous little sound.

"That's not an answer, Mate," he told her, keeping his voice low as amusement threaded through it. "Should I warn Wolfe that we need to call another tribunal?" A second later a sharp pinch to his waist had him chuckling.

"Go to sleep," she ordered, but her voice was sex soft and filled with sleepy satisfaction. "While you've been lazing the last two days away, I've been working. I'm tired."

He grinned again, remembering the security recordings Brim had shown him before he literally passed out.

"While the alpha's sleeping the coya's playing?" he asked her.

"Being your coya is damned hard work." She stretched as she spoke, a sinuous, almost feline movement of grace that had him pushing back the thought that perhaps he could fuck her again. Maybe this time slower, easier.

Tucking the sheet over her breasts she sat up and stared down at him, her hair touseled around her face, her gaze drowsy and filled with satiation.

"Coyotes aren't like Wolves," she told him as she bent her knees and rested her chin on them.

"Yeah, their work ethic sucks sometimes," he admitted. "We're turning hardened killers into techs and security personnel. Just because they have the knowledge to do it doesn't mean they have the temperament for it."

He'd acknowledged that even before they had approached the Wolves for an alliance. His plans were vast in comparison to the roadblocks he faced.

Then his mate shook her head. "That's not their problem at all." She stared at him, wide-eyed. "Their work ethic is every bit as dedicated as the Wolves or the Felines. They just like to pretend otherwise. They're working to create something and that means a lot to them. But they're more solitary. Working within a team is their problem."

Del-Rey propped his head on his hand as he lay on his side watching her.

"We weren't trained to work together," he told her. "We have more Coyotes coming in soon, pack leaders who have no problems stepping back in command, though their packs number less than the ten to twelve ours do. Mostly two-man teams.

Stragglers who are deserting the Council as quickly as they can. We'll have another dozen or more soon to add to the dozen coming in from the Middle East via the Bureau. Integrating them will be harder."

He watched as she frowned at the information.

"Are you returning to mission status now?" she asked him.

Del-Rey watched her carefully. "I'm not going back, Anya. I'm needed here."

"You say that as though someone disagrees."

He sighed at that. "The order of separation disagrees," he told her. "Until you inform the tribunal that you are accepting the mating and your status of coya, then I'm bound by my word, Anya." He reached up and played with the ends of her fiery hair. "Are you accepting your place now, or merely feeling your way?"

"You'd allow that?" She tipped her head to the side. "Time for me to feel my way?"

Him and his big mouth.

Del-Rey stared back at her and sighed heavily. "I'd give you whatever time you needed." He shrugged. "Would I have a choice? I don't want to force you into my bed or into your place here. I want nothing from you that isn't freely given."

She nodded slowly. "We have things to resolve," she said then. "With both of us. I notified those on the tribunal that the separation order is null and void, no matter your decision in the mating."

Satisfaction surged inside him.

"I think you know my decision on it," he told her somberly. "You're my mate, my coya. I haven't changed my mind about that. Nothing can change that for me."

She nodded again, though clearly there was more on her mind and Del-Rey hesitated to push her. Here, he felt on very unfamiliar ground. He would have once said he knew this woman and each move she would make. She had shown him differently from the moment he had taken her from Russia.

She was stronger than he had ever imagined and definitely more stubborn. More her own woman than she would ever be any man's lover or mate perhaps.

"We need to return to Haven," he finally said into the silence. "You at least need to take the hormonal supplements that will allow you a measure of freedom from the more extreme symptoms of the heat. I don't want you suffering."

She shook her head. "This is my choice." She turned to him again. "You suffered it."

"It's not as hard on the male, baby," he sighed. "It's endurable. For the females, it's not as easy."

She lifted her shoulders in a shrug. "So, I get horny. I'll just drag you from whatever you're doing and you can do your mating duty before anything else."

"Really?" His brow lifted. "And should I get horny?"

An impish grin crossed her lips. "It's not as hard for the males, remember?"

What the hell was that sudden tighteness in his chest, that emotion that gripped his throat and had him staring at her with a need to never have her out of his sight? To always see her eyes sparkling with mirth, that pursed little grin on her face?

She was, quite simply, adorable. And she was his coya. Not just his mate. Not just his woman. She was the other half of who and what he was as alpha of his packs.

She sighed then. "I believe, based on information I've gotten over the months, I have several hours before that luscious body of yours is going to be put to work again." She bounced from the bed before he could reach out and stop her. "I have to shower and get dressed. We have a meeting at Haven as soon as you're ready and an interrogation to watch. Wolfe agreed to hold the questioning of the bartender until you could be present." Her expression tightened as she turned back to him, brazenly naked, breasts firm and tipped with hard nipples, fiery curls gleaming between her thighs. "He meant to kill me. Why target you like that?"

Del-Rey's brow lifted as he rose from the bed, though fury clenched his gut. "That shotgun wasn't on me, sweetheart, it was on you."

"But all killing me would accomplish is whatever my death would mean to you," she pointed out. "Very few outside Haven know about the separation agreement. To the world, according to the tabloids several months ago anyway, we're the latest great Breed love match. The kidnapped Russian admin and the Coyote alpha. The stories were very romantic."

"Really?" He frowned back at her. He hadn't lied when he said he didn't read the damned tabloids. "How romantic?"

She gathered up her clothing as she shot him a look he couldn't quite decipher. One of those feminine looks that he'd often wondered about when he saw other men getting them. Normally when said male had done something that displeased said female.

"Excessively romantic," she snorted as she checked her link. "Ashley has some information I was waiting on as well; she's waiting for me."

She dumped the clothes in a hamper. Only then did he see the dusty state of her clothing.

"How did that happen?" he asked as she disconnected the link she had put through to her bodyguard to request clean clothes.

"Spelunking." She moved from the bedroom into the adjoining shower room.

Del-Rey frowned as he followed her. "Cave exploring? What caves? We've explored them all."

She rolled her eyes as she turned the shower on and adjusted the water. "Of course you have. You're just not using them all. You have more Breeds coming in, remember? Where are you going to put them? Will they have beds? Blankets? Towels?"

He leaned against the entrance and watched her, loving the graceful movements of her body, the way she tipped her head back, washing her hair, and still watched him.

"They would have found what they need." He frowned at the thought. "You're trying to cuddle the whole damned place, Anya. There's not enough of you to go around."

She laughed at that. "I don't have time to cuddle. But I do have time to arrange reasonable rooms for them. It will engender loyalty, Del-Rey, and a sense of thankfulness. There's nothing like a hot meal and a soft bed to remind a man of what he's fighting for."

He didn't like her seeming knowledge of men in general. She should only be aware of his needs, he thought with a hint of piqued pride. Dammit, she hadn't been cuddling him or taking care of his manly needs in the past eight months. Why worry about others? He was opening his lips to ask just that question.

"Hope and Faith have been forcing me along on their forays into managing Haven," she said then. "I know what I'm doing here."

He had no doubt of that and that wasn't his bitch. Simply put, he had no desire to share her time or her attention with the rest of the packs as a whole.

He was selfish that way, he admitted. Coyotes were bred to selfishness though, he assured himself; he had a reasonable excuse.

He was forming another protest when she began soaping, washing her body quickly, suds rolling over silken flesh, shimmering against her skin and holding his attention more surely than a weapon in his face would have.

Damn her. She had him tongue-tied. He'd be damned if he knew how to put his foot down here and settle the area of what her duties could or couldn't be. Cuddling other Coyotes, even impersonally, wasn't going to be one of her duties.

Unfortunately, before he managed to get a grip on his tongue or his wayward lusts, she was wrapping a thick towel around her and the soft peel sounded, announcing someone at the door.

"That's Ashley." She peeked around his shoulder to the monitor that looked out into the hall. "Get in the shower; she doesn't need to see your manly ass. She's ditzy enough. I don't need her getting worse."

He frowned back at her. Again. What did his ass have to do with Ashley's often apparent lack of common sense? Shaking his head, he moved into the shower though, determined to get a handle on his lusts so he could get a handle on his mate. He was starting to get the feeling that if he didn't do it quickly, there might be no hope for it.

◆　◆　◆

Anya gritted her teeth as she jerked the door open and pulled Ashley into the bedroom with a firm yank. Eyes wide, her lips open in a surprised little moue, the other woman stared back at Anya in confusion as she shoved an e-pad at her. "Just need you to sign at the X, Coya."

"He hasn't read the tabloid stories about that great and wonderful love affair we've had. Just exactly how much did the three of you pay those papers to plant those stories anyway?"

Ashley looked everywhere but at Anya for long seconds before pursing her lips and shuffling her feet. "Didn't have to pay them a damned thing," she muttered. "They just about orgasm when you give them dish. How did you know?"

"You might be subtle, but I've had a lot of years to figure the three of you out; I'm not stupid," she sniffed.

Ashley nodded slowly before peeking toward the shower. "Been a while since I've seen the alpha's bare ass. Can I sneak a peek? It's probably my birthday. It would make a great present."

Anya's eyes narrowed.

"Oookay," Ashley drawled as she shoved her hands into the back pockets of her jeans and rolled on the heels of the boots she wore. "So we heading to Haven in a bit?"

"In a bit," Anya ground out as she stalked to the bed and tossed the clothes on it.

She dried off quickly before pulling on panties and bra.

She quickly dressed in the snug black pants and gray sweater before sitting down and pulling on thin socks and shoving her feet into the black dressy boots.

"Hey, boss man." Ashley's voice piped up with amused appreciation. "Damn, look at those chest hairs. Damn sexy. Turn around and flash me some buns."

Anya's head whipped around to see *her mate*, striding from the shower room with nothing but a towel tucked at his waist.

"Watch the bleach in the hair dye, Ash." He grinned. "Maybe you should see Doc Armani. I think the animal genetics are recessing in favor of the human where you're concerned."

Ashley rolled her eyes. "You're just being mean to me, that's all," she griped good-naturedly before turning to Anya. "Sharone, Emma and I will be in the community room if you need us." She turned to go.

"No, you won't." Anya stopped her. "You're going to collect your co-conspirators and get the rest of the day's reports together for me. I'll go over them while Del-Rey and I are at Haven. Send them to my PDA and be ready to go whenever your alpha decides we're leaving."

"Perhaps your coya can tell you when we're leaving," Del-Rey said evenly. "She seems to have everything else planned out in her day."

"She's good like that. We taught her well, huh?" Ashley winked back at him before turning to Anya once again. "I'm on the run then, Coya. Files to PDA, prep for adventure in Haven. I wonder if Styx will try to pinch Emma's ass again. It's always fun watching her try to kick his bad ass."

Ashley turned and made a quick exit as Del-Rey growled low and warningly. The steel door slammed behind her, electronic locks engaging as Anya turned back to Del-Rey slowly.

"Brim should be here any minute," she told him. "He's been waiting for you to wake up."

"And will he have any reports for me?" Del-Rey asked her silkily.

"Most definitely," she promised. "And I should know, because I put most of them together. If you have any questions though, I'm sure he can answer them."

She watched as he dropped the towel and had to swallow tightly at the sight of his erection. Heaven help her, she wanted him again. She could feel the muscles between her thighs flexing, her panties dampening.

He looked back at her from beneath his lashes, his tongue touching his full lower lips, wicked lust filling his expression as he moved toward her.

"You dressed too fast." His voice deepened, his body tensed.

Anya shook her head, feeling her breathing escalate. She was still tender and she was heating up for him again.

"Um, I think . . ." She was saved from saying more when the security alert chimed again. "I think that's Brim. He has reports. And stuff." She backed to the door as he stilled, watching her with that predatory look of hunger. "Maybe you should get dressed." The security alert chimed again as the monitor showed Brim's impatient features. "Look, he's in a hurry."

Del-Rey's rumbled growl of discontent raced up her spine as he moved to the small dresser and yanked free a pair of white underwear before pulling them on. Jeans came next before he padded to the door, watching her intently, his gaze never leaving her until he opened the door.

Anya slid back to the side of the room and breathed out roughly as Brim stepped into the short hall.

"She's taking over. She's got the pack leaders panting under her thumb, and I'll be damned if she's not setting up quarters for the Coyotes heading here. She's even suggested hiring a damned cook, Del-Rey."

Anya bit her lip as she glanced over at her mate and smiled brightly.

She peeked her head around the edge of the wall and waved at Brim. "She's still here too."

He stopped in his tracks. He looked from Del-Rey to Anya, inhaled and shook his head wearily. "Hell, she even smells like you now. How the hell am I supposed to be on guard for her?"

"Why would you have to be on guard for me?" She opened her eyes innocently and stared from him to Del-Rey. "You're on guard for a threat, Brim, not a friend." She sighed with false hurt. "And here I thought we could be friends."

Brim looked at Del-Rey with curious pity as he jerked his head toward Anya. "What did you do, let her use Ashley's hair dye?"

Del-Rey's lips twitched, and Anya's flattened as her eyes narrowed back at the two men. "Remind me not to do you two any more favors," she muttered.

"I'll make a note to do that daily," Brim growled before turning back to Del-Rey. "We need to talk. Alone."

And Anya felt her heart sink. Here it was. The end. She hadn't stepped on anyone's toes but Brim's apparently, and he was second-in-command. He had the right to object to anything she had done. To cut her out of any meeting. To reduce her back to no more than caretaker when he and the alpha were absent.

"Alone doesn't work now, Brim."

Anya stared back at Del-Rey, shocked. "She's not just a mate; she's my coya. One whose responsibilities and duties will be discussed as time allows. Until then, she'll be present for all meetings. She can't make the decisions she needs to make should both of us be incapacitated for an extended length of time if she doesn't understand the decisions that need to be made."

He held his hand out to her. Such a simple gesture, but one that had her eyes dampening as she moved to him and laid her palm against his. She was his coya. He had made her status clear, and by accepting his hand, she accepted the position. And the man.

It was a step, she told herself. One step among many.

CHAPTER 16

Anya sat silently and watched through the two-way mirror into the interview room where the bartender was being questioned. His name was Ron Coley and he had been hired out of Dallas, Texas, for the party that had been meant to turn into a massacre. He didn't know who had hired him, just that he was to provide a distraction while the intended target was murdered by another member of the party. He'd had her picture, her name, nothing else.

"Who hired the staff for the party?" Del-Rey asked the Wolves' alpha leader, Wolfe Gunnar.

"A catering service out of Boulder," Wolfe murmured. "We screened the employees. He was listed as contract labor but his name and picture didn't raise any red flags."

Anya continued to watch as Jonas Wyatt, head of the Bureau of Breed Affairs, continued the, so far, civil interrogation.

"What about other employees?" Del-Rey asked. "Have they been detained or questioned?"

Wolfe gave a shake of his head. "Jonas has surveillance in place on the employees, but they were dismissed after formal questioning. Law enforcement in Boulder as well as in town are demanding answers to his detainment and inclusion in the interrogation. They were denied."

Breed Law gave the Breeds autonomy in matters of security and enforcement, to a point. Jonas's arrival made the detainment official; his questioning of the bartender was merely a formality. Notice of punishment, whether it was death or imprisonment, would go before the Bureau tribunal once he had his recommendations completed. That tribunal was twelve members, drawn from the four separate committees that made up the ruling body of the Breeds' society.

"Jonas isn't going to get the information we need here," Del-Rey murmured as they continued to watch. "The city council was in on this, Wolfe."

"We know that." Wolfe nodded as Dash Sinclair sat at his other side, eyes narrowed on the interrogation.

From where Anya sat at the side of the small room, she could see each man's expression. The alpha leader of the Felines had remained silent, but his gray eyes glittered with wrath as he watched.

"Don't imagine this will be overlooked, Del-Rey," Dash spoke up then, his voice cold as he watched the interrogation. "Your coya is no less important than the lupina or the prima. We won't let this go."

Anya stared at the Wolf Breed, father to the incredible young woman who had argued for Anya's separation from her mate. Cassandra Sinclair's father was strong, but that strength was tempered with compassion, though she could sense inside him an awareness that, sometimes, blood had to be spilled.

"We're going to have to deal with the town before we go much further," Del-Rey stated. "Raines is running unchecked. In the past days we've pulled in enough information on each man to fry them all. My soldiers have found evidence of the drug we're tracking in Raines's house as well as four other city council members' homes. The Coyote Cabinet is convening tonight to prepare a proposal on how to deal with this matter."

Wolfe glanced over at Anya. "I hear your coya ordered that move while you were healing. None of us considered the women's bags and wraps that were left there, and the fact that the council members in on this may have stolen those items knowing no one would be there to collect them. It was an ingenious plan."

Anya's gaze focused on Del-Rey. Male pride was a tenuous thing; she should have thought of that before having any military plan proposed. As Brim had told her while Del-Rey slept, she should have waited, presented it to the alpha then to the cabinet rather than ordering one of the soldiers to prepare the proposal.

Del-Rey's lips twitched in amusement as he glanced at her. "She ran Base with the same dedication and commitment that Hope and Faith showed her was her due as they overlooked Haven. I have you to thank for approving the time Hope gave her."

Anya sniffed at that. Damned manipulating Wolves and Coyotes. A woman didn't have a chance against them. They even taught their women how to scheme and manipulate. It should be illegal.

She turned her gaze back to the interrogation, barely restraining a yawn as Jonas Wyatt, the badass of the Bureau of Breed Affairs, asked the bartender again who his contact was and how he received his assignments.

"Man, look, I told you," the bartender sneered. "I ain't no damned Breed assassin, and if I was, I wouldn't get caught."

"You stink of blood, Mr. Coley," Jonas drawled. "I have your file; I know you better than you know yourself now. You're one of those disposable little peons. But even peons have information, and you *will* tell me what I want to know."

"Or what, you'll snarl and growl at me?" Ron leaned forward, his arms braced on the table as his pitted face screwed into lines of disgust. "Or you gonna bite me?"

Anya barely saw the blurred movement of Wyatt's arm. But a second later, claw marks, deep and bloody, swiped down the bartender's face, and he squealed like a gutted pig and jumped back as far as the chains would allow.

He stared into the two-way mirror, seeing the blood dripping down his face now, the marks that extended over his eye, then below the eye and down the cheek to his jaw.

Anya had never seen anything like it.

"Damn, Wyatt's getting pissed." The alpha pride leader

stepped closer to the window. They couldn't see Wyatt's face, only Coley's and his was filled with terror now.

"So, are you ready to answer my questions, Mr. Coley?" Jonas's voice was cool, unfazed as the bartender began to shake in reaction.

Coley's gaze jerked down to the table and he seemed to pale further. "That's not possible," he wheezed at whatever he was looking at.

"Look at me, Mr. Coley."

Coley's gaze jerked back to the Bureau director's face.

"Very good. You will stay on topic, or I'll make certain the next time I slice you that it goes to the bone, perhaps takes an eye. That's not a pleasant experience for the victim, and it's rather messy when I have to do it. I'd prefer not to have to resort to those means. Now, are you willing to give me the information I asked for?"

Coley swallowed tightly. "They said kill the girl. She was that Coyote's wife or something. Kill her and the Coyotes would start dropping out of that base. We might even be able to get a few back to the Council. I was supposed to have help. There were supposed to be six of us. We were to kill the women first as we made our way out of the ballroom. As many as we could, paying special attention to high-ranking wives or lovers. Kill them, they said, and you break the Breeds' backs. That's all I know."

"Who was your contact?"

Coley shuddered. "I got a kid." He lifted his eyes, his gaze tortured now.

"Why should I care about your kid?" Jonas asked coldly.

"She's only thirteen." He swallowed tightly. "I know things they didn't know I know. I heard about Breeds. You don't hurt kids, no matter what. You protect my kid, and I'll give you information I know you don't have."

"Such as?" Jonas asked him.

"The names of the city council members here and in Virginia near Sanctuary who are involved in a plan to take out the Breed leaders. And I got more. I got names of Breeds helping them." He was still staring at Jonas in horror. "God, man, stop doing that shit, please. I'll give you what you want, but you gotta protect my kid. I just do this for the money. That's all. Just for my little girl. I'll give it to you."

Anya stared into the room in horror. Her gaze flipped from the scene below to the cold, hard gazes of the Breeds watching as well.

"Gentlemen?" Callan Lyons turned to the others questioningly.

"His daughter is handicapped. Blind," Dash stated. "Thirteen years old."

"Call Wyatt back here," Wolfe said. "I suggest we send out a team, collect the girl and then requestion Coley. He's asked for asylum for his daughter of his own free will. Let's see what we can get."

They turned to Del-Rey.

"It's your decision to make, Del-Rey," Wolfe told him. "The hit was primarily against your coya."

He stared into the room as Anya watched him, knowing exactly what his decision would be. That knowledge was frightening; she knew, even before he spoke, the stance he would take.

"The child is the most innocent in this whole mess," he growled. "I'd like Brim on the team that goes after her. I'd suggest a team of enforcers only, fully sanctioned to retrieve the child at all costs. She'll be watched. They know we have the bartender; they may have already taken the child themselves to assure his silence."

Callan activated the speaker into the room. "Retrieval of minor child approved and sanctioned," he stated. "You have the full assurance of each alpha leader that her safety will be our top priority, Mr. Coley. As long as you cooperate." Callan winced at the last sentence, and the expression on each alpha's face assured Anya that no matter what Coley did, that child would never know anything but safety.

Children were the focal point of every Breed Anya had ever talked to. It didn't matter if it was a rare Breed child or a human child on the street. Breeds were always aware when a child was around and they were always protective of them.

Coley nodded as Jonas handed him a handkerchief. "For your face," the director stated, though Anya glimpsed the blood on his nails. "We'll get a doctor in here to look at those scratches. We wouldn't want your daughter frightened for you when she sees you."

Coley sniffed, almost in derision. "She's blind. She can't see them."

There were snorts from the alphas, contempt filling the sounds.

"Poor little girl," Jonas sighed. "She has a father that likely doesn't realize the talents she possesses. Why do you care if she's protected, Coley?"

Coley stared back at him in confusion. "Blind doesn't mean I don't love her," he stated harshly. "She's just a little scrap of a thing. You guys, you're at war with the world and you know it. You're adults. I don't want her hurt in it. She seems to think you bastards are cool or some shit."

Too bad the father didn't follow the daughter's instincts, Anya thought as she shifted in her chair, aware of a slow, building heat in her stomach, as well as the mass confusion that was filling her mind.

How had she known what Del-Rey's response would be? No one could have blamed him for wanting blood rather than to pledge his protection to a child whose father had targeted his mate and himself. Coyotes were sometimes more logical, less emotional than the other Breeds. They could be colder, less feeling. But Del-Rey's voice had deepened with his thoughts on the child's protection.

She clenched her teeth and rose to her feet as Del-Rey moved to counter her, standing as well and watching her with hooded black eyes.

He could smell the arousal, she knew. As it bloomed inside her, he would know that. A part of her was freaked out over that. Completely terrified that no emotion, no feeling, no hint of what she was doing or thinking could be hidden from him.

"Ladies' room." She swallowed tightly. "Should I meet you somewhere?"

"I'll await you here," he finally told her softly. "We'll return to Base soon."

Anya nodded before slipping quickly from the dark room.

In the hall, Sharone, Emma and Ashley surrounded her, their expressions concerned as they watched her.

"Wow, that heat stuff is bad again, huh?" Ashley stated.

"Shut up, Ash," Emma hissed.

"Well hell, it's not like she didn't know it was going to happen when she refused that last shot," Ashley retorted. "I mean, she's not going to, like, go to the tribunal again."

Silence followed Anya then.

"Will she?" Ashley finally whispered, almost horrified as Anya lifted her hand in a signal for the bodyguards to remain outside as she pushed into the ladies' room and moved to the sinks.

She turned on the cold water, stuck her wrists under the stream of water and laid her head against the cool mirror.

She'd tried to ignore the heat building in her. She should have had a few more hours before it became this bad. Before her breasts swelled, her nipples becoming so sensitive that her bra was painful. Her clit was so swollen, so engorged, it was touching the silk of her panties. Each move she made was agony now.

Part of her was cold, chilled to the bone and aching for Del-Rey to wrap his arms around her, and another part of her refused to ask, to beg for what she needed. She had made the first move. She had ignored Sofia's insults to begin with, then she had made the first move and initiated that sexual adventure they had taken. She was forcing back her pride and trying her damnedest to make up for the past months, but it wasn't easy.

And while that ice collected, she also burned. It was terrifying. Hot and cold at the same time. No, not just hot and cold. Icy and blazing. It was affecting her ability to think, to hold on to her composure and restrain herself.

Composure was everything. If she was going to take her place at Del-Rey's side, then she had to prove she was competent and able to make decisions when needed. If she let the mating heat do this to her, then she was going to fail.

She almost whimpered at the thought. The way she felt right now, she couldn't help him do anything but roll around in bed. What if they were attacked? What if Base was in danger? How could she do what she needed to do, and know Del-Rey had faith in her to do it while he and the other Coyote soldiers defended the inner caverns?

He wouldn't be able to trust her. She would be a liability again. Something to fuck. That would be the extent of her worth to him, and she couldn't bear that.

"Coya?"

She straightened quickly at the sound of Hope's soft voice

behind her. Dammit, she should have hidden herself before she gave into the ragged emotions filling her.

Straightening, she quickly shut off the water and pulled free several paper towels to dry her hands as she turned to face the other woman.

"Lupina." She smiled back at her friend. "Do you ever feel strange as hell when someone actually calls you by your name?"

Hope's lips tilted with charming amusement. "It's according to the person. I'm Hope to many, but I'm also lupina." She shrugged. "I'm the same person, no matter the name they use."

"True." Anya smiled as she inhaled slowly. "I'll get out of here for you." She headed for the door.

"I stopped in to talk to you." Hope's statement had her pausing.

"Why?"

"Brim informed our head of security, Jacob, that you were no longer on the hormone treatments, even those that still the more painful effects of the heat. You don't have to suffer, Anya. The base hormonal therapy controls the pain and conception until you're ready for it. What you were taking before controlled the heat itself. You have a choice in this."

Anya breathed in more roughly this time. "I made my choice, Hope," she whispered, staring back at the other woman intently. "It's just . . ." She swallowed tightly. "It caught me off guard."

Hope stared back at her in disbelief. "The heat is terrifying," she said. "I know well how bad it can be. Until Kiowa's mate, and then you to a greater extent, allowed our doctors and scientists to track how it works within our bodies, we knew that horror every month. We could feel it coming before we cycled, then as soon as that was over, we were hit with the mating heat cycle. And that doesn't even count that first month of mating, when it's like a vicious claw tearing at your mind and your body. It doesn't have to be that way."

Anya stared back at the lupina, the pain in her chest nearly brutal as she swallowed back her tears.

"What happens," she said, "if I'm not able to get to your doctor? If Base is on lockdown and we're under attack? If I don't know how to handle it, then how do I help Del-Rey? How do I keep from becoming something he has to protect above all things, rather than someone that can help him? You learned how to work through it; I've heard how well you take care of your duties, even in the middle of mating heat, while Haven is under attack. How you've worked within the secured areas to make certain everything is running smoothly while Wolfe and the others fought back the attacks. How can I do that, if I don't understand how to control my own body?"

"And being more than just a lover is very important to you, isn't it, Anya?" Hope said gently.

"Isn't it to you?" Anya asked, confused. "You were raised in Wolfe's labs. We've seen what awaits them if they're recaptured, what they came from. Protecting Del-Rey means everything to me."

"You didn't feel that way eight months ago," Hope pointed out.

Anya turned quickly away from her as she ran her hand over her forehead and propped the other on her hip.

"I couldn't think then," she whispered before turning back. "All I knew was the anger and this fear that only grew day by day. For three weeks I lived in this horrific little world where I couldn't control so much as a single thought." She shook her head as she shoved her hands in her pants pockets and stared around the feminine little outer room that led to the toilets beyond. "I fought through puberty to control my temper. Once I had it conquered, suddenly there was something worse that my body and mind could do to me, that I couldn't control." She blinked back her tears as she stared at the lupina. "And I blamed him, when I shouldn't have. I don't like that about myself, and I'm damned sure not going to let it happen again. But I'm also not going to let this reaction to what's going on between us make me a liability to him."

Hope tilted her head and stared back at her. "Because you used your logic, your composure, and the challenge you knew it would present to the Breed to draw his notice to you," she guessed. "Now you're terrified to let him see the real you."

Anya flinched. She stared back at the lupina miserably.

"I berate my bodyguards for maneuvering me into the position of coya. But I knew what they were doing, distantly, in a place where I didn't have to admit it to myself. I knew, because

I used the same wiles to make him notice me, to make him want me, to trust me. He thought he was choosing a woman that could help him establish his freedom. Instead he found he had married a child that couldn't accept the changes in her life. I don't want him to learn that she grew into a woman that can't even control her body long enough to make a rational decision."

Hope sighed and shook her head. "I can understand your reasons. But I can't countenance your suffering, Anya. There is help available."

"But it isn't help I can count on," she cried out, before capping her hand over her mouth. "God, listen to me. I can't even debate effectively. I won awards for my ability to debate when I was ten years old, and now I feel like sitting on the floor and sobbing like an infant."

It had been worse eight months before. A thousand times worse. Ten thousand times. She barely remembered those weeks, the fears driven so deep in her head that she couldn't escape them. She had sobbed then. Sometimes for hours, holding her hands over her mouth so the doctors and her bodyguards wouldn't hear her crying out Del-Rey's name.

And now she nearly had to bite her tongue to keep from screaming for him. She simply wanted him to hold her. Just that if nothing else, to do something to ease the ice inside her.

"I'm a mess, Hope," she whispered.

"Oh, Anya." The other woman's expression twisted in compassion. "You need to talk to him. Your body and your mind know what you need besides the sex. He could help you."

She shook her head as she forced back her tears and inhaled again, determined to get a handle on this.

"I have it. I'll be fine." She wasn't going to whine to Hope about the relationship that wasn't a relationship between her and her mate. That was her fault. She had to find a way to fix it.

"Yes, you will be," Hope said softly. "Tell you what, when you're feeling more up to it, give me a call. Prima Lyons and I were thinking spring would be a great time for your official ceremony. She's offered Sanctuary's grounds for the vows, or Haven's are available as well. I'd love it if you'd use Haven."

The ceremony. A wedding. She wondered if Del-Rey was looking for the rings. Of course, he wouldn't mention it to her if he was. He probably already had the damned things and wasn't even telling her.

"I would love Haven," Anya admitted. "And spring sounds wonderful. When Del-Rey finally gets around to mentioning it, I'll let him know."

Hope nodded. As she parted her lips to speak, the door pushed inward, leaving Del-Rey standing in the entrance, Wolfe behind him.

Del-Rey's gaze pinned her, his brows lowering into a frown before he held his hand out to her. "We're returning to Base," he told her. "The alphas will reconvene there later tonight to finish the plans that have to be made."

Because of her. Because her emotions were in such chaos that her mate knew he had to get her back to Base and fuck her. Her face flamed at the awareness that everyone else knew that as well.

"A temporary glitch." She breathed in deeply as she moved to him. "I'm fine."

"I know you're fine," he stated. "There's information we have to collect before we can finalize our plans. We're returning to Base."

Anya had a terrible feeling he was making excuses, but she couldn't ignore his outstretched hand. God, she needed the warmth of that much at least.

As he drew her from the room, he gave her more. His arm curved around her shoulders, drawing her to the warmth of his body and pushing back that chill that threatened to shake through her body and leave her trembling in weakness.

Anya kept her head high, her steps measured. Her expression composed. She leaned into him when he pulled her close, and wanted to close her eyes at the warmth that battled against the ice now. She hated herself for needing it. Hated herself for being unable to stand against the need for the pleasure that built like an agonizing fury inside her.

He hadn't needed a crutch in all these months. He had stood strong, battled against those that would have destroyed the Breeds, and kept his logic and his ability to lead intact.

Yet she couldn't. How much harder could it be for her than for him? The difference couldn't be such a wide divide, no matter what the doctors had told her. Male Breeds didn't allow experiments or tests. And they didn't take hormones to control that mating heat. How would the doctors know how much worse it was? Breed males were used to incredible pain. Pain a normal man could never survive.

As they stepped into the evening air, a military-enforced limo pulled up to the entrance to the underground bunker. Cavalier, one of Del-Rey's personal bodyguards, jumped from the passenger side and opened the door as Del-Rey pushed her inside.

And kept pushing her until she was flat on her back, the door slamming behind them as he came over her.

His lips were on hers immediately, the wicked, heated taste of his kiss infusing her senses, filling her with the hormone that had begun the mating heat to start with.

Her arms wrapped around his neck, holding on tight as her legs parted, allowing him to settle between them. They were fully clothed, but the warmth of his body seeped past the material, worked into her flesh, and she felt the warmth gathering rather than the ice.

She could feel the heat burrowing inside her, making the arousal deeper, stronger, but taking away the pain.

The arousal she could deal with. The aching need for his touch, she could handle that. But the pain, the ice, the confusion—she couldn't deal with it. The loss of complete control outside his arms? It terrified her.

The loss of control here, she could handle. The way his kiss filled her, stroked pleasure after pleasure across her lips, filled her senses with the feel and the taste of him as she moved against him. She was safe here. She didn't have to control this.

One hand held her head in place, the other touched her, pushed beneath her sweater, settled on her stomach, and the warmth there, it was incredible. It was like melting.

"When I needed your touch," he growled against her lips, "I grew icy here first." His hand pressed closer. "Cold until I felt my bones would shatter from the need of your warmth."

She gazed into his dark eyes, seeing the shadows of the pain and the cold he had endured for eight long months.

She shook her head, fighting the guilt that consumed her,

the evidence of what she had left him to suffer. Male Breeds, she had learned, had an instinctive, overriding need to protect their mates. To hold them against any pain, to shelter them as much as possible.

He kissed her again, sinking into her, his tongue stroking against hers as she whimpered against his lips in pleasure. He stroked her lips, licked at them. Each touch was filled with gentleness, with aching warmth as he held her against the effects of the mating heat that would have torn her apart.

His head lifted. "Look at me."

Her lashes lifted until she was staring into his determined, arrogant expression.

"Never do this again, Anya. Ever. When the mating heat builds, if we can't satisfy it at that moment, then my kiss will ease it until we can. No matter where we are, no matter what we're doing, my kiss is yours. My warmth is yours. Do you understand me?"

She had to battle her tears again, her guilt, the knowledge of what she had done to them both.

"Why?" she whispered. "Eight months, Del-Rey, and I stayed away. I made you suffer as well."

"And you think I should blame you? That I should revile you?" he asked as he pushed her hair tenderly back from her face. "Anya, do you think I don't know how terrified you were the day I took you and fired upon your family in front of your eyes? That I didn't know I had lied to you, betrayed the trust you gave me so freely? I never blamed you, little love. Myself yes. My own impatience and lust, most definitely. But never you."

"You should hate me." A tear slipped free. "You suffered and your base suffered; your people suffered because you weren't there. And you weren't there because of me."

"But you suffered because of me," he sighed. "And now it doesn't even matter if there is blame to be laid. You're in my arms. My mate. My coya. We'll struggle through this, Anya. Together."

His lips feathered over hers, parted them, slanted and took hers in a kiss that took her ability to debate, argue, agree or disagree. She sucked his tongue into her mouth, teased him, tempted him.

Her hips lifted, her sex rubbed against the hard ridge of his cock, her clit gloried in the heat racing between their bodies now.

Her hands moved, dragging down his arms, pushing beneath them to pull his shirt from his jeans and burrow beneath the cloth to the hard, heated flesh beyond.

Oh God, she loved the feel of him. She wanted to wrap him around her like a blanket and hold on to his warmth forever. It seared into her palms as his kiss seeped into her soul and left her quivering with the sensations building inside her.

How she had ached over the months, and refused to admit it. How she had worried, fought with herself, and fought the need that flowed between them, even before she had known about the mating heat. He was a part of her. And he had been a part of her since the moment his black eyes had met hers when she had been no more than sixteen.

Before they touched. Before that first kiss. Before the anger and the fear and the realization of the world she was entering when she entered Del-Rey's arms.

"I need to fuck you," he growled as his lips lifted from hers and traveled to her jaw, her neck. "I need to be inside you, Anya. So deep, so tight that there is no you, no me. Just this."

His fingers flipped over the closure of her pants, pulled the zipper loose. "I sat in that fucking dark room smelling your need for me and thought I'd burn out of control before I managed to touch you. Imagining how wet you were. You've always been wet for me, Anya. Always. Before the heat, before you were even old enough for me to touch, you've been wet for me."

A ragged cry left her lips as his finger brushed the saturated curls between her thighs.

"So wet your pussy clings to the silk of your panties." He nipped her jaw, then licked the little wound. "Your juices cling to my tongue the same way. Loving my touch. You love my touch, Anya."

"I love your touch," she gasped, her hips lifting into his palm as he covered it, cupped it. "Oh God, Del-Rey, I've always loved your touch."

"I love your touch," he growled. "I ache for it, dream of it.

I wake drenched in sweat yet freezing from the need of your warmth."

Two fingers curled, parted the swollen folds between her thighs and pressed, slowly, almost teasingly, into the aching depths of her body.

It was so good. So brutally good Anya jerked against him, his name a gasp on her lips as she felt her internal muscles clenching around his fingers. The heated warmth of her juices flowed around his fingers, slickening them, easing his way as he thrust them slowly inside her.

"I ached for this," he whispered at her ear, then slid his teeth down her neck. "The feel of you, the taste of you. Your sweet pussy opening for my cock, gripping me and pulling me in as your arms and your kiss hold me closer to you. I would have died for just one more night in your arms, my coya."

"Don't die," she moaned. "Just touch me, Del-Rey. Don't stop touching me."

Self-control wasn't important here, in his arms. There was no need to fight for lucidity. He could think for both of them here, because Anya knew she didn't have a hope of saving a single thought in her head.

She arched her neck as he dragged the loose neckline of her sweater to the side, found the mark he had left on her neck and then, amazingly, he lapped at it. His tongue licked with slow, sensual strokes over the wound that had become so incredibly sensitive to the lightest stroke that she felt her vagina flutter, then convulse around his fingers.

This shouldn't be possible. It shouldn't be so sensual, so erotic that she wanted nothing more than to be stripped bare before him and feel him stroking over every inch of her flesh.

"I don't know how to handle this." She arched, shuddered in his arms. "I don't know how to think, Del-Rey."

"Don't think, sweetheart," he groaned against the mark he had left on her, before kissing it gently. "Just feel. Feel me. This is all you need to do. I'll take care of everything else."

She had to trust him, because she couldn't control this. She didn't want to fight it, not anymore. She didn't want the hormone treatments blocking so much as a single sensation or a second of the need. She wanted it all. He had accepted it all, suffered for it, given her the freedom and the time she had needed to realize what she wanted, what she ached for. She could do nothing but let her senses fly and give herself into the keeping of the man she had chosen years before as her own.

She arched into the thrust of his fingers, her cries shattering the space around her as she fought not to beg for him to take her now, at this second.

They couldn't be far from Base. He would have to stop. It couldn't last much longer.

"God, you make me lose my head." He breathed out roughly, his head lifted despite her protests, his gaze narrowed on the window. "Come, sweet." His hand slid slowly from her saturated flesh.

"Not yet," she whimpered. "Don't stop yet."

"Just for a bit." His lips lowered to hers, brushed against them, and he was kissing her again, slowly, deeply. His tongue pushed against hers, encouraging her to suckle at it as he fixed her pants, her sweater.

He pulled her hands from his flesh, holding them above her head with one of his as the other smoothed down her side, gripped her hip.

When he lifted his head, she forced her eyes to open, to stare back at him.

"When you need me, come to me, Anya. No matter where I am, no matter what I'm doing. Suffer in silence again, and I'll make certain you understand clearly that it will not be permitted."

Her lips parted in surprise at the dominant, dominating tone of his voice.

"Getting awful bossy, aren't you, Coyote man?" She had to curl her fingers against the seat to keep from dragging him to her once again.

"I'm weak where you're concerned, Mate," he told her gently, but the tone didn't disguise the pure power beneath it. "But don't tempt me in matters of your safety or where your well-being is concerned. Be stubborn, I can deal with that. Take charge in the areas that are your own, that I can handle. Argue with me when you need to, yell at me if you must. But don't endanger yourself or allow something I can fix to harm you. That I won't tolerate."

"Is there a rule book?" She snorted as he helped her sit up.

"Or do I get to just stumble around on my own and mess up whenever?"

"Mess up whenever." He grinned. "I'll greatly enjoy showing you the error of your ways."

Charm, seductive humor. She loved his smile. The sheer wicked devilry in it, the warmth she had always glimpsed now flaring into heat.

"We're here," he told her as the limo pulled into the front of the caverns.

"We're going to clash soon," she warned him. "Very soon."

A frown tugged at his brow, though he nodded somberly.

"Yes, I know this, Coya. But know, even when we clash, you're my coya. And I'll ensure, even if it chances your wrath, that you're always safe. Now come." He gripped her hand as the limo door opened. "Let's go find our room. I have a need for your touch and your taste. And I'll wait no longer to ease that need."

· CHAPTER 17 ·

He didn't wait. Anya was rushed into the base, Del-Rey's arm still wrapped around her, and pulled through the tunnels until they were locked into their room.

She found herself against the wall within seconds, his lips on hers, his tongue pushing into her mouth again. The hormonal release from the glands beneath his tongue seemed spicier, more addictive than ever before.

She sucked at the taste, licked against his tongue and heard his rumbled growl as she tore at the buttons of his shirt and pushed the material from his broad shoulders.

"I love your body," she panted as his lips tore from hers and he shrugged the shirt free. "So hard and muscular." She ran her hands over his shoulders and wanted to whimper at the heat beneath his flesh. "And so warm. Always so warm. I need your heat, Del-Rey."

She needed *him*. How had she managed to stay away from him all those months? Denying herself the ultimate pleasure of just touching him, watching him move, or hearing his dark, rough voice.

"It's yours." His hands pushed beneath her sweater, lifting the material until he revealed the delicate lace of her bra.

He paused. Anya felt her breath hitch as his hands lifted to her breasts, his fingers curving around the mounds as he palmed them with delicious greed. The look on his face as he touched her was pure male hunger. Part lust, and part more. Something deeper, something that touched the feminine part of her soul and made her weaker, made her ache for more. It made her welcome the excruciating arousal that tormented her body, because she could see his nostrils flare, see him breathing her in as his hands flexed on her aching breasts.

"God, I love the scent of you wanting me," he groaned, reflecting her thoughts as his lips lowered to the mounds rising above the lace cups.

Anya shivered as he licked over them. His tongue rasped her sensitive flesh, coming incredibly close to the hardened tips of her nipples.

"Are you going to torture me?" She gasped.

"I'm going to torture both of us." A flush mantled his cheekbones as he licked over the lace that covered her nipples. "Because I need to taste you, Anya. I need to feel you against me, so sweet and warm. Lifting to me, needing me, Anya. Just need me."

And she did need him. She didn't have the option of blaming it on the mating heat. She had wanted him before he ever kissed her. She had wanted him after the hormone therapy had controlled the painful spasms of need. There hadn't been a time since she was sixteen that she hadn't wanted him.

Beneath her hands his flesh was heated and solid. Beneath his lips sensation sizzled against her flesh.

"Take this off." He pushed at her sweater as his tongue traveled into the valley between her breasts.

Her arms lifted to allow him to push the material over her head. No sooner had it dropped to the floor than his hands were at the waistband of her pants, flipping open the closure and lowering the zipper.

Mesmerized by the pleasure on his face, by the pleasure winging through her, she could do nothing but watch his expression as his hand slid past the material, beneath her panties and into the swollen, slick folds of her sex.

Her head fell back to the stone wall as her breath locked in her throat. Pleasure, ecstasy—it winged through her with such sensual promise that there was nothing left but to hold on to him as he stroked her. Caressed her.

"I need you naked," he growled against the rise of one breast, which he licked sensually. "Can you toe the boots off?"

The boots? She shook her head in confusion. What boots? She didn't care about the damned boots, not with his fingers slipping into the desperate, aching heat between her thighs.

His head lifted, fingers moving slowly, so slowly before stilling altogether. Anya's hips pressed into the touch, arching against his palm as she gazed back at him in desperate need.

"Toe the boots off." A grin tugged at his lips as the savage features of his face softened with sensual amusement. "Come on, baby. One foot at a time."

She whimpered in need, her foot reaching out for his.

"Ah, baby. Your boots," he groaned, his lips feathering over hers. "Toe your boots off."

Oh yeah. Her boots.

She lowered one hand, knee bending, fingers finding the zipper at the side of her low boot before fumbling and pushing one free of her foot. She repeated with the other foot until her toes were curling with the pleasure of his renewed, gentle strokes into the folds he possessed.

With his other hand he pushed the pants over her hips, dragging her panties with them as he went to his knees before her.

"Del-Rey, the bed," she gasped.

"Fuck the bed." His voice rasped along her nerve endings as pleasure quaked through her body. "I need to taste you now, Anya. My tongue in your sweet pussy." His lips feathered over the curls between her thighs. "So sweet and soft. So damned good."

Her thighs parted beneath the guiding force of his hands. Her fingers curled into the thick, coarse strands of his dark blond hair and she watched. Watched as his tongue licked through the saturated slit, ran around her clit and sucked the last of any chance of control from her sensation-ridden body.

Del-Rey licked, stroked, tasted. His tongue ravaged her flesh, left her shaking, shuddering as she fought to keep her knees locked, her body pressed against the wall.

"I'm going to fall," she cried.

"I'll hold you, baby." Sexy, wicked, an inhumanly erotic growl breathed against her clit.

She nearly came. Pulses of extreme pleasure rippled through her body at the sight, the sound, the touch.

"So close," he crooned in that sensual, graveled tone. "I can smell how close you are, Anya. Are you going to come for me, baby?"

She breathed in roughly, her breath hissing between her teeth as his tongue circled her clit again, before slipping it in and sucking it with deliberate, exquisite draws of his mouth.

There could be no pleasure greater than this. Her sensitive flesh rippled with the agonizing sensitivity. She could feel it, racing through her blood, traveling through her nerve endings and ricocheting through every cell of her body.

Just from the suckling of his mouth at her clit. His hands on her hips, holding her in place. The feel of his hair beneath her fingers. Electrical pulses of pleasure sizzled through her. She felt tight. She felt feminine and weak beneath his touch, beneath the need tearing through her.

"Mmm. So good," he crooned, licking again rather than suckling her clit to orgasm as she needed.

Her flesh was so sensitive she could feel the perspiration beaded on it. The brush of his hair against her stomach as he drew her clit into his mouth once again. And this time, he meant business.

His tongue flicked over the tender bud, his mouth sucked it, until she went to her tiptoes in a cataclysm of pleasure so desperate, so deep that nothing emerged as her lips opened in a soundless scream.

She lost the strength in her legs, and he held her up. She lost the will to stand on her own. Her head tipped back, her hips moving until the exploding little bud was deeper in his mouth, his lips rubbing against the sensitive folds and the world dissolving around her.

"Mine." Her hands slid from his hair to his shoulders, her upper body collapsing over him as her nails raked along his back.

He caught her, lifting her into his arms with a growl of triumph, and bore her to the bed.

She bounced against the mattress, rolling and coming to her knees. As he moved to come over her, she was waiting for him. She pushed at his shoulders.

"My turn."

She was weak from the pulses of ecstasy racing through her, and yet the need, the hunger that had nothing to do with the mating heat, flowed through her now.

"Mine," she repeated, lost in emotion and possessiveness, lost in the sheer perfection of his body, his touch, and the rising natural progression of what she had known was coming since she was sixteen years old.

And he went down for her. Naked, though she couldn't remember when he had undressed, splaying out on his back, those wicked black eyes watching her, the hint of blue stronger now, reflecting in the lights that gleamed from within the wall.

Moving over him her lips covered his, took the kiss she needed, sucking his tongue into her mouth to take the last of the spicy taste from the mating glands beneath it.

She flowed over him, lips moving from his, her tongue licking over his flesh, her teeth nipping at the heavy vein in his throat as his neck arched.

"Yours." The animalistic sound empowered her, sent a fierce rush of adrenaline and sensation burning through her.

Because he was hers. Her mate. Her lover. Her Del-Rey.

Her lips coursed over his shoulder. Her tongue licked over his collarbone, her taste buds going wild at the heady flavor of him. Perspiration and male excitement. It was rich, spicy, earthy. And she was addicted.

She licked at the flat, hard male nipples and felt him arch to her, felt his hands grip the thick strands of her hair, heard his snarl of impatience and let a smile curl her lips as she lifted her eyes and licked her way down his stomach.

"Coya," he groaned. "My coya."

"Your coya." It was a promise, a vow.

His teeth clenched, the sight of the savage, curved canines at the side of his mouth only intensifying the visual pleasure.

She licked, lowered herself, sprawled between his thighs and let a hungry moan pass her lips. His cock stretched from between his thighs to his lower abdomen, thick and powerful, engorged and iron-hard.

The heavy crown was flushed, beaded and damp with pre-cum, awaiting her tongue. She licked over it, and approved his taste with heavy sounds of delicious pleasure. She licked down the shaft, ignoring the hands in her hair, urging her to return to the sensitive crest. She licked down to the tight, throbbing sac below the shaft, where she played.

Running her tongue over the smooth, hairless flesh she dampened it, then parted her lips and sucked delicately at first one side, then the other. His groans, the low, graveled growls, filled the room.

"My alpha," she whispered as she moved back up the wide shaft. "My mate."

And she accepted. There was no escape, because in her heart, she had no desire to escape. In her heart, where she had hid the dreams, the memories, the wants and the pain of loss, he had always been hers.

"Yours," he snarled. "Now fuck me. Lose your control, Anya, because God help us if I lose mine."

She smiled, licked over his cock head, then drew it into her mouth.

Yes, that was what she wanted. No control. Not his, not hers. Just them, together, flying out of control and loving every minute of it.

"Anya, don't tempt this," he ordered, commanded. He was so good with that commanding tone that she shivered at the promise of the retribution his gaze held.

She sucked him into her mouth, flattened her tongue and rubbed, sucked, milked the sensitive crest with her mouth. She lifted her lips slowly, let him watch as her tongue swirled over the head and she watched his eyes. She watched the wildness fill them, felt it fill her.

She had been born for this. Born to touch this man, to steal his control, to lose hers. Born to be his mate.

"No, Anya." His hands pulled harder at her hair. When that didn't work, they pressed under her arms, lifting her until she let her teeth bear down on the tight flesh.

He paused, stared down at her, his expression agonized.

"It will be like the first time," he snarled. "Do you hear me? Like the animal I am."

No, like the man he was, the glorious male creature that

filled her fantasies and sent a rush of need through her, no matter the circumstances.

She let her lips grip him tighter, not in pain, but in warning,
until his hands moved from her and gripped the sheets beneath
him instead. His eyes glowed with acceptance, and with concern. His expression was savage, honed, flushed with lust.

She sucked him deeper, though the width of his cock made
it impossible to accept much more than the brutally flared crest
into her mouth.

He was delicious. A small spurt of pre-cum filled her mouth,
and she relished it. Minutes later another. Del-Rey's neck was
arched, the veins standing out clearly on it, just as they did on
his cock.

Another spurt, and she had only seconds to enjoy that taste
before he moved. There was no chance to react before he was
dragging her up his body, beginning to turn.

Her thighs clamped on his, her hips lowered, the slick, wet
folds of her sex rubbing against the hardened shaft as he suddenly stilled.

The warning growl that filled the air had her smiling as she
pressed her palms flat against his chest, slid her hips up until
the tip of his cock was poised at the entrance to the desperate,
hungry depths of her body.

"I take you," she whispered. "For my mate."

She pressed down, a whimper of ecstasy leaving her throat
as the head pressed inside her, stretched her, opened her.

"My coya!" It was a snarl, a demand. His hands gripped her
hips, his thighs bunched, and Anya screamed with the pleasure
as he thrust inside her. Heavy, hard undulations of his hips had
him buried inside her in three hard strokes, and he didn't stop.

This was supposed to be her ride, she thought hazily. And
she was riding, tossing, writhing above him as he lost the control she had felt chaining him before and gave her all of himself. Not just every hard inch of his cock, but his control, his
sense of self, and the power of his hunger.

The heavy lunges burrowing into her stroked nerve endings
so violently sensitive that she knew she wouldn't last long. She
could feel the pleasure tightening, building. She rocked against
him as he stroked into her, shafting her forcefully, groaning her
name, his hands holding her in place as she tipped her head

back and screamed his name and rapture imploded inside her, then exploded in a brilliant, outward force that had her tightening further on him, her nails digging into his hard chest, her pleasure a creature tearing from her body.

No sooner did it ease than Del-Rey stiffened beneath her and it began again. She felt him this time though, the fierce swelling in the center of his cock, pressing the convulsive tightness of her muscles apart, revealing yet more nerve endings, more pleasure receptors, and sending them into ecstasy with the fierce pulsing throb of the knot that now anchored him inside her.

With each spurt of cum that filled her, the thick swelling rippled and pulsed against her, sending her shaking and shuddering into yet more pleasure. It was never ending. An orgasm that eased only to explode inside her again, leaving her shaking, shuddering, and collapsed upon his chest long before it finished.

Del-Rey blinked up at the ceiling long, long minutes later, still fighting to breathe as the last pulse of release tore from his body and filled the depths of the too snug, too hot silken flesh gripping his cock. Her pussy was sheer rapture. It was pleasure that went so beyond pleasure that there was no way to put a name to it. And just as he had the first time he had taken her, he had lost control within her.

There was blood on her shoulder where he had bit her again. He lowered his head and licked at the wound he knew would never fully heal. Not simply because he couldn't keep from biting her when he took her, but because the hormones always filled that little spot, kept it sensitive, kept it ready for the pleasure he would bring her from his lips and tongue against it.

As he held her tight against his chest, his arms wrapped snuggly around her, he felt the fierce, secondary swelling of his cock pulse again, shuddering through him as she trembled in response and a low, broken moan came from her lips.

What the hell had she done to him? Surely something he had never known before. Never, even that first time that he had taken her, had he known this depth of satiation, this satisfaction that seemed to echo through every cell of his body.

Hell, a man, or a Breed, should never know this soul-deep sense of belonging. Because it was something he would always remember in battle, something he would always know waited to be snatched from his hands by fate or the cruelties of man. Losing this could destroy him. He would be no more than a broken shell of a man, and surviving that wouldn't be possible.

He would follow her into death, Del-Rey thought. He'd be of no use to his people if he lost her, because nothing mattered as much to him as this one woman.

Love. He scoffed at the word. This wasn't love. Love was his joy of a good steak, a hot bath. It was breathing in the mountain air and watching the mists in the valley. What he felt for this woman in his arms, this wasn't love. It was something he didn't have a name for, or a way to express. She was his freedom. She was becoming an extension to his soul.

"I have to move sometime this year," she mumbled against his chest, sweat-dampened and still breathing hard.

"In a minute," he promised, still locked inside her, feeling the fierce grip and rippling response in the muscles surrounding his cock.

"'Kay," she muttered drowsily. "But lying on your ass all day isn't going to get anything done."

There was the lightest thread of amusement in her voice, a teasing vein that he remembered often filled her eyes with impish delight. She had always teased him, flirted, made it damned near impossible to resist her.

"I could lie on your ass for a while," he chuckled as he felt the knot anchoring him inside her finally begin easing.

He grimaced at the sensation, another lingering pleasure that he didn't want to lose. He wanted to stay like this forever, buried inside his woman, his mate, knowing she was forever safe.

A long, low moan left her lips as the swelling finally eased, releasing them from the pleasure that seemed never ending.

Del-Rey lifted her from him, his body tightening as his semi-hard cock eased from her snug grip and she collapsed to the bed beside him.

Letting her go wasn't an option though. He turned and pulled her to his chest, wrapping his arms around her and holding her close as he kissed the top of her head.

"Will the heat ease for you soon?" he asked her then, knowing that for Wolf and Feline mates after the initial four- to six-week cycle of the heat, it would then ease and come back for only seven to ten days per month. It was when the females were most fertile and the chances of conception greater.

She lifted her shoulder in a light shrug. "I dunno," she mumbled. "I was different. Kinda."

"How were you different?" he asked her as he eased back enough to stare into her drowsy expression.

Her brows creased thoughtfully. "Several years ago, the Coyote, Kiowa Bear, mated with the then U.S. president's daughter. They learned then why the Wolves and Coyotes take so long to conceive. There's an additional hormone the males carry that continues to attempt to block conception, even as the other hormones work to create it. Then with Aiden's mate, Charity, they've only just been able to figure out why she conceived, based on the experiments the Council scientists did on her at the labs where she was held for a number of years. The hormone works to ready the ovaries and change the egg being prepared to drop, to ensure its compatibility with the Wolf or Coyote sperm. It gets complicated sometimes, the way the hormones work. That's why each hormonal therapy has to be different. Dr. Armani begins with a base, a therapy that's compatible across the board, then she has to add to it depending on the individual female and her heat."

"So each mating is different?" he asked as she settled more comfortably against him.

"Very much so." Anya nodded. "She has a lot of trouble keeping mine within an acceptable limit. For the first few months, the hormones she was giving me pretty much wiped out all emotion but kept me on the verge of panic. I couldn't function. The same hormone didn't affect the Wolf mates at all."

His frown deepened. "When Dr. Armani came to the caves that first time, she said I was the first Coyote to mate. Kiowa Bear is Coyote as well, yet he was mating well before that."

"Kiowa is what they call a hybrid. His mother was one of the women the Council kidnapped and tried to use for artificial insemination. It didn't work on her. Before she left those labs, one of her Coyote guards mated her, then released her. Kiowa was conceived and born naturally, and as I understand it, that creates a shift in the DNA that doesn't come about otherwise.

But there are other anomalies with him as well. His genetics are actually closer to the Wolf than the Coyote."

"Has Dr. Armani learned the differences in our mating yet?" he asked her.

Anya snorted at that as she pulled from him and rose from the bed. "Not hardly. Just as with repairing your wounded bodies, Coyote genetics and Wolf genetics are just separate enough to make it dangerous." She glared down at him then. "We need our own medical personnel."

"There's some still living?" he asked, surprised. "What the Council hasn't killed, I'm certain we must have. I told you, find one and I'll consider it." It had been a matter of pride for years to destroy those capable of creating more Coyote Breeds. If the Council left any for them to kill.

"If you can hide from the Council all those years, then I bet there are doctors as well as scientists that have managed to do the same," she informed him. "I'll find them."

His brow arched. The tone of her voice was a warning itself.

"And how do you think you'll do this?" he asked her silkily.

She was scheming. He had known Anya long enough to know when her brain was turning over a problem and working it out in a manner he was certain to disagree with.

"I have my own contacts." She shrugged as she pulled his shirt from the floor and pushed her arms through the sleeves.

Why it gave him a surge of satisfaction to see her wrapping his clothing around her much smaller frame, he couldn't say.

"You'll not be making contacts, Anya," he told her firmly. "I won't have you risking your life in that manner. If there are any doctors left, then they aren't ones we could trust anyway."

"What about Dr. Armani?" She propped her hands on her hips as she stared at him, the light of battle waging in her eyes. "She's human and she's dedicated her life to the Breeds she cares for. What about the doctors that work under her? They could be in the general public, probably making a hell of a lot more money than they are here. But they're here, and they're loyal."

"What about the two assistants—Breeds, Anya—who betrayed Sanctuary?" he asked her. "They drugged Dr. Morrey, nearly killed her, and were attempting to sell the secret of mating heat to a pharmaceutical and research facility that likely even now has doctors and scientists experimenting on Breeds to create a drug that controls us. Or, God forbid, something that can be used on humans. What about them?"

"What about Coyotes who have a code of honor?" she asked then. "Who have a soul when they were created to have none? What about them, Del-Rey?"

He frowned, knowing she was talking about his packs, but her point eluded him.

"What about them?"

"Others took a chance on you. There are good doctors, good scientists who have escaped the Council, who know the Coyote physiology and would give their eyeteeth to learn as much as they could within normal confines. To treat them, to heal them, and to protect their strengths and weaknesses. You find them, you choose the ones you have the best chance of trusting, and you use them. Keep up the way we're going here at Base, and eventually, we're going to lose our people because Dr. Armani can't treat them properly."

"Or we'll lose them because we're betrayed by the very people we've brought in to treat us," he bit out. "That's not acceptable to me, Anya. Dr. Armani will figure this out in time."

"If Nikki lives to be three hundred, she won't figure out the Wolves, let along the Coyotes," she argued back. "I have the contacts, Del-Rey. I can find acceptable candidates."

"No."

She gaped back at him. His expression had shifted from lazy satisfaction to full, dominant refusal.

"What do you mean 'no'? This isn't a no equation. It's something we have no choice but to consider."

"I've made it a no equation," he informed her arrogantly. "The risks are unacceptable."

"We need to discuss this, Del-Rey," she told him carefully. "You can't just brush the subject aside with an arrogant little refusal."

"That's exactly what I've done," he told her as he turned and headed to the showers. "This isn't up for debate, and it isn't arguable. I won't take that risk with my men or with you. Armani will learn enough."

"And if we have children?" She threw out a question that had been haunting her. "Will a doctor that knows nothing about your unique genetics be good enough to treat our child if he's wounded or sick? Will 'good enough' be enough for you then?"

He gave her a shuttered look before turning and jerking clean clothes from a dresser and striding into the shower room without an answer.

Anya bit off a curse, staring at the doorway and trying to figure this one out. She had seen over the months the complications that could arise in Haven, just with the Wolves and their unique DNA. Fevers from nowhere that Dr. Armani had to track down and find a way to treat. Wounds that were simple and should have been easily fixed that suddenly the Wolf genetics fought against. It was a crapshoot, Armani had told her, and the additional pressure of treating the Coyotes, a species just different enough to change all the rules, was driving the doctor to long hours and less and less sleep.

It couldn't continue.

But it seemed that getting Del-Rey to understand the problems they were facing wasn't going to be easy either.

CHAPTER 18

"You asked to see me, Coya?" Brim stepped into Anya's office, formerly her bedroom, three days later, his expression bland, his blue gray gaze quizzical.

Anya stood to the side of her desk and watched the Breed move with lethal grace into the room. Anyone daring to challenge this man could be in for a world of hurt, and she knew it.

She considered the best way to approach the problem she was facing.

"I'd like to apologize, Coya," he suddenly said.

Anya blinked back at him in surprise.

"For what?"

"You could have told Del-Rey that I had allowed Sofia into his room while he was healing. We would have fought. Fighting the alpha isn't always wise." His lips quirked as though amused by some thought.

She inhaled slowly. "Crying to Del-Rey would have accomplished very little in a meaningful way," she finally said. "This is something you and I need to discuss."

Arrogance was a natural part of him, and Anya was smart enough, intuitive enough, to know that, coya or not, she wouldn't be ordering him to do anything.

"I agree." Brim nodded. "It's nothing you have to worry about happening again. I promise you."

She tilted her head to the side and narrowed her eyes on him. "Why did it happen to begin with?"

His lips quirked. "Something or someone needed to piss you off enough to take what was yours. I convinced Del-Rey to give her asylum to achieve that end."

Surprise, surprise. Another Coyote Breed manipulating her. She was going to get pissed off over this soon.

"Brim, I would hate to ever have to consider you my enemy," she finally said quietly, staring back at him with somber determination. "But manipulate me again, in any matter, and that's the path we'll take. Do we understand each other?"

A hint of surprise filled his eyes. "You're not going to throw anything at me then?"

She shook her head, a smile trying to tug at her lips. "I reserve that for your alpha alone."

He nodded slowly. "Understood, Coya. No further manipulations."

"And when you find yourself in mating heat, watch out for me," she informed him in all seriousness. "Ashley and I have a plan. We're going to show you how to manipulate properly. Doesn't that suck for you?"

A hint of worry touched his gaze as he grimaced tightly. "I think I'd prefer to fight the alpha."

"Too bad. I like getting even much better." She moved behind her desk then. "I'd like your estimation of Sofia. A risk estimate."

His brows arched as he eased toward the chairs that sat in front of her desk and sat down. "In what way?"

"The attacks began when she arrived. I knew Sofia in the labs; my first thought is that she's not behind them. But I'd like to know what you think."

He was thoughtful for long moments. "I'm not ruling anyone out. I'm investigating the attack on you and your bodyguards while in the mountains, as well as the attack in town. It's clear we have a leak. I'm just not convinced Sofia is that leak."

"Because she helped you over the years?"

"That," he agreed, "but there's more to it. Sofia has always worked hard toward the rescues and used her position in the

Council's lower ranks to the utmost advantage. I can't see her betraying us now."

"Even if she's losing something she may have believed was hers?"

"The alpha?" Brim asked, shaking his head. "She's always known better. There was nothing serious on either end when it came to them. They're friends."

Anya nodded. "Do you have any ideas why Del-Rey has suddenly been targeted?"

"Strength," Brim stated. "Our team has been investigating those drugs, and someone could have learned of that investigation or what we found. It could also be something as simple as an attempt to weaken Haven. We've made a difference in their security. We've also been establishing a minor presence in town. Our men go to the bars there, while the Wolves pretty much stay more to their own packs. I'm looking into several areas."

"Any headway?"

"You would have been one of the first to know if I had anything yet," he promised her. "We brought in Coley's daughter last night and should be requestioning him within a day or so. Hopefully we'll have more then."

Anya nodded again. "I appreciate you sharing this information with me."

"Did you ask Del-Rey?" he asked her then. "I'm sure he would keep you apprised of the investigation if you asked him."

"He would have," she admitted. "But I wanted to discuss Sofia with you as well."

"And you'd prefer not to allow emotion to become involved in the discussion." He nodded as he rose to his feet. "I understand, Coya. But rest easy, you can place that responsibility on my shoulders."

She watched as he left the office, closing the door behind him before she turned to the computer monitor and the small light blinking in the lower corner.

She pressed the hidden button that revealed the digital keyboard inset in the desk and tapped another button to bring up the conversation box before sliding it into an encryption program her father had helped her to create.

We're worried about you, the message stated. *Your father is well?*

Father is well, she answered. *And he sends his regards.*

How did you find us? The question came quickly. *We've stayed well hidden.*

We're friends, Anya typed. *I used what I knew. Information I knew others wouldn't have.*

Doctors Chernov and Sobolova had hidden themselves well. But Anya knew the forums they inhabited online. It had taken her a few days, but she had finally managed to locate their on-line identities.

How may we help you?

Anya considered that question carefully. She had to be careful; if she had found this information, then others could as well, and if her encryption was cracked, then she could endanger them all.

I would like to meet, Anya typed.

Here or there?

Near.

The cursor blinked longingly for several seconds.

Is the welcome sign up or is it open season?

Unfortunately, it could still be open season without the answers I need first. I ask that you use caution but make the trip with all haste.

For you.

The answer had her closing in momentary relief. *This line is not always safe*, she typed. *Please contact secondary source, which will direct you from here on out.*

We appreciate your discretion in first contact. We hope to see you soon. The message ended and the screen disconnected as Anya closed the keyboard and breathed out roughly.

She could be making a mistake. She could be risking Del-Rey's rage, she knew. Hopefully, she wasn't risking the lives of friends as well.

Dr. Chernov and Dr. Sobolova were dedicated scientists and geneticists. Their work in the labs after they took over had been rumored to be some of the most advanced in understanding the Coyote genetics and many of the Breed's strengths and weaknesses.

Several of the Coyote Breeds coming in from the Middle East had been secretly trained in the psychology of the Coyotes as well as advanced medicines. The lab facilities there had been considered to be ahead of their time. The training there was rumored to have stirred controversy among the scientists within the Genetics Council.

It would be hard for the Coyote Breeds to accept any Council scientist into Base, but the situation was becoming intolerable. Dr. Armani couldn't treat both species. It wasn't going to work. The Breeds coming in didn't have the knowledge needed to work independently of a scientist proven in the areas of Breed physiology and genetic makeup.

Del-Rey had told her that if she could find someone she trusted her friends with, then she could have them. Then he had turned right around and forbade it.

Her lips thinned. The first promise was the one that counted, she decided, as she signed several more reports on the e-pad and sent them to the respective pack leaders awaiting them.

With that finished, she rose from her desk, tucked her cotton shirt into the band of her jeans and inhaled slowly. The heat had been easier today. Much easier. But then, Del-Rey had spent the past three days making certain that the hormonal releases she needed were given in quantity, as well as quality.

She flushed at that, then grinned. He was an incredible lover whether the heat was present or not. And as he had promised, he had more than made up for that first time that he had taken her.

As she moved for the door, e-pad in hand, the link at her ear beeped, a distinctive signal that had her smiling as she stepped from the room.

"Yes?" She answered her alpha's call with a surge of excitement as her bodyguards converged behind her with a snicker and Ashley muttered, "Lovesick."

"Are you well, Mate?" Del-Rey's voice was low, his tone like a whisper of rough velvet over her senses.

"I am," she answered, her voice just as low. "You?"

He chuckled. "How close is Ashley behind you? I'd hate to make her blush."

Ashley snorted.

"Close enough," Anya answered with a laugh as she glanced at her e-pad. "I'm heading to your office if you're free. I need to discuss some reports that came in this morning on the new construction in the lower caverns, as well as some shifts in duty I'd like to make with a few of the teams." And kitchen staff and uniforms. She saw no reason to list the full file of complaints she intended to face him with.

"We could discuss it this evening," he suggested.

"That's what you said yesterday," she told him. "We didn't get around to that discussion if I recall."

"Ah yes, other things definitely came up," he chuckled.

And they had. Hours' worth of pleasure. Her body still tingled with it.

"I'm headed up," she told him as they reached the stairs that led to the upper caverns. "Don't run and hide."

He laughed at that. "I'll be here, Mate. Maybe I'll even have a treat for you."

She shivered at the thought of that. She had become overly fond of Del-Rey's afternoon treats. The ones where he pulled her into his office or entered hers and showed her how hungry he was for her.

A nooner sounded good. But maybe after she got his approval on the things she needed and had him lift the restrictions on her limits of power within Base.

Command and Security she understood; the day-to-day running of the base itself was another matter.

After being delayed several times for different requests, she stepped into his office nearly fifteen minutes later, and came to a hard stop.

That scent. She almost quivered in longing. Coffee. Real, caffeinated, dark and rich coffee. She almost whimpered as she watched Del-Rey lift a cup to his lips and sip slowly.

"You hate me," she sighed, longing making her tongue almost curl. "Now I know you hate me."

He grinned back at her, black eyes dancing as he leaned back in his chair and lifted his cup up to her. "Want a drink of mine?"

She licked her lips. More than she wanted chocolate. She stepped forward slowly, eyes narrowed as his lips quirked. She bet he tasted like that damned coffee. Coffee and male heat and hunger. Tempting. Very, very tempting.

Her eyes narrowed. Cunning, calculating damned Coyote.

She smiled. "I'll take half a cup when I've finished."

His brows lifted. They both knew what that coffee would do to her within hours.

"You could have a sip of mine now," he offered.

Anya settled in the chair in front of his desk and stared back at him with a knowing smile. "Mongrel."

He laid his hand over his heart, his eyes widening despite the wicked laughter in the dark depths. "Coya, you wound me."

"I'm going to wound you." She barely managed to contain herself from rolling her eyes. "What are you trying to get out of, Coyote? Lifting the restrictions on my basic powers or the uniforms for our soldiers?"

Del-Rey took another sip of the coffee and regarded his mate over the cup. She was slick, he had to give her that. As bad as she wanted the coffee, and she did want it bad, she wasn't about to allow herself to be deterred.

Lowering the cup, he sat on the side of his desk and leaned forward. "We can incorporate a rotation of kitchen duties . . ."

Her hand lifted as her expression became shuddered. "Lift the restrictions on my duties, Del-Rey," she told him firmly. "Kitchen duties and our rotations there are not your department. I don't tell you how to run Command and Security, or how to train your men. I expect the same respect."

"This isn't about respect, Anya," he finally told her. "This is about maintaining a functioning military base here. This isn't Sanctuary and it isn't Haven. We don't have cuddly little cabins with pretty little flower beds around them."

She sat back in her chair, crossed her arms and stared at him silently. Hell, she was going to get pissed off.

"I run this base when you're gone. I've learned how to do what has to be done at any given time, and I do it with resources so limited they're laughable," she said calmly. "You have no right, Del-Rey, to keep a limit on my authority."

And he'd considered that fact. For days. Unfortunately, he and Anya differed in several areas regarding the base. Areas he knew would change if she were given the authority to change it. He didn't want to fight her. There had been too much conflict between them already. He liked her soft and sexy in his arms, not angry with him.

"Anya, I don't want humans in this base, neither do I want staff that we don't have control over. The Coyote soldiers coming in here from the Bureau rescues are going to feel out of place if they have beds, blankets and pillows without working for them. This isn't a Council facility. It's a military-run base. I can't lift the restrictions on the powers you have until I'm assured that you understand this. Until then, my signature will be required on any changes you request."

He could smell her anger simmering now. Low, fierce, barely held in check. But he felt her hurt, and it pinched in his chest.

"Is that why you haven't signed off on the requests I've sent you?"

"I don't believe the changes you're requesting are for the good of the base." He kept his tone soft, gentle. "It isn't so bad here, is it?" he finally asked. "A little rough at times, I admit, but your personal requests are never restricted."

She rose slowly to her feet, her chin lifted with that surfeit of pride he knew she had.

"Haven and Sanctuary are homes, to their alphas as well as their mates and children. If you prefer a military base rather than a home, then that's your choice. Excuse me for taking up your time Alpha Delgado. Perhaps if you find the time from all your duties to fuck tonight, I'll see you then."

"Anya." He came out of his chair as she moved from hers and headed for the door. "Dammit, that was uncalled for."

She paused and turned back to him. "Was it?" she asked, the hurt in her voice thick now. "I had more freedom when the separation order was intact. I've become the one thing I swore I would never be, Del-Rey. Your pet, nothing more."

"That isn't true," he growled. "Anya, you know better than that."

She shook her head slowly, her blue eyes dark and filled with sadness. That sadness struck him like a physical blow.

"You just proved it," she said softly. "I'll leave you to run your base now."

She swept from the room, head held high, shoulders straight, the subtle scent of her pain drifting back to him as he dropped into his chair and wearily wiped his hand over his face.

She knew better, he told himself. She would come to understand the necessity of this. Like a woman, she wanted ribbons and bows on everything. Coyotes didn't do well with ribbons and bows. If they did, fuck, they'd be Wolves. Coyotes weren't fucking Wolves.

He glared at the door as a firm knock sounded on it.

"What?" he snapped, knowing who stood on the other side.

Brim stepped into the office. "Well, how did you manage to fuck up?" He closed the door behind him as he smirked back at Del-Rey. "Wouldn't let her have the quilts over the plain blankets for the soldiers' barracks?"

"I refused the requests across the board," he snarled back. "Do you have a problem with it? Since when do Coyotes think they don't have to work for what they sleep on? How long did it take us to find a bed of our own? We appreciated it more for the fact that it was ours."

Brim's expression went blank. "I see," he finally said. "Very well. I'll leave you to your duties, Alpha." He opened the door.

"What the fuck has a stick shoved up your ass?" Del-Rey snarled. "We're a military base, not a fucking hotel complete with room service."

Brim turned back slowly. "If this is true, then perhaps you should return the females to Haven. That way they don't remind our men of everything they don't yet have, and everything they know their coya would do to make their lives less military and more normal. They'll remember they're animals then, rather than the men they want to be. Should I arrange to have the coya and her detail returned?"

Del-Rey rose to his feet with a primal growl.

Brim's brows arched. "Be a fool with your mate if you want to be, but stop excusing it. You don't want the changes because those changes threaten you, not the base, Alpha. And despite your determination to claim her heart, simply put, you're not willing to give her yours, or your trust, in the same measure. Poor coya. Maybe she'll become the soldier you need rather than the mate she thinks you want. Would you be happy then?"

He didn't give Del-Rey a chance to respond, but stepped from the office instead and closed the door quietly behind him, leaving Del-Rey alone with the knowledge that his second-in-command might be right. If she didn't make the base a home, then if he ever lost her again, there would be less to suffer for, less to miss. For all of them.

◆　　◆　　◆

"I need an escort to Dr. Armani's office," Anya told Emma as they stepped into the community room and headed back to the tunnel that led to her and Del-Rey's rooms. "Ask her to have the hormonal therapy to prevent conception prepared and to please pencil in a few moments to talk to me."

"Yes, Coya," Emma said quietly, using the comm link to access the outside line.

"Ashley, when is your nail appointment this week?" Anya asked.

"Alpha hasn't approved it." Ashley didn't pout; her voice was calm, composed. The airhead was nowhere in sight.

"I just approved it. You'll be accompanying me to my own appointment so we might as well make it a girls' day out. Have our security team advised and make certain the detail is comprised of at least as many of the soldiers that came out of Russia with us as it is of Del-Rey's men. Ensure that the other half are men who have been on that detail with us before. I want no complications."

"Fuck," Sharone hissed. "Now isn't the time for this, Coya."

"We can't wait forever," she told them. "Once our appointment is set, I'll need you to find an excuse to go into town, make contact and give them details. I'll talk to Armani this afternoon."

"The conception hormone is an excuse then?" Ashley asked.

Anya breathed in roughly. "I made a choice," she whispered. "It's a choice I believe in—to let this play out without the hormones. But that mangy Coyote tried to manipulate me. He tried to play me. Let's see how he likes playing his own game." She turned to Ashley then. "How long do you think Brim will give us?"

Ashley's smile was deadly. "I saw his face when we left. He'll wait until the last possible moment before telling the alpha. I'd guess, half an hour lead time as long as no one else blabs."

"No one blabs on the coya," Sharone grunted.

"Team is in place. We have five men, all are from the alpha's original team, ready and waiting at the south exit. They have an all-terrain ready to roll."

Anya changed direction. It wasn't necessary to change clothes before going to Haven. Jeans, boots and long-sleeved shirts were standard attire there.

"There's snow moving in," Sharone reported. "We may not

make it back tonight. All we have are the all-terrains; the heli-jet is still in tech getting repairs, but one is on loan from the military."

Wouldn't it just be too bad if the alpha didn't have his little sex toy to play with tonight, Anya thought furiously as they rushed to the waiting escort. Why, that just might break her heart.

Not.

· C H A P T E R 1 9 ·

Anya stepped into the examination room and faced the Wolf Breed doctor silently for long moments. Dr. Armani was exhausted. There were darker shadows beneath her chocolate brown eyes, and for once, her long, silky mane of black hair was tied into a ponytail rather than braided into all those tiny braids that normally covered her head.

She was a beautiful woman. Like many of the Breed specialists still living, she wasn't very old and was incredibly intelligent, with an above-genius ability in genetic engineering. The Council had spent years trying to blackmail her or force her into their ranks. She had spent just as many years in hiding, trying to escape them.

"Shots ready," Armani said quickly as she prepared the injection. "The hormone to prevent conception isn't complicated and it works quickly. I just need to take a few tests to make certain you haven't conceived."

"I don't need the test, Nikki," she said quietly. "I need to talk to you."

Nikki swung around, her brow wrinkling in a frown. "Is there a problem? Have you been experiencing any other symptoms that we didn't discuss?"

"No." Anya moved across the room slowly and took a seat at the end of the examination table. "This has nothing to do with mating heat."

Nikki's eyes narrowed. "What does it have to do with?"

She licked her lips slowly. "Treason."

Nikki stopped cold. "Are you going to kill that Coyote mate of yours?"

Anya let a smile tip her lips. "I haven't come to that yet."

"How serious is this, Anya?" Nikki pulled her stool closer and sat down. "I assume its fairly serious for you to make an excuse to see me."

"How desperate are you for Coyote specialists?"

Nikki's eyes widened. "I'd give my ass right now for just a few detailed notes. You don't want to know what I'd do for specialists. But why would I need them if you have them? Base would—"

Anya shook her head. "He refuses to allow Council-trained specialists into Base. He's made a career of killing them, Nikki. The ones he didn't kill, the Council did. With the psychologists and medical specialists coming in from the Bureau, specialist backing could make a difference in determining some of the anomalies in the Coyote Breeds. Am I correct?"

Nikki nodded slowly.

"Would Haven give them asylum over the alpha Coyote leader's objections?"

"Whoa!" Nikki's head jerked back in surprise. "You have some? Not just one?"

"Two. I've been in contact. They're currently in hiding, running for their lives from the Council. They were exceptional, Nikki. Compassionate, dedicated. They suffered when they were forced to allow Coyotes in that Russian facility to die."

"Oh my God," Nikki whispered. "Chernov and Sobolova are alive?"

"For now." Anya nodded. "I've tried to discuss this with my alpha, but he refuses to agree that the Coyotes need their own specialists." Or blankets and pillows, or a sense of belonging.

Nikki rose from the stool as she drew her jacket around her, crossing her arms under her breasts and turning from Anya for long seconds.

"I have limited time before my alpha jumps in here demanding answers," Anya sighed. "I need a decision soon, Nikki."

"You could get in a lot of trouble, Anya," Nikki whispered. "If these are Council plants, it could backlash on you."

Anya nodded. "I know this. Just as Hope knew the trouble that could arise when she contacted you, Nikki, and the Wolves gave you asylum."

Dr. Armani grimaced at that. "And you want Hope to consider giving these two asylum as well?"

"I can't discuss this with the lupina." Anya slid off the exam table. "But if you were to tell her that a confidential contact informed you of the possibility, then there would be no backlash to her, or to you, if it were discovered who your contact was. Your medical designation separates you from many of the laws that hinder me here."

One of those laws? Going against direct orders from a person's alpha leader. A mate could face serious charges if her alpha decided to go that far.

Would Del-Rey do that? She had to say at times, she simply didn't know. Trust was an issue between them. She couldn't be certain which way he would go in this. She hoped he would accept it, see the value of it and eventually trust that she was doing what was best for them, and any child they conceived.

"Why are you risking this?" Nikki asked her then.

Anya placed her hand against her stomach, feeling the twinges she knew to expect. "I'm still ovulating," she whispered. "If I conceive now, or in the future, then I want my child safe, Nikki. I don't want to risk losing Del-Rey's child on the off chance that the genetics decide to go haywire or something unforeseen comes up. He's an adult, an alpha. He can risk his life if that's his choice. I'm not nearly as accepting of that risk to any children we'll have together."

"I can understand that." Nikki nodded as a hard, sharp knock came to the examination room door.

Their heads jerked to it.

"Your alpha," Nikki said. "I'll talk to the lupina and contact you within the next twenty-four hours."

Anya lowered her head, closing her eyes briefly as Nikki strode to the door and unlocked it before pulling it open.

He was standing there, wild, irritated, alpha. It was like a slam of lust surging inside her without the physical pain. Or was the emotional wound just too deep right now to allow her to feel the physical?

She stared back at him, seeing the disarray in his long hair. He must have raked his fingers through it more than once. He did that when he was frustrated or becoming angry. His dark eyes were narrowed, thick blond lashes framing the wicked black.

"What's wrong?" He strode into the room. "Why have you decided you need the additional hormone shots?"

"I changed my mind." She gave him a bright smile as she jumped off the examination table. "I guess I just needed someone to talk to."

He stopped in the middle of the room, his gaze focused, intense on her now. "You have me and your bodyguards to talk to," he growled. "Why do you need someone else?"

"The restrictions placed on me don't bar me from talking, Alpha. Just from acting."

He frowned. "I have a name, Anya."

She paused and stared back at him silently for long moments. "And I have a brain, Alpha Delgado, regardless of what you think. Are you ready to go?"

She swept past him, moving from the examination room and rejoining the security detail waiting in the hall outside.

He turned to Nikki, staring back at her as though he could will her to give him the truth.

She shook her head, her somber expression giving him more to worry about than to find comfort in.

"You're making a mistake," she sighed. "But, with Breed males, I've learned, all you can do is let them beat their head against a wall. When it hurts enough or the blood gets thick enough, they stop." She shrugged.

"What the hell does that mean?"

"It means you're just as hardheaded as the rest of them." She glanced to the door then. "She's not as easy to manipulate as you think she is. And manipulating her is only going to hurt you worse. There." She threw him a bright smile. "The advice was free. Do you need anything while you're here? A shot of common sense perhaps?"

He clenched his teeth before turning on his heel, stalking from the examination room and moving to catch up with his coya.

She strode, shoulders straight, head high, pride draping her like an exquisite cloak as she moved through the underground steel-and-reinforced-concrete corridors to the ground level.

There was no dust here as there was at Base. It was brightly lit, functional, yet still there were areas of greenery built into the walls with growth lights. A small, miniature orange tree grew in one hallway; the controlled atmospheric settings around it kept it healthy and in its natural growth cycle.

Vines grew along one wall. There were glassed-in sunrooms with a complicated system of mirrors that opened along a wide tunnel to allow the sun's rays inside. Unlike the mountain facility that housed the communications that the labs were networked into, Dr. Armani's medical facility was warm, friendly. He could understand why Anya would want to visit. There were many things here that Base lacked.

But this wasn't a military facility, he told himself. Coyotes didn't care about a little dust and dirt, a few inconveniences. They had the bar, the kitchen, the television. Del-Rey had his mate.

His mate was human.

He nearly paused. When other Coyotes mated, their mates would in all probability be human as well. He pushed through the exit doors just behind Anya and her security detail, his frown darkening.

Dammit, he didn't trust humans. He trusted Anya and Armani and that was pretty much the extent of it. He was wary even with the lupina, Hope, and the Felines' prima, Merinus.

He didn't like humans and he didn't want them in his base. Except his coya.

Yeah, that was going to go over well.

Fuck!

He could feel it working through him now, the way that woman messed with his mind, made him think, made him want to give her anything and everything she desired.

He'd cross the bridge of the human mate problem when he had to, he decided. Until then, he was faced with another, very intriguing problem: figuring out exactly what his mate was up to. Because he had no doubt she was up to something.

◆　◆　◆

Anya moved into the bedroom ahead of Del-Rey as he opened the door and stood back for her to enter. Sharone, Emma and Ashley had been completely silent during the heli-jet ride back to Base. They had sat across from Anya and Del-Rey, and stared over his shoulder like good little military-trained Coyote soldiers.

Del-Rey hadn't been happy about it; she could tell. If she hadn't been so upset, she would have been amused.

She heard the door close behind her as she pulled the jacket he had forced on her off her shoulders and laid it over the chair at the side of the room, before turning to face him. She rubbed at the chill in her arms and fought to ignore the need for his touch.

She didn't want the chaos that came from his touch right now; she needed to think, to plan. So much was happening, and so many things she had envisioned happening weren't going to happen. And it hurt.

"What was so important that you had to talk to Armani as a snowstorm was brewing?" he finally growled as he pulled the comm link in his ear free and tossed it to the table at the side of the large bed.

"Evidently, something important." She shrugged. "Girl stuff."

She forced her arms down, forced herself to stop trying to rub the warmth into them once again. She'd been cold before; she was certain she would be again before it was all said and done.

"Would you like to tell me what you were doing in Armani's office?" he asked her. "Or should I begin questioning your bodyguards?"

Her brows lifted as she forced a smile to her lips. "I asked them to schedule an appointment for me, Del-Rey. I'm certain they'll be more than happy to tell you this themselves."

There was no lie there. A careful manipulation of the facts, nothing more.

He crossed his arms over his wrinkled shirt. He looked good scruffy, she had to admit. And he did look fine in that tux the night of the party. Del-Rey was a man that could pull off any look he wanted to, even the harried, irritated male.

He finally breathed out roughly as he stared at her, his gaze caressing her from head to toe. "I can smell your hurt," he said softly. "I can feel it. I'm sorry, Anya."

She waited, but nothing more came.

"But not sorry enough to change your mind," she said painfully.

His expression was heavy; his black eyes raged with emotions that she didn't know how to interpret.

"Fine." She shrugged. "What about our marriage ceremony? Or mating ceremony? We need to schedule that."

She was going to crawl into a hole and strangle on the pain. She watched his expression shift, become closed. She believed it was the worst rejection she had ever faced.

"You're not officially making me your coya," she stated hoarsely.

Sofia's words haunted her now. That it wasn't official. That Anya was living in a dreamworld, and somehow the other woman had known it.

"Anya, the ceremony doesn't matter." He pushed his fingers through his hair as he glared at her. "You're my mate. That makes you my coya. Period. It can't get any more official than the mating."

She stared back at him, forcing herself not to cry, not to scream in rage and agony.

Finally she nodded slowly. "Thank you for sparing me the preparations for the celebration that comes later. I'll answer Lupina Gunnar and Prima Lyons's inquiries into that in the morning and let them know that they needn't prepare for it."

Humiliation sang through her bloodstream. She wasn't going to cry, she promised herself. She was too tired to cry, too hurt to want to do anything but curl into a miserable ball of shame.

Hope and Merinus were already making plans. A spring ceremony, the white gown Anya had always dreamed of. A real wedding, just as their mates had given them. A ring. Every woman's dream, but in the world she now lived within, it would have been even more. It would have been an affirmation, and it came with a certain security where other mates, where the hierarchy of the Breed society, was concerned.

"Anya, dammit," he growled, his eyes flashing with an edge of anger. "What's happened to you? You're more logical than the pain I can sense coming from you. You're killing me with it."

She lifted her chin slowly and swallowed past the lump in her throat. "Sorry. Hormones probably," she finally whispered. "If you'll excuse me, Del-Rey, I think I'm not feeling very well. I'm going to go to my office for a while. Good night."

"The hell you are." His fingers looped around her arm—not hard, his grip wasn't tight, yet still, she flinched. It was almost painful, that touch, even through her clothing.

He released her just as quickly, staring at her as though confused.

"I hurt you." He frowned, perplexed, watching her carefully. "What's wrong? Is this why you went to Dr. Armani? Is my touch suddenly painful to you?"

Anya shook her head. It hadn't been pain. It hadn't hurt, not physically. Emotionally. The warmth she needed, the feel of him that she ached for physically, couldn't overshadow the pain she felt inside.

"I'm fine," she said again. "Please excuse me, Del-Rey. I just need to shower. Maybe eat." She gave him a false smile and edged to the door of her office. "Good night."

She opened the door, slipped inside the little room and nearly sank to the floor as her upper body spasmed with the need to sob. She was his mate, not his coya. Without the ceremony, she would never truly be his coya, his other half. She was just the woman he fucked and nothing more.

Exhaustion filled her, and for the first time since Del-Rey had returned, the mating heat didn't torment her. She lay down on the couch, pillowed her head on her arm and stared into the darkness until she slept.

She wasn't aware of Del-Rey stepping into the room or of him crouching beside her. She didn't know he reached out, touched the tear on her cheek and felt like sobbing himself.

"I'm sorry, baby," he whispered. "This way is best. For both of us."

He touched her cheek with the back of his fingers, feeling the silky, cool flesh as he felt a shiver work through her. She was cold, but she wasn't aroused. He could smell the hurt radiating off her in waves, even in sleep.

Sighing at the brutality of what he'd done to her, aching with it to a depth of his being that he didn't know existed, Del-Rey picked his fragile mate up in his arms and carried her to their bed.

Undressing her took a while. He moved slowly, carefully, unwilling to wake her from the exhausted slumber she seemed to have slipped into.

When he had left her that morning, she had been laughing, happy, teasing him. She had been making plans and he had known it. He had known it and hadn't wanted to lose the warmth of her laughter until he had no other choice.

Now he had lost it, and it felt as though he had lost a part of himself.

He stripped and eased into the bed beside her, curled around her cold body and fought to bring back the warmth in her. He was cold himself. Cold to the marrow of his bones, and he couldn't explain why. The chill had begun when she had walked from his office earlier. It had grown after she had left their bedroom for her office.

He had to protect her. Hope and Merinus lived with the threat of greater danger than Faith or the other Breed mates. More attempts were made on their lives than on the others'. Without the ceremony, the world would never know for certain if she was lover or true coya. Coyotes weren't Wolves, he told himself again. They didn't need a ceremony to make something like this official. And she would see in time that it would give her a greater security, and that was what mattered.

She was hurting now, but later, later she would understand, he promised himself. He would find the words to explain it. He'd find a way to make her understand. She had to understand, because her safety was more important to him than a misunderstanding.

He had seen with the first attempt on her life in the mountains that he was going to have to put his foot down. He had to be responsible for keeping her by his side, keeping her safe and well. Nothing else mattered.

◆   ◆   ◆

Del-Rey awoke the next morning as Anya eased out of his arms and left the bed. He waited, listened, inhaled her scent and still detected no arousal, no need for his touch.

He restrained his concern. Coyotes were different, he told himself again. It could simply be a cycle of rest that the hormones were allowing her, nothing more.

He lifted his lashes enough to watch her pick up the dirty clothes he had left on the floor the night before. Her expression was calm, composed. Okay, she should be all right. The vivid scent of pain wasn't overpowering his senses. Perhaps it had simply been hormones.

He waited, listened as she took the dirty clothes to the bathroom. Perhaps he'd join her in the shower.

Dresser drawers opened as she collected clean clothes, then he heard the door to her office open, close. Lock. She was using the shower in the other room and had ensured he wouldn't be following her without her knowledge.

Hell. He didn't like this. This distance that suddenly seemed to separate them, this feeling that made him cold and irritable, made him wonder what the hell he was doing where his mate was concerned.

Son of a bitch, he'd rather he use in a fistfight than face her this morning, because God only knew what he would do if he saw that pain in her eyes again. He just might end up crying for her.

◆   ◆   ◆

Hope Bainesmith Gunnar stared at the message in her inbox. The email was surprising, saddening.

Lupina Gunnar. Prima Lyons. It has been decided that there is no need for the official ceremony of status. Anya Kobrin, mate to Alpha Delgado.

So much in such a simple email. So much pain and such a loss of dreams. Hope knew this ceremony was one Anya had looked forward to since accepting her place at Del-Rey's side, but this decision was perhaps not surprising after the discussion she'd had with Dr. Armani first thing that morning.

Hope wasn't surprised either when the satellite phone she had laid on her desk rang. Caller ID showed Merinus's number.

"You got the email," Hope sighed as she answered.

"Tell me it's a joke," Merinus said quietly. "Even Callan was hopeful that this ceremony would take place soon and cement Anya's position. Without it, her standing among Del-Rey's people will be weakened. Their respect for her will erode."

Hope shook her head. "I'm afraid it's not a joke."

"Have Wolfe talk to him," Merinus urged. "This ceremony is too important, Hope."

Hope thought about that, she considered it. She sighed. "This is something he'll have to see for himself, and it's a fight Anya has to face alone. We can support her if she needs us, Merinus, but there's little else we can do."

"Damned stubborn Coyote," Merinus cursed. "Pain in the ass."

"For both of us," Hope said quietly. "Hopefully I can get to the base and talk to her soon. I'll let you know what I learn."

Merinus sighed. "I'll call her soon. That email broke my heart. She needs time I think before talking to me."

Hope nodded. "I'll give her a day or so. Until then, we'll pray."

"And pray," Merinus stated. "Poor Anya."

Poor Anya.

Poor Del-Rey.

Because Hope knew this was going to cause more trouble for the alpha than he could have considered. The mating for an alpha was one thing; acceptance by the men who followed him was another, as she and Wolfe had both learned. For some reason the wedding ceremony that meant so much in the human world meant just as much in Breed society, perhaps more so, especially for an alpha.

If an alpha didn't accept his mate, then his men wouldn't accept her either. The past eight months, the order of separation and Anya's refusal to accept her alpha hadn't seemed to faze the Coyote soldiers. They had accepted her despite that. Because they had believed the decision was out of Del-Rey's hands. Once this was learned, Anya's position at Base would erode, and the problems she faced wouldn't be easy.

Not for Anya. And most definitely not for Del-Rey.

Hope emailed the only other person she could think of that could help with this particular problem. The one man that might have enough sway to convince his alpha of the error of his ways.

His brother.

Brim.

◆　◆　◆

Brim stared at the email, at the forwarded text plus the lupina's message, and felt a curl of anger unfold within him. Son of a bitch. Maybe this time they would fight after all.

CHAPTER 20

Del-Rey checked on Anya after she left their rooms. A frown pulled at his brows when he learned she was in the kitchen area. Striding through the base, he moved past the community room and into the kitchen.

With only the sound of movement and four women working in silence, the damned place was eerie. There was an air of heaviness, tension, a subtle scent of pain and anger and an underlying chill that he couldn't put his finger on.

Anya lifted her head from the bowls and ingredients she was working on. Her eyes were dark, and perhaps there were shadows under them.

"There are cold cuts in the fridge if you need a sandwich," she told him. "I'll have egg and assorted meat biscuits in an hour if you'd like to wait."

"You don't have kitchen duty." He hardened his voice.

"No one has kitchen duty." She shrugged. "Cleanup is a far cry from making certain there's actually food on base and certain items ready to eat when your teams get hungry, Del-Rey. There are well over sixty soldiers here at last count with several dozen more coming. Someone has to make certain supplies are kept up with."

"Add it to the duties with rotation," he ordered her.

He watched her pour milk into a huge bowl of flour and begin working it in. Her head was lowered, her expression calm and composed, when he knew she was anything but.

"Doesn't work that way." She shook her head.

"Then make it work," he bit out. "We have things to discuss that require both our attention, not you standing elbows deep in a bowl of flour."

She looked up at the clock on the wall. "You can table your discussions for two hours," she decided. "Pencil me into your schedule after that and let me know what time to meet you where."

"So we're scheduling in fucking now?" he snarled, ignoring the other women.

Her head jerked up, a flicker of pain crossing her face. "If that's the discussion, then I guess that's what we're doing."

He felt almost helpless. He remembered that feeling clearly from his youth. So clearly it punched into his brain and left a growl rumbling in his throat. With a steel cage surrounding him, he had watched, so many times, as his brothers and sisters were murdered before his eyes. Coyote Breeds that were considered flawed, because they had mercy, because they reached out to one another. Children no more than babies that cried for attention or for food when there was none left. Cut down before his eyes. And if he tried to fight, if he tried to save them, then others died as well. They hadn't been kind enough to go ahead and kill him and put him out of his misery.

They beat him. Lashed him with a whip. Hooked electrodes to him after chaining him to the wall, and tortured him with the electricity they flayed his body with.

He was an example to the others the same as the killings were. They meant to break him, to destroy that mercy he had inside him and prove that a Breed had no soul, honor or principles.

They had failed. But in some ways, they had won as well.

"Excuse me, Alpha." Ashley moved around him as she stepped from the small closet that held countless cooking implements.

He glanced down at her, saw her shorter nails and frowned.

"Didn't I just send you to the damned salon?" he growled.

Her eyes widened. "I had dishes last night. A few popped off."

"What do you mean you had dishes?"

She fidgeted in front of him and looked to Anya.

"It was Ashley's turn to load the dishwasher and clean the pots and pans," Anya answered.

"I have a fucking rotation for kitchen duty." His voice was harsh, primal, causing the three female Coyotes to flinch.

Anya shrugged. "When I checked the closet, the dishes hadn't been cleaned well. They're soldiers, Del-Rey. Men. They don't understand rinsing first, nor do they understand cleaning. Sharone, Emma and Ashley spent hours in here fixing it. Your rotation isn't working." Her head lifted. "Unless the Felines are doing it. They seem to have a clue. But I imagine Alpha Lyons wouldn't be pleased if we used the Feline Breeds for kitchen duty only."

She dumped her flour mess on the counter and began working it into a ball. A huge ball. He glared at her.

"You are not a servant," he snapped. "This is not where you belong."

She paused, stared at the dough and lifted her head. Her gaze was shuttered, but God, what he felt coming from her. Emotions were almost locked inside her, giving him only the smallest hint of the roiling, overwhelming anger, fear and need that twisted in her dark blue eyes.

"I'm busy, Del-Rey," she finally said. "Schedule a time and I'll be there. Until then, let me finish if you don't mind. Or is this something else I need your permission to complete?"

Fury slapped him. He could feel it building inside him. The need rose inside him to force her submission, to carry her back to their rooms and fuck her until she didn't have the energy to defy him. And another part, a saner part, the human part, paused as he sensed more than the animal wanted to see.

He turned on his heel and left the room. They would fight this out later. Once his orders were implemented, she wouldn't find herself in that kitchen cooking for the whole damned base again. He'd be damned if she would. She wasn't the fucking cook. She was his mate. His coya. She could oversee until hell froze over, but it wasn't her job to do the actual work.

He slammed his office door closed, stalked to his desk and

sat down. He looked around the office. Dust was accumulating. Files were stacked here and there haphazardly. It hadn't been like this when he'd arrived. His office had been immaculate. The scent of his mate had filled it.

He ran his fingers through his hair and blew out a hard, rough breath as Brim's knock sounded at the door. He knew his second-in-command's knock and the anger behind it.

"What?" he snarled out.

The door opened.

Military straight and perfect, Brim moved into the room. His gaze was icy, his manner stiff.

"What kind of stick has been shoved up your ass?" He bared his teeth at the other man.

Brim handed over an e-pad. "I need your signature."

Del-Rey jerked the pad out of his hand, glanced at it, then felt a haze of red wash over him at the memo awaiting his approval.

Re: Official notification of reversion of duties from Anya Kobrin to Alpha Delgado. Status coya, revoked. Status mate, revoked. All due authority hereby revoked.

He stared up at the other man. "What the fuck is this?"

"By order of separation she only held her title if you didn't rescind it."

"I still haven't rescinded it," he informed Brim, his tone guttural. "What the fuck is this?"

"You should have read the separation agreement more fully perhaps," Brim stated. "Anya posted the memo this morning to Lupina Gunnar and Prima Lyons as well as to their alphas. A decision that the mating ceremony tentatively scheduled for spring was being canceled. She lost her title when that memo went out. Word of it is already filtering through Base. She's no longer coya and therefore your pack leaders need a directive from you."

The memo was a directive all right. It rescinded all powers that Anya had previously held to command in his absence. It also directed her status to below those pack leaders, rather than above them as she had once held.

He stared at it.

"If she's officially my coya, I paint a target on her back for any Coyote that has managed to fool us, or betrays us in the future. They'll strike at her first."

Brim shrugged. "That isn't my call, Alpha. All I need is the order signed so Base runs properly. Military structure must be adhered to."

Del-Rey's jaw clenched.

Before Del-Rey could control the impulse, he picked up the e-pad and threw it. A vicious, savage swing of his arm, and it shattered against the stone wall to his side.

Brim stared at the destruction before turning his gaze back to Del-Rey. "A copy was sent to your PDA. You can sign it from there. If you'll excuse me now." He nodded to Del-Rey with all due military respect.

Perfect, smooth, coordinated.

Del-Rey was out of his chair before Brim could stride across the room. In the next second he had his second-in-command against the wall, his arm braced across Brim's throat as a snarl echoed from his throat.

"What is your fucking problem?" He stared into Brim's eyes and saw nothing but that cool, emotionless facade.

"I wasn't aware I had one." And he wasn't fighting.

Brim wasn't a man that allowed even his alpha to throw him against a wall. But there he was, relaxed, cool. Del-Rey felt as though a volcano was ready to explode inside his own head.

"Erase that fucking memo," Del-Rey bit out.

He could imagine Anya's pain if she saw it, once she read it. He could almost feel the loss he knew would burrow inside her.

"I can't do that, Alpha," Brim stated. "This is a military base, and the rules have to be adhered to; otherwise, our men are going to become confused and uncertain. They'll choose sides. Her people against your people. We can't allow that."

Del-Rey released him slowly. "Delete that fucking memo or I'll do it for you," he commanded.

Brim shrugged. "It's already gone out to your pack leaders. Protocol demanded it be sent. Just as it's gone out to the Wolf and Feline pack leaders. You're showing weakness in refusing to send it out yourself. As alpha, you can't afford to show that weakness at this time. A separation of packs could destroy us, Alpha. The alliance will go to hell and we'll be left fighting in the jungles for meals again. That wasn't as much fun as we pretended it was, I don't believe."

"Get out of my office," Del-Rey ordered him coldly. "Now."

He turned his back on Brim, listened until the other man walked to the door. Brim paused then and Del-Rey tensed further, knowing he wouldn't like the other man's parting shot.

"I'm your brother."

Del-Rey flinched at the reminder.

"We lost our sisters in that hellhole. We lost brothers. Do you know, Del-Rey, until I received that memo this morning, I actually resented you for refusing to acknowledge that tie between us." There was amusement in his voice.

Del-Rey turned back to him slowly.

Brim shrugged at the glare he directed to him. "I've decided it really wasn't personal. Nor was it the fear for your brothers' lives that caused you to deny those few of us still living."

"And you decided this based on what?" Del-Rey could feel the fury building inside him, tearing through him.

Brim's lips twisted into a cold smile. "You've just rejected your coya, Alpha Leader. Any man that could do that doesn't have a soul. He doesn't have brothers, nor does he have sisters. I think I'll simply count myself lucky you have enough honor that you didn't drown those of your bloodline while we were still pups."

With that, Brim opened the door and left the room, closing it slowly behind him, a second before Del-Rey's snarl of fury echoed through the room.

Fuck them. Fuck them all. He had a soul. A soul that cringed in horror at the memories, a soul that writhed and bled at the bottom of his guts at the thought of everything he had lost over the years. A soul that wept for everything he couldn't have.

Because having meant losing. And God help them all if he lost his coya.

◆　　◆　　◆

Anya sat down at her computer hours later, weariness tugging at her as she pulled up the keyboard and activated the hologram monitor.

One email. Private and encrypted.

She pulled it up, noted the date and time of the meeting,

confirmed, and then deleted it. She covered her face with her hands as she rested her elbows on the desk and forced back her tears, as well as the need beginning to burn inside her.

She'd received her copy of Brim's memo that morning before going to the kitchen. She felt as lost now as she had then. She felt as though spring had been canceled. As though the warmth she had so looked forward to had been snatched away from her forever.

"Coya?" Her office door opened and Sharone, Emma and Ashley stepped inside.

Anya swallowed tightly as she lowered her hands and stared at the women who were the same as sisters to her. They had been reassigned by their pack leaders. She had received that particular memo as she moved from the kitchen back to her rooms.

"Don't," she whispered, shaking her head. "You can't use that title any longer, Sharone."

"You have to do something," Sharone demanded fiercely. "Do you think a lack of title is going to save your life? He can't be as insane as to believe that."

Anya shook her head. "You've been reassigned. You still have your scheduled off hours by my request. We'll have our last girls' day out in one week. We'll make a party of it," she told them. "Dr. Armani and hopefully Lupina Gunnar will be joining us as well. Be prepared for that."

Sharone's eyes widened as the meaning behind Anya's words became clear.

Ashley slouched against a wall while Emma sat on the couch, her head down as she stared at the floor of the small office.

"And after that?" Sharone asked. "We can't leave you undefended. Anya, the Breeds that came out of Russia with us are incensed. They're muttering about leaving the alliance the alphas have built. This is the worst insult he could have dealt you."

Anya shook her head. No, the worst insult he had dealt her was when he convinced her to come to him, charming her, seducing her with his lies. She was his coya. She was his life. She reaffirmed that he had a soul.

"Coya," Ashley whispered, her voice heavy. "What he's done is wrong."

Anya held her hand up slowly. "Please. Tell the others it's my wish they remain with the alliance. They pledged their loyalty to Del-Rey under certain rules. That I be his coya wasn't one of those rules. They can't afford to break their word in this world, Sharone." She shook her head and had to swallow back her tears. "Please. Report to your pack leaders as they asked. I'll be fine here."

Ashley moved. She jerked the door open and slammed it closed with a strength that had Anya flinching. Emma rose from her seat and left more slowly, her hands shoved in the pockets of her jeans as Sharone stared back at Anya with a pain-laden expression.

"Tell him," Sharone said softly. "If you're harmed, he's made enemies, Anya. More than he could ever imagine."

Sharone turned and left the room as Anya felt her breath hitch. She was going to miss them. They were more than friends, and they had always been together. Since she was a little girl and had first found the cells where the five Coyote females were being held.

She, the princess of the Chernov facilities even at age five, had twisted the scientists and doctors around her little finger until the girls she wanted to play with were given partial freedom. They had then formed a bond that had never been broken.

They had never been separated, until now.

"Anya?"

She stiffened at the sound of Del-Rey's voice at her side. She turned her head, staring at him, seeing the heaviness in his expression, a heaviness reflected in her heart.

"You would have hurt me less had you used that knife you held at my throat in Russia," she said, breathing out roughly.

"I'm a Coyote," he said, his voice low. "The most hated and feared of the Breeds, across the world. My coya will live in constant danger. If the world perceives that she is no more than my lover, if the other Breeds perceive that she holds only my body, then she's safe. If I make a mistake and allow a traitor into our midst here at Base, then you're safer."

"Will our children be safer?" she asked.

"Kiowa's wife hasn't yet conceived," he stated. "She doesn't use the hormone for conception either. We have time to work this out."

It seemed he had already worked it out.

"I didn't ask for explanations." She rose to her feet and disconnected the computer.

There had been no emails, no Breeds asking for advice or assistance. None of the often dozens of requests that filled her inbox. There had been a single email, nothing more.

Just that easily she had been wiped away.

"Anya." As she moved around her desk, he stopped her, moving to her, his body pressing against hers. "You are every part of my soul. I can't risk you."

Keeping her back to him, she closed her eyes at the pain in his voice, at the pain that vibrated through her own soul.

"I understand that," she finally whispered, and perhaps a part of her did understand. "I'm your lover, nothing more."

"Only in others' eyes." His hands slid around her. "What's between us is between us, Anya. You're my mate. My coya. No matter what the world sees."

But she wasn't his coya. That power, that privilege, had been taken from her. She was his bedmate. In the eyes of the world, and now in his eyes as well. Because the benefits she would have brought to his life as anything more had been stripped from her with a single memo.

She was crying inside as his lips pressed against her neck. Crying as the familiar need began to burn low in her stomach, began to curl through her body and rage through her nerve endings.

And still she couldn't deny him.

As his fingers lifted the hem of her shirt, drawing it over her head, she couldn't deny him the touch he sought. When he turned her in his arms and pressed his lips to hers, she couldn't deny him the kiss she needed herself. The taste of him, that little bit to hold on to. A part of himself he couldn't steal from her, simply because nature demanded that he take satisfaction from her alone.

Her arms twined around his neck; emotion seared her insides. This man was her life; every ounce of her belonged to him, no matter how much it hurt. She had realized that in the past two days. He owned her. She, who had sworn she would never be owned, was owned by this man, this Breed.

"God yes," he growled as she softened against him. "Hold me, Anya. Hold me close, baby."

His flesh seemed to warm against her, hers heated beneath his touch. She pushed her shoes from her feet as he released her jeans and drew them over her hips.

She grew hungrier for his kiss, desperate for this connection. The one thing that couldn't be stolen from her, that couldn't be taken.

She was sinking beneath the waves of pleasure as he pulled back and turned her, pressed her along the desk until her fingers were curling against the broad forearm he laid beneath her head.

He surrounded her. Not like that first time, when he had just been behind her. As he bent her over now, he surrounded her. His lips were at her neck, licking, biting, sending flash flares of heat surging between her thighs as she felt the crest of his cock tuck against her.

"I need you." He nipped at her neck. "I need you until I can't breathe for the need. Until I'm dying inside for you."

Her chest tightened, ached at the emotion in his voice, the torment that filled them both now, bound them, held them together.

One hand gripped her hip as he turned her head to him, took her lips and worked the thick length of his cock inside her. Slow, steady strokes filled her flesh. He stretched her, burned her until she was gasping against his lips, her legs parting farther, her lips and tongue moving against his in a kiss that bound her spirit to him.

"So sweet. So giving," he groaned into their kiss before taking her lips in a hungry exploration that mimicked the firm, delving strokes of his cock.

He stroked nerve endings so sensitive from the pulses of pre-cum that she burned for him. He touched her, inside and out, he held her to him, his hips bunching, moving, grinding into her as the spiraling sensations of need began to tear through the last barriers of control she possessed. The last barriers against the emotions twisting inside her.

"Hold me, Anya." He tore his lips from hers, embracing her fiercely as he made the male demand.

His cock dug inside her, deep, burrowing thrusts that had her gasping, pleading for release. Her muscles clenched around him, spasmed, milked him as she felt herself climbing higher, always higher. She burned in his arms like wildfire and couldn't halt the destructive force of it within her mind.

It tore aside any chance to remain aloof, from the man or from the pleasure. Both wrapped around her, spurred her own hungers.

She pressed back, opened herself and screamed out his name as she felt his lips, his tongue, the scrape of his teeth against the mark he had left on her flesh.

Shudders worked through her body. Her nipples ached as the lace of her bra rasped them; her clit was burning, throbbing mindlessly for release as he pounded into her from behind.

Shaking from the need, she gripped his arm as she felt his other hand move between her thighs, as though he sensed, as though he knew this position alone wasn't going to afford her the relief she needed there.

"Love me again, Anya." His head pressed against her shoulder. "Please, baby. Love me, just one more time."

His palm covered the hard bud and ground against it. Quaking tremors of response began to build inside her. Warmth surrounded her now, every part of her. It moved inside her, heated the cold spots and eased the agony that resonated through her soul.

She loved him. She loved him until nothing else mattered, until she was lost inside him and she knew she would never fully escape.

"Love me," he whispered again.

The pleasure built inside her until it was a whirlwind. Until it raced through her blood, centered at her clit, in her vagina. Until she was exploding with a force that lifted her to her tiptoes and had her teeth biting into his arm as he sank into the bend of her shoulder, his tongue lashing at the mating mark as she felt him swell inside her.

Agonizing throbs of pleasure tore through her. Perspiration dampened both of them, and between them rioting flames of release seared across their nerve endings.

She was shaking in his arms. Shudders that seemed to go to the bone trembled through her as she felt the deep jets of his semen pulsing inside her. Filling her. Completing her until she knew that living without him wasn't possible. Existing without him wasn't going to happen.

Anya heard herself whimper as he lifted her in his arms and carried her to the bed long, long minutes later. He finished undressing her, undressed himself, then moved over her.

"I need you again."

He was still erect, still hard.

Her thighs parted as she felt him move inside her, working slowly into the swollen tissue as they both cried out at the pleasure of it.

"Sweet Anya," he groaned as he filled her.

Dely-Rey had never known pleasure as sweet, as rich as fucking her. Sliding his cock inside her, feeling her pussy clench and tighten around him, those convulsive, sucking little motions destroying his control.

The scent of sweet female cream and male lust filled the air as his lips feathered over her lips, then moved to her tight, hard nipples.

She arched to him as he sucked first one, then the other of the hard tips into his mouth. He drew on the tight tips, feeling her nails digging into his shoulders, her legs wrapping around his hips.

This was what he needed from her. All of her. All of her centered right here, in his bed, taking him, needing him. Loving him.

Sweet God, he was losing himself in her and he couldn't help it. He couldn't hold it back. He needed more and more, until he shafted into her with hard, hungry thrusts. Until he felt her exploding, heard her screaming his name as he locked inside her again, spilling his release and growling her name like a demented animal that could find sanity nowhere else but in this woman's arms.

He had hurt her, wounded her pride, he knew that. Her safety was more important. His peace of mind was more secure knowing the risk of being his coya was no longer something he needed to fear.

Instead, he had only to fear that strange, quiet place inside her that he could feel growing darker. The animal knew it was there. Knew its mate was holding back, holding on. And it, as well as the man, demanded all of her.

He would have all of her. Or he would never survive it.

CHAPTER 21

Anya moved through the community room three days later, pausing to pick up newspapers, magazines and various items of trash that now littered it.

She'd been relegated to being a fucking housekeeper, it seemed. Nothing was picked up anymore, nothing was put away properly, and she was doing it herself. At least when Sharone, Emma and Ashley were with her, there were able hands willing to help with the process.

There was none of that now. She hadn't seen the girls in three days, and she missed them.

"Jax, hand me your empty bottles please," she asked one of the Coyotes sprawled on a couch as he watched the huge television mounted to the wall.

Jax leaned to the side instead to see around her, and gave her room to pick the bottles up herself.

"It would be easier if you handed them to me," she told him with an edge of amusement.

His gaze slid back to her. "Be easier for me if you pick them up yourself."

Anya froze at the deliberate disrespect and straightened, leaving the bottles where they were sitting.

"Come on, Anya, you're in the damned way," he growled. "Let me watch television."

It was deliberate, a reminder that she had no rights above even the lowest of the soldiers at the moment. She was no longer coya; she wasn't even an acknowledged mate. She was Del-Rey's lover, nothing more. There was no male willing to stand for her, and that left her at the mercy of the beasts who would push her, taunt her and eventually force her to either stay out of their way or risk their lives if she tattled on them.

They were testing her, and she had known it was coming; she just hadn't expected it to come so soon.

She left the bottles on the table and moved through the room, leaving the rest of the disarray as it was. She was aware of the other Breeds watching her as well, eyes narrowed, some in disapproval, some in curiosity, as she moved into the kitchen.

But there was one gaze that had shame curling in her stomach. Sofia. She was still there, and the other woman knew.

Anya disposed of the garbage she carried into the kitchen, then stared around at the dishes piled haphazardly in the large sink. There were dirty skillets and cookers on the stoves and cabinets. The door had been left open on one of the ovens.

The kitchen was a mess.

"Who has rotation this week?" she asked Cavalier as he stepped into the room from another door.

He looked around the room. "Wolves and Felines were taken off rotation. One of the pack leaders was assigned to keep rotation in here, but I'm not certain which one."

"Thank you," she said tightly as she moved to the sink and felt her shoulders want to sink in despair.

"You could stop this," Cavalier said behind her. "One word is all it would take."

"And what word would that be?" She shook her head.

She turned on the hot water, stopped the sink and prepared a soak for the dishes before putting them in the dishwasher.

"We swore loyalty to him because of you," Cavalier told her. "Because you were by his side and your scent reassured us that no matter the problems you were having, he was still loyal to you. He's no longer showing that loyalty."

Anya turned around slowly.

"He's an able commander and alpha," she said roughly.

His dark face was stoic, his eyes fierce as thick, long, burnished dark blond hair framed his face.

"He is at that." He nodded. "But a man isn't judged on his abilities to lead well, Coya."

"Don't call me that, Cavalier," she whispered. "I'm no longer your coya."

"You are our coya," he stated, a flare of anger filling his voice now. "We followed him, we swore our allegiance to him, because he was yours. Not because you belonged to him. He doesn't shit on what we claim as our own and still command that loyalty."

"No," she said fiercely. "You just don't understand his reasons. Let it go, Cavalier."

"All we need is a single word, and we walk," he stated. "If he's mistreating you, none of us will remain under his command."

How could she ever have considered this Breed dead inside? When she first met him, he'd had the same look on his face as he had now. Expressionless, his eyes cold—but in those cold amber eyes there was more than she had ever seen.

She saw it now. A feral fury, a dedication and complete loyalty. She had read his file from the other lab. She had known he'd been marked for death when she convinced her father he was a candidate for the training program at the Chernov labs.

She'd been fourteen. He had never reached out to her or anyone else, until now.

"He doesn't mistreat me," she swore.

He growled fiercely. "Neither does he show his respect for you. Until he does, there's not a single Coyote, except those who knew you before, that will show you respect. There will be fights." He glared at her. "Blood will spill. Because there's not one of us that will stand by and allow it."

He swung away from her then and stalked from the room.

"Dissension in the ranks, how interesting," Sofia drawled from the other doorway. "Shouldn't Del-Rey know about this?"

Anya swung around in surprise and faced the other woman. Great. Perfect. Just what the hell she needed.

"Whatever you think he needs to know," she bit out before shoving dishes into the water to soak.

Silence filled the room.

"He's not doing you any favors, Anya," Sofia said then. "Del-Rey can be damned strange on a good day, and he has all these quirky little ideas about protecting the people he cares about. He's not protecting you like this. He just thinks he is."

The quiet reflection in the other woman's voice had her head lifting, her eyes meeting Sofia's surprisingly somber gaze.

"He'll do what he thinks he should."

"He'll get you killed," Sofia warned her.

"He knows what he's doing," Anya gritted out.

Sofia smiled. At first, a sad, wistful curve of her lips, then one of the mockery Anya was more used to.

"Oh well, if you die, I guess we'll find out if Breeds really can mate a second time. I heard Mercury Warrant did. Maybe a Coyote Breed can as well."

She turned and strolled from the kitchen then, flipping her hair over her shoulder with an air of interest, as though she were determined to find out one way or the other if she had a chance of playing coya now.

Anya stared down at the water before her, blinked back her tears and pushed back the hurt. Hurting wasn't going to fix it.

During the hours she spent with Del-Rey in their rooms, she knew the man she wanted, the one she couldn't help but love. Once those doors were open and the alpha emerged though, she found that the commander, the leader, was a much different man.

Her status at Base had changed drastically with that memo stating that there had been a change of plans in the official ceremony. The order of separation had demanded her status as long as their relationship remained unresolved. It had been a protection for her, the other alpha leaders had explained. She had never imagined it was an illusion that would dissolve as quickly as the separation order had been dissolved.

Yet it had. The relegation from a place of respect to one of watchful challenge grated on her pride. But then again, few Breeds of any species gave respect where their alphas didn't. Anya, a human, weaker physically and for all intents and purposes without another Breed officially accepting responsibility for her and her actions was then less than the dirt on their feet.

It was the way of the world in which she now existed, and

she had no idea how to change the impression they had been given.

◆   ◆   ◆

Del-Rey read the morning reports, signed off on memos and sipped his coffee as he frowned over the day-to-day admistrative end of his job. He had shit in his inbox he'd never had before. Complaints. Requests. Bitches over the Feline and Wolf teams. Ingratiating emails that always ended with a request. Hundreds of them.

He sat back in his chair and glared at the holographic computer screen, before activating the link at his ear.

"Yes, Alpha?" Brim's voice was calm. Too calm. The same tone he had used for three days now. It was pissing him off.

"Get in here," he ordered.

When the door opened, he glared at the other man as he waved his hand to the computer screen. "What the fuck is this?"

This. Two hundred and twenty-seven emails from pack leaders, soldiers, Breed Enforcers and others that he had no way to identify.

Brim moved around the desk and stared curiously at the screen.

"Ah yes," he finally said. "The reversion of duties." He shrugged.

"What the fuck," Del-Rey snarled, "is that?"

Brim crossed his arms over his chest before he leaned against the wall beside Del-Rey's chair.

"Reversion of duties," Brim stated. "The responsiblities of the coya, Del-Rey. There is no longer a coya. Her email address was revoked and all emails addressed to her are returned to their proper owner. Namely, the alpha."

"You did this?" Del-Rey growled.

Brim's eyes widened. "Not I," he chuckled. "That happened at Haven when the memo went out. The server processes the emails. When the official ceremony was called off, Haven had no choice but to cut off the email address. It's part of the bylaws of the society. Didn't you read them?"

No. He hadn't read the fucking bylaws, because he wasn't

part of the society. Protocol bullshit. Societal responsibilities. They were a military base, not a fucking home for wayward Breeds.

"Assign someone to answer this bullshit." He waved his hand to the computer. "Anya's probably ecstatic she doesn't have to deal with it anymore."

Brim was silent.

Del-Rey stared at the emails again and blew out a hard breath.

"I could assign someone," Brim finally stated. "Sofia should still be lounging around somewhere; I'll put her to work."

Del-Rey stared back at him slowly, his lips lifting in a silent snarl.

Brim shrugged. "As you stated, Anya was probably glad to be rid of the responsibility. It leaves her more free time to spend with you."

Del-Rey turned and stared at the screen again, saying nothing.

"Should I assign that duty to Sofia, Alpha Delgado?"

"No," Del-Rey snapped. "Just get the hell out of here."

He waited until the door closed behind his second-in-command before activating his link to an outside line. He waited until Wolfe Gunnar came online.

"How can I help you, Alpha Delgado?" The other man's voice was cool.

Fuck he was getting tired of this.

"Fuck with me, Wolfe, and I'm going to come down there and rip your dick off. We'll see how much your lupina enjoys you then."

There was the faintest chuckle before the sound smoothed out. "That doesn't tell me what you need."

What did he need? Besides Anya, besides that something missing inside him that felt so fucking lost he couldn't figure out where the hell to find it.

"The interrogation of the bartender. Why have you rescheduled it yet again?"

"We have new intel we're awaiting," Wolfe told him. "That was forwarded to your email yesterday evening. You should have received it."

"I'm sure it's in that mess somewhere," Del-Rey growled.

Wolfe's chuckled was amused. "Yeah, if it weren't for Hope, I'd be overrun with complaints and requests. I assume you're dealing well with them though. A military base is a hell of a lot more convenient than home, I would imagine. I don't envy you the mass emails though. Have you assigned an assistant yet?"

Del-Rey pinched the bridge of his nose. "Just bring me up to speed if you don't mind."

"We're awaiting more intel that Cabal St. Laurents, a Bengal Breed with Sanctuary, is looking into. I'd like to have that intel, which involves the possibility of a Breed having planned these attacks to begin with. If he can identify the Breed and the bartender can confirm involvement, then it would help us pin Engalls and Brandenmore. I'll give you a call when that information comes in."

"Thank you, Alpha Gunnar," Del-Rey bit out. "I'll await that call."

He disconnected before Wolfe could make another jibe at him, and activated a personal line.

"Yes?" Anya's voice was wary. It had been wary for days whenever she answered their personal line.

"I have coffee?" He tried to tease her. God, he needed her beside him at that moment.

"The coffee wouldn't be very good for me right now," she replied. "But if you need me, I can meet you in our rooms."

If he wanted to fuck. He could almost hear the undercurrent of that statement.

"I need you in the fucking office," he bit out. "If I wanted to meet you in our rooms, then that's where I'd be."

"I'll be right there then."

The line disconnected as he growled furiously. He was horny, discontent, and he'd be damned if he knew how to fix any of it at this moment.

She didn't understand. Brim didn't understand. Losing her would kill him. He was ensuring her safety, that was all. Attempts were made against Hope and Merinus regularly. He couldn't imagine the hell their mates went through.

A small knock at his door moments later had him tensing. He could smell her. Sweet, so soft.

"Enter."

She stepped into the room and closed the door. She was

dressed in jeans and a sweater. Boots. Her hair was as soft as always, her creamy flesh looked as silky. But there was something different. Something he couldn't put his finger on. As though something inside his precious Anya had been snuffed.

"Did you need me?"

"Lock the door." He was suddenly impossibly aroused.

Her gaze flickered as she locked the door slowly and he darkened the room's windows. His tongue throbbed to kiss her, to taste her. Nothing mattered but the hunger razing his body and mind now. The ache in his arms to hold her, the chill that seemed to spread through his chest.

He'd been too long without her. Too long since he had touched her. Loved her. He rose from his desk and drew his T-shirt over his head, his hands going to his belt.

"Undress," he ordered her desperately. "Now, Anya. Give to me."

Give to him.

She had given him everything, and he wanted more. Anya wondered if she had more to give after the hell she had trudged through today.

She unlaced her boots and slid them from her feet before undressing slowly. Tomorrow. Tomorrow it would all end. He would learn how she had conspired against him.

He would turn against her then. He despised Breed scientists. He tolerated Dr. Armani because she had managed to hide from the Genetics Council; she had refused them through the years she was also doing her own research into what they were doing.

He would never accept Chernov and Sobolova. And he would hate her for bringing them to Haven. For exposing his people to them.

Naked, aroused herself, she moved to where he stood by the desk, tall and golden, powerful in his sexuality and his nudity. One large hand was wrapped around the shaft of his cock, stroking it leisurely as his chest moved with heavy breaths.

She loved his body. She loved the man. She understood what she didn't want to understand, and she ached for both of them, because she knew it was going to blow up in their faces soon. Until then, she wanted her mate. Her lover. Her alpha.

"My coya," he whispered as she came to him, breaking her heart with a title that would never be hers.

"Alpha." She accepted him for who he was, what he was as she moved against him, rubbing her forehead against his chest, letting her lips drift over the hard muscles as she felt his palms curve around her hips.

She touched him, smoothed her hands down his chest, his abs. The fingers of one hand gripped his pulsing cock as she lifted her head for his kiss.

It was sheer power. Black magic. He kissed her with a hunger that sank inside her as surely as his tongue pushed between her lips.

Heady spice filled her senses. The taste of the mating kiss, smooth and whiskey-hot. It wrapped around her senses and reminded her of hot Colorado summer nights when she had lain alone, thinking of him, dreaming of him.

But this was no dream. This was Del-Rey. So powerful. So much hers and, yes, so separate from her.

She moved back, tearing from his kiss to find a breath. Her lips moved from his lips to his chest. That fine sprinkling of chest hair mesmerized her. Light, lighter than the dark blond on his head. Almost a burnished gold. It was soft to the touch, tempting, warm.

She rubbed her cheek against it and felt the small grumble in his chest. Not hardly a groan, a rough sigh of pleasure as his hands threaded through her hair.

"I want to touch you," she whispered.

She needed to touch him. Everything was spinning out of control. He was the only thing she had left to hold on to as the world unraveled around her. Around them both.

"Touch," he sighed. "Sweet baby. My coya."

His coya in private. His whore to his men, nothing more. How much longer could she bear this?

She caressed the hard length of his cock with slow, easy strokes. Her fingers moved from base to shaft, stroked lower and curved around the heavy sac of his balls. She licked his chest, nipped it, kissed it.

She loved him the only way she knew how. With her touch, with her kiss. Moving lower, knees bending as she knelt before him and licked the engorged crest.

She stared up at him, sucked him into her mouth and watched as his head tilted back, his long hair falling over his shoulders. The broad planes and angles of his face were tight with need now, his lips heavy with sensual hunger.

"God, your mouth," he groaned, staring down at her again. "Suck me, Anya. Sweet coya. Take me into your mouth."

His coya. She was his coya here, but nowhere else.

Her lips parted as she drew the thick head inside. Immediately a pulse of pre-cum filled her mouth. As warm as heated syrup, tinged with lightning and male promise. She loved the taste of him. Loved the power and the promise in his taste, in his touch.

His fingers in her hair, the tight flex of his thighs, the throb of heavy veins beneath the silken flesh of his cock.

"Anya. Yes, damn you, I could die in your mouth it's so good."

His hips moved, pressing inside the heated depths as she opened for him, took as much as she could and sucked him, lashed the sensitive underside with her tongue. Another pulse of heated fluid and she was wilder, hungrier. Another and she was desperate, whimpering, reaching for him.

And he was there. Lifting her into his arms, laying her across his desk. His lips played with her nipples, first one, then the other. Hunger enfolded them, surrounded them, sank into their pores as they fought to devour each other.

Her lips were at his shoulder, his on her breast. His hands stroked her thighs, moved between. Calloused fingers rasped through the silken folds as her head tipped back, a strangled cry leaving her lips at the pleasure washing over her.

"I need to taste you." Heated, rough, his lips moved down her stomach. "All that sweet cream I can smell. So hot and sweet, Anya."

His lips caressed, licked, kissed to her thighs. Pushing her legs farther apart, he moved to the aching flesh there, his tongue swiping through the wet center as she cried out his name.

She arched, begged. Her legs fell over his shoulders as his hands gripped her rear, held her to him, and he ate her with a pleasure she couldn't contain. Heated, hungry lips, his tongue an instrument of pleasure and lust. He licked and stroked.

Electric pleasure whipped through her, left her writhing beneath each caress.

Her fingers tightened in his hair as his tongue circled her clit, his lips surrounded it, and the suckling, heated pressure began to draw ecstasy to its pinnacle.

The explosion that rocked her had her screaming his name. She ground her sex tighter against his hungry lips, fought for more and then arched into the sensations as they consumed her.

Damp with perspiration, she was waiting for him when his head lifted, his hands dragging her legs around his hips as he lifted her to him.

Thick and hard, his erection was pressing inside her as he collapsed in the chair behind him, drawing her legs around his back as he began to work inside her.

Anya gripped his shoulders, stared into her lover's eyes and saw all the desperate pleasure, the aching need and loneliness she felt inside herself.

"Too slow," she moaned. "Harder, Del-Rey. Take me hard and fast."

His hands clenched on her rear, fingertips delving into the narrow cleft there.

Anya clenched her muscles around the flared head as it lodged inside her. A hard, heated spurt of pre-cum had her whispering his name again. Another had her trying to force him inside her.

"Now," she panted. "Hard, Del-Rey. Take me hard. Give me everything."

His black eyes, hints of blue, were fierce with the insatiable need that poured between them.

"Fuck me, wild man."

He growled, hips flexing, his cock driving deeper, and he didn't stop. Thrust after thrust until he was filling her, and he didn't stop.

Holding on to him, Anya moved with him, her arms wrapping around his neck as her lips took his kiss, smothering both their cries as she moved against him. Taking him, loving him. Her sex sucked his erection inside her as she sucked his tongue into her mouth.

The deep, penetrating thrusts raked and caressed exposed nerve endings. She could feel the pleasure building, ratcheting up with each thrust, until she was mindless with the need blazing through her like wildfire.

She needed.

She braced her feet on the chair behind him as she lifted and fell with him, his hands on her ass, his fingertips clenching on her rear, pressing into sensitive nerve endings there. His lips took hers, caressed hers. They were buffeted by a storm of sensation that caught them off guard, left them fighting for release, bucking and thrusting until Anya tipped her head back and cried out in a perfect, burning orgasm that sent her flying.

Mindless. Bodiless. She was pure sensation, pure pleasure burning in his arms as he thrust into her full-length and that deep, burning swelling filled her until she was shooting into the stars and exploding into a white-hot center of pleasure.

She was aware of him following her. The way he growled her name, jerked her to him and bit into her shoulder again. To hold her in place, she thought hazily. That bite held her body in place where he wanted her, in perfect alignment with his, his seed spurting inside her, filling her so deep, with such hard, burning spurts that she knew she would never be the same.

She collapsed against his chest when his teeth finally released her. His tongue licked over the wound, each caress sending a racing shiver through her as she shuddered in his arms, his cock still locked inside her.

"I need to hold you," he whispered, his lips caressing her neck. "Just like this, Anya. Just in my arms."

Her head rested on his shoulder, turned away from him as she fought back her tears. Just like this, just in his arms, and separate everywhere else.

It was like being torn in two. Always on the outside staring into what had been or what could have been and knowing he wanted nothing more than this.

◆　◆　◆

Del-Rey watched an hour later as Anya moved from the private bathroom attached to the office—dressed, she was beautiful but her expression was somber.

That was what was missing, he thought, her smile.

"I'll see you tonight?" she asked, fiddling nervously with

the hem of her sweater as she pulled it over the low-rise waist of her jeans.

"Tonight," he promised.

"Maybe we could shower together?" There was something lost in her voice, something that cut him to the bone.

"Are you okay?" He moved from the desk to cup her cheek in the palm of his hand. "Do you hate me, Anya?"

Her lips trembled. "I love you, Del-Rey," she whispered, staring up at him with those sad blue eyes. "I'll always love you."

He dropped his hand as she moved quickly away from him then and escaped as he stood in shock and surprise. He had known she loved him; he could feel it in every touch. He had known it since she was sixteen, had burned for it when she was twenty. But he hadn't expected her to admit to it.

Following her to the door, he opened it and watched her leave. From the shadows across the wide cavern that led into Communications, he glimpsed someone else.

Ashley.

She stood, eyes narrowed on him, a knife sheathed on her thigh, the olive gray uniform he had rarely seen her in giving her a harder, merciless look as she turned her head and stared back at him with a cold, level gaze before moving to follow her coya.

He didn't like seeing Ashley in drab olive green. The next time he saw her, he'd have to ask about that. He much preferred the flirty Ashley in color and tripping around with her pretense of ditzy fun.

This Ashley, he sighed heavily, like Anya, reminded him of everything he could feel he was losing.

CHAPTER 22

Anya had hoped to delay a confrontation for herself or between the now opposing factions of Coyote soldiers. She felt as though she and Del-Rey were in the middle of a very silent war. Hers against his. She could feel everyone's determination, like her own, to leave the alpha out of it. It wasn't his fight. It was hers.

A fight to keep the Russian Coyote Breeds within the alliance that had formed and to hold on to the tenuous peace she could feel unraveling around her. A peace she had worked eight months to ensure. The battle between his and hers. The Coyote soldiers that had followed Del-Rey for so many years and the ones she had fought tirelessly to gain freedom for.

As long as she had been coya, peace had reigned. Now those of the Russian pack saw an insult in the reversion of rights and her lowering of status. She saw Del-Rey's reasons, almost understood them, but to make them work there was no way that the packs could know the reasons.

That left them at a stalemate she feared wouldn't last much longer.

It was evening by the time she made it into the kitchen. There had been an attempt made to load the dishwasher. It was haphazard at best.

The kitchen was the biggest problem in the whole facility. None of them wanted to clean up their own messes. Soldiers were always in a rush, teams rushing in to eat, then back out. Some came in weary and tired, fixed what they could, then went to sleep, exhausted. She couldn't fault them, but she couldn't keep up with them either.

At least someone had tried.

She was straightening the dishwasher when Jax stepped into the kitchen. Tall, light blond, with darker streaks and dark blue eyes. He was as handsome as the others. Breeds were created to be perfect in every way.

He wasn't cruel with it, or even mean. But like the other soldiers, he pushed and he tested his boundaries. He hadn't tested her as coya, but it seemed he was determined to test her now.

"You didn't make biscuits," he noted as he moved to the fridge and set out a plate of thickly sliced sandwich meat. "Morning teams missed them."

"I was busy this morning," she sighed, straightening the dishes in the machine.

"Yeah, Del-Rey's a horndog when he gets started," he snickered. "I remember a coupla years back, he wore three women to exhaustion and was looking for a fourth before the night was out. Damn, he was fun then."

Anya stiffened. "TMI, Jax."

He snorted at that. "Come on, Anya, you know what he's like yourself. You checked out his rep before you came to that bar when you first met him. You were a cute little thing," he commented. "I wouldn't have waited so long if I'd been Del-Rey. I would have done you that night."

Anya straightened slowly and turned to face him. He was standing behind her now, his expression controlled, his gaze cool.

"Don't do this, Jax," she said softly.

"Why? Because Cavalier likes to warn those of us that followed Del-Rey what a little angel you are? What happened, Anya? How did you betray the alpha enough to force him to revert your authority?"

She shook her head. "Ask your alpha. But let this go tonight, Jax."

"You betrayed us somehow, Anya," he growled. "No Breed

turns his mate away for any other reason. He stripped you of status. Why?"

She tried to edge away from him. She hadn't expected this, and surely Del-Rey hadn't either. That the Breeds who followed him would suspect she had done something to harm them.

She could feel the fear clogging her throat now. Jax wouldn't hesitate to take her throat out. Suspicion was as good as proof to the Coyote Breeds. And Del-Rey had provided them with plenty of suspicion.

She was nearly at the corner of the counter, almost far enough away to escape him, when he grabbed her wrist and jerked her back.

Agony streaked through her at his touch. She barely held back her scream as he jerked her back into place, and released her just as quickly. Her hip slammed into the counter as she drew in a hard, pain-filled breath.

"You aren't screaming in agony, Anya," he pointed out. "Are you even his mate? What? Did you play the alpha's guilt and somehow convince him he was your mate?"

There was no meanness; there was determination. Jax was convinced she was a threat, and in his eyes, he was doing what needed to be done.

"Please, Jax," she whispered. "Ask your alpha. Don't do this."

"You think because he still likes fucking you that you can convince him to cover for you?" Jax snorted. "Answer the damned question, bitch. What did you do?"

She shook her head, then waited until he moved and tried to run.

A dirty kitchen was a dangerous kitchen. There was a fine film of flour or maybe sugar on the floor. Her foot slid as he caught her by the hair, throwing them both off balance. She found herself thrown again, this time against the wall. Her head struck the stone, her wrist bent against it painfully as she cried out and tried to keep herself from falling.

She managed to find her feet, jerking around only to stop, eyes wide at the sight of Cavalier and Ashley. Cavalier's knife was against Jax's jugular, Ashley stood at his back, a long, wickedly sharp knife in each hand as she faced off against three of Jax's teammates who had run into the kitchen as well.

"No. Cavalier. Stop." She stumbled across the room, nearly falling as she realized she had managed to somehow bruise her leg. There was blood on her jeans, a slice across the material.

Cavalier snarled in Jax's face as the knife bit into the other Breed's neck.

"Coya, return to your rooms." Cavalier's voice was an echo of death.

Anya inhaled roughly as the other Breeds turned to her, their expressions hard, suspicious, accusing. She wasn't coya, yet the Russian Coyotes refused to accept the alpha's directive. Refused the loyalty they swore to him.

"Back up, Brazon," Ashley snarled as one of the pack leaders tried to edge closer. "I'm hell with this blade, you should remember that."

Brazon stopped, his amber eyes measuring his chances before he turned to Anya.

"Cavalier," Anya whispered hoarsely. "You once swore you owed me for your life."

Cavalier growled furiously. "Don't."

"You owe me his life." Her breathing hitched painfully. "Swear to me you'll let him go. I'll leave the room, but you swear to me you won't harm him." His pride was fierce. If she made him back down while she was there, he would suffer for it. His pride, his sense of honor, would suffer.

"He struck against his coya," Cavalier snarled.

"I'm not his coya." The first tear fell. "Please, Cavalier. Swear it."

She couldn't stand it. She couldn't hold up, and there was no way she could let Del-Rey see her tonight. Not like this. He would kill Jax. She couldn't fight any longer. She was tired, she was lost, and on the inside she felt broken.

"Don't ask this of me," Cavalier bit out. "No matter your title, he had no right."

"They think I betrayed them," she told him. "He'll learn better. Swear it, Cavalier, or I'll leave this base and I'll never return. And I'll leave alone."

Without friends or security. Without the men and women

who'd sworn their lives to her. A mate undefended. Cavalier would never risk that.

"I won't hurt him." His voice was primal, enraged. "This time." There was a warning there she prayed Jax would heed.

She turned to the others. "Go to your alpha for explanations. This fight ends now."

They stared back at her silently.

"Brazon." The pack leader had once been her friend. "Please."

His nod was slow in coming. "This time, Anya. This time only."

She would have to leave. She had no choice. If she didn't, blood would be shed and the Coyote alliance and Del-Rey's dreams would be gone forever.

Grief churned in her stomach, sickening her as she limped from the kitchen and hurried through the community room. She was aware of Sofia watching quietly, another lash to her pride. By the time she reached the tunnels, she was sobbing with the pain. It was tearing through her, breaking her down until she didn't know if she could survive the agony flaying her.

◆   ◆   ◆

Cavalier waited until she was gone. His knife still at Jax's throat, he stared into the other man's eyes. "You're his brother," he said softly, speaking of Del-Rey. "I smell the bond between you and the kinship. He doesn't claim you, whelp. Does that make you a traitor?"

It took only seconds for Jax's eyes to widen in horror. Long enough for Cavalier to pull back and slide into a defensive position. Long enough for Ashley to move. She moved the wrong way.

A snarl of fury, a howl of anguish left her lips, as she turned, jumped the counter until she balanced behind Jax, jerked his head back, and sent the knife swinging on a hard, downward arc.

When she was finished, blood coated Jax's neck and half his ear was missing, as Ashley jumped from the counter and ran from the kitchen. Cavalier covered her, staring back at the silent Breeds as he lifted his hand and activated a private channel on his link.

"Yes." Brim answered on the first beep.

"First blood has been shed," Cavalier warned him. "I believe a medic might be needed."

◆   ◆   ◆

Anya stumbled through the caverns and tunnels, feeling her way for a while as sobs tore through her and tears washed over her face. One hand wrapped around her stomach as the pain seemed to lash at her there as well. She felt the cold as she neared her destination. A cold that seeped into every pore, and yet was warmer than the ice building in her soul.

She collapsed at the mouth of the small cave that overlooked Haven. Covered with snow, it looked peaceful below. A warm glow seemed to extend around the enclosed valley, wrap over it, and tease her with the promise of something she would never have.

She pulled her knees to her chest and rested her head against them as she cried. Everything was lost. She couldn't fight any longer. She couldn't make herself endure this, the pain was too agonizing. If she wasn't here, then Del-Rey would quickly get a handle on the divisiveness beginning to tear the base apart. Without her as a distraction, something to secure, he would see the mess in the making and draw his men together again.

And she would be alone. So alone.

She wished she could howl with the pain ripping through her. With the thought of sleeping alone, always cold, always searching for what wasn't there.

This was her fault and she knew it. If she hadn't allowed herself to lose control when Del-Rey had kidnapped her, then this wouldn't have happened. This division wouldn't have occurred if she had never been given the status of coya while Del-Rey was gone.

She should have seen then the illusion it was. No Breed left his mate, everyone knew that. The tribunal would know that. His enemies would know that. He would have never allowed her to stay at Haven while he was on base, he would have never left her care to others. He had depended on that and the perception that he had not accepted her as his mate to protect her.

Her own arrogance in believing she had a place here had

been her downfall, her ultimate humiliation and the loss of the man who held her soul.

She sobbed at that loss, cried out for it until she felt as though her spirit were breaking from it.

"Its okay, Coya." Ashley's voice had her head lifting in shame, in shock. That these women should see her so broken, so weak, sent a ragged shaft of agony through her soul.

"You need to be warm." Sharone spread a blanket over her, her own face wet with tears.

Emma hunkered beside her, crying as well as she laid her head at the stone wall beside Anya's.

"Anya." Precious Ashley. Her face was pale, her lips quivering, tears streaking her face as she knelt in front of Anya, then curled into a small ball on her side, her head in Anya's lap. "I don't like this," she sobbed at Anya's knee. "I don't like this. They separated us. They took you from us," she cried. "I don't like this, Anya."

Anya sobbed with her.

"Don't let them take you from us," Emma whispered tearfully. "Please, Coya. You've always been our coya. You've always been our leader. Don't let them take us anymore."

Her fierce, ditzy little Ashley. Anya buried her hand in the girl's hair as she laid her head against Emma's, then reached up and drew Sharone to them.

Untamed, so filled with pride, and yet tears streamed down Sharone's face as she laid her head against Anya's shoulder. And not for the first time, they cried together, and they grieved. Because freedom was supposed to mean they would never lose one another. That never again could an order separate them. And yet that was exactly what had torn them apart. The order of the man Anya loved.

It was almost over. Tomorrow, it would finish. If she could manage to hold on, just a while longer, then it would be over. She would be the traitor and the Coyotes that had once followed her would once again follow Del-Rey.

And Anya would finally, irrevocably, be alone.

◆　◆　◆

Del-Rey stepped into the infirmary slowly. Rage was burning a hole in his mind as he listened to the reports on the comm link.

Anya hadn't been found, and neither had her bodyguards. She had gone into the caverns and simply disappeared.

Sitting on a gurney was his brother, the youngest, the one Del-Rey had despaired of saving when the boy was no more than a babe. And now, Del-Rey wanted to kill him.

Jax sat on the gurney, wincing as Regan stitched a part of his ear back where it belonged. Cavalier was there, under guard, willingly.

There were six Coyote soldiers covering him, but behind them were six others, the Russian Coyotes, and they looked furious.

He stared at Jax as the other man stared at the floor, refusing to lift his head.

"Ashley cut his ear off," Brim reported. "Cavalier nicked the skin over his jugular."

Cavalier was leaning against the wall, eyes narrowed, arms crossed over his powerful chest.

This was the man who never stepped out of line. He followed every order, fought like hell, and Del-Rey knew, he would fight to the death. He had never so much as struck at any of the men who had sworn loyalty to Del-Rey.

"That pup," Cavalier spoke first, nodding to Jax. "The next chance I get, I'm slitting his throat. When I do, I'm going to watch him bleed like the gutless rat he is, Delgado."

Delgado. Not alpha, not Del-Rey. The subtle insult was acceptable, but grating.

"Where is my mate?" That was all that concerned him. He'd find Anya, then figure this out.

Cavalier laughed at that. A harsh, grating sound that had a growl coming from his throat.

"Ask that little whelp brother of yours what he did to your mate." Cavalier sneered at the title. "What he called her. Your whore I believe it was."

Jax flinched as Del-Rey turned on him. He gripped his brother's hair, jerking his head back and staring into his blue eyes. Eyes like the woman that birthed them. A deep, dark blue that swam with misery.

"What did you do?"

Jax was often impulsive, but he was never cruel. And he was intelligent, too smart to do anything to harm Del-Rey's mate.

God save him, Del-Rey prayed. He would hate to kill his own brother.

"I didn't understand," Jax said, making no apologies, knowledge of his own death filling his eyes. "I thought she had betrayed us. That you had rejected her because she was a traitor."

Del-Rey felt every bone, every muscle clench in his body. "What did you do?"

"He touched her," Cavalier snarled. "He caused her to slip when he gripped her arm to jerk her into place. When she ran out of here, there was a knife wound at her thigh. I think I heard her wrist snap and I know I heard her head hit the wall. That motherfucker hurt our coya, you son of a bitch, and if you're going to kill anyone, put the gun to your head first."

Bleak, desperate fury lashed at Del-Rey. He heard the snarl that left his throat as he threw his brother from him to keep from killing him.

Cavalier laughed. "You can't even protect her against your own men. You make her stay and play your whore for what?"

He jumped for the other man. Jax didn't have a prayer of surviving his rage. Cavalier might.

He heard Brim curse. Suddenly there were bodies blocking him, enraged growls and curses as his men were pushing him back, Cavalier's men holding him back.

Snarls filled the room, primal, enraged.

"Enough dammit!" Brim shouted above the din. "Damn you two." He turned on Del-Rey. "What the hell did you expect, you stupid bastard? You insult her in front of twenty Coyote Breeds that she all but gave her life for and expect them to take it lying down when your stupid fucking brother abuses her."

Del-Rey spun, fists flying, feet lashing; within seconds he had taken down the Breeds trying to hold him back, just as Cavalier did.

They faced each other now.

"My coya is a target," he told the other man, realizing in a flash of insight what he had done. "What I did may have been foolhardy, but it was to protect my mate. My coya."

Cavalier paused.

"I would give my life for her."

Del-Rey stared into the other man's eyes. He wouldn't fight

him unless he had to. He would never fight the man that would stand and face death to protect the coya, Del-Rey's mate.

"We swore loyalty to you, because of her," Cavalier informed him, and it was no more than what Del-Rey had already known. "She was our coya before you mated her."

Del-Rey nodded. "I know that, Cavalier. Now she's hurt. I have to find her. Help me find her."

Cavalier sneered at that. "If you hadn't taken her bodyguards, you wouldn't have to search for her."

Del-Rey's eyes narrowed, fear flashing through him. "Her bodyguards were not reassigned."

Surprised looks turned on him. Two pack leaders' eyes widened.

"Alpha, the rescending of status took her bodyguards. They've been reassigned since the memo went out."

Del-Rey turned on him. Icy, murderous fury filled him.

"Find her," he growled. "If I don't have the location of my coya within the next twenty seconds, the lot of you can pack your asses out of this base and get fucked. You stupid bastards," he yelled back at them. "Did I tell you to do this? Did I tell you to endanger my fucking mate?"

"No, Alpha," Brim answered for them, the sneer in his voice unmistakable now. "You rescinded her status. By refusing to accept her official vows, you rejected her." Flipping on his own link, he began barking out orders as Del-Rey's jaw clenched in fury.

Hell, he'd managed to fuck this one up royally. He stared at every man in the room now.

"Within the next fucking hour, you will receive memos," he snarled. "My mate, my coya, will be making her official vows this spring. And pray to God she's alive to make them, or every damned one of you will die for being stupid."

"And you, Alpha?" Cavalier growled furiously. "You did this to her, not those of us who face you now. You placed suspicion on her shoulders by rejecting her. Your men only followed your lead."

Del-Rey pinned him with primitive fury. "I'll already be dead, Cavalier," he informed him. "A man doesn't live without his soul. Take that woman from me, and that's what you'll see.

Exactly what the Council strove for. A Coyote without a soul."

With that, he strode from the infirmary. Fuck this. He knew how to find his mate. He knew her scent unlike anyone else could know it. He knew his mate, her pain and her tears. And that was the scent he followed.

To no avail. Before the night was over, the caverns echoed with his howls of rage. Coyotes were searching the mountain, the heli-jet was in the air, and teams were dispatched to Haven.

Del-Rey's coya had disappeared along with three of her female Coyote bodyguards. And some feared she had disappeared forever.

CHAPTER 23

Dr. Armani didn't slip Anya into the main portion of Haven. She met her and the three bodyguards as they pulled to the bottom of the mountain in a stolen all-terrain.

Sharone and Emma helped Anya into the passenger seat before the doctor slid into the back with Ashley and Emma as Sharone drove, lights out, to a hidden entrance into the medical facility.

The cut from the knife that had fallen from the table and grazed Anya's leg was deeper than she had at first believed. Her wrist was broken and the side of her head ached from its impact with the wall.

Nikki was silent as she applied a skin adhesive over the leg rather than the antiquated stitches used for smaller injuries. Anya's wrist was placed in a hard plasti-cast and secured in place before the doctor cleaned the abrasion at the side of her head and carefully applied a film of adhesive there as well.

"I can't believe he allowed this to happen." Nikki's voice was rough with unshed tears. "I need to get the lupina in here. She has to see this. There's no way the Breed tribunal won't grant you complete safety against those monsters, Anya."

Anya lifted her head in shock. "It wasn't their fault, Nikki," she whispered. "They think I betrayed them."

"Fuck them!" The harsh fury was followed by a hard grip to Anya's shoulders as Nikki shook her fiercely, a tear slipping free and running down her dusky cheek. "Look at you, Anya. It doesn't matter why. Jax laid his hands on a woman. A human woman, weaker than himself, unable to defend herself, and he let her be harmed. That is not Breed honor, that is a monster."

Anya shook her head. "It was an accident."

"It was fucking abuse," Nikki yelled in her face as Sharone, Emma and Ashley paced the room. "Abuse, Anya. There is no excuse; there is no forgiveness."

Ashley snarled as she jerked the doctor back, her enraged face nose to nose with Nikki's. "Your hands hurt her. Keep them off her unless you're treating her."

Nikki stared back at the younger girl, and Anya saw the torment in her face.

"Ashley, I'm okay, it didn't hurt," Anya whispered. "Come here, little sister."

Ashley was breaking apart on her. The feral animal she fought to keep hidden was breaking free at the rage and pain filling her. Anya hadn't been the only one betrayed. These young women who had so hoped for a normal life, for freedom and laughter, had been betrayed as well.

The others hurt, but Ashley, who had so depended on Anya's laughter, her support and affection, had suffered the most.

The younger girl tore herself from the doctor after a last warning look, but rather than coming to Anya, she paced again. As though her slight body contained too much energy, too much power for her to contain.

"Ashley's right," Nikki admitted roughly. "I shouldn't have touched you. It was no better than what that fucking Coyote did."

Nikki was cursing. It was supposed to be a bad thing when Nikki cursed.

"Doctors Chernov and Sobolova will be at the spa in Advert late tomorrow afternoon." Anya swallowed back her tears. "Del-Rey is going to be watching for us. We have to get Alpha Gunnar and the lupina there for this meeting and get asylum requested." She pushed the fingers of one hand through her damp, mussed hair. "Jax messed my plans up."

Ashley snarled viciously, a primal, animal sound that caused Anya to wince. "And Ashley needs her nails done. She gets rabid when they chip."

Poor Ashley, her nails were bare and natural, the polish gone, the pretty little designs painted on them had disappeared. They had been filed to sharp little points that were strong enough to lay open flesh.

"I should have killed him rather than cutting the side of his ear off," Ashley bit out. "I should have done what Cavalier was unwilling to do and sliced his throat."

"That wasn't what I wanted, Ashley," Anya whispered. "The alliance has to stand. We agreed to that; it's the only safety for the Coyotes."

"Anya, once Wolfe sees this, there will be an inquisition," Nikki told her fiercely. "This will not pass. If Del-Rey doesn't control his men, then Haven will break the alliance. You know this as well as I do."

Anya shook her head. "It was only one."

"Bullshit!" Emma burst out in an uncharacteristic display of feral defiance. "It was all of his men. His men, not ours. Do you know the trouble we got from the team leaders for trying to cover you? They disobeyed even their pack leaders and assigned the Russian Coyotes as far as possible from you. This was not just a few men. It was his entire fucking base of rabid mongrels."

Anya lowered her head and shook it wearily. Even her bodyguards didn't see what Anya had known.

"They're soldiers," she whispered. "Completely dedicated to their alpha, just as the three of you are to me. They believed I had betrayed Del-Rey and the base. Their only safety." She lifted her head and stared back at them painfully. "Jax didn't mean to hurt me. I slipped and everything went to hell from there. It would have never happened if they hadn't been certain Del-Rey was rejecting me rather than attempting to protect me."

"You're a fucking bleeding heart," Nikki muttered. "You'd die for any of those bastards."

"Yes. I would," Anya sighed. "Their freedom is worth dying for, Nikki. I know them. I know Jax. He was protecting Del-Rey and the packs. He would have never deliberately hurt me."

She tried to convince herself of that. Wanted to, but she had been terrified as she faced him.

"What time is that damned fucking meeting?" Nikki cussed again.

"At three," Anya told her. "Coyotes will be all over the place soon. We're going to have a hell of a time getting out of Haven."

"Then we better move you out of here before they start swarming like flies over the dead," she snapped, turning to Sharone. "There's a vehicle in the back, get it ready to roll. There are weapons in the locker of the garage, easy to find. I have a safe house. I'll take the four of you there, then come back here and talk to the alpha and the lupina."

Anya didn't want to be here for that conversation. She caught Nikki's arm, glaring back at her fiercely. "This was an accident, Nikki. I wouldn't lie to you about it."

"Yes, you would," Nikki snapped. "Remember, you said it, Coya, you think they're worth dying for."

Anya stared back at her intently. "You listen to me, Dr. Armani. If you tell Alpha Gunnar I was abused, I will deny it. I'll scream it. I don't lie, even for my people. Freedom isn't served by lying, and the freedom of my people is more important than a lie for a single Breed that could bring it all down."

Nikki's lips tightened. "Sharone, get that vehicle ready to roll. I'm making a call. Three female Wolves I know will protect Anya with their lives. They're our best. They'll drive you out of here, and no one will question them or think to follow them."

Anya released her wrist.

"Alpha and Lupina Gunnar will be at that meeting as well as every Wolf Breed ready and able to roll."

Anya nodded as she slipped off the examination table.

"Del-Rey will be here," she whispered.

"Delgado can get fucked," Nikki snarled. "I'm so pissed off with him I could shoot that bastard myself. Damned stupid men. I hate Breed males. I fucking hate them."

Nikki stomped to the counter, slipped her comm link over

her ear and made her call as Anya wrapped her arms over her chest.

She was cold again. So cold. The arousal wasn't back though, and honestly, Nikki's examination hadn't hurt. Evidently the cycle for the mating heat was easing. If she was lucky, she'd get through the next day without too much difficulty.

"Vehicles and weapons are ready." Sharone stepped back into the room, her expression hard, composed as she stared back at Nikki. "Our coya needs to eat. She hasn't had anything since morning."

"There's food at the safe house." Nikki nodded. "Satin or one of her enforcers can go for takeout if you prefer."

Anya nodded wearily. She didn't care about the food. She was exhausted. She wanted to sleep. She wanted to curl into Del-Rey's arms and she wanted to be warm, and it was never going to happen again. After tomorrow, he would reject her in truth for betraying him.

The Coyote Breed scientists had tried to strip the Coyotes of their humanity in ways often more destructive than what had been done to the other Breeds. Psychologically, their scars were so deep, so bloody, that Anya knew they would never attain the quiet surety the Wolves and Felines had attained.

Coyotes would always be rougher, the baddest of the bad boys. They didn't just struggle with the two opposing sides of their genetics, animal and man; they also struggled with the very idea of their humanity. They were created to be animals, thinking, walking, talking animals, whereas the other Breeds were created to be strategists, thinkers, plotters and killers.

The Coyote was created simply to kill other Breeds. To track them, hunt them, torture them. That was all. It had bred distrust among the packs and prides before the alliance was ever formed. A charge of abuse from one of those Coyotes could decimate that alliance.

"Del-Rey should have protected you," Emma hissed, turning to her. "He shouldn't have had us pulled from your protection."

Anya shook her head. She understood his reasons. Neither of them had considered the chance that one of the Coyotes would believe she was a traitor. Del-Rey would have never left her undefended if he had thought, even briefly, that such a thing would happen.

The result of it was breaking her heart in two. It was leaving
gouging wounds in her soul, and fighting back that pain was
killing her. She wanted to scream out at the injustice of it, the
unfairness of everything she was losing. And she wanted
Del-Rey to hold her, just one more time. Just one last kiss. Just
something to hold on to.

◆   ◆   ◆

Del-Rey strode into the alpha residence, stopping just inside
the door as Brim, Jax, Cavalier and six other enforcer-level
Coyote Breeds stepped in behind him.

Alpha Gunnar was waiting for him, along with Jonas Wyatt
and Dash Sinclair.

"Bring two men with you." Wolfe's amber eyes were icy
with contempt and rage. "And that one stays outside my home."
He punched his finger in Jax's direction. "I'd suggest he protect
himself in an all-terrain."

Del-Rey's jaw tightened, but he turned and nodded to the
others, leaving Brim and Cavalier at his side. Wolfe's eyes narrowed at the Russian Coyote before he nodded in approval and
turned away, leading the way into his office.

Lupina Gunnar was waiting in the corner behind her mate's
desk, standing, arms crossed over her breasts, her blue eyes
glaring at Del-Rey.

"I tracked my coya to Dr. Armani's medical facility," Del-
Rey stated as the door closed behind them. "She refuses to inform me where Anya went from there."

Wolfe took his seat as Jonas and Dash stood ready and prepared at each side of the desk and Del-Rey and his men faced
them.

"So you want me to order my doctor to turn over information on your abused coya?" Wolfe's voice throbbed with power,
with fury. "Then you insult me by bringing that man into my
home where my mate, my lupina, resides?"

Del-Rey could feel the shame curling through him, and the
fury. He'd fucked up. He'd not just hurt his mate, but he'd endangered her, left her without his protection or the protection of
the women who would have prevented this. Out of his igno-
rance and his belief that his men would never treat her any differently than they ever had, he had endangered her.

"The fault was mine, Alpha Gunnar," he bit out. "I take responsibility for it and will face whatever inquisition comes after I locate my coya. So yes, I insist that you order your doctor to give me the location where she has hidden my mate." By the time he finished, the growl in his voice was primal.

"Alpha Delgado," Dash spoke quietly, "Anya's injuries weren't piddling. A gash in her thigh from a blade. A broken wrist. A possible concussion. Injuries delivered by your man in response to your rejection of her status as coya. This is an animalistic society. You rejected your mate, what did you think your men would believe?"

"We are not just animals," he snarled. "Jax realizes what he's done and punitive measures will be taken in accordance to Breed Law. I stand by the alliance we signed. Unless you refuse me access again, to my mate."

Jonas sat down slowly on the corner of the desk, his gaze going to Cavalier. "You witnessed what happened?"

"I came in as he grabbed her." Cavalier nodded. "She slipped, causing a blade that had been laid at the side of the table to slice her leg. Jax tripped and, as he tried to right himself, more or less threw her across the room. I admit, it was an accident. There was no clear intent to harm, only to frighten."

A growl rumbled in Del-Rey's throat. "And that is still unacceptable," he snapped. "No man on my base has leave to touch a female in any such way, no matter the reason. Jax knew this, and he knows the punishment for it. He will be dealt with."

"And you have him with you in your search for your coya," Wolfe pointed out, his voice ice.

"Because he's the best fucking tracker I have," Del-Rey snapped. "He found her. A vehicle left the house and left Haven's grounds. I want to know where my coya is."

"Safe." Hope spoke up. "From you and from your men until such time as she deems herself ready to face you again. Go back to Base, Del-Rey," she said scathingly. "Maybe her absence will make your heart grow fonder."

He stared back at her silently, long enough that the male Breeds in front of him began to bristle. His fingers ached to curl into fists beneath the leather of his gloves, and he could feel his hackles rising as he faced off with the other men seconds later.

"Do you know where my coya is?" he asked one last time.

Breaking the alliance wasn't something he wanted to do, but he'd be damned if these Breeds were going to rule his life.

Wolfe stared back at him unblinkingly.

"You kidnapped your mate," Del-Rey snarled. "I've heard the tales, Wolfe. You tied her to your bed and kept her there until you killed her demon mother in front of her eyes. Should I read into that what I want to? Should I decide you raped your mate and forced her compliance? Don't forget, Alpha Gunnar, I know well the ways of twisting words and events to suit my own designs. Don't play this game with me and don't consider yourself more than my equal in this game we're playing within the alliance. You will not control me simply because you think you control my mate."

Jonas and Dash turned to Wolfe as he stared relentlessly back at Del-Rey. Finally the Wolf Breed alpha sighed. "Nikki won't even tell Hope where she's located. All we know is she's safe and protected outside Haven. Where you can't reach her."

"Where I can't reach her," Del-Rey repeated, staring back at the other men with a sneer. "Fuck the three of you. To my knowledge out of this whole damned society Dash Sinclair is the only Breed to have treated his mate with any honor once he came in contact with her. I did my research. You can rail at me as you wish. Anya and I will feel our way through this mating the same as you were given the chance to. Unless your damned doctor manages to get her killed first."

Wolf winced and looked at his wife. Hope was still glaring at Del-Rey, still furious.

"She came to us hurt and requested our help," Hope snarled. "Did you expect me to simply send her back to you?"

"I expected you to allow me to see that my fucking mate was safe!" He throttled the demented screams that built in his throat. "I expected a chance to clean out my base and fix this problem. The same as any Wolf pack leader would be given. You have no right to do this."

"She needed medical care." Hope shrugged as though unconcerned, though he could smell her concern. It was thick, fierce. "You don't have medical in that base that would safely treat a mate in mating heat. Her bodyguards brought her to a doctor who could treat her. She requested protection for a period of twenty-four hours." Her smile was mocking. "I'm lupina. Trusted. My alpha's equal where my responsibilities are concerned. I have the authority to grant that protection for a short amount of time." She tipped her head to the side inquisitively. "Did your coya have even enough authority to order your man's hands off her?"

No, she didn't, because of his stupidity, because of his lack of knowledge in what he had done by stripping her of status in his attempt to protect her.

"The second I learned of her confrontation with Jax, her status was reinstated," he growled. "The second, Lupina. Whoever the traitor is that I've been tracking in my base, he is now aware of her importance to me. Two attempts have already been made on her life. She was safe as long as she had no status outside my lover. Is she safe now that she's in your care?"

Wolfe reached out and caught his wife's hand. His fingers twined with hers as her lips thinned and he turned his gaze back to Del-Rey.

"For the moment, your coya is safe, of that I have no doubt," he sighed. "But you're right, Alpha Delgado, you have the right to ascertain that yourself. I'll talk to Dr. Armani myself and see if we can't learn her location. We'll go in together."

Del-Rey's lips twisted mockingly. "I have forty Coyotes heading to Advert. Be kind enough to give your Wolves guarding my mate the order not to shoot them on sight." His expression hardened. "I hear Satin and her enforcers believe the only good Coyote is a dead Coyote. I'd hate to see one of my men die because of her trigger-happy little fingers."

"If you know where she's at and who she's with, then why come here?" Wolfe asked.

"The alliance bylaws demand it," Del-Rey informed him. "That alliance means everything to me, and to my mate, as well as our people. You've been informed, Alpha Gunnar, I'm going to find my mate."

He turned and stalked from the office, Brim and Cavalier following silently as they left the house.

Jonas turned to Wolfe. "Do you know where she's at?"

Wolfe shook his head. "Nikki isn't saying. We have a meeting scheduled for this afternoon, but she hasn't given us the location yet."

"She's a rogue," Jonas bit out. "She needs to be reined in."

Wolfe snorted at that. "Sure, Wyatt, you go for reining her. Let me know how that works out for you."

"We need our own men in Advert," Dash stated then. "Cassie's afraid this is going to end in bloodshed. She's pacing the floors, Wolfe."

Wolfe grimaced. Cassie, or Cassandra, Sinclair knew things she shouldn't know. She saw things she shouldn't see, and if she was scared, then there was a hell of a risk.

"I want every enforcer available," he told Jonas. "Feline, Wolf, Coyote, I don't give a shit. Get them ready. I want half sent to Advert and half ready to fly with us. Whatever the hell is going on, we need to be prepared."

"Doctors," Hope whispered.

Wolfe looked up at her with a frown.

"She's meeting with two council scientists she helped hide in Russia. The very two Nikki has been searching for to bring to Haven. Chernov and Sobolova. Her father is bringing them into Advert. She requested asylum for them."

"Did you grant it?" Wolfe asked carefully.

Hope shook her head. "Nikki just told me before Del-Rey showed up. But that's why Anya ran. She's afraid Del-Rey will kill them. He expressly forbade her to contact them. She's breaking Breed Law and she knows it. She contacted Council scientists without the express permission of one of the alphas of the ruling cabinet."

Jonas cursed, Dash breathed out roughly, and Wolfe felt a sigh of regret pass his lips. They had no choice but to give asylum to the doctors. Giving asylum to Anya wouldn't be as uncomplicated.

"She had my permission." Jonas shrugged, as though surprised. "Didn't you get that memo?"

Wolfe's head jerked up. Only one alpha had to be contacted. Responsibility then went to that alpha to contact the others.

"We've had server problems," Wolfe said softly. "Had to shut everything down."

"Ah." Jonas's eyes widened as he spread his hands. "Well, that explains it. Consider yourselves informed."

"You informed Alpha Delgado?" Wolfe asked.

"Same memo." Jonas smiled.

Wolfe chuckled.

"Manipulating bastard." Dash accused him with a grin. "Remind me to watch the two of you more carefully in the future."

"Hmm," Hope murmured. "Dash is put out. He must not have gotten his memo either."

Male chuckles filled the room, but there was a hint of worry there as well. The Coyote alliance was important to the Breed society as a whole, but more than that, Del-Rey and Anya were their friends. Their future was important to them too.

"Let's get it together," Wolfe said moments later. "Find out where Satin and her women are holding the coya and get a message to her. Let's see if we can do this without killing anyone."

"Let's pray we can get this done without any of us getting killed," Jonas sighed as he moved for the door. "It would look damned bad on the Bureau if we have to wade out of a war in Advert."

And it would plain piss Jonas off, because war was the last thing the Breeds needed right now.

· CHAPTER 24 ·

Daylight was riding the mountains as the all-terrain moved over back roads, following satellite imagery of hidden cabins that could possibly be Breed safe houses. There were many in and around Advert, Del-Rey knew, though he didn't know the locations of each as he should have.

He liked to say Coyotes were lazy and shiftless, that they were more rogues than warriors; otherwise, they'd be Wolves. It wasn't true. They liked to play the game. They liked to convince the world they were that harmless, but the truth was, they were exacting in their deliberate sloppiness.

"Team one." The general link opened to his comm. "Alpha, we've scoured this side of the mountain," Brazon reported. "We found two cabins, empty. One with a vacationing family. Thermal imagery gives us a single adult female, an adult male and two minors. That's it."

"Turn north," he ordered. "There are five cabins on the slope. Thermal tracking picked up smoke from two of them."

"Heading north," Blazon acknowledged as Del-Rey propped his elbow on the side of the door and ran his hand wearily over his jaw.

God, where was she? Was she as cold as he was?

He stared at the thick, heavy blanket of snow that covered the mountains around them, and for a moment he was back in time. He was ten, staring out the bars over his windows as he watched the soldiers chain Brim by a collar around his neck, in the middle of a snowstorm.

There had been a doghouse to huddle in. There had been no warmth. The five-year-old Brim had been naked and depending on Del-Rey to save him. Because Del-Rey had sworn he wouldn't let the boy die.

Brim was blue by the time the soldiers dragged him into the warmth of the cells. He had shaken and shivered for hours as Del-Rey coordinated the Coyotes in the cell so there were two to warm him and the others to hide it.

It had taken him nearly six hours to manipulate the guards and the scientists into deciding to bring him in. There had been so many others he hadn't been able to save.

What if he couldn't save his mate now? After the years he had trained to protect his people, would fate laugh in his face and let him fail with his mate?

God, where was she?

"Team six," he spoke into the comm link. "Any sign?"

"Negative," the team leader reported. "We have four and five working a grid through town, but nothing's shown. City council seems to be meeting today. Strange for a Sunday, don't you think?" the leader mused.

"Keep your eyes open, cover the back roads out of town as well. I want her found."

"We'll find her, Alpha," the team leader swore. "We won't let our coya go unprotected."

But they had, and it had been his fault. He should have thought. The animal genetics were too close to the surface. He'd thought the Coyotes that knew him, trusted him, would see what he didn't tell them. That he was protecting his coya as he protected his brothers. By denying her. Instead, they had seen suspicion and distrust. She was a human, not a Coyote, and he'd rejected her despite the fact that she was his mate.

"Alpha Delgado, this is Base." The communications supervisor came on. "Switch to private."

Del-Rey flipped the link to a private channel, including Brim in the transmission.

"Delgado here."

"Alpha, we found a transmission, erased. I was able to track it from the coya's computer."

"And?"

"Alpha, the transmission originated from her private computer to a public forum and bounced to France. Transmission was to Dr. Jekyll and Mr. Hyde. Separate identities. Another transmission tracked from Austria to the coya's line in private chat arranging a meeting and then confirming said meeting for today. I ran the identities myself. Doctors Chernov and Sobolova from the Russian facility. She's contacted Council scientists. Were you aware of this?"

God love her. He closed his eyes, battling his fears for her. Her drive to protect the Coyotes was going to get her killed.

He thought fast. "You didn't get that memo?" Protecting her was his prime importance.

"No, Alpha, pack leaders did not receive their memos in regards to this," the team leader stated soberly. "But there was that communications blackout and shutdown."

"That explains it." Del-Rey's throat felt tight with emotion. "Your coya was contacting doctors she thought would aid our unique genetics."

"So why meet them alone?" the pack leader asked.

"I don't know, because she was fucking attacked in her own home?" Del-Rey snarled. "Stop asking me damned questions and find her. I want the location of that meeting."

"There was reference to a secondary contact, Alpha," he was told. "The only person she speaks to by phone or link is her family."

Del-Rey's eyes narrowed. "Track down her father and those three useless cousins of hers. Find out if they're where they're supposed to be, and if not, find out where they went."

"On it." The link disconnected as Del-Rey cursed viciously.

"Head to town," he ordered Brim. "She's in town or close. She wouldn't risk a cabin to meet those doctors in. It wouldn't be secure enough."

"She's intelligent," Brim agreed. "She a strategist as well. She would choose a place she feels she knows, one she thinks she can control."

Oh yeah, that helped a lot. He'd be damned if he knew where Anya went when she went to town.

"Team three." He contacted the team that had served as her primary security off base. "List known locations your coya traveled to in town."

The list was like a fucking map of the town.

"What the hell was she doing in every fricken bar in the damned county?" he snarled, glaring at Brim.

Brim shrugged. "I was with you. Wasn't my fault. Alpha Gunnar was supposed to supervise that."

He plowed his hands through his hair as the vehicle surged through the snow that had begun falling again, and headed into the town outside Haven.

He could feel the tension tightening inside him, a sense of fear gripping him whenever he thought of her out there alone, arranging meetings with Council scientists without his protection.

Why hadn't he paid more attention to her insistence, her fear for the people she called her own? His arrogance and ignorant pride were cutting at him now. He should have never stripped her of her title, her authority. He should have listened to her.

Hell, she had contacted a ghost when she was sixteen, and walked into a bar filled with the worst humanity had to offer. She had done it bravely, with confidence and courage, and faced him even after he informed her he was going to kill her.

He should have known that courage hadn't been extinguished. He should have seen her determination to ensure a stable life for the Coyotes. For him and their children.

"We'll find her, Del-Rey," Brim repeated. "You can fix what's been wounded."

"Can I?" he asked his brother then. "Is there any way to repair what I've done to her, Brim? I didn't just strip her of her status, I stripped her of her pride."

"And still she came to you every night." Brim shrugged. "Remember this the next time you're riding high on your own arrogance, and it will bring you back fast. She'll forgive you."

It was a good thing forgiveness wasn't linked directly to whether or not that forgiveness was deserved. Because Del-Rey knew he, least of all, deserved it.

"We're moving into town," Del-Rey announced into the link as he thought of something else. "Team Leader Four, put two men on that city council meeting. That has my hackles rising for some reason."

He couldn't figure out why either. He turned to Brim. "Inform Alpha Gunnar of that little meeting. It's Sunday for God's sake. Since when did they start meeting before daylight on a Sunday morning?"

"Good time to do it," Brim stated. "Wouldn't be too many to notice it. We don't patrol town, just the area around Haven."

Maybe that should change. Maybe some of the money the Coyotes had in their coffers should go toward Breed-friendly politicians in this town.

He grimaced, fighting back his impatience, his fears. He'd find Anya, he told himself. He had to. There was no other answer acceptable; there was nothing else he could live with.

♦　　♦　　♦

The cold had seeped into her bones. Anya sat in the small basement of the safe house, huddled in a heated blanket, and wiped her tears away as she glanced at the clock once again.

Three hours before they made the journey from the house to the spa. Del-Rey was surely looking for her by now. What price had Jax paid for the confrontation in the kitchen? Was Cavalier well? Was Del-Rey warm?

She shuddered at the questions that had tormented her through the night.

They had listened to the heli-jets moving overhead for hours that morning. Satin Belle and her Wolf Breed female enforcers reminded her too much of Ashley. They joked, laughed, did their nails and compared clothes. But Ashley hadn't joined in.

The younger Coyote Breed female was still silent, her gray eyes hard as she cleaned her weapons. Sharone and Emma had followed suit, checking their weapons, going over their plan and watching the Wolf Breed females closely.

Satin, the obvious leader, was brazen. She was sharp-tongued, sharp-witted and, like all Breed females, so beautiful it almost hurt to look at her.

"We have confirmation Alpha and Lupina Gunnar are in

place and prepared for the meeting," Satin stated as she finished drying her nails, after listening closely to whatever was going through her comm link. "We have Director Wyatt in town, Alpha Lyons and Alpha Delgado." Satin's brows lifted as she turned to Anya. "He sounds pissed and he sent a message."

Anya stared back at her.

"He says to tell his coya he made a mistake. It will be rectified the moment she returns."

Anya shook her head. It was too late; she had gone too far to turn back now, and he would never allow this.

"Respond to his message," she said painfully. "Say, 'There is nothing to rectify.' "

Satin stared at her soberly for long moments before nodding and sending the message. A second later her eyes widened, she winced, then cut the link.

"Wow, Coyotes know how to howl," she stated in awe. "That was a good one."

Anya flinched. Coyotes howled only in rage as far as she knew.

"Let him howl," Ashley growled. "This is his fault. Let him suffer."

"Ashley." Anya hardened her expression. "This is not his fault. He wanted to protect me."

"Against what?" she sneered. "His own arrogance? What was there at Base to protect you from except his stupidity?"

She shook her head. "Tonight, I'll ask that question. When this is over, I want the three of you to return here and stay secure until I know the punishment for this. I won't have you suffering further."

"Oh yeah, we're just going to tuck our little tails and hide under our beds while our coya wades into danger headfirst again," Ashley snorted. "Get real!"

"That's an order, Ashley," she said firmly.

Ashley leaned back. "I didn't get the memo making you coya again. Technically, that order's not worth shit, Anya. And even if I had gotten such a memo, you can forget it. Where you go, I go. Period."

Anya inhaled roughly before turning to Sharone for help.

"I'll not be taken from your side again, Coya," Sharone

stated. "Neither will Emma. We've discussed this and we agree. Whatever your punishment, we'll share it."

Would she have done any less? Anya knew she wouldn't have, but it hurt to know that by nightfall, she could be sharing space with them in a cell.

"Hey, you gotta be tough to be a cowgirl, Coya," Satin stated. "Get ready to pony up and ride. I want to be in place ahead of time."

Anya rubbed at her arms. She had received the message earlier from her father that he and her cousins and the two scientists were in place and waiting to head to their meeting.

The spa on a Sunday was the perfect place to meet. It wasn't overcrowded, but it drew a fair crowd from surrounding counties. The enclosed gardens were secluded and made for privacy and relaxation. Tea parties were held there as well as private luncheons at the time Anya would be there.

They would slip into the gardens and into the spot they had selected for this meeting. Alpha Gunnar would be given the location once they arrived, and he would move in with his enforcers.

She unwrapped the blanket and struggled to pull her shoes on.

"Coya, let me help." Emma was there, taking the shoes from her and unlacing them before helping Anya slide them over her feet.

Her entire body screamed in protest at each move. The bruises from her fall, the broken wrist and the wound at her thigh were little when compared to the headache that blazed in her skull.

"Pony up," she whispered achingly. "I'm tired, Emma."

Emma stared into Anya's white face and felt fear curdle in her stomach. She was a Breed that had never known fear until these past days, but she knew it now. Her coya was drained, freezing with a chill, running a fever. Emma could feel her pain, and she could smell something more that she couldn't put her finger on, something that had her instincts screaming out in warning.

"They're doctors," she said, swallowing tightly. "They'll fix you."

"Can you fix a broken heart?" Anya asked, her uncasted hand reaching out to lay her palm against Emma's cheek.

Anya had done that long ago, when they were children, when she had found the girls, dirty, sleeping on rags, naked. She had petted Emma's face and promised her a bed. She had promised Ashley pretty clothes. She had promised Sharone that one day, she would smile. Anya had kept her promises even at the worst cost to herself.

Emma lifted her hand and touched her coya's face then. Her friend. Her protector. "One day, you will smile again," she promised.

The curve of Anya's lips was sad, almost broken. "I hope you're right. So." She breathed in roughly, breaking Emma's heart as she gathered her courage around her. "Shall we pony up, my friends?"

◆   ◆   ◆

Satin Belle stared at the little human who fought to pull herself to her feet, despite her exhaustion. She inhaled slowly, made certain her senses weren't lying to her, then made another call to her alpha.

"Yes?" Gunnar came online as Satin moved into the other room.

"The coya is breeding," Satin said softly. "I advise against this. We should meet with teams, get her to Haven and take care of this ourselves."

Gunnar was silent for long moments. "What's her status?"

"Feverish, weak, extremely pale. I can scent conception, Alpha. I don't know how her bodyguards are missing it, and it's sapping her fast. I've never seen anything like this."

"Teams three, eight and ten are converging on your location. Has she told you where she's meeting the doctors?"

"Not yet. I'll contact you when we have it and move in then. We can't wait much longer, she's going to collapse . . ." She paused.

"Satin?" Wolfe's voice snapped into the link.

Satin moved to the door, stepped into the main room and cursed at the sight of her two Wolf Breed enforcers unconscious on the floor.

"Son of a bitch," she cursed. "They've flown. My girls are down, I repeat, my girls are down and the others have flown the coop. Get those teams in here now."

◆　◆　◆

"I knew better than to trust those bitches," Ashley snarled as she helped Anya sit up in her seat, holding her upright as Sharone maneuvered the car they had stolen the night before from its hidden parking place. "Damn them."

Anya tried to shake awareness into her head. Something was wrong, she could feel it. She needed Del-Rey. She was so cold her teeth were nearly chattering. She was off balance, feverish.

She couldn't believe what they overheard. That Wolfe and Hope would betray her. That the Wolf enforcers she had been sent to would be ready to turn her over to security teams so quickly.

Armani was going to be pissed off.

"Something's wrong with her." Emma worried. "She's getting too weak."

"We're going to meet with damned Coyote doctors," Sharone cursed. "They'll know what's wrong."

Anya hoped they did. She felt off balance, dazed. She needed Del-Rey's touch, but the sexual intensity of the mating heat was missing. She could feel herself inside, crying out for him.

"Call him," she whispered.

"What?" Ashley's voice was frantic. "Anya, you have to sit up. You can't be sick. Tell me what's wrong."

She forced her eyes to open. "Call my mate. Call him, Ashley."

Her eyes widened in distress. "Coya, I don't have a link," she whispered. "We didn't bring links."

She shook her head. "When we reach the spa, take me to my papa and call my mate. I need my mate. Now."

"We need to find Del-Rey," Sharone insisted. "The meeting is only an hour away; we'll have just enough time to get in place."

"There are Breeds scouring the city," Emma hissed. "Let me out. I'll find a team and radio Del-Rey. What's wrong with her?"

Anya could feel fear skating over her now. She shuddered, shook with it. She needed his touch desperately. She felt as though she were going to die without it.

She inhaled roughly. "The spa," she said again. God, she could surely make it that far. "Get me there. Call from there. I need Del-Rey."

"We're nearing the spa, Coya," Sharone answered, worry thickening her voice. "We'll call him from there, I swear it."

♦　♦　♦

Del-Rey lost control at Satin's message. His mate was pregnant and she was without him. She was ill, feverish, reacting with the same symptoms as a Coyote Breed with a life-threatening wound.

"Find her." He turned on Brim. "Find her now."

Brim was staring around the street they were on, his expression intense, furious.

"She would go somewhere she thought was safe," Brim muttered. "A place she could feel comfortable and protected in without her security force."

"Where?" Del-Rey snarled.

"The spa." They turned on Jax where he sat in the backseat with Cavalier.

"What?"

Jax swallowed tightly. "Her security force could only surround the spa. They couldn't go in. Women only. Out back is a huge garden area. Secluded little places for lunches and stuff, all kinds of evergreens and sheltered grottos. They went there a lot. All-day trips."

"Edge of town." Brim hit the gas. "That fucking spa. We had a dozen reports from the team leaders of her security force concerning their inability to adequately protect her there."

"She's a fucking woman. Women like spas," Del-Rey snarled. "I had it on the list to disapprove when Wolfe called laughing at me and asking about flowers for my funeral. They like to be girly. They can't be girly with a man hovering over them." He repeated Wolfe's words.

"Get there," Del-Rey ordered. "Get there now. Those city council members managed to slip past the two men we had on them. My fucking neck is itching, Brim."

"Alpha, this is Communications," a voice barked at his ear. "Sofia has the identity of our problem but lost sight of it. Subject of interest is missing. Estimated flight at an hour and a half. Sofia is trying to track but we fear he's headed to your location. I'm sorry, Alpha, we lost him in the confusion here."

Fuck. Fuck. Sofia had finally found the spy in Base, only to have him slip free. Enduring the pain her presence brought to Anya had been bad enough. Sofia was brash, angry that Anya had refused him eight months before, but she had been his only chance to identify that leak. She had played the disgruntled and rebuffed lover, when nothing had been further from the truth. She had played it too far. And now Anya was paying the price.

"Find them," he growled. "Find them now."

He looked at Brim, fear eroding his control further. "The city council's going after her. They know where the meeting is; they won't bother kidnapping her—they'll kill her."

The vehicle's speed increased as Brim cursed.

Del-Rey clenched his fingers around the weapon he carried and clenched his teeth in rage. He'd known there was a leak in Base. The attack on Anya that night in the mountains had begun his suspicions. Only a member of the base would have known her schedule, her habits. And only one that worked Communications would have been able to give out the locator codes on the comm links.

He had been betrayed from within. Being careful, cunning, weeding the chaff from the harvest hadn't worked in this case. He'd chosen the wrong Breed and placed him in the wrong team. Once again, he'd failed his mate.

He ran his hand over his face, wiped away the sweat and swore he could feel himself bleeding on the inside. Anya was suffering, ill and carrying the child he knew she had ached to give him once she had gone off the hormonal therapy.

As though that child meant more to him than she did. She couldn't know that nothing meant more to him than she did, because he hadn't shown her that. He hadn't proven it with his love. And now she didn't trust him enough to have him at her side.

CHAPTER 25

Anya managed to find the strength to follow her bodyguards into the secluded gardens of the spa and to the sheltered privacy of the grotto they had reserved under a false identity.

Her papa was there, her cousins and the two nervous doctors.

"Anya." Her papa moved swiftly for her, his craggy features twisting into a distressed frown, his blue eyes filling with concern as he pulled her to him. "My baby girl. You are ill."

He kept his Russian accent out of stubbornness, she knew. Her father could sound as American as one born to it, yet he refused to.

A shock of dark red hair fell over his brow as his large hand cupped the back of her head and held her to his chest.

"Papa." She held tight to him. It had been months since she had been able to see him.

His steady strength bolstered her, his courage and bravery. So many years he had worked with her, subtly telling her how to rescue her friends, pointing out weaknesses, strengths in his force, teaching her to see more than just people, but also resources and courage.

He had been her rock after her mother's death. He had been

her hero until Del-Rey, and even now, he was the man she knew would soothe all her hurts if possible.

"Little girl." So Russian, his voice was a whisper of her childhood. "Look at you, so pale and ill. It is good, huh, that I bring your friends."

She pushed away from him, unable to bear his touch for long. Ashley was there to steady her as she turned to Dr. Alexi Chernov, and his niece, Katya Sobolova. They were young, protégés of Alexi's grandfather, and so damned intelligent they were scary.

"Katya." Anya reached for her friend's hands.

Katya wasn't much older than Anya; she was barely thirty. Her clear, unlined expression was tight with worry though, as her too perceptive topaz eyes went over Anya's face.

"Anya, I agree with your papa, you are not well," she said haltingly, a frown marring her brow.

"I'll be fine soon," Anya promised her. "Alpha Gunnar is on his way to this meeting. Asylum is being granted to you and your uncle but under very strict rules. You'll have little freedom."

Alexi shook his head. His brown hair was longer than it had been in the lab facilities, his green eyes worried. "We have no freedom now, Anya. We run in fear of our lives. The Coyote Breeds were our lives, not just our research. To work with them again . . ." He shrugged philosophically. "From what your papa says, we will have more freedoms than we did with the Council, yes?"

"Well, you won't die for stepping outside for that cigar you like so much," Anya promised him. "Though you might have company."

Alexi's eyes crinkled in humor. With his and Katya's arrival in the facilities and their eventual control of it, conditions had changed drastically. They had made Anya's job of aiding the rescue much easier.

"Sit, Anya," her father encouraged her. "Your cousins, they are waiting for your Alpha Gunnar. Why are you ill, child? You are never ill."

"The inoculations we gave her as a child should have made her immune to nearly every virus known to humans," Katya stated, watching her carefully.

"I was inoculated?" Anya blinked back at her. "With what?"

"We all were," Katya confirmed. "Alexi and I developed the immunizations before coming to the labs. We finished them there. The Breeds are immune to all viruses known. We used that inoculation on ourselves as well as you, your family and Sofia. There was no danger involved. We'd been lab testing on certain animals for years. But it has allowed us never to grow ill. Even your papa has not known illness. You should be well."

Anya shook her head. She would get to that later. She turned to Ashley. "Has Emma made that call?" God, she needed Del-Rey.

"We dropped her off before coming here, Coya, remember?" Ashley reminded her gently.

She remembered. She swallowed tightly and focused on her father and her friends again. "You'll be taken out under armed escort."

"You will go with us," Katya said with an edge of fear. "Won't you?"

Anya shook her head and turned to her father. "You and the cousins must leave now, Papa, before Del-Rey arrives."

"Why, will he shoot my leg again?" Petrov Kobrin asked with a snort. "I will not leave you while you are ill, Anya. I will return with you or these Breeds you protect will learn a father's anger. I will stay until you are well."

"We have a Feline Breed arriving, advance scout," Sharone told them. "He's coming armed."

Anya nodded and forced back a cry. Del-Rey had allowed an advance scout rather than coming himself.

"Coya." Fear laced Ashley's voice a second before there was a rustle of greenery, a scuffle, and suddenly, they were surrounded.

She stared at the weapons trained on her father's head, and Ashley's. The Feline Breed stepped into the grotto.

"Douglas," Anya whispered.

The junior-grade soldier that hadn't yet made enforcer. He was young, younger than Anya. Close-cropped dark hair, brown eyes. He was dressed in an enforcer uniform though. A Wolf Breed Enforcer uniform.

He smiled, displaying his canines as he lifted the butt of his weapon and brought it down hard on the back of Ashley's head.

"Ashley," Anya cried out as she moved to kneel beside the girl.

"Come here, bitch." Hard fingers wrapped round her wrist and through the blinding pain she saw the blow delivered to her father next.

Where was Sharone? Anya looked around desperately; feeling dazed, confused. Sharone should be here. Instead, she saw only city council members and the Feline.

Seven humans and one Breed and leading the pack was the mayor, Timothy Raines.

"I hear you're breeding," he sneered as two others tied the doctors' hands and placed gags over their mouths. "I was just going to kill you. I think I'll give you to those nasty Coyotes that have offered us a damned fortune a piece for a Breed mate. Only mates can breed, right?"

Breed? He thought she was pregnant?

She shook her head. "Someone lied to you."

He chuckled. "I don't think so. But we'll get what we wanted anyway. Your fucking kind out of our county. We break the Coyotes' backs, then Haven will fall. That's the only thing saving them right now. Bastards. The alliance will never stand when a Wolf Breed is seen escorting the Coyote's mate out of this spa just before she disappears forever. We'll win. You'll lose."

Sharone and Emma. Where were they? Where was Del-Rey? A sense of vertigo gripped Anya as she swayed.

"The bitch is sick," one of them cursed. "She could be contagious."

"Get her, Douglas. Let's find your damned Coyotes and get our payment."

The fingers that wrapped around her arm were like a manacle of agony, needles driving into her flesh. She went to her knees with a scream, and she swore hell opened up and loosed demons that howled in fury.

"Coya, come with me. Now."

Jax. She lifted her head to stare at the Coyote dragging her across the ground, his expression tormented as he lifted her, carried her as fire flashed around her.

"Coya, you're safe," he growled.

"Papa . . ."

"Cavalier has your father and the doctors. Move. We have to move." He pushed her through the snow-shrouded evergreens that surrounded the next grotto, dragging her through them, pulling her from the sound of gunfire.

"Ashley . . ."

"Taken care of dammit," he growled. "Hurry, Coya. If you get so much as a scratch, the alpha is taking my throat out. Do you want that?"

He steadied her as she tried to crawl, handicapped by the broken wrist and her own weakness.

"Clear," he snapped, his arm wrapping around her waist. "Let's go. We have enforcers just ahead waiting on you."

He rose, and before they could move, they found themselves facing what Anya knew were not the good Coyotes. She swore she could smell them. A stink like blood and death as they smiled coldly.

"Well, it's the princely whelp," one of them sneered. "Move away from her."

Jax pushed her behind him instead. Anya stumbled against the fence before gripping the back of his coat.

"Let him go," she cried out. "Leave him alone."

She couldn't let Jax be hurt. For whatever reason, the young Breed was more important to Del-Rey than the others. He made Del-Rey laugh. She couldn't let that be taken from him.

She pushed to the side, sidling away, knowing the Coyotes would follow her. She could hear the shouts, the roars and howls of rage now filling the gardens.

"Coya, no." Jax held his hand out, trying to push her back. "Dammit, Del-Rey will take my fucking throat out."

"If there's a throat left to take out." The Coyote lifted his weapon. "Good-bye, little prince."

Anya jumped, pushing at Jax as the shot fired and she felt the flames that suddenly enveloped her body.

Jax screamed out to her. Howls of rage filled her mind as she felt herself go to her knees and the ice inside her seemed to fill her veins.

"Anya!" She heard Del-Rey scream as she looked up.

The two council Coyotes were on the ground, bloody, dead. Del-Rey threw himself to her, sliding in beside her on his knees, his hands reaching for her as she looked down, down, to her side and the blood soaking her shirt.

"Del-Rey?" She blinked back at him, crying, desperate when she saw the pure, startled horror that filled his face. "Smile for me," she whispered as the lethargy began to sweep over her. "One more time, smile for me."

♦　♦　♦

Del-Rey caught her. His head tipped back as agony poured from his throat in a vicious, horrible howl. He shook with the grief, the rage as he picked her up, barely aware of Jax screaming out for doctors. Barely aware of anything but the smell of his mate's blood.

Howls joined his, Coyote howls, ripping through the gardens, echoing through the mountains as he stumbled to his feet, holding her to his chest, and searched desperately for the doctor that had come with them.

"Armani!" he screamed out as he rushed inside the spa.

She was here. They had left her in the protection of the building.

"Del-Rey." The doctor was there, rushing to his side. "Heli-jet is in the street, hurry."

By her side were the two Coyote doctors. They were jabbering about inoculations, blood loss and fevers as he jumped into the jet.

"Lay her here." A carrier was stretched out at his feet. "We have to get her to Medic. I have to stop the bleeding."

Her shirt was ripped open and Del-Rey felt the fear that tore through him.

"Move, Ghost." Alexi Chernov pushed him to the side. "Let me in there. Blood clotting should go fast," he snapped to Armani as Del-Rey fell back. "The inoculations saved our lives when the Council nearly caught up with us. The boost to immunity has resulted in surprising little extras."

"The blood flow isn't as hard as it should be. We don't know if the bullet hit an organ. Did it go out the back . . . ?"

The three doctors were shouting at one another as they surrounded her. The heli-jet lifted off, banked and shot through the sky to Haven as Del-Rey wiped his face with shaking hands and found tears on his cheeks.

His mate, his heart. She was bleeding, wounded. Her flesh was like fire to touch, her lips nearly blue. As Brim's had once been. So cold.

He edged around until he was at her head, bent and laid his lips at her brow. "I love you, Coya," he whispered. "Live for me, baby. Live for me. Because I can't live without you."

He stayed like that. He could warm her no other way. He held her head steady, his lips pressed to her forehead, and told himself it was the dampness of sweat that dripped to her brow rather than his tears.

◆　◆　◆

Nikki Armani stood back in the surgical room of the medical facility in Haven and watched Chernov and Sobolova work steadily to stabilized Anya Kobrin.

Del-Rey sat by her side, his arm stretched out, a transfusion of his blood moving slowly from his strong wrist to his mate's. His head rested beside hers, and sometimes, she swore she heard the big, rough Coyote praying.

Jonas, Wolfe, Callan, Hope, Dash Sinclair, his mate and daughter waited in the observation room, watching silently, their expressions somber.

"The hormonal fluctuations are too severe," Katya Sobolova stated. "You can't give such hormones during the fever. We need to counteract them."

"She's conceived," Nikki argued then. "We can't afford to mess with the hormones; it could harm the child."

"You don't give hormones to Coyotes in heat," Katya stated. "It results in pregnancy every time. This we didn't want the Council to know. From the creation of the first Coyote, our grandparents knew they were exceptional. Different in all ways. Their true potential was always hidden. That was the reason for the practice of killing their creators. That directive was given to them, even as babes. Their escapes resulted in their creators' deaths. Destruction of all records. There were very few who could manipulate those genetics."

Nikki stared at the other woman in shock. "That's why the Council has been searching for you."

Katya smiled. "We are two of the few Coyote scientists left living. There are no known records of the Coyotes now. Normally, Coyotes themselves took care of killing us. If not the Coyotes, then the doctors assigned to us. They knew their duty." She glanced fondly at Anya's still face. "This one, she hid us during that rescue. The doctors searched for us, but we stayed where she placed us for days, and finally we found another hidden exit from the room."

"If the geneticists that worked on the Coyotes were Council, why make that directive?" Nikki shook her head in confusion.

"The past generations, our fathers and grandfathers, they, like us, could not tell the Council no. They would kill the families of those scientists as well. Our grandparents destroyed records and placed false ones instead. They reported that the Coyotes were as the Council wanted. Soulless, without mercy. They are without mercy, no doubt, but it was always easy to know those who would kill without compunction and those who would kill only when needed. So few Coyotes were created compared to other Breeds, that we were able to work together, pull those we knew were worthy to only certain labs where they would have a chance at life." She shrugged. "Some of us succeeded, some did not. In Russia and in the Middle East, we succeeded. I hope you saved the scientist in charge there." She glanced at Nikki. "Simply amazing. She was the brightest in our field for her young age. As though the Almighty reached down his hand and opened her mind to this area in a way no mind had ever been opened. Incredible."

"There are no reports that she survived," Nikki said.

"Ah." Katya shook her head. "This is too bad. She was an angel sent to know things the rest of us only have questions about. We were attempting to contact her when Anya found us."

"Bleeding is contained," Chernov said quietly, nodding to Del-Rey. "Take him loose."

Nikki shut the valve off and eased the needles from both their arms as Del-Rey refused to take his eyes from his mate.

"Give her a few hours to stabilize," Chernov ordered as he applied the skin adhesive over the wound. "We'll need blood samples then. Several. If you don't get her off those hormones, she will go straight back into heat as soon as this babe is born. You don't want that."

"We have another mated Coyote," Nikki said. "His wife hasn't conceived."

Chernov snorted. "She was not inoculated as this one was with an immunization created from Coyote blood. Coyote females will breed, Dr. Armani. We've always known this. This is why so very few females were allowed to live. We couldn't risk it."

"Why the girls in Russia?" Nikki asked.

Chernov sighed. "My grandfather adored this child." He patted Anya's arm. "We lost my sister when she was but a babe. He saw Anya and lost his very old, cynical heart. I believe perhaps we all did. She has a way about her. She gets what she wants, and she wanted those girls as her friends. We reported their deaths and kept them alive." His head lifted. "We were monsters, Armani, do not doubt it. We killed when we were ordered. We researched with demonic practices when we had to. But every doctor in that lab knew what our true goal was. The survival of those we had arranged to have brought to us. Those five girls, they are the future of these creations. They are amazing."

"Created to breed," Nikki said in horror.

"No. No." Chernov shook his head violently. "Created to be natural. The inability to conceive was coded into the Breed genetics. The records of how they did this were lost so future generations could not undo it. My grandfather and several others learned the secret with the Coyote Breeds. They managed to take this unnatural coding out. How will it work?" He shrugged. "We do not know. If it can help the other Breeds, we cannot say. But the Coyotes are natural. Natural man. Natural animal. We have yet to see what this will accomplish."

"A miracle," Nikki breathed. "If we could figure this out, we could figure out the mating heat. We live in fear of the public taking the tabloid stories seriously. World opinion could go to hell if they figure out it's true."

"Eh. People." Chernov eased back and gently disconnected the saline solution that had dripped into Anya's other arm. "They are fickle. Breeds will always live in fear of this."

He sighed heavily. "She must rest. We need heat packs around her. Her fever is high, but that is natural. The chill is what worries me."

"She needs me." Del-Rey's voice was rough, primitive. "Let me lie with her. She needs to be warmed. I warm her."

Chernov shrugged. "As long as she is allowed to rest for the next week, the wound should be fine. Nothing strenuous." He eyed Del-Rey warningly. "She must be treated as though she would break with a breath, Ghost."

"Del-Rey," he growled.

Chernov grunted. "As though I did not know about those transmissions this child sent you. Six years you waited, though I told Sofia countless times she must tell you the truth of who she was. Chaff from the harvest." The doctor scowled back at him. "As though we were not doing this. You did not research as you should have."

There were a lot things he hadn't done as he should have, Del-Rey admitted to himself.

"She needs a bed," Chernov said. "She needs comfort and care now. Is there a room available here? I do not want her transported for two days at least. Where she goes, we must go as well. With the child she carries, her condition is too delicate. We must watch her closely."

Dr. Sobolova touched Anya's hair gently. "I believe my girls Sharone, Emma and Ashley are awaiting us now," she said. "I have missed them. I would make certain they are well and not suffering from their injuries."

"Petrov Kobrin is demanding to see his daughter, Dr. Armani," Wolfe announced through the intercom. "When she's stable enough, could you please meet with him? I have four crazy Russians consuming vodka in the community center, and Breeds joining in. We're going to have a mess soon if we don't do something."

Nikki nodded. "We have a private room just down the hall. We'll transfer her there and see if her mate can warm her." She glanced at Del-Rey with a cool little smile. "I have a gown she can wear."

Del-Rey didn't rise to the bait. He nodded, rose and was at the head of the bed as they wheeled it to the room.

Nikki jerked the blankets back on the double bed as they maneuvered it into the room.

"Very gently, Ghost," Chernov advised worriedly as they

lifted the blanket Anya rested on. "We'll monitor her for infection, though I do not expect such a thing to develop."

They eased her onto the bed, then pushed the gurney from the room as Nikki helped Del-Rey ease his mate into the soft cotton gown she had pulled from a dresser.

"She'll sleep for a while." Nikki patted his shoulder as she moved for the door. "If you need me, there's a link on the bedside. Rest yourself, Del-Rey."

Rest.

He undressed and eased into the bed on her uninjured side, wrapping himself around her as he pulled the blankets over them.

He flinched at the feel of her cold flesh and rubbed her shoulder, her arm, gently.

She was breathing slow and easy, but her lips were still blue. She was cold, so cold. He eased her legs between his, his arm beneath her head, and all but surrounded her. If he didn't get her warm, he wouldn't be able to keep the knot clogging his throat from choking the hell out of him.

"Come back to me, baby," he whispered at her ear. "Warm me, Anya. I'm cold, love. So cold."

As cold inside as her flesh was on the outside. He kissed her forehead again, then laid his head at her shoulder before gently kissing the little wound he had left there.

"I love you," he whispered. "My sweet Anya. How I love you."

CHAPTER 26

She was warm. Toasty warm from head to toe. She could feel the warmth wrapped around her, like a brush of flesh, like Del-Rey.

It felt like Del-Rey. It didn't feel like death. She didn't feel feverish. She didn't feel cold and in pain. She didn't feel weak and lethargic.

Actually, she was damned hungry.

She opened her eyes as a rumbled growl of hunger caused a flush to heat her cheeks. How long had it been since she had eaten?

A warm, broad palm whispered over her stomach. She felt a bandage on her side and the tight sensation of flesh adhesive.

Memory rushed over her then. The meeting, the attack. Ashley and the girls.

Her eyes opened to meet the gentle, black gaze staring down at her.

"About time."

She stared into his face. There was a rough, rakish growth of beard on his lower face. His lashes were heavy as though he had just awoken himself. Broad shoulders were naked, looming over her side as his fingers lifted to her cheek, his thumb whispered over her lips.

"Don't move too fast," he said softly. "The shot missed vital organs but you bled a lot. The doctors want to be careful that you don't experience more shock." His expression twisted. "The baby's safe."

She blinked back in shock. "Baby?"

"Those doctors you risked your life for—" he cleared his throat—"they knew so much that we didn't, Anya. So much." He shook his head. "I'll let Nikki explain it all later. But you need to be careful at least until our child is born."

His lips crooked into a grin. "I told you, they knew so much we didn't. You were right, Coya, we needed them. You were right about so many things and I refused to listen." He shook his head. "Later. You need food."

She watched, silent, uncertain where to allow her thoughts to land as he slid from the bed and tucked the blankets carefully around her.

"Ashley," she whispered. "Jax?"

He swung around as he pulled a pair of cotton pajama bottoms from the chair and dragged them over his powerful thighs.

"Jax is currently sitting out in the hall, his proverbial tail tucked between his legs as he guards our door. Ashley is fine. A bump on the head to match Sharone's. They were distracted by your illness. They didn't have time to react to the attack." He frowned at her lightly. "That's why I demanded a security force when you left Haven, Mate."

She stared back at him. "You took my girls," she whispered.

He shook his head. "The pack leaders made a mistake in that unsigned memo Brim sent out. A mistake that will never happen again. A signed memo went out the second I learned what happened in that kitchen, Anya, reinstating your status and scheduling our ceremony for spring. Unfortunately, you had left and the Feline Breed that betrayed us all was able to get out of the base." He shook his head. "I should have told you my suspicions, but I didn't want to worry you."

"We were betrayed?" She licked her dry lips in confusion. "What the hell happened while I was gone, Del-Rey?"

"Everything went to fucking hell," he suddenly snarled in

male irritation. "My whole fucking base came down around my damned ears. I'm a general, Coya, not a fucking nursemaid. You need to get well to take care of their gripes and complaints before I start knocking their fucking heads together. You've slept for two days. I've spent that time in that bed." He pointed to her side. "With a laptop, answering a million damned hysterical emails from Coyote Breeds who can't seem to make a decision on their damned own."

Her lips twitched. "All it takes is an occasional kind word, Del-Rey. They're really very responsive to a little emotional pat now and then."

He glared at her without heat. A hint of humor lit his eyes.

"Prove it, Coya."

"Feed me first," she demanded. "And God, I need to use the bathroom."

He helped her to the bathroom first. He carried her in despite her protests, waited just outside the door, then carried her back when she was finished.

She had managed to wash her face and brush her teeth. She felt almost human again as he tucked her back beneath the warm blankets.

"The girls are bringing your food." He sat down beside her gingerly, touched her face again. "I almost lost you."

"I tried to contact you before the meeting," she sighed. "I made them leave their links behind though. When Sharone borrowed one from Satin's enforcer, she heard Satin talking to Wolfe about stopping us. We ran but lost the link in the flight. I couldn't stop, Del-Rey." She stared back at him desperately. "I couldn't stop. We had to have those doctors."

"Shh. The doctors are here, safe and making lists of equipment needed for Base. They're our doctors. They know us, Anya," he said softly. "I never saw so many things. Never suspected that a scientist could be more than a monster. They showed me differently. They showed me what we are, and what we were meant to be as Coyotes. But it wouldn't have mattered. They saved your life. Nikki couldn't have done it. She would have killed you trying to save you, and I was too damned arrogant to understand that."

She shook her head. "Too concerned for your people," she

sighed. "This isn't a blame game, Del-Rey. We survived, right? Jax, Brim, the girls? Everyone?"

"Several wounded, none of our people are dead, though seven city council members and one traitorous Feline Breed were killed." He shook his head at that. "Douglas was hand-picked by me. He wasn't even drugged; he just hated Coyotes. Nothing mattered but that hatred."

She barely knew who Douglas was. He had stayed out of sight for the most part. Now she knew why.

"You have a lot to explain to me, don't you?"

"Quite a bit." He grinned as a soft knock sounded on the door. "Ashley is refusing to let me pay for her nails until she sees you. Sharone is still glaring at me, and Emma is playing with her knives every time she sees me or Jax. I think you should reassure them."

"That ceremony." She stopped him. "Why?"

"Because I love you," he said simply. "You're my coya, Anya. I won't deny that any longer. Denying it was killing both of us, and driving a wedge between our people. And I will re-mind you, I sent out a memo to that effect before you left Base." He frowned down at her. "Not because you were hurt or be-cause of our child. Because you're mine, and I no longer deny what is mine."

With that he rose, opened the door and let in her girls.

They eased into the room. Their faces were bruised, Emma was limping a bit.

"Em? What happened?"

"Stupid Wolf tripped me when I tried to rush to you," she snarled, her gray eyes flashing. "Bastard wrenched my ankle and held me down until the shooting stopped."

"Son of a bitch sheriff slipped up on me while I was trying to sneak into the shrubs and blow that fucker Douglas's head off," Sharone snapped. "Knocked me out cold as hell about the same time Douglas caught Ashley by surprise." A tray was set on the bed beside Anya, the scent of food beneath the metal dish covers making her mouth water.

"Milk," Ashley growled. "Doc says you need the calcium for that little hell-raiser you've conceived. Geez, Anya, don't you know about birth control? Do you know what a kid of his is going to be like?" She jerked her head to Del-Rey as he leaned against the wall and watched the Coyote girl show with something akin to male horror. "Hell, he probably doesn't know how to breed girls either."

Del-Rey winced and lifted his gaze to the ceiling as though he were praying.

She ate and listened to the girls fill her in. Between bites of chicken soup, baked potato and perfectly grilled steak with icy cold milk, she slipped looks at her mate. He listened and watched with complete male fascination and fear as they talked.

"Well, at least that arrogant pup Jax knows his place," Ashley finally bit out. "I should have kept his earlobe as a trophy."

Anya almost lost a drink of milk at that one. Del-Rey winced again.

"And on top of it all, they bring in those two totally uptight doctors from Russia. Katya refuses to go to the spa with us, and Alexi is just as stick-up-his-ass as he ever was," Emma inserted.

"Yeah, but man, Petrov is as damned cute as he ever was. Forty-two looks good on him, Anya," Sharone all but purred.

Anya winced. Sharone had a thing for her father that Anya had just never understood.

"I'll shoot you if you sleep with my dad," Anya warned her.

Sharone only laughed, her eyes twinkling in a way that made Anya throw Del-Rey a desperate look. Since when the hell did he let her father in Haven? Why? Why now? She was not listening to any more of Sharone's perverted fantasies about her father. It so was not going to happen. Anya had suffered enough after Del-Rey had shot her father. Sharone had mooned over him for months.

She finished her meal, her eyes growing heavy as the girls argued over ceremony colors and shoes. She found herself drifting off, thinking of the white dress she had her heart set on, walking down the aisle on her father's arm. Her cousins and their families there.

She felt warm. Liquid warm and excessively happy. For the first time in so long, the daydreams returned. Seducing her Ghost. Loving him. Touching him. Sharing things with him she had always longed to share. Sunrise and sunset. A caramel apple. The fights, the yelling, the loving. And wasn't there something about sex that Wolf and Coyote Breeds just loved?

She opened her eyes and stared at him, imagining it, feeling a tingle of warmth where she knew she shouldn't. Something so wicked, so forbidden.

Her gaze slipped to his thighs as the girls' chattering finally stopped. Would he, when she was well? she wondered. Would it be safe?

"Girls, time to go." His voice was husky, rough now as he moved from the wall. "Ashley, get the tray please."

"Oh man, there they go getting all hot and bothered," Ashley said and pouted. "I'm going to tell Armani on them. She'll rein his ass in."

"It's not his ass that's the problem," Emma snickered as they moved from the bed.

"Night, Coya." She was surprised by Ashley's quick kiss to her cheek. "Kick his ass before you give him some. He was such a male Breed."

"Yeah." Anya grinned in delight. "He is, isn't he?"

Ashley rolled her eyes as the girls left laughing. They were laughing. They were happy. And her mate was happy.

He moved to the bed, beside her, his lips lowering to hers gently, whispering over them. "No sex for three weeks," he told her. "Doctor's orders."

She pouted. "I won't last three weeks."

"Three weeks," he repeated.

But his lips slanted over hers, his tongue touched her lips, slipped between them. That taste of the mating hormone wasn't there, but the heat, the hunger, the need still filled her.

This was her Coyote. Her mate. Her lover. He would be her husband. But first, damn, three weeks. She might not survive it.

◆   ◆   ◆

"Four weeks was uncalled for." Anya was sniping when she entered her and Del-Rey's rooms.

She threw her PDA in a chair and turned to face him. "What did you do to her this time? What did Brim do to her? Four weeks, Del-Rey. She's made me wait four weeks."

"Just get your damned clothes off," Del-Rey snarled as he jerked his boots off. Black eyes gleamed in hunger.

"Get 'em off or I'm ripping them off," he snarled in complete male dedication to the arousal that had been about to drive them insane for weeks.

She jerked her sweater over her head.

"Brim's been harassing her again, hasn't he?"

"Hell if I care," Del-Rey grunted as he ripped the buttons on his shirt in his desperation to get it off. "Stop bitching and get ready to start fucking."

Her bra clip broke as she tore at it. Grimacing, she flung the piece of lace across the room before jerking her shoes from her feet.

Damn, Del-Rey was beating her. His pants were almost off. She tore at the snap on hers and pushed them, along with her panties, over her thighs. She was barely stepping out of them before she found herself picked up, gently, and moved to the bed. On her back.

He jerked the jeans off her legs and threw them behind him. He stopped then, stared down at her.

His fingers reached out and touched the small pink scar at her side.

"Don't start, Coyote Man," she ordered fiercely. Del-Rey could get rather intense over that scar. "We're here to fuck, not stress over something that didn't happen."

"I can stress later?" He lifted his gaze to hers. "If I never forget, Anya, then I'll never let my arrogance get out of hand again. I want to always remember what I nearly lost."

"Later. Fine." She thumped her hands on the mattress, then lifted them to his hair. "Kiss me first. Then do that wicked, naughty thing I made you blush over in the doctor's office."

He blushed again, his black eyes going wild just as they had in the office when the doctor had slid that little look his way. The one that was equal parts amusement and curiosity.

"You tease," he groaned. "You weren't serious."

His erection assured her he was very seriously interested.

"Are you gonna turn it down?" she teased him.

"Ah God. Turn that ass up to me and its fucked," he groaned, his lips sliding over hers. "So damned fucked."

She loved it. She'd heard of it. Hope and Faith had snickered over it a time or two. They had no idea what caused it. Defiance could get it for them. They argued, they yelled, they got their way in the form of their mates going all super dominant and showing them who was boss.

Nikki Armani had been confused by it. She called it a Breed thing. Something about submission and seduction and dominance. The forbidden. She had shaken her head and shrugged.

Anya hadn't tried that with Del-Rey yet. They yelled, they argued, but she'd been saving the defiance stuff for later. Maybe after the baby was born. But this, she didn't want to wait any longer for this kind of intimacy.

She wanted him though, she wanted that. She wanted it until it had tempted every fantasy she'd had for four weeks. Every one. To the point that she had awakened to his heartfelt groans as he rolled from the bed at the scent of her arousal. Refusing to take her, refusing, until the doctor signed off on it.

Well, the doctor had signed off on it.

"Kiss me, wild man," she groaned. "Hard and deep. Convince me."

He chuckled, a rough, sexy sound. "You need convincing?"

"You never know," she moaned, reaching for him, dragging his lips to hers. "Please me, Mate, like you've never pleased another."

His lips stole hers, like the first time. A deep, slanted, tongue-thrusting kiss that had her moaning, arching against him, her juices easing from her sex, preparing her for later. Definitely later.

"Let me taste you," he growled, moving from her lips to her nipples.

They were sensitive, so sensitive that she nearly orgasmed as his tongue lashed them, his lips suckling them gently.

His kisses wandered down her stomach then. He kissed her scar, kissed her belly, then laid his cheek against it for long, breathless moments before he spread her thighs wider and took her with his tongue.

"Del-Rey!" She screamed his name as she arched to him, feeling his tongue thrusting hard and deep inside her.

Wicked, slashing forks of pleasure raced through her sex, to her clit. She writhed beneath him, feeling him taste her, lick her. His tongue was ravenous, his moans fueling her desire as she felt his fingers moving lower.

He parted the cheeks of her bottom, tempted her there. He caressed and massaged the puckered little opening of her rear.

Oh, she liked that. She arched at the spike of pleasure, the tingle of incredible heat as he smoothed her juices back and the tip of his finger pierced her slowly.

She lifted, moaned for more.

"Ah hell, you're going to give me a stroke," he groaned against the wet folds he was devouring.

"Breeds don't have strokes," she panted. "Good hearts. Remember?"

"I'll be the first," he breathed out roughly. "Ah fuck."

She cried out as his finger slid inside her.

"Ah hell. Baby. Anya. This is for the heat cycle."

"No. For now." She twisted against him as his tongue circled her clit. "Oh yeah, that's so good."

A second finger pierced her and she wondered if she could pass out from the pleasure. She felt herself stretching, relaxing. Eager. Oh, she was so eager for this.

"I should spank you for this," he growled.

"Yeah, spank me." Her hands gripped his hair as she rode his lips. "Do it. I dare you."

Don't dare a Coyote. It should be on a plaque on every wall in Base. "Never Dare A Coyote."

His free hand landed on her raised rear.

Anya froze, felt the tingling burn and gave a low, drawn-out moan.

"Dare ya to do it again," she panted.

Before he could do more than gasp, she found herself rolled to her stomach. Hips lifted. His hand landed on her rear and she felt something better than mating heat.

Oh damn, this was wicked, and she loved it.

One hand moved between her thigh, palmed the wet flesh, his fingers stroking her clit as he held her in place and delivered another little slap to her rear. It wasn't painful; it was hot. It was sexy and wicked, and she wanted more.

She rolled her hips, cried out his name and lost count of the heavy caresses. She didn't lose count of the burn though. It was racing through her bloodstream, sensitizing every nerve ending in her body. Oh yes. She loved this. She was dying for him. She wanted more and more and she wanted to sink beneath the onslaught of pleasure/pain she could feel was coming.

"I can't wait." His fingers slid back to her rear.

One finger eased in, then out. Two pressed inside her, stretching her. He gathered her juices, drew them back, teased her with the little strokes that weren't really strokes. Just stretching, just easing her.

"Don't wait," she cried out. "Oh God, Del-Rey, please."

How long was she supposed to bear this torment? She needed. She had needed for four weeks.

"I'm ready dammit. Oh God, do something."

She was dying for him. Her thighs were slick with her wet need. She was hot, so slick that when he gathered more and eased it back, he was able to press three fingers inside her as she screamed out his name.

"Oh yes," she cried out. "I'm so close. So close."

His fingers eased back. A second later she felt the blunt, wide tip of his cock press against her in the same spot.

Immediately a spurt of pre-cum shot from his cock against the little entrance. She felt it burn brighter. Her back arched as the tingle in her rear became hotter, deeper.

"Hell," Del-Rey snarled as he eased against her, pressing slow and easy. So slow. So easy.

His cock jerked as it spilled again, shooting into the opening he had created. The tingles turned into something more. Something that ached and burned and eased his way as the essence created a lubrication that made her even slicker, easier to penetrate.

Another. Another.

She was screaming his name as he stretched her, pressed inside her. His hands were hard on her hips, holding her still as his muscular legs pressed hers apart.

"Fuck. What the hell have you done to me?" He groaned as the fluid shot inside her again.

He shuddered behind her, his cock jerking, and more filled her. He was sliding slow and easy inside her now, stretching her until she swore she was going to come from the pleasure-pain of that alone.

It was exquisite. It was more pleasure, more intensity, a

naughty, thrilling sensation of submission and being dominated. Of complete trust and the need for a pleasure so extreme that the border between it and pain dissolved.

She was begging by the time he filled her. Tightening on him, trying to milk him deeper inside her, to suck all the pleasure from the act that she could bear.

"Baby." He rose over her as he filled her, his arms catching his weight, his lips going to her neck.

Sensation tore through her as his lips found the mating mark, caressed it. The sensitivity there was almost too much to bear. He laved it with his tongue, sucked at it and slowly began thrusting, fucking inside her rear with deep, slow thrusts.

She hated slow. She bunched the blankets in her fists and screamed out at the need.

"Faster," she cried out. "Harder."

She needed faster and harder. Oh God, she needed to come. She was going to come, if he would just *move*.

"Anya, baby." He kissed the mark as she stared back at his tightly clenched expression. "God. I'm trying here. Stay still, sweetheart."

Stay still? Was he kidding?

Her hips writhed beneath him. It was agony, it was pleasure. It was so many sensations she wasn't certain she would survive it.

"Now, dammit," she cried. "Please, Del-Rey. Now. All of you, now."

He pulled back. He meant to go slow. Del-Rey commanded himself to go slow. Slow and easy. But she was killing him. Clenching on him.

He clamped his lips on the mark, licked and sucked at it as he began to move. He could feel the spurts of pre-cum, the mating fluid that normally eased her snug, hot little pussy but was now spilling into her rear, easing her there. She was burning tight around his dick, milking him, destroying him. One hand gripped her hip, the other found her hand.

Holding on to her, he fucked her. Deep, powerful thrusts that sent an agony of pleasure sizzling up his spine. He wouldn't last long. He was going to take her until she found her release. Only until then. He wasn't going to find his own release here.

The swelling mating knot was thick, hard. He wasn't going to hurt her. Never again. His mate would never hurt again.

He worked inside her, fighting to push her over the edge as he teetered on it himself. His hips thrust, driving his cock inside the snug channel, feeling her tighten, her throaty cries growing deeper. She was clenching, convulsing; she was screaming in orgasm, tightening on him as he fought to draw back.

Too close. Too close.

"Ah fuck!"

His teeth pierced her neck. He slammed in hard and felt his cum spilling, that additional swelling locking him inside her, spreading her farther until he swore he filled not just her rear, but that tight little pussy as well.

Anya lost awareness. She felt him spurting inside her, her release catching her off guard. She felt him swell, lock into her, and amazingly, incredibly, she felt that swelling press against the thin tissue between her rear and her vagina. She felt stuffed with him. Filled from one end to the other as another explosion tore through her, shattering her mind as every nerve ending in her body pulsed in response.

She tried to scream his name, but she could only manage strangled cries. Her fingers locked with his, her teeth bit into his forearm, and another explosion rocked her.

She was lost within this pleasure, lost where she needed to be, surrounded by him, held and anchored by him as she flew, free as the wind, and shattered into an exhausted heap beneath him.

"My love," he whispered.

"Hm. My love." She kissed his arm, turned her head for the gentlest kiss he had ever bestowed upon her and grinned back at him drowsily. "Dare you to do it again later."

He chuckled roughly. "We're going to start limiting your dares," he warned her. "You get your way too often."

She had dared him to buy the beds and quilts for the new Coyotes who had arrived. They watched her like the sun and the moon set on her. She dared him to find a decent cook that he could tolerate. He ended up with a full kitchen staff. Humans. He would have shuddered at the thought, but they were damned good cooks and he never had to worry about finding his coya stacking the damned dishwasher.

She did nothing more strenuous than carry her PDA or e-pad. The girls made certain of it. If she tried to do more, they called him.

She distracted his thoughts as she stretched beneath him, causing a groan to tear from him at the pleasure in the heat still wrapped around him.

Finally, long minutes later, he eased back.

"I'll move later," she murmured. "After I sleep."

He smiled. She made him smile. She made him warm. She made him happy and made him look forward to each day and the surprises she had in store for him.

Shaking his head, he moved to the bathroom, washed up, then carried a damp cloth and towel to the bedroom. Despite her grumbling, he cleaned his seed from her, kissed a pale buttock, then patted her rear gently before crawling into the bed beside her.

Immediately, she was curling into him. They shifted and tussled for position for long minutes, until finally he was curled around her, her head pillowed on his arm, his cheek against her hair.

Sleep came easily. It came with a sense of security. It came with warmth.

"I love you, Del-Rey," she whispered sleepily. "With all my soul."

"I love you, Anya," he said. "You are my soul."

· E P İ L O G U E ·

The bride wore a long gown of white lace and satin with the traditional one hundred pearl buttons running down the back. She looked like a fairy-tale princess as she walked up the rose-strewn aisle.

The groom was dressed in black. It suited him.

The bride's father, tall, proud, still broad and strong at forty-two, wore black as well, a good contrast to his dark red, nearly auburn hair.

A spring snowstorm couldn't cancel this ceremony; weather-equipped heli-jets were parked for miles outside Haven, and the underground sports facility at Haven was packed to capacity with Breeds and humans alike who were there to witness the joining of the Coyote alpha, Del-Rey Delgado, and his mate, Anya Kobrin.

Vows were spoken. Those were important. Rings were exchanged. It was said that the groom, or alpha, had had the rings specially made by a master jeweler in Russia. It was said that there was an inscription inside each: *Let the past not be forgotten. Let the lessons not be in vain.*

It was the wedding of the year. Journalists from around the world were in attendance, and when it came time for the bride to go to her knees and swear her loyalty to the alpha of the pack she had just married into, the alpha shocked them all.

He went to his knees. His hands clasped hers.

"You proved your loyalty, countless times over. As a child fighting for your friends' freedom. As a woman fighting for her mate's heart. As coya fighting for the peace we all dream of. I pledge myself, Alpha Del-Rey Delgado, to my mate, my wife, my coya, Anya Kobrin Delgado. May our future be filled with promise and may your smile always light my way."

There wasn't a dry eye in the house, as a reporter, Cassa Hawkins, even checked to be sure. Well, maybe there was one dry eye in the house, besides hers. The large Breed that stood in the shadows across the room. His eyes were, like hers, scanning the crowd, watching, as though he were waiting, hunting.

What, my beautiful Bengal, are you hunting?

Unfortunately, despite her wicked, wicked fantasies, she had a feeling he wasn't hunting her. Too bad. She heard he was a wild man in bed; she'd never had a wild man in her bed.

She almost snorted at that thought. It had been a long damned time since she had had any man in her bed.

Her attention was drawn back to the ceremony as howls and roars, cheers of goodwill and laughter echoed through the cavernous underground arena.

Del-Rey and Anya had turned, hands clasped, to face the crowd watching them while the priest that officiated over the ceremony pronounced them man and wife.

It really was a beautiful affair.

What made Cassa's heart clench, though, was when Del-Rey turned his bride back to him, lowered his head and took her lips in a kiss that looked more like a promise.

As Anya Delgado arched in his arms, Cassa's brows lifted at the small, rounded mound of her tummy as it became visible. Was it possible? Was this mate actually pregnant? She looked closer.

"You don't want to put that in your little article."

She jerked, her eyes widening at the voice in her ear. Her head swung to the side. Oddly striped gold and black hair met her cheek. It grew long around his face, silken, tempting to touch. His eyes were green, jungle green and flecked with gold.

His scent wrapped around her, spicy and male, and tempted her to lick her lips.

"Meaning?" she drawled as she felt his hand touch her hip, his head move closer until his lips were at her ear.

"The suspicion I see in those pretty gray eyes," he murmured. "Any additional announcement will come when the time is right. You can be a part of the group allowed into that announcement, or you can be strangely uninvited to that one as well as many others."

She sighed. Okay, no telling about that intriguing little bulge.

"I want an exclusive," she demanded. "Someone else will beat me to the punch. You'll owe me."

His chuckle stroked over her senses. "You might get more than you bargained for."

Her lips twitched. "And you might be biting off more than you can chew."

♦   ♦   ♦

The newly wedded couple turned, clasped hands, but stared into each other's eyes. Black eyes met perfect blue, and Del-Rey knew that in this woman he had found peace.

Now, if only peace could be assured in the world they were fighting to belong within.

Turn the page for an exclusive look at
the next title in the Feline Breeds series
by Lora Leigh

BENGAL'S HEART

Coming soon from Berkley Sensation!

Cassa Hawkins slipped silently through the shadows of Haven as she tried to ignore the misty rain falling and her own feelings of anticipation. She felt like a ghost, like a shadow, unseen, unheard. It was a heady sensation as she slipped past Breed after Breed, undetected.

The chill night air wrapped around her and penetrated the black clothing she wore. Even the snug black cap that covered her hair did little to keep out the cold or the dampness. It added to the thrill, to the sense of danger. She was insane, creeping around like this, and she knew it. She couldn't get far. It wasn't possible that a drug had actually been created that could fool the Breed senses and allow her to sneak past the sentries posted throughout Haven.

Someone was playing with her, allowing her to get only so far. That was the only explanation for the distance she had gained between the cabin where she was staying and the main offices of the compound without being caught. The Breed guards had an incredible sense of smell. They were chosen for their positions simply because they were impossible to pass.

It wasn't possible that such a drug could have been created—was it?

According the anonymous emails she had received and the small bottle of round white pills that had arrived at her apartment the week before, it was definitely possible. And she had been crazy enough tonight to actually take one. To slip it onto her tongue, to allow it to dissolve and enter her system before she left her cabin.

Her own recklessness had concerned her, but only for a moment. As many of her fellow reporters knew, Cassa had often been known to dare death. It was one of her faults, many said. She considered it one of her strengths. After all, her days were numbered and she knew it. She may as well get away with as much as possible until the day of reckoning arrived.

In this case, intuition had spurred her on though. The pictures of bloody bodies, the emails that had warned her that a rogue Breed was taking vengeance for some unknown crimes, and the pills that arrived with a message stating that the past always returned and wouldn't she like to know the truth before it knocked on her door had pushed her into this choice.

The past was always hovering at her shoulder and now she had a feeling that someone might possibly know the secret she had fought to hide for so long.

The truth. The truth was, Cassa had spilled blood herself. The truth was, once her secrets were revealed, she would die. The Breeds would never allow her to live once they knew the truth.

She slipped past yet another Breed guard. Mordecai. One of their best trackers, rumored to be one of their most merciless Coyote Breeds. On silent feet she moved slowly through the shadows, along the wet ground, heart racing, mouth dry until she was a safe distance from him.

The chilly winter air gave no hint that spring was just around the corner. The cold penetrated flesh and bone, but nothing could still the excitement racing through her now. It was working. They hadn't scented her; they hadn't *scented* her.

God, this couldn't be possible.

Pressing her back tight to the thick trunk of a pine, she stared up at the moonless sky and whispered a silent prayer that at least one of the Breeds patrolling the area would scent her.

A drug like this could be deadly, just as her source had warned her it was.

Pushing away from the tree, Cassa skirted around several maples bare of leaves and dripping a chilly rain as she slid through the night.

There was a whisper of voices ahead, the sound of soft footfalls coming nearer. Ducking behind the evergreen shrubs that grew around an enclosed picnic area, she waited for them to pass.

"Are you certain of your information?" Jonas Wyatt's voice came through the night clearly as the pair grew closer.

"Five dead, Jonas, that's hard to mistake. Each one was rumored to be part of a twelve man hunting party that came together several times a year to hunt down escaped Breeds. Each one was killed in the same manner, using the same pattern. There's no mistake."

The voice that answered had Cassa's heart tripping, then speeding up in awareness. She fought back the response, bit her lip and prayed that little miracle pill would cover the scent of arousal as well.

Cabal St. Laurents had a voice that made women want to melt to the floor in a puddle of orgasmic bliss. It rasped over the senses with a velvet cadence Cassa had never been able to ignore.

"Hell." Jonas paused, no more than four feet from where she crouched.

As bad as she wanted to peek over the border of shrubs, she didn't dare. The scent of her body may be masked, but there would be no way in hell it would affect the men's exceptional eyesight.

"That's a good description of what we're facing," Cabal answered the curse. "It's not over. The hunters are becoming the prey, and if the first five are any indication, we could be looking at some pretty high-profile individuals. The former mayor that was killed last week was a well-known individual throughout the nation. We're looking at a PR nightmare here."

"PR is your brother's area," Jonas growled. "I'll let Tanner worry about the sugar coating. I want the killer caught, Cabal. That's your job."

"It's hard to do a job when there's no evidence to go on, Jonas," Cabal snapped, his voice irritated. "There's no DNA left on the scene, and no scent. We were notified within hours of the mayor's death. When we arrived, you could smell the scent of his terror, but the scent of his killer was no where to be found."

Cassa felt her mouth go dry. The former mayor that had disappeared recently was David Banks, a proponent of Breed rights. David Banks had gone for his evening walk one night in the little town of Glen Ferris, West Virginia. He hadn't been seen again. His body hadn't been found. There was no trace, no clue where he might have gone. Until now. He had argued for Breed Law, and had been known to host several charity parties a year in honor of the Breeds. Now, he was also rumored to have been a member of a group of men that once hunted Breeds?

She could believe it. She had never liked Banks, but she knew his popularity, his smooth, charming smile and his soft voice had fooled more than one journalist.

"Find something, Cabal," Jonas ordered. "We're working on borrowed time here. If you don't find the killer before news of this leaks to the press, then we're fucked."

"It looks to me as though we're fucked either way," Cabal informed him, his voice cold. "Horace Engalls and Phillip Brandenmore are making certain of that."

Brandenmore and Engalls. The owners of a pharmaceutical and drug research company were under indictment for the drugging of the Breeds' doctor, Elyiana Morrey, and for conspiracy to murder in several Breed deaths. They had been caught attempting to buy research conducted by Dr. Morrey from her two assistants and were rumored to be conducting research into an aging phenomena the Breeds and their wives were supposedly experiencing.

There was no supposition to it. Cassa knew the truth of it. The Breeds were experiencing a slow down in the aging process once they went into mating heat. The phenomena was making Breed doctors crazy as they tried to figure it out, and sending the breed ruling cabinet into a frenzy each time the gossip tabloids came up with another angle to tell the story.

So far, it wasn't being taken seriously. But that couldn't continue much longer. It had been ten years since the Feline Breed alpha had announced the existence of the breeds. Ten years since he or his wife had aged in any noticeable way.

Cassa was one of the few people who knew the truth, and

she knew the consequences of ever writing that story or revealing her knowledge of it. The non-disclosure agreement she had signed in return for special consideration in interviews and breaking Breed stories had been frightening. She may have signed away her soul, her first born child, and her cat's blood. Or something close.

"Engalls and Brandenmore are being dealt with," Jonas drawled, his tone one of pure ice. "I'm more concerned with a rogue Breed's indiscriminate killings. Find him, Cabal, or we could all be up shit creek without a paddle."

Cabal grunted at that. "I thought we already were."

"No, at the moment, we have a paddle," Jonas informed him sarcastically. "Now find that bastard before he kills again. I'll be damned if I want to try to clean up another mess like Banks. I'm certain there are still pieces of him missing."

Cassa forced herself to remain silent. She had the pictures of that killing; she was certain she did. That one, and four others. Pictures that had been sent via secured emails, accusing the Breeds of hiding a killer.

She hadn't doubted the Breeds were capable of it; she just hadn't imagined that even a Breed could do the damage that had been done in those pictures.

Trepidation built inside her as she felt the sweat that began to trickle down her temple at the thought of being caught now. She knew Breed Law, and she knew the price of eavesdropping on this conversation. Like David Banks, she could disappear and her fate would never be known.

"You're pissing in the wind, Jonas," Cabal informed him. "We have nothing to go on here. No suspects, no clues. Until I have one or the other, we're screwed."

"Get it." Jonas voice became dangerous, clipped. "Quickly, Cabal."

"Yeah, I'll get right on that, Director, just as soon as you tell me who the hell I'm looking for." Cabal's voice lowered until it vibrated with suppressed menace. "Until then, there's not a hell of a lot more I can do."

"Banks was from Glen Ferris. Get back there; see what you can find out. We're supposed to be searching for him. Investigate it from that angle."

"Just what I need, you telling me how to do my fucking job," Cabal grunted.

"I could be telling you how to find your mate," Jonas drawled with a hint of amusement. "I'm certain she's around here somewhere. What do you think?"

A dangerous growl filled the air as Cassa felt her heart sink in her chest. Cabal was mated? No, that couldn't be true. Breeds did not ignore their mates, and they sure as hell didn't flirt with other women as Cabal had flirted with her earlier in the day during the wedding reception.

He wouldn't have watched her as he had, nor would he have followed her to her cabin later.

Jonas had to be talking about a mate in general, not one in particular. Such as, seek and ye shall find. A why aren't you looking for your mate type thing. That had to be it.

"Don't fuck with me, Jonas," Cabal warned him. "I'm not in the mood."

Jonas chuckled. It wasn't a comfortable or amused sound. It was frankly frightening.

"I'm not the one you have to worry about fucking with you, my friend," he drawled. "I do believe though that our intrepid little reporter, Ms. Hawkins, could give you lessons in it."

Cassa felt her lips part in shock. There was a hint of amusement in Jonas's voice now but none in Cabal's rumbled snarl. The sound was sexy as hell even as it sent chills racing up Cassa's spine and a flood of warmth between her thighs.

"Drop it, Jonas," Cabal warned him.

Yes, Jonas, please drop it, Cassa moaned silently. She was becoming aroused despite her best efforts. She had a feeling that whatever the pill did, it would be little defense against the scent of her need. And she was definitely needy. In the ten years since her husband's death, she had never been so turned on as she was when she was around Cabal St. Laurents.

"Fine, consider it dropped." She heard the shrug in Jonas's voice. "The heli-jet will be ready to fly you to Glen Ferris in the morning. Investigate Banks's disappearance. We might get lucky and you'll find a suspect while you're there."

"Keep hoping," Cabal grunted. "Trust me, Jonas, if they're hiding a feral Breed in their midst, they're not going to turn him over simply because I ask nicely."

"You know how to ask nicely?" There was a wealth of sarcasm in Jonas's voice.

"Go to hell." There was a wealth of arrogance in Cabal's.

Cassa wanted to laugh at the confrontation but stifled the impulse.

"I'll return to hell, you check on our nosy reporter," Jonas's voice echoed with command once again as Cassa gave a small start of fear. "She was too jumpy at the reception tonight. Make sure she's where she's supposed to be."

Cassa sensed the hesitation that filled the area on the other side of the shrubs.

"Is she becoming a problem?"

She definitely didn't like the flat, cold tone Cabal used now.

"She's always a problem when she's here or at Sanctuary," Jonas answered.

Cassa's eyes narrowed. She was never a problem at Sanctuary. The Feline Breed stronghold was homier, and a damned sight more welcoming to her than the Wolf Breed compound she was in now.

"You don't know how to handle her," Cabal injected.

Handle her? No one handled her, period.

"Only with a whip and chair," Jonas growled. "Callan and Merinus give her much too much freedom in Sanctuary. She thinks she deserves it elsewhere."

"And this is my problem how?" Cabal argued. "She's a reporter. You should have known better than to allow the invitation she was given to stay, to stand."

Bodies shifted. Cassa was dying to look over the top of the shrubs, but leaned to the side instead to try to get a view through the opening in the foliage.

The glimmer of light from a nearby building revealed the two men. Jonas was still dressed in his tuxedo, Cabal though had changed into jeans, a T-shirt, a rain resistant jacket and boots. His black-striped golden blond hair dripped with the misty rain and fell long to his shoulders.

His shoulders were broad, his waist lean, his thighs muscular and his legs long. Standing there in the rain, he looked like the male animal he was. In his prime, ready for action. Sexy as hell. Mouth-wateringly male.

She breathed in slow and easy, and felt the familiar slick warmth between her thighs.

"Just make certain she's in her cabin and well guarded, if you don't mind." Jonas ordered in a drawl heavy with mockery.

"And if I mind?" Cabal asked carefully.

Jonas's teeth flashed in a hard, cold smile as the chilly rain dripped along his face and saturated his short, clipped hair.

"Then I might make you part of her protection detail rather than sending you to Glen Ferris. Come to think of it, that might be a good idea after all."

Cabal's brilliant green eyes narrowed, and Cassa could have sworn she saw the glitter of the amber flecks within the green as he stared back at the other breed.

"I'll check on her." The hard fury that echoed in his normally cold voice surprised Cassa and sent a chill racing down her spine.

She had to get back to her cabin before he arrived. If he found her sneaking around in the rain, or God forbid, found her missing from her cabin, she could just imagine the consequences.

She slid back from her position silently. Heart racing, she fought to move slowly, carefully.

She was running out of time anyway. The single pill she had taken only gave her a small amount of time. Two hours, the information had warned. She had spent most of that time testing it against the Breeds patrolling the compound.

Once the time limit was reached, her natural scent would return quickly—that meant she had less than half an hour to get back to the cabin.

She couldn't let Cabal know she hadn't been there all along, and she damned sure couldn't face him while that drug was still in her system.

They continued to discuss her, much to her dismay, as she slowly retreated. She could hear their voices, but not what they were saying. Once she reach a safe distance, she straightened again and moved hastily through the shadows back to her cabin.

She used the heavy trees that grew throughout the compound to hide her return. Skirting the areas she knew the Breeds were prone to guard more heavily, she made it back to her cabin in twenty minutes. The delays were nerve-wracking as she waited for sentries to move slowly past her or when she was forced to backtrack to avoid them.

Rushing back through the unlocked window of her cabin, she raced to the bathroom as she heard a vehicle pulling up in the small driveway outside.

Twisting the knobs to her shower, she quickly adjusted the water and stripped the wet clothes from her body. Tossing the saturated fabric into a nearby closet, she grabbed her scented shampoo, squeezed a large amount into her palm and worked it quickly into her long hair before snatching the bottle of bath gel from a shelf and soaping up a sponge.

She needed scent, lots of it. Pear scented shampoo in her hair, apple scented bath gel. Lather built over her body from head to toe as she fought to make damned certain Cabal had plenty to smell when she faced him.

Rinsing quickly, she beat back the racing of her heart, forced herself to calm and assured herself the drug would have time to get out of her system by the time she conditioned her hair, rinsed it and shut the water off.

Minutes later she left the bathroom, her hair bound in a towel, a heavy robe wrapped around her and plenty of apple scented body lotion smoothed over her.

Normally, she would have used the products sparingly. She preferred unscented shampoos and conditioners, even soaps. The heavy scents bothered her, as well as Breeds. Tonight was an exception, and she was thankful her assistant had once again slipped the scented stuff into her overnight back.

Kelly thought everyone should smell like a fruit stand just because she did.

Calm and poised, Cassa stepped out of her bedroom into the wide living room and came to a stop at the sight of a damp haired, much too handsome Breed as he sat in the large easy chair across the room.

It was no more than she had expected, and it wasn't the first time she had walked into a room that should have been hers alone to find a Breed waiting for her. Though, she admitted, it was rarely this particular Breed.

"A little late for a visit, isn't it?" She tugged at the towel around her hair as the mocking question passed her lips.

She didn't miss the flicker of his eyes to her hair as it fell around her shoulders, curled down her back and fell just above her waist. Damp, riotous curls snaked over her shoulder and fell down the front of the robe to lie over her breasts. His gaze touched there, and Cassa was suddenly thankful for the thick robe. It hid the hardening of her nipples, but she knew nothing could hide the scent of her arousal now.

Cabal's nostrils flared, his eyes narrowed, and his muscles bunched as he rose slowly from the chair to a very impressive height of at least six feet four inches tall.

She felt dwarfed by him, despite her own five feet eight inches. She felt too feminine and too physically weak. She felt like those silly little twits that cooed and ahhed at the sight of him. The ones she hated because they lusted after him with such determination. The slinky little redheads that hung to his arm. The vapid little brunettes she had seen him squire around. She detested each and every one.

"You're normally up rather late," he stated, his voice low as his gaze flickered to her laptop. The one she hadn't turned on all day. "I expected you to be working on whatever story you were coming up with." There was an edge of suspicion in his voice.

Could he smell her nerves along with her arousal? Probably. But who wasn't nervous around him?

"I was restless tonight." She shrugged, moved across the room and headed to the open kitchen. "I'm going to fix a pot of coffee. Interested?" In the coffee, she should have said. She wished he was interested in something more.

She felt him follow her. Like a heated breath of air at her back, she could feel him behind her as she moved into the kitchen and headed for the counter.

"Nothing for me."

No coffee, tea, or me, she thought sarcastically.

She lifted her shoulder negligently. "Suit yourself."

Silence filled the room as she programmed the coffeemaker and flipped it on. Within seconds the scent of hot, rich coffee began to fill the room.

Cassa turned then and faced the one man, the Breed, she couldn't seem to help but be fascinated by.

He looked far different now than he had nearly eleven years before during his rescue from the labs in France where he had been held.

There, he had been bloodied, slashed, bruised, near death but still fighting to survive in a pit filled with stakes and slashing blades. His pride had fallen around him. Women, children, young men. His screams of rage still haunted her nightmares, as did the knowledge that she had played a part in him being there.

Guilt seared her with a slash of pain that raced across her chest and a sense of fear that never failed to weaken her knees. And he sensed it, just as he always did. She watched his eyes darken, his body tense as the scent of it reach him.

"You're always frightened of me. Why?"

After all these years, he had finally asked. Strange, she'd always imagined that question, and she'd always had a glib reply ready. Now, the words wouldn't come. Her tongue felt heavy, her mouth dry as she stared back at him and fought back the truth.

"Feminine wariness?" She asked a question rather than giving an answer. Breeds could smell a lie, and she wouldn't give him the satisfaction of smelling hers.

"And arousal?" His head tilted to the side as though the knowledge of it were a curiosity to him.

"I bet a lot of women are aroused by you." She was careful to keep her tone even, calm. No nervousness, no hint of guilt. She'd learned over the years how to cover most of her responses when around Breeds. They sensed too much, knew too much. And Cassa had far too many secrets.

"That doesn't answer my question," he stated as he continued to watch her much too closely. "Why the fear?"

Cassa could only shake her head. And stare. She stared at those golden flecks in his eyes, unable to break the hold they had on her. She wanted, no, she ached to touch him, and that was by far the most dangerous impulse she had ever known.

"You should leave," she finally forced herself to say, to speak the damning words she always hated voicing.

His lips quirked mockingly. "You're always running from me, Cassa. Why is that?"

Why was that? Possibly because he was the most dangerous individual that she could ever have in her life?

Shoving her hands into the pockets of her robe, she pressed her lips together and forced herself to look away from him. A second later, her gaze flew back to him, her eyes widening as he stepped closer to her.

Heat suddenly raced through her veins in a frightening wave of pure lust. Cassa felt her hands fisting in her pockets as she fought to step back, fought to keep from touching him.

Cabal paused as he watched her, his eyes narrowing on her as he watched her pale. He had never seen so many expressions race across a female's face before. Fear, trepidation, lust and confusion. She was tense, fighting herself and the arousal he could smell reaching out to him through the fruity scents of her shower.

He wanted to wash away the unnatural scents. He wanted to smell the fresh, sweet scent he knew she possessed and called her own. A scent headier than that of sunrise in the summer as it touched upon the mountains around them.

He knew what was at play here, as well as what was at stake. He should have never waited for her to come out of the shower. The moment he knew she was there, he should have left. But something had intrigued him.

As he had stood outside her bathroom door listening to the water running, he had been unable to smell her. Until the scents of shampoo and soap had filled the heated air, there had been nothing but the smell of water for long minutes.

He could smell the woman now, beneath the layers of pears and apples, it was there, drawing him, tempting him. But it hadn't been there when he had first arrived.

He stepped closer, smelled her fear increase, as well as her arousal.

Damn her. She was wet. He could almost taste the silky heat he knew would be dampening her thighs. How wet was she, he wondered. How hot?

His fingertips itched with the need to press between her silky thighs and find out. To feel the silken rain of dampness, to draw his fingers through it, then his tongue. The need to taste her was almost overpowering his need to simply touch her.

"You're not answering me, Cassa," he reminded her of the question he had asked. "Why are you always trying to run me off?"

She inhaled roughly, then her tongue, pink and damp, raced across her lips. Soft, pink lips. Lips he longed to lick himself.

Hell, this was getting out of control.

"Look we're both aware of the freaky stuff going on with the Breeds right now," she finally stated. "Mating heat and uncontrolled, frenzied sex. I prefer to keep a safe distance between myself and all of you."

"We're both also well aware of the fact that once mating heat begins, it doesn't stop," he reminded her. "It becomes painful." He felt his voice lowering as the heavy length of his cock throbbed in anticipation. "You can't deny it. Do you feel the need to rub all over me Cassa? Do you want it so bad it hurts?"

God, he did. He wanted it until nothing else mattered. It enraged the animal within him that he denied himself the taste of her, that he denied the heat he knew awaited them.

She snorted at the question and rolled her expressive gray eyes. "Get real."

Such a deceptive little baggage. He almost smiled at the knowledge that she was trying to hide her need from him.

Cabal allowed his lips to quirk in amusement and forced himself to step back. Her scent was there where it hadn't been before. Perhaps something else had been at play to fool his senses earlier, he thought, though he doubted it.

He looked around the kitchen, searched for answers where he knew none existed, then turned back to her.

"When are you leaving Haven?" he finally asked. "I have the heli-jet in the morning, we could drop you off at your offices in New York if you wish."

Her brows lifted. "That's very generous of you, but I'm meeting with the lupina and prima in the morning."

The alpha mates, Hope Gunnar and Merinus Lyons. Both were present at Haven after the joining ceremony of the Coyote alpha and his mate.

He nodded slowly and turned to the door. "Perhaps next time," he offered instead.

"Yeah, I'll remind you of that." Her voice was cockier now that he was retreating. Cabal found it amusing, and definitely intriguing.

"You do that, Cassa," he drawled, as he stopped at the door and turned back to her.

His gaze raked over her robe clad form. Brillant red little toenails peeked out beneath the long, thick robe. They curled against the warm floor and the scent of her became heated and filled with desire.

"Good-bye Cabal," she hinted strongly.

Yes, she wanted him out of her cabin, out of her life. As she had stated, she knew about mating heat. She had to suspect the reason for the strength of her desire. Just as she was denying it.

Anger surged through him at the thought of it, as it always did each time she avoided him or went out of her way to let him know he was encroaching on her space.

"Until later, Cassa," he said softly. It was a warning rather than a promise.

He'd thought he was meant to be alone, that finding his mate would be something that would never happen, at least not this quickly. The year before, at his brother's mating, Cabal had felt the loss of the only true connection he'd had in his life. Until he'd met the reporter who had insisted on interviewing his new sister-in-law. She was pushy, inquisitive and too damned tempting. And she was his mate. He'd sensed it, known it, even though he hadn't wanted to admit it to himself during that first meeting.

In the months after that, he'd stopped denying it. He'd accepted it. And now, he was losing the battle in his attempt not to force her to accept it.

"Until later, Cabal."

Was that regret he heard in her voice, he wondered as he opened the door and returned to the rainy darkness beyond? Did he hear knowledge in her voice, as well as hunger?

He shook his head and closed the door carefully behind him, blocking out the scent of her, though there was nothing that could block his need for her.

He had a job to do. He didn't have time for a mating. He had a killer to find, not a mate to claim.

The darkness stretched ahead of him. Darkness as shadowed and bleak as the life he led. And still, he walked away. From his mate.

COMING SOON IN PAPERBACK

Fourth in the *New York Times*
Bestselling Nauti Series from
LORA LEIGH
Nauti Intentions

Since he saw Janey Mackay taking a dip in her
bikini, Major Alex Jansen has had to quell the
fire she ignites in him. Even touching her would
mean death at the hands of the Mackay men.
Until now, the girl of his dreams—and fantasies—has lived in a vacuum of affection, shying
away from the danger she thinks men represent.
Alex sets out to prove her wrong, with his torturously slow caresses.

But when someone starts leaving spine-chilling
notes, Alex won't rest until she's completely safe.
And completely his—body and soul.

M340T0908

The *New York Times* bestseller from
LORA LEIGH

Dawn's Awakening
A Novel of the Feline Breeds

The runt of the lab she was created in, Dawn
Daniels endured years of torture by her pride
brother and the Council soldiers. Finally freed
from her torment, she's now a Breed Enforcer,
in control of her own life. That is, until she's assigned to protect the one man destined to be her
mate—and realizes it's far too easy to lose total
control.

> "When I'm in the mood for a steamy
> romance, I read Lora Leigh."
> —Angela Knight

M279T0408